FIRST MEETING

Flintlock lay helpless with a bullet in his leg inside a smoky deerskin lodge. Pimoacan was looming over him with a knife, and Nathaniel's first thought was that this was the end.

"The bullet must be removed," the Delaware said.

Pimoacan placed a strip of rawhide between Nathaniel's teeth. Flintlock clamped down hard on the rawhide as the blade pierced his already torn and tortured flesh. The ground seemed to fall away beneath him and he was plummeting down through a black hole, leaving the scream and the pain somewhere up above.

An eternity—or was it a minute?—later he heard, very faintly, voices shouting outside. He opened his eyes to see the face of the young Delaware woman who had been heating the knife. Then he made out what the shouting was saying.

"Tecumseh! Tecumseh!"

"He is here," the woman said, with a kind of reverence.

And Flintlock knew he was at the mercy of the legendary leader who had none. . . .

SUSPICION OF INNOCENCE

by Barbara Parker

This riveting, high-tension legal thriller written by a former prosecutor draws you into hot and dangerous Miami, where Gail Connor is suddenly caught in the closing jaws of the legal system and is about to discover the other side of the law. . . .

Available now from **SIGNET**

THE
BORDER CAPTAINS

Flintlock, Volume 2

by

Jason Manning

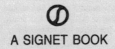

A SIGNET BOOK

SIGNET
Published by the Penguin Group
Penguin Books USA Inc., 375 Hudson Street,
New York, New York 10014, U.S.A.
Penguin Books Ltd, 27 Wrights Lane,
London W8 5TZ, England
Penguin Books Australia Ltd, Ringwood,
Victoria, Australia
Penguin Books Canada Ltd, 10 Alcorn Avenue,
Toronto, Ontario, Canada M4V 3B2
Penguin Books (N.Z.) Ltd, 182–190 Wairau Road,
Auckland 10, New Zealand

Penguin Books Ltd, Registered Offices:
Harmondsworth, Middlesex, England

First published by Signet, an imprint of Dutton Signet,
a division of Penguin Books USA Inc.

First Printing, February, 1995
10 9 8 7 6 5 4 3 2 1

REGISTERED TRADEMARK—MARCA REGISTRADA

Printed in the United States of America

To my agent, Ethan Ellenberg,
who warned me that I would not have time
for a long African safari

AUTHOR'S NOTE

For a wealth of information on Tecumseh and the Shawnee Indians, the author is deeply indebted to Allan W. Eckert and his excellent history entitled *A Sorrow in Our Heart: The Life of Tecumseh*. Sections of this work dealing with national affairs were enhanced beyond measure by reference to Volume I of *The Papers of Henry Clay*. Letters attributed to Clay in this work are compilations of actual documents.

CHAPTER ONE

Tecumseh

I
(1768)

When his second son was born, the Shawnee chief Pucksinwah was on his way to Chillicothe, the principal town of the Chalahgawtha sept.

Pucksinwah had hoped to arrive in the village before the birth, but it was not to be. A makeshift shelter was erected for his wife, Methotosa, and a bed of evergreen boughs spread on the ground for her to lie on. With his twelve-year-old son Chiksika, daughter Tecumapese of ten years, and six women of the clan who volunteered to stay behind to perform midwife functions, Pucksinwah sent the rest of his followers—six hundred of them, including several hundred of the finest Kispokotha warriors—on to Chillicothe. He sent word, too, that on the morrow he would be present in the council house, the *msi-kah-mi-qui,* where he and the chiefs of the other four Shawnee septs would discuss the current crisis.

Pucksinwah sensed that this was to be an extremely important council. Which was why fully two-thirds of the population of Kispoko Town, located many miles away on the banks of the Scioto River, had accompanied him. For five years now the council had been meeting to discuss the problem of the white man. In violation of treaties between the Shawnee Nation and the

Great White Father, the frontiersmen were spilling over the mountains and taking the fertile land of the Monongahela and Allegheny river valleys for their own.

Each of the five Shawnee septs performed a specific task for the nation as a whole. The Thawegila and Chalahgawtha septs were in charge of political matters. They were the two most powerful clans, and from one of them the principal chief of the Shawnee Nation was always chosen. Right now, the principal chief was Hokolesqua, of the Chalahgawtha, who was also called Cornstalk.

The Peckuwa sept controlled religious and ceremonial matters, while the Maykujay clan was in charge of health, medicine, and food. The Kispokotha sept— Pucksinwah's clan—was in charge of warfare, particularly the training of warriors.

As the cold black shadows of night filled the woods, Pucksinwah waited anxiously a respectful distance from the shelter within which lay his wife. He was worried about Methotosa, of course, but he was just as worried about the upcoming council. Since Chillicothe was the largest of the Shawnee villages, and centrally located, five thousand Shawnee men would be there. Pucksinwah knew he had to be there, too.

Cornstalk and the Chalahgawthas, along with the Maykujay, would speak for making peace with the Long Knives—the *Shemanese*. They would argue that there were too many of them to fight. Pucksinwah knew in his heart that there never could be peace between the whites and his people. The whites would not honor a new treaty. Sure as day followed night they would continue to encroach on Shawnee land, along the wide *Spay-lay-wi-*

theepi—the Ohio River. And this would bring them into the sacred hunting grounds of *Can-tuc-kee.*

So Pucksinwah was resolved to speak for war. War was inevitable. Better now than later. Cornstalk was right about one thing—every year more and more of the *Shemanese* crossed the mountains. Why wait another summer or two? There would just be more Long Knives to fight. Strike now, and maybe the whites to the east of the mountains would think twice about invading the land of the Shawnee. Being the chief of the sept responsible for the training of warriors, Pucksinwah's words would carry great weight. He believed he could rely on the council representatives of the Thawegila and Peckuwa clans to side with him.

Cornstalk would be the main obstacle. Pucksinwah had great respect for the principal chief of the Shawnee. Cornstalk was a peace-loving man, who had the best interests of his people at heart. Pucksinwah loved peace, too. He dreaded the thought of war. But this matter had to be resolved. The white men had to be stopped, now. Pucksinwah's most fervent prayer was that his children would be able to live long and happy lives in a time of peace and plenty.

But sometimes he saw this for what it was—a forlorn hope.

Standing there in the night-shrouded forest, Pucksinwah prayed to *Moneto,* and when he was done he looked skyward. To his amazement, a meteor flamed across the star-studded, violet-blue sky.

This shooting star was an omen, a great spirit the Shawnees knew as The Panther.

From the shelter, where his beloved wife lay giving new life, came the sharp cry of a newborn infant.

Pucksinwah could scarcely contain himself, but he

waited until one of the women emerged from the shelter and, with a gesture, informed him that he could enter.

As he stooped to enter the shelter, the midwives departed, leaving the chief with his family. Methotosa lay on the boughs of evergreen, covered against the chill of the late-winter night with a buffalo robe. In her arms lay the newborn. The women had smeared the infant with bear oil.

Methotosa smiled wanly at her bright-eyed husband. "You have a son," she said.

"A son . . ." Pucksinwah was so filled with pride and wonder and love that he could hardly speak.

"Father," said his daughter, Tecumapese, "did you see The Panther?"

"I saw it. It is the child's *unsoma*."

Methotosa nodded. By Shawnee custom, a child was not to be named for ten to twelve days after its birth, during which time some notable event—the *unsoma*— would occur. In this way *Moneto* indicated what He wished the child's name to be.

Yet neither Pucksinwah nor Methotosa doubted that *Moneto* had provided their boy-child with an *unsoma* this very night. The fact that he had done so at the moment of birth was a sign of great import.

"He will be called Tecumseh," declared the Kispokotha chief. "The Panther Passing Across."

II
(1773)

Moneto ruled the universe, and bestowed His blessings on those upon whom he looked with favor. He was not to be confused with the Great Spirit. *Inu-msi-ila-fe-wanu,* the Great Spirit, was busy making a net, the *skemotah,* which one day, at *Moneto*'s command, would be thrown over the entire world. Those who were worthy would be taken up in the net and transported to a world of eternal life, where there would be peace and plenty forever. Then the old world would be destroyed, along with all those left behind.

A Shawnee was expected to be absolutely honest with the rest of his tribe. There could be no lying, no stealing, no dishonorable conduct of any kind suffered by one Shawnee at the hand of another. This was the fundamental rule that guided every action. A Shawnee, man or woman, who deceived another would be banished from the tribe, and for a Shawnee, death was preferable to exile.

This Shawnee golden rule applied only within the tribe. As for conduct toward outsiders there was no standard. A Shawnee had no responsibility toward a white man, or a member of another tribe.

These and many other things Pucksinwah taught his youngest son, Tecumseh—things that had to be inculcated at an early age. But it was not just Tecumseh who had to learn. There was Blue Jacket, as well.

Blue Jacket had been born white. Two years ago he had been taken captive, at the age of seventeen. His *Shemanese* name was Marmaduke Von Swearingen. He and one of his six brothers had been out hunting when eleven Shawnees stumbled upon them in the forest.

Duke, as he was called, and his younger brother would have perished then and there but for the fact that Duke spoke the Shawnee tongue. This came as quite a shock to the Indians. They could not have known that all his life Duke had admired the Indian way of life.

He had learned many Indian words from a neighbor, an old trader who was happy to share his vast store of knowledge about the red man with Duke.

To a man the Shawnee hunting party was impressed by Duke's fearlessness. He palavered with them for over an hour, and when all was said and done, he promised to accompany the warriors to their village. The Shawnees had come to the conclusion that they ought to adopt him. That suited Duke just fine. His brother did not want to see him go, but Duke convinced him that it was the only way either one of them would live to see another sunrise.

"Don't worry, little brother," said Duke. "You know this is what I've always wanted."

"But what about Ma?"

"Tell her that someday maybe I will see her again. You, too."

"But Duke . . ."

"I'm not Duke Von Swearingen any longer. They've already given me a new name." He rattled off six syllables of Shawnee that sounded to his brother like a bunch of snorts with a couple of grunts thrown in for good measure. "I like it much better than my old name."

"What does it mean?"

Grinning, Duke fingered his blue linsey-woolsey hunting shirt. "Blue Jacket."

When the hunting party arrived at Kispoko Town, Duke was required to run the gauntlet. If he showed fear, or faltered, he would be refused adoption. The consequence of that refusal, of course, would be death. Duke knew this. The old trader had acquainted him with many of the Shawnee customs. But he was unafraid, and did not falter.

It took him a fortnight to recover from the brutal beating he endured in the gauntlet. Later, he was painted from heel to hairline in a variety of colors and taken down to the Scioto River. Pucksinwah uttered a brief litany before the assembled village. Three squaws led Duke into the river and took mischievous pleasure in scrubbing and scouring him with sand until every bit of the paint was gone. By this ritual they symbolically cleansed him of every bit of white man.

After that painful ordeal, Duke was brought to the huge council house. He was dressed in buckskin with beads and quillwork. Hundreds of Shawnees looked on as Pucksinwah presented him with a pipe tomahawk adorned with feathers. Duke and many others smoked their pipes, and the pungent aroma of kinnikinnick—a mixture of tobacco, dogwood, willow, and sumac—filled the council house. Finally Pucksinwah formally welcomed him into the tribe with a long and solemn speech. The chief adopted him into his own family.

It was Pucksinwah's duty to instruct Blue Jacket on the social customs, politics, and religion of the tribe. Blue Jacket was a quick and enthusiastic study. Soon he had mastered the Shawnee tongue. He showed the utmost respect not only for Pucksinwah but for all the Shawnee and their ways. In return, the Shawnee treated him as though he had been born an Indian. This was immensely gratifying to Blue Jacket. As for Pucksinwah, he was convinced that *Moneto* had been in one of His mischievous moods on the day of Blue Jacket's birth, to have ordained that his adopted son—as true an Indian on the inside as he was himself—was to enter this world with white skin.

Blue Jacket became an extremely popular member of the Kispokotha clan. The warriors admired him because he excelled in sports and hunting. The young women liked him because he was tall and good-looking. His blue eyes and ready smile melted their hearts.

Perhaps Blue Jacket's closest friend was Pucksinwah's own son, Chiksika. A few years younger than Blue Jacket, he looked up to the chief's adopted son. They were very close, and it pleased Pucksinwah to see this. Even little Tecumseh, three years old, adored Blue Jacket.

III
(1773)

At the great meeting five winters ago at Chillicothe, Cornstalk with his talk of peace and accommodation had won the day, despite the somber warnings of Pucksinwah and others that war with the *Shemanese* was inevitable. As a result, the Shawnee nation had signed the Fort Stanwix Treaty. This treaty guaranteed that the land north and west of the Ohio River would remain to the Shawnee, inviolate forever.

Now, five summers later, a Long Knife named Bullitt arrived in Chillicothe and informed Black Fish, chief of the Chalahgawtha sept and second only to Cornstalk, that the white men were going to settle in *Can-tuc-kee,* the sacred hunting grounds of the Shawnee. Bullitt had been dispatched by Lord Dunmore, the White Father of Virginia, to inform the Shawnee of this *fait accompli.* He brought gifts—calico, beads, twenty new skinning knives—as a token of friendship. And he assured Black Fish that the land north of the Ohio River would not be coveted by his people.

Black Fish frowned at the buckskin-clad frontiersman sitting opposite a small fire from him in his *wegiwa*.

"But the *Shemanese* have already come across the river. They have killed some of my people. It has not been easy keeping our young warriors from the warpath."

"Isolated hunting parties," said Bullitt. "They know if they get caught they would be punished for breaking the treaty."

"Tell that to the widows of the dead. Have any of these men been caught? Have any of them suffered for killing Shawnee?"

"Not unless you caught them," admitted Bullitt. "I believe I saw some white topknots on that scalp pole out yonder."

"Perhaps," said Black Fish, with a shrug.

"We don't object. Any hunter crossing the Ohio forsakes his rights."

"How *could* you object? This is our land. Our laws prevail here."

Bullitt nodded. "We respect that."

"But now your people have come down the *Spay-lay-wi-theepi*, as far as the great falls, and they are turning up the earth, and building *wegiwas* made of logs and mud."

"Only in *Can-tuc-kee,* south of the river."

Black Fish grimaced. "We do not own that land. No one can, not even you. It belongs to the ghosts of the Azgens, an ancient people from the eastern sea."

"They were white people, weren't they?"

"So it is said."

Bullitt wondered if the mysterious white people the Indians called the Azgens could possibly have been members of the Lost Colony, Sir Walter Raleigh's settlement at Roanoke, which had vanished two hundred years ago. Most assuredly the eastern sea of which Black Fish spoke was the Atlantic Ocean.

"The Azgen protect the game in *Can-tuc-kee,* and it will always be plentiful, as long as we honor the claim of the ghost people upon that land," continued Black Fish. "Our grandfathers killed the Azgens, but their spirits are very powerful now, and we fear them. If we attempted to live in *Can-tuc-kee,* or killed more game than we needed, the ghosts would come out of their caves and with their magic turn brother against brother, and neighbor against neighbor, until we had all killed ourselves."

Bullitt did not believe this superstitious nonsense about ghosts and magic, but he evinced the utmost respect as he listened to Black Fish, because it was obvious the Shawnee chief believed it.

"We cannot give you permission to live in *Can-tuc-kee,*" Black Fish said solemnly, "as it is not ours to give. But we will continue to hunt there as before."

"Of course. There is enough game for all. Never has there been a more bountiful land, Black Fish."

The Shawnee chief was skeptical. "Perhaps. But be warned, *Shemanese,* that to survive the Shawnee must kill enough game in *Can-tuc-kee* to feed our women and children, and get enough plews to trade for our blankets, our rifles, and our gunpowder. If your people try to keep us out of *Can-tuc-kee,* there will be blood spilled between us."

"We will live in peace."

"Maybe so. And if any more Long Knives set foot on this, our land, above the *Spay-lay-wi-theepi,* they will be put to death."

Bullitt let Black Fish have the last word, and took his leave. The Shawnee chief dispatched five braves to follow the Long Knife and make certain that he crossed the river, leaving their land.

Led by Peshawa, the warriors trailed the unsuspecting Bullitt to the banks of the Ohio, where he was met by fifteen men in four canoes. All the *Shemanese* headed downriver. Peshawa and his companions shadowed them, riding along the northern bank, remaining hidden in the forest.

Bullitt's party contained surveyors commissioned by Lord Dunmore to chart the land south of the Ohio and in the vicinity of the great falls. There was another surveying party at work near the mouth of the Scioto. Bullitt left eight men and two canoes on the south shore of the Ohio at the confluence of the Great Miami River, and continued on down to the falls.

Peshawa decided to stay near the mouth of the Miami River and watch the men Bullitt left behind. So neither he nor the eight *Shemanese* across the river could know that two days later Bullitt met disaster at the great falls, wrecking both canoes against the rocks. No lives were lost, nor many provisions, and the surveying equipment was saved. Bullitt and his party remained at the falls to do their surveying, and then had no choice but to walk back up the river to rejoin their comrades. This delayed their scheduled arrival, and the eight-man detail began to fret.

They decided to get into their canoes and paddle out to the middle of the river, where they could see past the point of land where the river bends—and, with any luck, spot Bullitt's party returning from downriver. In putting into action this bit of wishful thinking, they discovered that the middle of the river would not do—

they would have to go to the northern bank, or close to it.

Even then, there was nothing to see downriver. Disappointed, they landed on the north shore and talked things over. Clearly Bullitt and his companions had met with mishap. Should they stay put, or head downriver and try to find their missing friends? But if it was Indian trouble, what could eight men do? It was decided that three men would take one of the canoes upriver. Somewhere near the mouth of the Scioto was another surveying party. These men would be enlisted in the search for Bullitt, since there was a kernel of truth in that old axiom, strength in numbers.

Peshawa and his four brother warriors saw the three Long Knives depart in the canoe, leaving five behind. The Indians had patiently waited and watched the white men across the river ever since Bullitt had departed for the great falls. Black Fish had instructed them to do so until the *Shemanese* were gone. But now the white men were on the Shawnee side of the river. The chief of the Chalahgawtha had been explicit in his instructions—henceforth, any white man who stepped foot on Shawnee soil would have to leave immediately, or pay the consequences.

The Shawnee braves discussed matters. Their decision: They would wait until the sun had crossed the sky before taking action, giving the white men every opportunity to leave of their own volition.

But all day the anxious *Shemanese* lingered on the northern bank of the mighty Ohio, watching for Bullitt. They had forgotten all about their surveying job across the river. Bullitt was overdue, there was trouble, and they were worried. The Shawnees again conferred, and deemed it prudent to wait until sunrise.

The sun rose to find the five *Shemanese* still camped on the northern bank.

"I will ride in alone," said Peshawa. He handed his rifle to one of the others. "They will see that I come in peace if I am without this."

"Do you think that is wise, Peshawa?"

Peshawa was grimly resolute.

"They must be given the chance to leave in peace. I will tell them they must go."

And so the brave young warrior rode down out of the forest into the camp of the whites. There was no stealth in his approach, but still the nervous *Shemanese* did not hear him coming. When he called out to them they almost jumped out of their skins. One of them grabbed up his flinklock.

"Don't shoot, Ward!" exclaimed one of the surveyors, the first to notice that the Shawnee was not only alone but unarmed.

It was too late. The man named Ward fired, and the bullet caught Peshawa just above the left eye, killing him instantly.

IV
(1774)

Pucksinwah was finally going to have his war with the *Shemanese*.

He derived no pleasure from the fact. Unsure that this war could be won, nonetheless he knew it had to be fought. Several events, though horrible and tragic, conspired to give his words greater weight in the council than those even of the peaceloving Cornstalk, the principal chief of the Shawnee Nation.

Last spring, a party of frontiersmen had appeared across the Ohio River from a small encampment of Mingos. It so happened that among these Indians was Shikellimus, father of the great Mingo chief Logan. Shikellimus and his son had always been friends of the white man. In fact, James Logan had been named after a white man, James Logan, a colleague of William Penn. Quakers like Penn and James Logan kept faith with the Indians, and James Logan had developed a close personal friendship with Shikellimus.

Chief Logan's reputation as a peacemaker was well-deserved. He had refused to allow his tribe to become embroiled in the French and Indian Wars. He had declined an offer to join Pontiac's ill-fated uprising. And recently he had respectfully refused to join the Shawnees to fight the Long Knives who were pouring into *Can-tuc-kee* by the hundreds.

Pucksinwah had already paid Logan a visit at the Mingo village on Yellow Creek. Aware that Logan's words were heeded by the Delawares and Wyandots as well as the Cayugas and Senecas, Pucksinwah had hoped to persuade the Mingo chief to join him in the war that Pucksinwah had long deemed inevitable. It was in Pucksinwah's mind that if he could sway Logan, Cornstalk would reconcile himself to war. Cornstalk's chief argument against taking the warpath was the indisputable fact that the Shawnees by themselves could not hope to prevail against the whites. There were perhaps a thousand Shawnee warriors in all the septs. The Long Knives greatly outnumbered them.

Pucksinwah's dream was a confederacy of all the tribes to the north of the Ohio River, and Logan was the key to achieving that end. If Logan and the Mingos picked up the tomahawk, so would many other tribes. Together they would stand a fighting chance.

But Logan had politely refused to sign on with Pucksinwah.

Then, only weeks after Pucksinwah's visit to the village at Yellow Creek, the party of frontiersmen, led by the notorious Jacob Greathouse, had come calling on Shikellimus, all smiles and words of friendship, inviting the old Mingo to bring his people across the river and share their rum, and even perhaps engage in a friendly shooting match.

Shikellimus did not wish to offend these *Shemanese*. But as his small band was about to break camp, with the intention of traveling to Logan's village on Yellow Creek, he could send only five braves to represent the tribe. Greathouse returned across the river, and a little while later the Mingos arrived in their canoe—the five best marksmen in the band. They were accompanied by the daughter of Shikellimus, Logan's pretty sister. An added bonus, mused Greathouse, as he broke out the rum.

The Indians were encouraged to drink their fill. Then they were invited to shoot first in the match. A strip of cloth tacked to the trunk of a tree was the target. The Mingos fired their rifles, one at a time. Already well on the way to inebriation, only one of them came close to the mark. Their poor shooting struck them as amusing.

When all of the Mingos had discharged their weapons, Greathouse gave a signal, and his five companions raised their flintlocks and fired into the Indians. Three warriors were killed outright. The other two—having failed in their rum stupor to reload their rifles—drew their knives and tomahawks, but pistol fire finished them off. Logan's sister ran screaming for the river. Greathouse caught her. He and two of his men had their rough way with her. Then Greathouse opened her up from sternum to crotch with one vicious swipe of his tomahawk.

All six Indians were scalped. What Shikellimus had not known was that Virginia had recently offered a bounty on Shawnee scalps. Greathouse was fairly certain that the authorities in charge of collecting the scalps and paying out the bounty would not be able to distinguish between Mingo and Shawnee topknots.

To Greathouse's delight, Shikellimus and twenty warriors rushed to their canoes and crossed the river to investigate the yells and screams of red prey and white predator. The frontiersmen proceeded to pick them off in their birchbarks like sitting ducks. Not a single Mingo reached the south side of the Ohio, and only a handful made it back to their village on the north bank. Shikellimus perished. Some of the bodies were fished out of the river for their scalps, but most of the corpses were swept away by the strong current.

When word of this treachery reached Chief Logan, he led a war party from the Yellow Creek village. But Greathouse and his scalphunters were long gone.

The grief-stricken Logan addressed his warriors with the scalped and ravaged body of his sister in his arms. There would be no more peace for him. He would not put down his tomahawk until he personally had taken ten white lives for every Mingo murdered here. The Mingos vowed to follow him to their deaths.

Logan did not return to Yellow Creek, but traveled instead to Kispoko Town, where he agreed to ally himself with Pucksinwah.

And then, a fortnight later, Cornstalk, too, changed his mind about war.

The Fort Pitt Indian agent, Colonel Croghan, sent an envoy to the principal chief of the Shawnee, inviting Cornstalk to come to the fort and talk peace with colonial representatives.

Cornstalk agreed, convinced that this would be his last chance to secure peace on the frontier. He appeared at Fort Pitt with his brother Silverheels and his sister Non-hel-e-ma. The latter was known as the Grenadier Squaw by the whites. Over six feet tall, this redskin Amazon could fight better than most male warriors.

In only a few short years the town of Pittsburgh had grown up around the stronghold. There were dozens of homes, as well as stables, taverns, and stores. The population was swollen now by hundreds of whites who had abandoned isolated farms and outposts to seek the security of Fort Pitt, as the past few months had witnessed an increase in violence on the borderlands.

As Croghan's messenger escorted the three Shawnees through the town, heading for the main gate of the fort, where the colonel awaited to greet his guests with the utmost pomp and ceremony, a crowd of hostile frontiersmen gathered. Harsh words were spoken, and then the buckskin-clad *Shemanese* rushed the Indians. Colonel Croghan led a detachment of redcoats from the fort to disperse the frontiersmen at the point of the bayonet. But it was too late for Silverheels, who was seriously wounded by a knife thrust into his chest.

The mortified Croghan apologized profusely to Cornstalk, and promised that Silverheel's assailant would be brought to justice. But Cornstalk would not listen. In stony silence, he and the Grenadier Squaw took their leave. Non-hel-e-ma carried Silverheels all the way back to Chillicothe. He survived his wound. But in the fall, when again all the septs met for the great council, Cornstalk was not so outspoken for peace as he had been on previous occasions. This time, Pucksinwah prevailed.

Scouts informed the council of the enemy's disposition. Lord Dunmore himself was leading several hundred militiamen across the mountains from Virginia, having finally decided to heed the pleas for protection from the settlers in Kentucky. And there were several hundred frontiersmen assembled at the Great Kanawha River, under the command of Colonel Andrew Lewis.

Cornstalk listened to these reports and made up his mind.

"Several suns must pass overhead before Dunmore can join the Long Knives at the Kanawha. We must strike quickly before the *Shemanese* are all together. If we hesitate, we will lose the advantage of numbers."

In an hour's time seven hundred Shawnee warriors were on the warpath, led by Cornstalk himself. They carried dozens of canoes, each strapped between two horses. Behind the principal chief rode Pucksinwah and his friend Black Snake. The Grenadier Squaw was there, too, as was Pucksinwah's eldest, Chiksika. So was his adopted son, Blue Jacket.

They were headed southeast through the rolling, wooded hills of Ohio, making straight for the mouth of the Great Kanawha, and the camp of the unsuspecting Long Knives under Colonel Lewis.

V

Colonel Andrew Lewis was well-respected by the frontiersmen who had placed themselves under his command. Lewis was fearless, but not foolhardy. An accomplished Indian fighter, he did not ask of his men anything he would not attempt himself. He was a natural-born leader. And he had the utmost faith in his men.

The camp he had chosen to await the arrival of Dunmore and the Virginia militia was on the banks of the Ohio, a place called Point Pleasant. This triangle of wooded land was bordered on one side by the Ohio and on another by the Great Kanawha. The point itself presided over the confluence of these two rivers.

On Sunday, October 9th, Colonel Lewis conducted noon services for his men, reading to them from Psalms and leading them in a prayer for final victory over the red savages who posed an unacceptable threat to their families. Unbeknownst to them, seven hundred Shawnees were at that very moment crossing the Ohio a mile upstream in the canoes they had transported all the way from Chillicothe.

Having studied the *Shemanese* position from across the Ohio, Cornstalk decided that the only way to attack was by getting across the river undetected and trapping the Long Knives against the rivers on Point Pleasant.

By dawn on the 10th, all the Shawnees were across the river and advancing through the woods. One of Lewis's scouts brought word to the camp. Calm and collected, Lewis called for his company commanders. A half mile from the point, the frontiersmen formed a line and advanced to meet the Indians. As morning

27

sunlight began to slant through the trees, the two forces met. A rolling crash of gunfire from one end of the line to the other signaled the beginning of the battle.

At first, the Shawnees seemed to be getting the better of it. The frontiersmen were pressed back. But they refused to retreat very far. Finding concealment behind rocks, logs, and trees, they laid down a withering fire which sent the Indians reeling backward. Seeing the Shawnees falling back, they jumped up with a whoop and holler and gave chase. But Pucksinwah and Cornstalk rallied their warriors, and it became the frontiersmen's turn to waver and fall back.

So it went, a back-and-forth battle that raged until noon on a front a half mile wide and only two hundred yards deep, because while both sides bent, they would not break. Colonel Lewis saw his brother Charles fall, mortally wounded. Blue Jacket distinguished himself, taking seven scalps, using his long rifle until he was out of powder and shot, then his bow until the quiver was empty, and finally resorting to knife and tomahawk.

Chiksika fought valiantly beside his father, and so was present when Pucksinwah fell with a bullet in his chest.

"Drive the *Shemanese* across the mountains," Pucksinwah told his son with his dying breath. "Do this thing, so that your brother Tecumseh can live in peace."

And so the Kispokotha chieftain, the great warrior who made war in order to have peace, died in the arms of his eldest son.

A hundred men, red and white, died that day. The shooting tapered off early in the afternoon. Cornstalk's scouts reported the approach of a large force of

Shemanese. Assuming this was Dunmore, and that the initial reports received at the great council in Chillicothe were in error, Cornstalk reluctantly called for withdrawal. He was discouraged, too, by the death of Pucksinwah. He could not know that Lewis's exhausted frontiersmen were nearly out of ammunition. One strong, concerted push might have broken the line of the Long Knives and driven them into the rivers. And he could not know that the advancing *Shemanese* were not Dunmore and his three hundred Virginians, but rather a band of forty buckskins come to join their friends and neighbors.

The Shawnees quickly crossed the Ohio and headed home. Lewis did not hesitate to engage in hot pursuit. He dispatched a runner to Lord Dunmore.

"Tell him we are marching on Chillicothe," said the grim, fierce border captain, his buckskins stained with the blood of his dead brother. "If he wants to share in the honor of destroying the Shawnee threat forever, he had better hurry."

Vengeance motivated Andrew Lewis to such audacious action—pursuing a superior force into their own land with weary men whose powderhorns and bullet pouches were almost empty. But not a single frontiersman balked. Many of them had lost loved ones to the Indians—loved ones whose murdered souls cried out for vengeance. And being outnumbered had never fazed these stalwart bordermen.

Crossing the Ohio delayed Lewis, as he had relatively few canoes available. But cross he did, and struck out on the trail of Cornstalk's Shawnees.

Upon reaching Chillicothe, Cornstalk was dismayed to learn of a strong sentiment for peace among the men who sat around the council fire.

"I am ashamed to hear such words from the mouths of the Shawnees," exclaimed Cornstalk, as he chastised his warriors. "If you wanted peace, why did we go to war? For years you have clamored for the blood of the Long Knives. I spoke against it, but you did not want to listen then. Now that you have tasted their blood you want no more of it?"

"We must seek peace with the Long Knives," replied one of the other chiefs. "If we do not, they will come to our villages and kill our women and children."

Blue Jacket stood up to speak. He had never spoken to the council, but now that he had distinguished himself in battle he had every right to do so.

"My mother, Methotosa, is sitting in her lodge with the body of the great Shawnee warrior, Pucksinwah, in her arms. Listen! You may be able to hear her wailing, as she grieves over her *wahsiu*. You should have listened to my father long ago. He was *nenothtu oukimah*—a great warrior chief. He warned you many winters ago that it was time to fight the Long Knives and drive them from our hunting grounds, before they became too strong. But you would not listen."

"Now they *are* too strong," confessed one crestfallen warrior. "We must ask for peace, or the woods will be filled with the wailing of hundreds of Shawnee women."

Blue Jacket's eyes flashed with cold blue fury.

"Better that we kill all our women and children ourselves, and then go out to die like Shawnee warriors should, with our faces to the enemy."

But the council would not hear of such extreme measures.

A runner was sent to Lord Dunmore, to inform the White Father of Virginia that the Shawnees wanted peace. Dunmore was vastly relieved, and hurried to intercept Lewis and his frontiersmen before the vengeance-seeking buckskins could reach Chillicothe. He only just made it in time. It wasn't easy convincing Lewis that the war was over. Dunmore had to resort to threatening the infuriated border captain with his sword.

"It will never be over until the Shawnees are destroyed—or we are," warned Lewis. "They will make peace with you today, and you will disband your militia and go home, and then next year they will be on the warpath again, killing our women and children. Mark my words. Better to finish it now, one way or the other."

But Dunmore would not heed such brutal advice. He and Cornstalk met and hashed out a treaty agreement. It would be as before. The Shawnees would retain their land north of the Ohio, and would be allowed to hunt in *Can-tuc-kee*. But only the most optimistic on both sides truly believed that this was anything more than an armistice. There would be more killing.

VI
(1777)

The nine-year-old Tecumseh crouched outside the long *msi-kah-mi-qui* and listened to the debate raging inside. Over three hundred chiefs, sub-chiefs, and warriors representing all the Shawnee clans were meeting once again to discuss the problem of the *Shemanese*.

Resentment was running high, and it was best expressed by Black Fish, chief of the Chalahgawthas. Black Fish voiced the complaints shared by the entire congregation. The buffalo and the elk were being slaughtered in the hundreds by the Long Knives, killed for their tongues and their hides and their horns. Ever since the treaty at Camp Charlotte, which had ended Lord Dunmore's War two years ago, the *Shemanese* had come pouring over the mountains. They shot at every Indian they saw. Hunting parties sometimes never returned from *Can-tuc-kee*. This state of affairs could not be allowed to continue. Had the Shawnees no pride?

Cornstalk rose to remind the council that they had given their word at Camp Charlotte to keep the peace. Were the Shawnees without honor? They could not defeat the *Shemanese*, who were too numerous. An unpleasant fact, yes, but one which had to be acknowledged. To go to war now would result in the destruction of the Shawnee Nation.

The chief of the Thawegilas addressed the assembly next. The Thawegilas would not fight another war against the Long Knives. If the Shawnee Nation decided to fight, the Thawegilas would cross the Mother of Waters to the west, never to return.

This gave the other delegates pause. It was what they feared most—the splintering of the nation.

But Blue Jacket was not long plagued by second thoughts. He rose and spoke forcefully for war.

"Now is the time to drive the Long Knives from *Can-tuc-kee*. The whites are at war with each other. No longer can the colonists depend on the redcoat soldiers for protection. We may never have a better opportunity. The destruction of our people, our nation, our way of life is inevitable if we do not fight. We have nothing to lose by taking up the tomahawk and striking the war post, because if we do not, we have lost everything anyway."

Listening from outside, huddled in the January cold, Tecumseh was proud of his adopted brother. He admired Blue Jacket. But it was Chiksika who had taken upon himself the responsibility to teach Tecumseh the history, traditions, customs, and laws of the Shawnee, taking up where Pucksinwah had left off. None of these things were written down. They had to memorized—and memorized perfectly, with nothing added or omitted—and passed down from generation to generation.

Blue Jacket loved Tecumseh, but he had little time to spare for the boy. He was often away from Kispoko Town, down in *Can-tuc-kee,* ostensibly on hunting trips, but Tecumseh, a smart lad, knew better. Blue Jacket hated the Long Knives. The death of Pucksinwah had darkened his heart. He and a handful of warriors crossed the river many times with the intention of breaking the treaty. They burned cabins and killed livestock and sometimes they ambushed the settlers. Men, women, and children fell beneath their tomahawks. Chiksika never stopped trying to persuade Blue Jacket to cease these acts of violence. They only made things worse, hardening the hearts of the Long Knives against the Shawnee. But Blue Jacket called it retribution, and he refused to stop.

Tecumseh was a quick study. He was highly intelligent. Under Chiksika's able tutorship, he mastered the art of tracking, how to build a *wegiwa,* how to find edible roots, as well as those useful in the treating of wounds or an illness. He learned that buzzard feathers were best for plugging a wound, and should always be carried. He learned that white oak made a smokeless yet very hot fire. He learned to commune with nature. When birds flew low to the ground and made no song, it meant a bad storm was rising. When the blackbirds flocked to fly south in the summer, then the coming winter would be a harsh one, with much snow. When the leaves of the maple turned over there would be thunder and lightning. If there was no dew on the grass at twilight it would rain during the night.

Tall and lithe and strong for his age, Tecumseh excelled at all sports. He could run faster, and swim farther, than all of his friends. It seemed perfectly natural that he assume the mantle of leadership among the Kispokotha boys of his generation. He excelled with the bow. He could ride like the wind.

From his elder brother he learned how to master his emotions. "Blue Jacket allows himself to be ruled by his passions," Chiksika ruefully informed Tecumseh. "They will destroy him. That is not to say he is wrong in what he feels. But you, Tecumseh, should learn from his errors. Always think before you speak or act. Never reveal your innermost feelings unless you are certain it is to your advantage to do so. Never let others know what is in your mind until you are ready for them to know."

From Chiksika, too, Tecumseh learned that honor was everything to a Shawnee. If he lied or cheated or stole he would forfeit his soul. He must be honest always, to himself as well to all others.

In his tenth year, Tecumseh would be ready to learn the ways of the warrior. To prepare him—to make him physically and mentally tough—Chiksika started him on a daily regimen. Every morning, Tecumseh would strip naked, run to the river, dive in, swim to the bottom, and then emerge to run back to the *wegiwa*. This he did, every day, without complaint, rain or shine. Summer passed into autumn, and autumn into winter. The river became icy cold. Sometimes, he had to break through solid ice just to make the dive. This ordeal tested Tecumseh's endurance and courage to the limits.

And when winter had passed, in the month of the Green Moon, Chiksika began to teach Tecumseh the art of warfare, which he himself had learned so well from Pucksinwah.

VII

1777—the Year of the Three Sevens—would forever be remembered by the Long Knives of Kentucky and their descendants. It was the year of savage Shawnee attacks, unequaled in ferocity and frequency by anything that had come before. A year when the woods were filled with the crack of rifle fire, the war whoops of painted braves, the screams of women, the crackle of flames. It was a year that gave new meaning to the Kentucky nickname—the Dark and Bloody Ground.

The Shawnee raids resulted in the abandonment of isolated outposts—McClelland's, Leestown, St. Asaph, Danville, and others. Dozens of pioneer families were slain. The rest rushed to the relative safety of Kentucky's two major settlements, Boonesboro and Harrodsburg. The latter suffered three major attacks, all of them led by Black Fish himself. With only seventy-five fighting men, short on food and ammunition, Harrodsburg somehow held out. The weather was a factor. A storm of snow mixed with hail disrupted the first attack. When, days later, the skies cleared, Black Fish attacked again. Yet in an hour's time dark and angry clouds again blotted out the sun. A driving sleet came, and the temperature plummeted. For ten days it rained. For ten nights the temperature fell below freezing. And on the day that Black Fish launched his third desperate assault, the temperature dropped to well below zero. His suffering warriors began to mutter that *Moneto* was protecting the settlement of the Long Knives. Discouraged, Black Fish withdrew.

The attack on Bonnesboro followed. The defenders were even fewer in number than at Harrodsburg, but among them were two of the greatest Indian fighters— Simon Kenton and Daniel Boone.

Boone was wounded in the initial attack, and would have perished beneath a Shawnee tomahawk but for the bravery of Kenton, who rescued Boone, who had been caught out in the open. Kenton killed four warriors with four shots, and a fifth with his own hatchet. His marksmanship was phenomenal and deadly, as the Shawnees would discover in the days to come. Every bullet that left the barrel of Jacob, Kenton's famed longrifle, claimed another Shawnee life. With Kenton's inspiring courage, and the older Boone's wise counsel, the outnumbered frontiersmen held out for days against repeated attacks. Finally, the disheartened Shawnees retired, taking their dead with them.

Returning to the Ohio, Black Fish discovered that the outpost at St. Asaph was reoccupied by the *Shemanese,* who, having fled to Harrodsburg and survived the attacks there, presumed the danger was passed. When seven of the white women emerged one morning to milk the cows in the pen adjacent to the stockade, they were cut down by Shawnee rifle fire from nearby woods. The distraught men of St. Asaph could not retrieve the bodies until nightfall, due to the

continual fire of their unseen foe. That night the Shawnees crept up and scalped and mutilated the bodies of
the women before the men inside the stockade could
summon up the grit to venture forth. But the next day
the Indians were gone, having refused the order of
Black Fish for an all-out attack on the weakly defended
outpost. They had learned their lesson the hard way at
Harrodsburg and Boonesboro.

The bloody campaign of Black Fish in the spring
and summer of 1777 accomplished little for the Shawnee cause, and the killing of the St. Asaph women
hardened every Kentucky heart against the Indians.

At the end of the summer, Cornstalk appeared at
Fort Randolph, a stockade erected on Point Pleasant
where, three years earlier, the one and only battle of
Lord Dunmore's War had been fought. Seeing again
those thick woods, where too many Shawnee warriors,
including the brave Pucksinwah, had perished, made
Cornstalk's heart heavy with grief.

His heart was heavy, too, because of all the blood
that had been spilled during this Year of the Three Sevens. It seemed as though the world was turned upside
down. He had labored so hard and so long for peace.
And yet peace eluded him and his people. So he had
come here out of a sense of honor, to inform the Long
Knives that he could no longer control the young men
of the Shawnee nation. With him was his son
Elinipsico, and a sub-chief by the name of Red Hawk.

The officer in charge of Fort Randolph's small garrison, Captain Arbuckle, was willing to listen to what
the great principal chief of the Shawnees had to say.

"Three years ago," began the grave Cornstalk, "I
gave my word that the Shawnee would keep the peace.
I promised that my people would not fight the

Shemanese who came over the mountains to live on our hunting grounds of *Can-tuc-kee*. I have come to tell you now that I cannot keep that promise."

"We figured as much," replied Arbuckle sourly. "Seeing as how your bucks have been burning and butchering all up and down this country for the past few months."

"My young men have been provoked beyond the point at which I can restrain them."

"It's the British, isn't it? They've been urging you to attack our settlements. They've got you fighting their fight for them. They've been providing you with rifles, powder, and shot. Can you deny that?"

"Why should I deny it? It is the truth."

"You think the British are your friends?"

"Once I thought you were all British. Once I thought you were all friends of the Shawnees. And yet my people are shot and killed when all they are doing is hunting in *Can-tuc-kee,* as their fathers had done before them, and their fathers before them. They are shot and killed when all they are doing is standing on the banks of the *Spay-lay-wi-theepi* when your people pass by in their boats."

"They're being shot at because my people never know when they're going to get ambushed and scalped. Isn't it true that the British are offering a bounty for our scalps?"

Cornstalk shook his head. "I have heard of no such bounty. The only bounty I ever knew of was the one the White Father of Virginia placed on the scalps of the Shawnee."

"Lord Dunmore was British."

"Are you not?"

"No. I'm an American."

"I do not understand."

"It doesn't matter," said Arbuckle coldly. "It seems our differences, yours and mine, are irreconcilable."

Cornstalk nodded sadly and rose to go.

Arbuckle summoned the guard. "Escort these three Indians to the guardhouse. Since we're at war with the British, and the Shawnee Nation is allied with England, we'll hold them as prisoners of war."

It was then that Cornstalk realized his mistake—possibly a fatal one. He had come here to do the honorable thing, assuming that the whites would be equally as honorable, and let him go, as he had come, in peace.

The Shawnees were tossed into the guardhouse. A little while later they heard angry voices from beyond the walls.

Cornstalk turned solemnly to Elinipsico.

"Neequithah—my son—we are about to die."

"I know, Father."

Elinipsico's quiet courage made Cornstalk's heart swell with pride.

The guardhouse door burst back on its leather hinges. Several men, armed with rifles, entered.

"My God, it's true," breathed one. "That's Cornstalk, right enough."

He raised his rifle. Red Hawk launched himself at the frontiersman, acting instinctively to defend his chief. He fell, shot through the heart.

Cornstalk and Elinipsico stood straight and unflinching as the rifles swung toward them and spat flame.

A dozen men entered the guardhouse to discharge their rifles into the corpse of the great Shawnee chief. When it was done, they would all boast that they had slain Cornstalk.

VIII
(1778)

The killing continued.

Daniel Boone was captured by the Shawnees, at the salt springs of the Scioto, and taken to Detroit with another frontiersman. On the way, Black Fish became so impressed with Boone's courage and composure that when it was time to surrender his prisoners he could only bring himself to sell Boone's companion, and not Boone himself, even though the British Governor Hamilton offered a king's ransom for the famous border captain.

Boone respected the Indians, and thoroughly understood their ways. Black Fish expressed a desire to adopt him into the tribe. Boone consented, and became known as *Sheltowee*—Big Turtle. He seemed quite content living in Chillicothe. He outhunted and outshot every warrior in the village. They admired him tremendously for his prowess in these things, and they were beguiled by his apparent contentment.

Of course, Boone kept his eyes open for a chance to escape, and escape he eventually did, bringing word to Boonesboro that Black Fish and over four hundred warriors were preparing to attack the settlement. What really burned the frontiersman's bacon was the fact that two redcoat officers were accompanying the Shawnees this time. Nonetheless, the siege that followed ended as had the one the previous year, with the Shawnees giving up and going home.

While Black Fish was besieging Boonesboro, Simon Kenton and a few hardy colleagues slipped into Shawnee country to steal back some of the horses the Indians had pilfered. But the frontiersmen were caught, and all but Kenton slain. His reputation saved him. For the Shawnees, his capture was a tremendous coup. They paraded him from one village to the next, so that all could see with their own eyes this great enemy. At each village Kenton was forced to run the gauntlet. He was kicked, beaten, whipped, stoned, tortured, and humiliated. Yet he remained defiant through it all, never begging for mercy. Arriving finally at Chillicothe, he was tied to a post in front of the great council house. Black Fish had returned empty-handed from Boonesboro, and Kenton was declared *cut-ta-ho-tha*—a condemned man.

Among the crowd that gathered to gawk at the bruised and bleeding body of the great *Shemanese* was Tecumseh. All the septs were gathering in Chillicothe at this time. As Tecumseh watched, women and children ventured as close as they dared to Kenton, cursing him, spitting on him, or beating him with sticks. Kenton never once cried out in pain. And if an Indian ventured *too* close, Kenton lashed out with his long legs and sometimes managed to inflict some pain on his tormentors.

Tecumseh did not take part in the torture of Kenton. In fact, he was disgusted by the whole sorry spectacle. He was greatly impressed by the frontiersman's courage. If all the white men had such strong hearts and minds and bodies, then the Shawnees indeed were doomed.

The council of five hundred warriors, sub-chiefs, and chiefs from all the septs condemned Kenton to die at the stake. They did not even consider adopting him, as they had Boone. Big Turtle had fooled them. They could not afford to let Kenton escape. He had killed too many Shawnees. No, Kenton would be burned at the stake.

Preparations were being made for the execution

when Simon Girty arrived in Chillicothe. Girty's black heart was cursed roundly by every white man in Kentucky. He was a traitor to his race, having led the Shawnees on their raids against his own kind. Or so the Kentuckians said.

Truth was, Simon Girty had remained loyal to King George III, and he genuinely admired the Indians. He was also Simon Kenton's blood brother. They had hunted and scouted as a team prior to the outbreak of hostilities between colonists and crown, and had gone so far as to pledge their lives one to the other. Upon finding Kenton condemned to death, the renegade made an eloquent plea before the council, announcing to his Shawnee friends that Kenton was his brother, and reminding the Indians that he had served their cause faithfully, never asking for anything in return for that service. Never until now.

Another vote was taken in the *msi-kah-mi-qui*. This time Kenton was given a reprieve, but only by a slim margin. He was taken to Detroit to be made a prisoner of the British. It was the best Girty could do for him. The Shawnees were adamant on one point—Kenton could not be set free, to return to *Can-tuc-kee* and resume the killing of Indians.

Winter came, and during those months of idleness, when the snow that covered the warpath remained undisturbed, there was much talk in the villages of the Shawnee nation. Many people were weary of war. Nothing had been accomplished. The Long Knives were growing stronger, while the reverse was true of the Shawnees. Hundreds of warriors had perished in the past few years. And for what purpose? The *Shemanese* could not be driven from *Can-tuc-kee*. Better to ask for peace and adopt the white man's way and survive.

Others disagreed. To adopt such a course would be to live without honor. There would be more dignity in death.

The following spring witnessed the event that all Shawnees had been dreading. The nation was irrevocably divided. Leaving the Ohio country forever were most of the Thawegilis, the Peckuwas, and some of the Kispokothas, almost five thousand in all. What remained of the Kispokotha sept moved to Chillicothe, joining Black Fish and the Chalahgawtha Shawnee to continue the war against the Long Knives. Among these were Blue Jacket and Chiksika. The former's hate burned as strong as ever against the whites, the slayer of Pucksinwah. Chikshika remained with his adopted brother out of loyalty.

Tecumseh, of course, stayed with his brothers—and so was present that terrible summer when the Long Knives attacked Chillicothe.

IX
(1780)

It was blind luck that brought Colonel John Bowman and his two hundred and sixty militiamen to Chillicothe on a day when many of the warriors were away at a council meeting at Wapatomica. But even though they were outnumbered, the handful of Shawnee men and boys who remained put up a valiant defense of their village. Bowman's losses were heavy. The Shawnees fell back to the great council house in the middle of the village and made their stand. The militiamen could not budge them, so they gave up trying, and turned to looting. Then they set fire to the abandoned *wegiwas*.

Bowman did not press the attack. Carrying their plunder—furs, blankets, silver ornaments, and anything else they thought might be of some value—the militiamen retired, taking with them over two hundred Shawnee horses.

But the Shawnees weren't done.

Rounding up what few horses that were left to them, they proceeded to harass the column of militia, nipping at Bowman's heels. Before they were finally driven off for good, thirty white men had been killed.

The Indians had suffered only light casualties. Yet one of them was the principal chief of the Shawnee nation, Cornstalk's successor, Black Fish. A bullet had shattered his hip. Black Fish lingered in great agony for three months.

Bowman's attack hardened the hearts of the Shawnees who remained on their Ohio lands. A thousand *wegiwas* had been destroyed. Chillicothe would never be the same. And Black Fish had been much loved by his people. It was decided that full-scale war would be waged against the Long Knives—a war that would be fought to the bitter end, with no quarter given or expected.

Envoys were sent to the British at Detroit. Would the redcoats help the Shawnees attack the Kentuckians? In November, Captain Henry Byrd met in council on the Upper Sandusky with representatives from the Shawnees, the Hurons, the Wyandots, the Chippewas, and the Delawares. An invasion of Kentucky was planned, and set for the following summer.

True to his word, Captain Byrd returned in the summer, with a hundred redcoat regulars and seventy green-coated Canadian Rangers. They were joined by eight hundred Indians, who were pleased to see the six cannon Byrd had brought along. The forts of the Long

Knives were very strong, but surely they could not withstand such weapons. The Indians had high hopes. Never had such a force been brought against the Long Knives. At last they would have their revenge.

The British and their Indian allies marched into Kentucky and struck first at Ruddell's Station. The cannon knocking the stockade down around their ears, the Ruddell brothers, John and Isaac, raised the white flag and discussed terms with Byrd. The honorable British officer and gentleman promised that while the men would be taken as prisoners back to Detroit, the women and children would be permitted to travel in safety to the nearest settlement. The Kentuckians accepted these fair terms.

But as soon as the Long Knives laid down their weapons the Indians struck. Before Captain Byrd could stop them, twenty of the settlers had been murdered—men, women, and children. John Ruddell's son was snatched from his mother's arms and hurled into a fire. Mrs. Ruddell was tomahawked and scalped.

Captain Byrd was furious. While his regulars protected the survivors of Ruddell's Station, the outpost was ransacked and burned by vengeful Indians. Cold-eyed, Byrd watched his redskin allies at their worst. Then he called a council and demanded a promise from the chiefs that they would not allow their warriors to commit another such atrocity. The chiefs gave their word—and kept it at Martin's Station, the next settlement to fall to Byrd's cannon.

By then Byrd had several hundred captives—more than he could feed and protect. And the horrors he had witnessed at Ruddell's Station had soured him on the invasion. He decided to turn back, intent on delivering his prisoners to Detroit. The Indians were irate. They felt betrayed. Several prisoners were murdered during the long trek north, as the Indians vented their frustration, and in spite of Byrd's best efforts to protect them.

The invasion of Kentucky and the massacre at Ruddell's Station triggered an immediate and violent response from the Kentuckians.

A thousand mounted men under the command of George Rogers Clark crossed the Ohio River. Among Clark's company commanders were James Harrod and Benjamin Logan, stalwart Indian fighters. Simon Kenton was present as well, having escaped from Detroit, and now commissioned as captain of scouts.

As Clark's formidable army approached, plans were made to evacuate Chillicothe. The Chalahgawtha Shawnees had partially rebuilt their principal town, burned last by Bowman's militia. Now they put it to the torch themselves, destroying everything they could not carry with them in their flight north. Byrd and his soldiers had gone on to Detroit. The disgruntled Wyandots, Chippewas, Hurons, and Delawares, bickering among themselves, had gone home. That left the Shawnees alone to face the wrath of the *Shemanese*.

Clark marched on to the Shawnee town at Mad River. A few hundred Shawnees tried to make a stand there but were routed. The Indians scattered, and the frontiersmen burned the Mad River town and all the crops they could find, an act that would bring great hardship to the Shawnees the following winter.

When the snows came, Tecumseh listened to the cries of hungry children. Down deep inside him was a slow-burning rage. The once great Shawnee nation had been crushed by the Long Knives.

One day, he vowed, *I will avenge my people.*

CHAPTER TWO

Jonathan

December 15, 1808

Dearest Rebecca,

I have this day arrived safely in Frankfort. The weather is dismal—snow and rain—and the roads even worse, but there were no mishaps during my journey here, though the conditions made the trip much longer than should have been the case.

Frankfort is not at all what I expected for the capital of the state. Far fewer amenities here than one can find in Lexington, for example. The streets are quagmires. The state house is a rather austere structure, and has the look of a cross between a church and a hotel. I understand that on several occasions the attempt was made to relocate the capital to Lexington, without success, of course, and I suspect that this is due to a suspicion that the people's representatives would succumb to such temptations as the cockfights, horse races, and gambling dens which flourish in that town, ignoring their responsibilities to their constituents as a result. There are no such temptations here, and so we have no recourse but to keep our minds occupied with the state's affairs.

I must admit that my mind is most frequently occupied with thoughts of you, dearest Rebecca. An unspeakable misery has had me in its grasp ever since we parted company. How are you faring without me? I find myself distracted beyond description without you. Is little Christopher well? Give him my love. You must write me every day. To know that a letter from you will arrive on each morrow will give me the strength to get through each night. I have found a room at McCall's Boarding House. Address your letters there, rather than to the state house, as they would in all likelihood be lost in the flood of correspondence which the representatives receive at the latter place. I am told that a great many such letters, addressed to my unfortunate predecessor, are awaiting my attention. I pray that Elisha Ferguson may rest in peace, as I suspect he never had a moment of it in the Kentucky House of Representatives.

As God is my witness, I rue the day I consented to having my name tossed into the hat as a candidate to complete Ferguson's term. What possessed me to perform an act so rash? I suppose I considered it an honor. Yes, I was flattered. But I never really expected to be chosen. Why, we've only lived in Madison County for three years. There are many other gentlemen better qualified and who have resided there most of their lives. I never seriously thought that the people would choose me. A hero of the war against the Barbary Pirates? I was there, certainly, because it was my duty, and I performed no heroic deeds. Yet you would think I had vanquished the Pasha's bodyguard and captured that debauched old corsair single-handedly, the way people talked. And in what manner does the fact that I captured the traitor Aaron Burr qualify me for this office? I know nothing of politics and, frankly, have no desire to learn. All I want is to be with you, my beloved wife. If there was a way to resign this post with honor, I would do so in a minute and fly back to Elm Tree, never to leave your side again.

I must stop writing and post this letter. Picture in your mind a melancholy man in a gloomy room waiting anxiously to hear from his lovely wife. Do take care of yourself and Christopher.

Your loving Husband,

Jonathan

December 19, 1808

My Dearest Husband,

It breaks my heart to hear of you so unhappy. I could scarcely refrain from calling for Gilly and telling her to pack my things, and telling Isaac to prepare the carriage, and then coming immediately to Frankfort. To think that only a few days travel separates us! But, instead, I sit here, sending you my love by this letter, bearing in mind that we agreed I must remain here—that it would be better for our darling son were he to be home, and that I must tend to our affairs while you serve with distinction (and I know you will) in the Assembly. You must rest assured, my darling, that my heart is with you, and my thoughts always on you, to the point of distraction. I was inconsolable the day you left, and that night was the most awful I have spent since the Shawnees carried me away. So long ago, and yet to think of it makes me shudder! But, had it not happened, would we have met? Some good comes from the worst of events, don't you agree?

Do not concern yourself with Christopher's welfare. He is the fattest, happiest, most rosy-cheeked little bundle of joy in the world, perfectly healthy and with a perfectly awful appetite! Nor must you worry about affairs here. All is well. There was snow on the ground this morning, and the ponds froze over during the night, but it is clear today. Have some of the hands chopping woods, others in the corn. Yesterday Nelly, Gilly, and I pulled up all the turnips and potatoes, and it is a good thing that we did so before the freeze.

The day after you left, Mary Bucknell came by. She could see I was desperately unhappy, and suggested we go into town, and I decided that would be a good idea, since the shoes we ordered for the hands had arrived at Cochran's. We visited Mrs. Thomas, whose rheumatism is much worse, poor woman. We also saw Stephen Cooper. Do you remember him? It was quite a shock to see him striding along the street, I suppose because the last time I laid eyes on him he was so near death. Mary tells me he has married, and has a place down on Hunter's Creek, where he grows tobacco and horses. I was going to cross over and speak to him but Mary begged me not to. She seemed a little frightened, and says he has something of a bad reputation. Rumor has it that he is extremely unkind to his wife, who is a frail and passive creature, as well as to his hands, whom he treats abominably. He likes to gamble on his horses, says Mary. He has a terrible temper, and has fought several duels on account of it.

Of course, I don't know that I believe all of that. I am not much for gossip, and it certainly sounds nothing like the Stephen Cooper I once knew, but then I suppose people can change. He did not see me, and perhaps that is for the best, considering the circumstances. Mary said it wouldn't be proper for a married woman to approach a man in such a brazen manner, but I would have liked to have at least said hello. After all, Stephen did very nearly lose his life trying to save me from the Shawnees. It startled me that he lives so near. That I knew nothing of what Mary told me makes me aware that I scarcely ever get away from Elm Tree. Not that I want to. I have been so completely and impossibly happy here with you and, now, little Christopher, and I confess sometimes I actually resented any visitors intruding upon our idyll. Isn't that selfish of me?

Oh, I do wish you were here with me, dearest Jonathan. I miss you so. I miss those strong arms holding me tightly. The nights are so cold! It isn't very ladylike, is it, being so shamelessly bold, even in a letter, but I can't help it. Please see to your health, my husband, and hurry back to your devoted wife as soon as your duties permit. With all my love,

Rebecca

December 28, 1808

Dear Rebecca,

I am sorry not to have written sooner, but have been incredibly busy. The day I arrived there was quite a heated debate in the House regarding the Embargo Act. Humphrey Marshall spoke scathingly in opposition to a resolution penned by Henry Clay, which applauds President Jefferson's administration of his duties as Chief Magistrate, and expresses the general assembly's approval of the embargo itself. "Highly judicious" I believe are the words Clay used to describe the embargo, and the only honorable expedient short of war as a response to the unprincipled, I might say *piratical,* depredations carried out by the British. The manner in which they seize American ships and impress our seamen is so outrageous that I admit I cannot think of it without my blood boils. They are as bad, if not worse, than the Barbary corsairs. At least the latter did not pretend to be a civilized nation. The utter disrespect with which England treats our flag has the House in a perpetual uproar. Were an expedition announced today, for the purpose of invading Canada, I doubt we could even fetch a quorum the following day—everyone would have volunteered for the endeavor. Everyone, that is, but the Federalists, like Marshall. But then, they have always been Anglophiles. I hear the New Englanders actually have the gall to continue in a brisk trade with the British, in violation of the embargo, and I daresay that if war ever *does* break out between England and this republic I wouldn't be at all surprised if New England broke away from the Union and allied herself with the enemy. I am told that the national Congress is on the verge of passing a Force Act, which will permit federal officials without warrant to seize goods suspected as destined for foreign trade. That will make the Federalists see red!

I don't need to tell you that I voted with the majority to adopt the resolution. Clay has quite a way with words. "Resolved, that the general assembly of Kentucky would view with the utmost horror a proposition, in any shape, to submit to the tributary exactions of Great Britain or to acquiesce in the violation of neutral rights, and they pledge themselves to the general government, to spend, if necessary, the last shilling, and to exhaust the last drop of blood, in resisting these aggressions." Yes, I know it by heart, every stirring phrase.

In addition, we have had the sad case of Rebecca Winchester to consider, afraid that her own property might be subjected to the payment of debts incurred by her sorry excuse for a husband, who gambled away his family's future. We passed a resolution permitting her to acquire and hold property *femme sole*. It makes me proud to be a member of this body when it performs such noble service to one so much in need. I cannot but feel that it is the purpose of government to help those who are truly in need. By the same token, it ought to leave to their own devices those who are trying to make their own way, and who are fully capable of doing so. We have in addition passed a resolution relaxing the summary course of the law for the recovery of debts. Every case is different, and it is simple compassion to acknowledge that sometimes extenuating circumstances merit consideration.

Mr. Clay has been by to see me this evening, and invited me to accompany him to Lind's Tavern. That establishment seems to be a favorite haunt of many of my colleagues, but none more so than Mr. Clay, who has a fondness for cards and billiards. He is quite a charismatic fellow, that Mr. Clay, tall and thin, with pale hair and the keenest pair of blue eyes in a face that a hawk would be proud of. He has a way about him which induces others to follow his lead and trust in his judgment. But he could not induce me to join him at the tavern, as I am weary in the extreme. I think he wants to get me in line for his resolutions supporting a strong response to the British. But I am already in line for that, and assured him of my support.

Though we had never met, he knew me, as the man responsible for the capture of Burr, and with a deprecating smile he remarked that he had defended Burr before the court of Kentucky, on the occasion when Burr was acquitted for lack of evidence. He told me of the letter which Burr had written him, assuring him that the charges were false—a letter which Clay has felt compelled by circumstances to present on numerous occasions since as proof that he was not involved in that traitorous conspiracy. I informed him that I had no doubts regarding his patriotism, and that it was my personal opinion that if war was necessary to persuade England to respect our sovereignty I was ready for it. This pleased Clay immensely. "Good!" he exclaimed. "Another

Kentucky War Hawk. We will have the world's respect, and Canada, too, if I have anything to say about it!"

Spending Christmas without you, my darling, was a miserable ordeal, one I have sworn never to endure again. Tell all that I have no desire to return to the assembly next year, as I hear that the good people of Madison County may be considering electing me to come here of my own right. I do not wish to be honored in that manner, nor will I serve if chosen. All I want is to live at Elm Tree with my family.

Your Husband,

Jonathan

January 2, 1809

My Dearest Jonathan,

The heavy snowfall has delayed the mail, and so I have just received your last letter. All this talk of war causes me the greatest anxiety, as I fear that if it occurs, duty to your country may compel you to leave me again and place yourself in harm's way.

Everyone is well pleased with the job you are doing in the assembly, and indeed, there is talk of electing you next year in your own right. I have to admit I am relieved by your determination to decline such an honor.

All is well here. Christopher is as healthy and happy as always. Rexica dropped her foal. And Nelly gave birth to a girl child. She had a difficult time of it, and I summoned Doctor Mattson. The baby is healthy, and Nelly is recovering nicely.

While he was here, Doctor Mattson mentioned that he had just called on Emily Cooper. He was quite angry when he spoke of it, as he suspects that her injuries may be the result of abuse. Mrs. Cooper insists that she fell down a flight of stairs. I cannot believe that Stephen would be so brutal—at least not the Stephen I once knew, but Doctor Mattson is convinced that he is the culprit. Of course, nothing can be done as long as she continues to lie to protect him, if that is in fact what she is about. Her father is a very well-to-do Tennessee planter, apparently, who purchased the estate on Hunter's Creek for his daughter and her groom upon the occasion of their marriage. That explains how the son of a poor backwoods farmer has done so well for himself in such a short time.

Do take care of yourself, Jonathan, and take comfort in the knowledge that my thoughts are always with you. With all my love, I am your devoted wife,

Rebecca

January 6, 1809

Dear Rebecca,

On the 3rd instant, Mr. Clay presented before the House a Resolution to Encourage Use of American Manufactures, which declared that henceforth my colleagues and I will clothe ourselves exclusively in garments made in this country, abstaining from the use of cloth or linens of European fabric until those nations respect our sovereignty. National interest requires that all Americans show preference to articles grown or manufactured in this republic, and I was glad to vote for the resolution, as was a majority of the assembly, just as I am glad to wear simple homespun. We do this in the hopes of leading by example.

Debate on the resolution led to a dangerous quarrel between Clay and his archenemy, Humphrey Marshall. It was Marshall who denounced the "tyrannical" behavior of the President in calling for an embargo. He is the

cousin of Chief Justice John Marshall, who, in my
opinion, subverted justice when he acquitted Aaron Burr,
doing so merely to spite Mr. Jefferson. That, they say, is
a consequence of the President's attempt to impeach all
the Federalists in the Judiciary. At any rate, there is bad
blood between Humphrey Marshall and Henry Clay. Clay
once tried, unsuccessfully, to have Marshall declared
unfit for a seat in the legislature, alleging that Marshall
had engaged in illegal measures to demonstrate the
fraudulent ownership of a piece of land that he himself
was interested in acquiring. Marshall accused Clay of
demagoguery with this resolution. The two men
exchanged insults on the floor of the House, much to
everyone's shock and chagrin. Then Marshall called Clay
a liar, and Clay lunged at him. At that point we
intervened. Clay attempted to calm himself, and
apologized to the members. But Marshall, unwilling to
leave well enough alone, called his apology one a
poltroon might offer. That evening Clay challenged
Marshall to a duel. Imagine my surprise when Clay called
upon me to act as his second. I could not in good
conscience refuse.

As a result, I was asked to acquire a brace of good
pistols, which I attempted to do, without success. The
weapons used were produced by Marshall's second,
Colonel Moore, and I believe they are the property of
Joseph Hamilton Daveiss, who you might remember as
Kentucky's district attorney, and as such was the man
who brought Burr to trial in this state. Moore and I
agreed upon and wrote down the rules of engagement.
The next day we crossed the Ohio near Shippingport, and
found a likely spot near the mouth of Silver Creek, as it
was the expressed desire of the principals that the blood
of her sons not stain the soil of Kentucky. They took their

positions at ten paces and the word was given to fire when ready. Marshall's pistol misfired. Clay wounded him slightly. Preparations were made at their mutual insistence for a second fire, even though Colonel Moore and I both tried to persuade them that honor had been upheld. Again Marshall fired without effect. Clay's pistol snapped. A third preparation was made! The two men seemed firm in their determination to kill each other. Marshall fired first, and Clay suffered a flesh wound in the right thigh. He fired without effect, and insisted on yet another fire, but Colonel Moore and I had seen quite enough foolish bravery for one day, and called an end to the affair.

Both gentlemen conducted themselves with cool courage. I was somewhat mortified that Clay's pistol snapped twice, though I am certain that I loaded the weapon properly. All agree that the pistols were less than satisfactory, as Marshall's also misfired twice. I must admit I am glad that such was the case. Only two shots out of six were fired, to which I attribute the fact that both men are alive today.

The legislature felt obliged to officially censure Clay, Marshall, and myself as members of that august assembly, for engaging in the practice of dueling, yet privately all the members have gone out of their way to congratulate me on the manner in which I conducted myself. Both Marshall and Clay are recuperating, and should be able to return to their chairs in the House before adjournment. I disapprove of dueling in general, but it seems necessary on occasion for the sake of a man's dignity, and I do not see how Clay could have done otherwise, in light of the remarks made by Mr. Marshall in the presence of the entire legislature.

I am exhausted, my dear, and can scarcely keep my

eyes open, so I will close now and go to sleep, to dream of you, beloved wife. Give Christopher a kiss for me. With the Deepest Affection and Respect,

Jonathan

January 11, 1809

Dear Husband,

I had heard about the duel between Henry Clay and Humphrey Marshall even before I received your letter. Such sensational news travels swiftly. The sentiment is overwhelmingly in favor of Mr. Clay, and the incident has certainly done nothing to affect his responsibility. They say he is bound for the national Congress. On the other hand, I know of no one who speaks favorably of Marshall and Daveiss and the Federalists. Or, if one had the desire to, he would do so at the risk of tar and feathers. There is an association in the minds of the people between the Federalists and the British—an association which will prove fatal to the political aspirations of men like Humphrey Marshall.

While I understand why you had to become involved in the affair, I must confess, Jonathan, that I was dismayed. Dueling is so ludicrous! What is honorable in the cold-blooded, premeditated killing of another man? You should have considered the effect your involvement would have on the voters of Madison County. You are very nearly the hero that Henry Clay is, in their opinion. I daresay, the people will re-elect you whether you like it or not. When they do, how could you refuse them? Wouldn't the honorable course of action be to abide by their wishes?

Rexica's foal is perfectly healthy. Christopher has absolutely fallen in love with it. I thought we would call it Jumper, after its grandsire, the horse my mother and father brought to Kentucky with them. Perhaps, so christened, it will someday perform some historic deed on a par with its namesake, when the first Jumper carried my father to Monticello to warn Thomas Jefferson of the approach of Tarleton's Tory Rangers. At the very least the new Jumper ought to win a race or two. Do you approve of the name?

Clay's resolution regarding the use of American manufactures was read in the square yesterday. I was in town on errands, and I witnessed firsthand the enthusiasm of the people for the measure. I will most certainly do my part, and pray all the while that the measure, and the President's embargo, will work a change in the attitude of the British. I would sacrifice everything to avoid war. Unfortunately, there are many who clamor openly for war. They want the British driven out of Canada, and I can't say that I blame them for the sentiment, as it is undeniably true that the British are actively inspiring the Indians to attack us, and have for years been supplying them with the rifles, powder, and shot with which to do so. But I have a feeling that some want war merely for an excuse to conquer Canada and bring that vast territory into the republic. The American people are the greatest on earth, but we have our faults, and one of those is this unquenchable desire to have every square mile of the continent for our own. What in heaven will we do with all that land, Jonathan? Why, it would take forever to fill it with farms and towns. We want British Canada just as we want Spanish Florida, and who knows what else when we've got them? I know it may sound odd coming from a woman who was once a victim of a Shawnee raid, but I can sympathize with the Indians. It seems to me that there is more than enough land in this country so that they could keep theirs.

Speaking of Indians, I am sure you remember Quashquame. On the same day that I received your letter, I received one also from my mother. She and my father are well, although my father has been made despondent by the departure of Quashquame, his friend of so many years. Apparently, the Delaware village where Quashquame's sister lived was attacked by white men, for what reason no one knows, and his sister was slain. She was all the family Quashquame had left, apart from us, of course, and so you may imagine his grief. Quashquame has always been a true friend to our race, and the bond between brothers has never been stronger than the friendship between him and my father. But the senseless murder of his sister, not to mention the slaying of other defenseless Delaware women and children, wrought a change in Quashquame which my mother says was terrible to behold. The end result is that Quashquame is gone. Mother fears it is for good. The news brought tears to my eyes. When I was growing up Quashquame was like an older brother to me. He is a noble, brave, and generous man, and my heart bleeds for him. He has suffered great tragedy throughout his life, and I suppose this last horror was more than he could bear. Why, oh why, Jonathan, do our people commit such atrocities?

I miss you terribly, my husband, and try to console myself with the knowledge that in another month's time you will be home. I am counting the days. They pass so slowly! All my love,

Rebecca

January 18, 1809

Dear Rebecca,

I am truly sorry to hear the news about Quashquame. If it is true that white men attacked a defenseless village, then it is a despicable act which shames us all. I say if, because I have made a few queries among my colleagues, and thus far have gleaned no information on such an event. They may not have been Kentuckians. I pray not. But it would not surprise me. There exists such enmity between the Indians and our Kentucky brothers and sisters that I fear an ocean of blood could not wash it away. The Indians have committed their share of atrocities, my dear. One wrong does not justify another, but alas, it is only human nature to seek revenge. Where did it all start? Who committed the first atrocity? I do not know, nor do I know where or when it will all end. I do know that if there *is* war between us and the British, there will be Indian trouble the likes of which Kentucky has never seen. And, if there is to be war, as much as I would regret being apart from you, I would feel obligated to offer my services, not merely for the honor of my country, but for my home and family, as well. I know it will cause you grief to read these words, but surely you can understand my position.

In several of your letters you have mentioned Stephen Cooper. I made no mention of it in my letters to you, but I will confess, ashamedly, that news of his proximity to you inspired some jealousy on my part. I have always wondered, were it not for those Shawnees, if you and I would be married today. Somehow I think not. You would have married Cooper instead. Your heart belonged to him before you gave me your hand.

Yet I have never spoken to you of these feelings of mine, and would not now, even after Cooper's unwelcome appearance in your letters, except for the fact that yesterday I received a letter from Dr. Mattson. He informs me that a week ago Saturday, while in town, he witnessed a scene involving you and Stephen Cooper. The good doctor claims that in appearance both of you were agitated, and though he was not near enough to hear any of the conversation that passed between the two of you, it seemed to him that you were quite upset. Dr. Mattson assures me that he is not one to interfere in the affairs of others, and I know of no occasion when he demonstrated anything less that the utmost discretion, but he felt it behooved him, nonetheless, to write me with a warning about Cooper.

According to the good doctor, Cooper is a man with a notoriously violent temper, and certainly no gentleman when it comes to members of the gentler sex. He relayed to me the information he had previously shared with you regarding Cooper's relationship with his wife, when he called on Elm Tree to attend to the delivery of Nelly's child. He also informed me that it has come to his attention that Cooper is also cruel to his slaves, and—I can think of no way to be delicate in this—considers the young Negro women his own private *hareem*.

Dr. Mattson was motivated solely by concern for your welfare when he wrote me the letter, Rebecca. Having no inkling that you were acquainted with Cooper, he was surprised to see the two of you engaged in such an earnest exchange—the kind one does not see pass between two strangers, or even casual acquaintances. He is in hopes, I think, of prompting me to advise you as husband to wife against any further association on your part with Cooper—again, out of fear for your safety.

Suffice it to say that I have never presumed to dictate to you on the matter of your acquaintances. I do not consider it my place to do so, though I believe many men in my position would do precisely that. Yet I must confess to being perplexed that you made no mention of your chance encounter with Cooper in your last letter, which by the date it bears I gather you wrote the day after that encounter. It never occurred to me that you would try to keep anything secret between us, Rebecca, so the question plagues me mercilessly. Why did you not tell me?

Your Husband,

Jonathan

January 22, 1809

Dearest Jonathan,

Your letter caused me such acute distress that I wept after reading it. Your tone was so abrupt, your parting so curt! Are you angry with me? I cannot bear the thought that you are. I have done nothing wrong.

I am sad, yes, and angry, too. Angry at Dr. Mattson. I cannot agree with your assessment of him, or his self-assessment, as a gentleman who does not relish interfering in the affairs of others. He has certainly interfered in ours, and I fear that his ill-advised letter has caused you to jump to conclusions about me and Stephen Cooper.

It is true that I met Stephen, quite by chance, in town, that Saturday. Gilly was with me, and we had just emerged from Chadwick Fuller's store when Stephen happened by. He recognized me instantly, and appeared surprised to see me. For a moment both of us were speechless. Then he inquired after my health. I assured him that I was well. "I have heard that your husband is in Frankfort, in the assembly," he said, and I confirmed that this was so. "I would think," he said, "that you would have better sense than to be married to a politician. They are thieves and scoundrels, every one." I replied that you were neither a thief nor a scoundrel—that in fact you were the most honest man I had ever known, next to my father. I spoke sharply, and my tone seemed to antagonize him. "But then I shouldn't be surprised that the man who stole you from me has gone on to Frankfort, where he can continue his thieving ways in the legislature, this time at the expense of the hardworking, decent people of Kentucky."

Jonathan, I was taken aback by his vehemence. There seemed to be a mad glimmer in his eyes. It was quite a shock. The man bore so little resemblance to the Stephen Cooper I had once known! Had I not seen it with my own eyes, I would have refused to believe that anyone could change so completely.

As I have said, Gilly was with me, and as you are well aware, she has quite a temper herself, and is so intensely loyal to both of us that it should come as no surprise to you when I tell you that she leapt to my defense. I think, too, that she could see I was frightened. "You ain't one to call nobody else a scoundrel," she told Stephen in no uncertain terms. "Not if what I hear is gospel."

Stephen looked at her as a cat might look at the mouse pinned beneath its claws. I shall never forget the expression on his face. I could sense the violence, barely restrained, raging inside him. I was suddenly afraid for Gilly, and she could sense it, too, but, to her credit, she stood her ground bravely, having imposed herself between Stephen and me.

"You're a pretty little nigger hussy, aren't you?" he said, and leered at her with such a wicked smile that it makes my skin crawl to remember it! "You should lend this one to me, Rebecca, and in a fortnight I could break her of this damned insolence."

I informed him, coldly, that he should address me as Mrs. Groves. It was only proper, and even if it wasn't, under the circumstances I would insist upon it. "Mrs. Groves!" he exclaimed. "After all we've meant to each other!" I told him that we had been childhood friends, but that this did not give him license to speak to me, or to Gilly, in that fashion.

The dark anger left him then. "Well," he replied, "what's done is done. If I have offended you, then you have my apology. But I will not apologize to this nigger wench. She should have a care how she talks to a white man."

I believe our impetuous Gilly was going to say something which would only infuriate him, but I grabbed her arm and squeezed it so tightly that she let out a small cry of pain. Stephen left us without another word.

There you have it, Jonathan. I remember every word, and have left nothing out. I did not write of it in my last letter because I was afraid you would take offense to Stephen's comments. Not the ones about you, but what he said to me and to Gilly. I suppose I could have just mentioned meeting him in town, but then . . . well, I was afraid, too, that you would find it peculiar, to say the least, that I wrote of him in three consecutive letters. After all, I meet many people when I go to town. If there was nothing remarkable about an encounter with Stephen Cooper, why would I write to inform you of nothing more than the fact that we had met? All I could think of were your words from the letter in which you described the duel between Mr. Clay and Mr. Marshall. *I disapprove of dueling in general, but it seems necessary sometimes for a man's dignity.* Do you think your dignity requires you to challenge Stephen Cooper for the manner in which he addressed your wife? If you do, which I fear may be the case, then there you have the reason I tried to conceal the encounter from you.

Your devoted—and devastated—wife,

Rebecca

January 28, 1809

Dear Wife,

Four days ago the legislature officially censured Mr. Clay, Mr. Marshall, and myself, but nothing more will come of it. It is anticipated that the session will be concluded within a fortnight, and I will be exceedingly glad when adjournment comes. I look forward to returning to Elm Tree, and to my family.

I pray with all my heart that you will forgive me, Rebecca. I wrote my previous letter in a state of high emotion, dismayed that you had kept something from me, but I understand now why you did so, and am ashamed. When I read what Cooper said to you I actually ran from my room and was halfway to the livery where my horse is kept before realizing the foolhardiness of attempting to travel the roads in the middle of a night which saw the heaviest snowfall yet this season. Resolving to set out on the morrow, regardless of the weather, I returned to the boardinghouse. I was scarcely able to sleep, but did manage finally to doze, and in the morning light I began to see things differently. To challenge Cooper to a duel would be to imply that he is a gentleman—and that he most certainly is not. Were it not for the fact that such action would upset you, I would go to his home and take a cane to the scoundrel immediately upon my return. Yet, having had time for further reflection, I would almost feel sorry for the wretch, but for the pain he inflicts upon others. He must have been quite a different person before the Shawnees came within an inch of killing him, else you would have had nothing to do with him, and I realize it must sadden you to see him in his present incarnation.

I am all for letting the whole matter drop, if you will just consent to forgiving me for having made you cry.

We are not accomplishing much here in the assembly, and I am anxious to leave. As soon as the adjournment I will depart for Elm Tree, with but one brief detour. Henry Clay has invited me to Ashland, his estate in Lexington. I believe he is intent on sharing with me an opportunity to invest in the hemp industry. What do you think? It is a burgeoning business, by all accounts. Kentucky hemp will be used to bag cotton from the Gulf States, and, as you know, cotton production has been vastly increased in the past few years. I think there is money to be made in the manufacture of cotton bagging, and I promised Clay I would pay him a visit on my way home, but I will not stay long, perhaps overnight, because my arms ache they miss you so much.

Love, your penitent husband,

Jonathan

April 12, 1809

Dear Mother,

I hope you and Father are well. We are all fine here. It has been raining for days now. The creeks have jumped their banks, and the bridge into town was washed away yesterday. A most fearful storm last night, with terrific lightning and thunderclaps so violent that they actually broke several panes of window glass. The stables are beginning to flood, so we have moved the horses into the house, an extreme measure, but we cannot leave them to stand in water. It would ruin them. What hands are not shelling corn for seed are working to keep the rain out of virtually every structure on Elm Tree, as the boards are swelling up, that is how bad it's been. Are you nearly drowned over at Boonesboro? I wonder if this letter will even get to you. We had just finished plowing and listing and carting stable manure out to the fields, but I'm beginning to think the whole world is going to wash away. I take comfort in the knowledge that Almighty God promised Noah that he would not destroy the world with a second deluge. One of our mares had a colt last night, dark bay on brown, with a dark line down the back and a white hind foot.

Of course your grandson is fit as a fiddle. The child is robust, and has hardly been ill a day in his precious life. I still hope that we can come to visit after spring planting. You won't believe how much Christopher has grown. Jonathan is doing well. He sends his regards. He has made an investment in a hemp farm, going into business with Henry Clay, no less, and several others. We need more room here. What isn't taken up in pasture we use for corn. Should have at least eight colts this year, and will sell all but two or perhaps three of them. Elm Tree colts are fetching a good price.

I believe that Jonathan will return to the legislature next winter. We both hate being apart, but the people are insistent on having him serve as their representative.

Miss you terribly, and hope to see you soon.

Your Obedient and Affectionate Daughter,

Rebecca

P.S. It has been two days since I began this letter, and still no means to reach town to post it, but the rain has finally begun to let up. I have never been so glad to see a ray of golden sunlight! The storms have caused much damage. The fields are a swamp. We will need at least a week of good hot sun to dry them out.

Gilly is missing. She was last seen yesterday morning. We have had everyone searching for her, but no sign as yet. Jonathan says she must have run away, but I just don't believe that. Gilly would never leave me of her own volition. She has been devoted to me ever since we came to Elm Tree, and I to her. Old Elisha claims he saw a cloaked figure roaming the grounds late at night several days ago, at about the time Gilly disappeared. He saw this figure only for an instant, in a flash of lightning, and then it was gone. Elisha is convinced that "the Devil hisself took Miss Gilly." I do fear that some evil has befallen her, and my heart is breaking. I can't explain it, but I have a strong feeling that we shall never see her again.

May 2, 1809

Dearest Rebecca,

I have just now received your letter, and am sorry you have had so many troubles of late at Elm Tree. Please do come see me, for I am terribly lonely. Nathaniel left three days ago. He has gone to find Quashquame. I begged him not to go, but cannot blame him for doing so. For months now he has suffered in silent anguish over the manner of Quashquame's leaving, and he is concerned for our Delaware friend's welfare. But it is so dangerous for a white man north of the Ohio! They say there isn't an Indian born can best Flintlock Jones, but what good is a reputation? It won't turn a bullet. I am worried sick. Do come visit me.

Amanda

CHAPTER THREE

Nathaniel

I

The Indians passed within fifty yards of where Nathaniel Jones stood in the sun-dappled forest. It was a testament to his woodsmanship that they had not an inkling of his presence.

They were Mingo. Logan's people. And warriors all. A dozen of them, and not a hunting party. On a mission, surmised the frontiersman, but not a mission of war, because they weren't painted for the warpath, and they were heading north, deeper into Indian country, and as far as Nathaniel knew no tribes were in conflict.

Bad luck for him. They were headed in the same direction as he.

Standing there, behind a forked tree, he was tall and straight in his buckskins. His soft doeskin shirt was rubbed with ash and charcoal, giving it a gray-dun color. His buckskin leggins were tight at calf and ankle for silent running. He wore double-soled moccasins of dirty yellow buffalo hide. A Kentucky long rifle, primed and loaded, lay in the cradle of his arm. His yellow hair was long and tousled. His blue-gray eyes were keen as a hawk's as he watched the Mingos. He watched them until they were out of sight, swallowed up by the forest, which seemed to go on forever.

Nathaniel breathed a sigh of relief. Then he thought

about Amanda, alone in the cabin not far from Boonesboro, but far indeed from where he now stood, and he had second thoughts about his mission. He had no business leaving her like this, venturing deep into enemy country, making the chances of his safe return more slim with every stride north. What would she do without him? They had relied on each other for twenty-eight years now.

What Amanda feared most of all was surviving him, having to live out the rest of her life in solitude, and perhaps losing her mind as a result. She had never forgotten the crazy old woman they had met on this side of the Cumberland Gap, when first they had come to Kentucky—the woman who lived alone deep in the forest, and who thought, on storm-swept nights when the wind was high and howling, that she could hear her long-dead husband calling to her from the grave.

Poor Amanda. He had suggested that she go stay with Rebecca at Elm Tree while he was absent, but she would have none of it. No, she would stay home, where his presence was strong, and watch for him every day, and be there to come running down that long bluegrass slope to him when he broke free of the woods and hove into sight, and he could picture her in his mind's eye, as pretty and willowy as she had been on the day they had married. It gave him something to look forward to, coming home to her instead of to an empty cabin, and of course she knew what that would mean to him, which was why she refused to go to Elm Tree.

He considered turning back. If he did, he could not only hasten that day of reunion but also virtually guarantee it. There were no such guarantees available if he traveled much further north. These forests were swarming with Indians, and no matter if they were Shawnee or Mingo or Delaware, like as not they would lift his scalp. That was how bad things had become. It was white man against red and the devil take the hindmost. In Nathaniel's opinion the current state of affairs was a crying shame, because he had always believed that there was more than enough land and game for all of them, and not so much difference between the red man and the white, when you thought about it, that they could not learn how to live together in peace. Most of his neighbors at Boonesboro would disagree with him on that score, and Nathaniel couldn't rightly blame them. Many had lost a wife or a son or a brother to the Indians. He'd been lucky in that respect.

Of course, the Indians had lost loved ones too. Quashquame had lost everyone in his family. For the millionth time Nathaniel wondered if it would not be better to just let his Delaware friend go his separate way. But no, he couldn't do that. Quashquame was more than a friend. He was like the brother Nathaniel had never had. Or the son. Together they had been through so much, resolute in their loyalty and devotion to one another, through thick and thin, and quite a lot of it, come to think on it, saving each other's life time and again. Quashquame had always been there for Nathaniel, and now Nathaniel sensed that it was his turn—whether Quashquame wanted anything to do with him or not.

He had to go, regardless of the risks.

Nathaniel was forty-six years old. There was some gray streaking his hair these days. The lines on his lean, sun-bronzed face were deepening. Sometimes, on particularly cold and damp mornings, his bones ached something fierce. But he could still move with the lethal grace of the panther, making no sound to betray his presence, and leaving no sign to tell of his passage, blending so perfectly into his environment that a dozen sharp-eyed Mingos could not distinguish this tall, brown-garbed, brown-skinned leatherstocking from the trees.

He knew all the tricks of his trade. Prior to leaving his cabin he had smoked his buckskins over an open fire, eliminating any trace of a scent of home and hearth and loving wife which might give him away in the forest. He could still go days without food, and nights without sleep, and he could still run from sunup to sundown without respite. He knew the ways of the Indians, and the secrets of the woodlands, as well as any Long Knife alive.

And as he continued on his way north, making for the village of the Delaware where he hoped to find Quashquame, Nathaniel had a hunch he would need every bit of his skill as a frontiersman to make it home with his skin and scalp.

II

Nathaniel trailed the Mingos straight to the Delaware village, on the banks of the Hocking River. He did not dare enter while they were there. Logan and his people had for years been the implacable foes of the white man—ever since Jacob Greathouse and his scalp-hunters had murdered Logan's sister.

As for the Delawares, it was hard to say how they would greet him. Sometimes they fought with the Shawnees and the Mingos, while at other times they stayed home. There had always been a deep division within the tribe on the subject of waging war against the Long Knives. Nathaniel was well aware that the same senseless atrocity that had cost him his friend Quashquame might have hardened all Delaware hearts against the whites.

So he had no alternative but to wait and watch.

Time worked against him. The village was a large one, sixty or seventy lodges, several hundred inhabitants, and so there was much coming and going. The longer Nathaniel lingered on the outskirts of the village, the worse his chances of remaining undetected. He knew that. But he had to find Quashquame, and he had to find out what the Mingos were up to. He was willing to bet that whatever it was, it bode ill for the white man.

The Delawares greeted the Mingos like long lost friends. The Mingos met with the old Delaware chief, Blue Turtle, who took one of them into his lodge for a private palaver. They were inside for over an hour. The rest of the Mingos remained outside the chief's lodge, sitting cross-legged on the ground, and were visited by many of the Delaware warriors, while the Delaware women brought them food and water. That they did not disperse into the village led Nathaniel to believe that their visit was all business. Perhaps the Mingos had come to ask the Delawares to join them on the warpath.

Nathaniel kept his eyes peeled for Quashquame, but did not see him, and was beginning to worry that his friend was not here at all when a commotion drew his attention to the west end of the camp.

It was the arrival of four Shawnees.

No, make that three Shawnees and the renegade, Simon Girty.

Girty could easily be mistaken for an Indian. He had completely adopted their dress and speech and mannerisms. Nathaniel might have been fooled, except that he had once met Girty.

That had been at Zanesville. Nathaniel had been there when the Shawnees attacked, without warning, a few years back, and he had helped Ebenezer Zane and Lew Wetzel beat back the fierce Indians assaults. Then Girty had appeared under a flag of truce, a lady's undergarment tied to the barrel of his rifle, asking the defenders of the station to surrender. Of course, Zane had no intention of surrendering to the likes of Girty, even though the renegade gave his word that no harm would befall the settlers. There wasn't a man alive in Kentucky who would take Simon Girty's word for anything—except maybe Simon Kenton. Though they were outnumbered three or four to one, and running dangerously low on powder and shot, the men of Zanesville chose to fight to the death. The next day the Shawnees resumed their attacks on the stockade. Those had been grim hours, as Nathaniel recalled. Plans were being made to kill the women and children rather than let them fall into Shawnee hands, when suddenly the Indians withdrew. A large party of frontiersmen from nearby Wheeling had gotten wind of the attack and come to the rescue.

Girty's presence among the Shawnees here at the Delaware village convinced Nathaniel that there were some big doings in store. The frontiersman did not know any of the Shawnee warriors, but he could tell that one was a chief by the eagle feathers in his scalplock, and the deferential treatment he received from his Delaware hosts. Girty and the Shawnee chief disappeared into Blue Turtle's lodge. Nathaniel was itching to know what was being said in there, but he wasn't willing to lose his topknot to find out.

The day waned. Nathaniel began to despair of finding Quashquame here. He had a bad moment when three young Delaware bucks coming back from a successful hunt—a doe and a mess of wild turkeys—almost stumbled over him. Slinking off into the darkening forest, Nathaniel counted his blessings, and found a new and better vantage point from which to watch the goings-on in the village, nearer the rushing river than his first location.

Shortly thereafter, Blue Turtle, Girty, the Mingo, and the Shawnee chief emerged from the lodge of the Delaware headman. The latter called for a feast. A bonfire was built. Many of the Delaware braves sat in a large circle around the fire with their Shawnee and Mingo guests. Much food was eaten. Pipes were smoked all around. A good time for all. The night-shadowed woods, alive with fireflies, rang with the shouts of lusty laughter from the throats of a hundred warriors. One after another, the men stood to speak, bestowing compliments, or simply singing their own praises, or cursing the Long Knives in inventive ways, or hoping for a brighter future, or wistfully recalling a happier past.

It was then that Nathaniel spotted Quashquame.

The frontiersman was at least a hundred yards away from the big fire, but he knew his old friend at once, and his heart sang with the joy of seeing him alive and well, as Quashquame emerged from a lodge and stepped into the light of the blaze. The other Indians implored him to address the circle. Quashquame was reluctant, but finally consented. Being mute, he used sign language to communicate. But Nathaniel could not wait around to decipher the signs.

Simon Girty was slipping away from the crowd, with his arms around the slender waist of a Delaware maiden.

They were making for the river.

A daring plan exploded full-blown into Nathaniel's mind, and he slipped though the night shadows, silent as death, to intercept Girty and the girl.

He shadowed them until, on the banks of the river, the girl broke away from Girty and began to run. Laughing, the renegade gave chase. The girl was swift of foot. Darting nimbly through the trees, she lengthened her lead as Girty stumbled and fell sprawling over an exposed root. That gave Nathaniel the opportunity he was looking for.

The frontiersman moved in like a predator cat, leaving his long rifle propped against a tree. This was no place for shooting.

The Delaware maiden was looking behind her, wondering what had become of her suitor, and slowing down, so that she did not see Nathaniel emerge from darkness until it was entirely too late.

She ran straight into his arms, and opened her mouth to scream. Nathaniel bore her swiftly to the ground, got a hand around her slender throat and squeezed. She flailed away with hands and legs, squirming to escape, but his weight pinned her to the ground. Careful not to crush her windpipe, he searched for the big artery in her neck with his long, powerful fingers, and applied just enough pressure to cut off the flow of blood to her brain, while his thumb lay across her larynx and kept her silent. She was unconscious in less than a minute. Nathaniel lingered a moment to monitor her breathing, putting an ear to her chest, listening to her heart. He had done no permanent damage.

Bounding to his feet, he turned, crouching, as the sound of Girty crashing through the brush reached him. When the renegade loomed out of the darkness, Nathaniel launched himself at him, carrying him to the ground. But Girty was quick to react and, driving a knee into Nathaniel's groin, flipped the frontiersman over his head. Nathaniel landed painfully on the base of his spine, but scrambled to his feet nonetheless. Girty had a knife in his hand now, and tried to gut Nathaniel as he lunged forward. The frontiersman avoided the knife thrust and caught Girty across the back of the neck with a forearm. It was as effective as hitting the renegade with a block of wood. Girty crumpled, out cold. Retrieving his rifle, Nathaniel rolled Girty over on his back, got a grip on the collar of the renegade's buckskin hunting shirt, and dragged him into the shallows of the river. Sticking close to the bank, he headed away from the village, keeping to the water, and making sure Girty's head remained above the surface.

He didn't want Simon Girty dead.

Not yet anyway.

III

Some distance from the Delaware village, Nathaniel stripped Girty of his Indian attire, and then securely bound the renegade with strips of rawhide, wrists and ankles. Girty was wearing a strip of calico around his forehead to keep long, greasy locks out of his face;

Nathaniel used this to gag his prisoner. If Girty came to, he didn't want the renegade raising an alarm.

The frontiersman shed his buckskins and donned Girty's clothes—fringed leggings, beaded moccasins, and a sleeveless tunic adorned with Shawnee quillwork.

His plan was fraught with risk, but he thought there was a chance he could make it through the Delaware village disguised as Girty and reach the lodge from which Quashquame had emerged. And as long as there was any chance at all he would take it.

The biggest problem that he could foresee was his yellow hair. Girty's hair was dark. Nathaniel scooped mud from the bank of the river and then ran his fingers through his hair. At close quarters the deception would undoubtedly fail, but he could only hope that most of the Indians would be sufficiently distracted by the festivities.

As for Girty, Nathaniel had every intention of returning for him and taking him to Kentucky, and justice long-overdue. The only other option would be to kill the renegade, here and now. Nathaniel could not bring himself to commit cold-blooded murder. That would make him just as bad as Girty. He realized that most of his fellow Kentuckians would not suffer a solitary pang of conscience in killing Girty. The renegade was responsible for the murder of whole families. Yet Nathaniel deigned not to take Girty's life—and resolved not to do so unless circumstances dictated. He would kill the renegade only if by not doing so he would be permitting Girty to continue his bloody career.

Returning to the place where the unconscious girl lay, Nathaniel tore strips from her deerskin dress and used them to bind her hand and foot. He gagged her, too. Then he proceeded boldly into the village.

He kept his Kentucky rifle. Girty hadn't carried his rifle out of the village, but Nathaniel didn't expect anyone would notice the difference. Initially keeping to the outskirts of the encampment, Nathaniel made his way through the *wegiwas*. Most of the lodges were empty, as the majority of the Delawares had congregated in the center of the village. A mongrel dog rushed him, yapping fiercely. Nathaniel picked up a stone and hurled it, striking the dog in the flank and sending it away in a scurry, tail tucked.

Nerves on fire, heart pounding in his chest, Nathaniel managed to stroll in full view through the lodges, even as his instincts screamed at him to dart quickly from shadow to shadow. A handful of Indians looked his way, but none were near him, and from what little they could see of him in the darkness there was nothing to alarm them.

It was with vast relief that he reached Quashquame's lodge and ducked inside. The last fifty feet of this, the longest walk of his life, had brought him to within a stone's throw of the crowd gathered around the bonfire. The few who took note of him did not give him a second thought.

The lodge was empty. A fire in the circle of stones at the center of the lodge was burning low. Nathaniel crouched in the shadows near the entrance and waited.

He did not have long to wait.

IV

When the Indian cast aside the deerskin flap and stooped to enter the lodge, Nathaniel didn't wait to see who it was. The frontiersman used the stock of his long rifle to knock the man's legs out from under him. The Indian fell, sprawling, and Nathaniel pounced like a big cat, pinning the Indian with a knee at the base of the spine and clamping a hand over his mouth.

Only then did Nathaniel identify the man as Quashquame.

"It is I, Nathaniel," rasped the frontiersman.

Quashquame ceased his ineffectual struggling. All the tension left his body, and he lay still.

Nathaniel removed his hand from the Delaware's mouth, and lifted the knee from his spine. He did not bother to ask for assurances from Quashquame that he would not try to escape or raise an alarm. He had to believe that their many years of friendship would count for something. If they did not—if Quashquame betrayed him to the other Indians—then, Nathaniel figured, it would be time to die, and he would go gladly, as those things that made life worth living, things like honor and friendship and trust, would be proven not to exist after all.

Quashquame rolled over and sat up. He stared at Nathaniel's borrowed garb, at the mud in his hair, and then at the keen, bronzed face he knew so well.

And smiled.

Relieved, Nathaniel sat back on his heels. "Sorry about the rough treatment, Quashquame."

The Delaware was actually grinning now.

"What's so funny?" snapped Nathaniel.

Quashquame signed, *I no speak*. Then he put a hand over his mouth while pointing at Nathaniel.

Nathaniel understood. "Reckon it is kind of funny, now that you mention it. But I wasn't sure who'd be the first to come in here, and I wasn't taking any chances."

Like Shawnee you look, signed Quashquame.

"These belong to Girty."

He dead.

Nathaniel shook his head. "I aim to take him back to Kaintuck with me, assuming I get out of here alive."

Why you come.

"To see you, old friend. I couldn't let things stay as they were between us." Nathaniel gazed pensively into the glowing orange embers of the fire behind Quashquame, picking his words with care. "After what happened to your sister, I reckon I couldn't blame you for hating all white men. But I . . . well, I have to know something. Are we enemies now, Quashquame? When and if there's another war between our peoples, are you going to go on the warpath? I want to know if one day we're going to wind up trying to kill each other."

We no enemies, signed Quashquame. *Friends always.*

"Thank God for that."

There will be war.

"Is that what Girty's doing here? And Logan's Mingos?"

There is Shawnee Chief, signed Quashquame. *Tecumseh. His brother the prophet. Tecumseh will lead the people to victory over Long Knives. The prophet speaks with* Moneto, *and* Moneto *has sent Tecumseh to save all tribes.*

"An Indian Messiah," mused Nathaniel. "Are your people going to fight in this war?"

Many want war.

"Can't say as I blame them, after all that's happened. What about you, old friend?"

I talk peace.

"I'd have been surprised to learn otherwise. But that puts you between a rock and a hard place, doesn't it?"

Quashquame shook his head. He reached out and clutched Nathaniel's arm, then signed, *You and family go quick. Leave this land.*

"I reckon not," said Nathaniel, taken aback. "Kaintuck's my home, and will be till the day I die."

All Long Knives will die.

"Look here, Quashquame. We've fought the Shawnees plenty. The Wyandots and Mingos, too. We won't be run out of Kaintuck. You've got to make your people understand, there's no victory in store for them. We've got to keep the peace, or it's the Indians who will be driven from their lands. Peace is your only chance, Quashquame. I say that because I don't want to see any more blood shed. You know that."

Quashquame nodded. Despondently, he signed, *No peace. War. All tribes will follow Tecumseh.*

Nathaniel sighed. "I've met this Tecumseh, and I'm pretty sure he's no messiah sent by *Moneto*. He's just a chieftain, like Cornstalk and Black Fish and Blue Jacket. They've all tried to drive us out of Kaintuck, but we're sticking, like it or not. Now, I don't know if we ought to be there, but we are, and there we'll stay."

All tribes, repeated Quashquame.

"When do you reckon? This summer?"

Quashquame shrugged.

"Well, I'm grateful for the news. Grateful, too, that you won't be on the warpath against us. But I don't guess there's much point in asking if you'll ever come back to us."

Quashquame looked morosely into the fire. Then he shook his head and signed, *I no fight my people.*

"Then I reckon it's good-bye," said Nathaniel, with

a heavy heart. "I was worried about the reception you'd get, since you've been consortin' with the Long Knives for so long. But by the looks of it, they think highly of you here. Not surprised. So do I."

He stuck out his hand.

Quashquame clasped it with his own.

Nathaniel was reluctant to let go. But he did, and slipped out into the night without another word.

There were no words adequate to describe the loss he felt.

V

Somehow Simon Girty had escaped.

For a moment Nathaniel stood there in the black shadows of the forest, stunned. He was certain this was the place he had left the renegade, trussed up like a turkey bound for the Sunday dinner table. But Girty was gone, and so were Nathaniel's buckskins. The frontiersman could scarcely believe that Girty had managed to free himself from the rawhide binding him at wrists and ankles.

It seemed likely, therefore, that once free, Girty had hastened back to the village. Which meant they had passed each other in the night. It also meant that the Indians would be after him. Nathaniel could only hope that they would wait until morning to begin their pursuit.

Resolved to put as much distance as possible between himself and the Delaware village before sunrise, the frontiersman turned to the river and began following it downstream, wading through the shallows. For hours he remained in the water, until his feet were frozen. When he could bear it no longer, he climbed up onto the bank, peeled off his moccasins, and rubbed his feet vigorously to restore the circulation.

Though tired and hungry he would not stop, returning to the river for another hour. Girty would bring the Indians back to the place where he had been bound, assuming that Nathaniel would return to that spot. They would also assume that he had stuck to the shallows to hide his trail, and they would follow the river for a time, searching both banks for any sign of him. They would not, however, expect him to remain in the river all night, and Nathaniel was hoping that after going some miles without finding any sign of him the Indians would double back, thinking that somehow they had missed his trail.

An hour before sunrise Nathaniel left the river and headed due south. Daybreak found him ten miles from the village, and moving swiftly in spite of his weariness. Assuming Girty and the Indians had not departed the village until first light, he felt he had a comfortable lead. By midmorning he had slowed to a walk. By noon he felt good about his chances, knowing that by nightfall he would arrive at the Ohio, with Kentucky only a long swim away.

He heard the bullet, burning the air inches from his ear, a heartbeat before the crack of a rifle from somewhere behind him, alerting him to the nerve-shattering fact that his comfortable lead had been a possibly fatal fantasy.

Running with great long strides, he threw a quick look over his shoulder. He was crossing a meadow, and the Indians were exploding out of the forest a hundred yards behind him—at least thirty warriors, and of course there was Girty in the lead.

Damn that renegade! Nathaniel had a hunch Girty was responsible for this. He had performed the impossible once by freeing himself from Nathaniel's bindings, and he had done so again by tracking Nathaniel through the night.

More rifles cracked, more bullets sizzled the air, or plucked the waist-high grass around the fleeing frontiersman. Nathaniel did not stop to turn and fire back at them. To pause would be fatal. He ran for all he was worth and got across the big meadow unscathed, plunging into the forest only to find himself confronted by a steep, rocky slope. His heart sank. He was exhausted. How could he scale this incline? Yet without pause he started up it, his powerful legs churning, his heart pounding in his chest, his lungs heaving like a blacksmith's bellows. As he neared the top he had to reach down deep and find a reserve of strength. His legs had become heavy like lead. Every muscle and joint in his body screamed for mercy. The breath rasped harshly in his throat.

His pursuers were at the base of the ridge now. Their blood-curdling whoops and panther screams spurred him to even greater exertion. Almost to the top! He stumbled, gathered himself up, strained to reach the crest, and when he did he let out a gasping shout of pure exultation. Now he paused, bringing the rifle stock to shoulder, drawing a bead, squeezing the trigger. The white powdersmoke blinded him for an instant, but he heard an Indian cry out—and it was the scream of death, a primordial sound that sent an icy chill down Nathaniel's spine. The Indians responded with a ragged volley of rifle fire, but Nathaniel was abruptly gone from the rimrock, and their angry bullets sang harmlessly off rock and tree.

As he raced across the top of the ridge Nathaniel reloaded. He did not have to break stride to do so. Holding the ball of Galena lead in his teeth, he poured the charge from powderhorn into barrel, spit the bullet down the barrel, and struck the stock of the rifle against the ground in lieu of using the hickory ramrod.

Reaching the other side of the ridge he plunged down the slope, lost his footing, and fell. He couldn't stop rolling, head over heels, and figured it was nothing short of a miracle that he didn't snap his spine in two against the trunk of a tree, or break his skull open against a rock. He lost his hold on the rifle, and at the end of the long fall he hurtled off a twenty-foot cutbank into a ravine. The bottom of the ravine was sand, providing a sufficiently soft landing, but the descent had dazed him, and he lay there a moment, dimly aware that precious seconds were being lost, but hurting so bad that he didn't honestly think he could get up.

Then he heard another shrill cry, issuing from the throat of an Indian somewhere on the slope above, and the sound acted like an electric charge through his body. He got to his feet, and the world tilted, but he kept his legs beneath him and realized, with a sickening knot in the pit of his stomach, that he had lost the long rifle—the very one Daniel Boone had given him so many years ago, and which had never failed him in all this time, so that it had become more than just a tool of his trade to him, more than maple and iron and brass all in one handsomely fashioned and lethally efficient work of art. He hated to leave it behind, as he would hate to abandon a trusted friend, but there was no help for it. *Linger here and you die.*

So he ran.

Ran for an hour, for two, and then for a third, and he

managed to actually increase his lead, but not enough, because they kept coming on, two hundred yards back, three hundred, a quarter of a mile. He ran until he could not go any farther, until all his strength and stamina were used up—and then he kept running, and the sun slid slowly down the azure sky. All he could think about was Amanda—poor Amanda, alone in their cabin, wondering why he never returned, and the image of her sad and lovely face framed by that golden hair only just a little streaked with gray was enough to keep him going. He just could not, would not, quit.

And as the sun finally sank below the wooden heights to the west, and its dying light turned pink and orange and crimson to form a backdrop for purple strips of clouds, he came abruptly to the brink of a sheer precipice, and his dulled brain registered the majestic sweep of the wide and rapid Ohio a hundred feet below him, the color of blood in places, a deep velvet blue in others, and he did not even break stride, for of late the Indians had been gaining ground on him. Some of them fired their rifles at him, and then he was gone, hurling himself over the edge.

When they reached the rim, Simon Girty and the Indians scanned the surface of the river for quite some time. There was no sign of their prey.

"He is dead," said one of the Indians, disappointed.

The others concurred, and turned back for the long walk home.

Only Girty lingered. Clad in Nathaniel's buckskins, he smiled slightly at the darkening waters of the *Spay-lay-wi-theepi*. He paid unspoken tribute to the frontiersman—truly, a worthy foe.

"I reckon we'll meet again," murmured the renegade, and turned to follow his Indian friends.

CHAPTER FOUR

Tecumseh

He dreamed of years gone by ...

I
(1783)

The Shawnees had ambushed the thirteen *Shemanese* on the banks of the Ohio River, and he had been among the warriors, though only fifteen years of age. Boys taking the warpath—indeed, it was a sad thing, bemoaned the elders, but this was what the once great Shawnee Nation had been reduced to after so many years of fighting the white man.

The battle had been fierce, fought at close quarters, and Tecumseh had narrowly escaped death, while slaying four of the Long Knives himself. For that reason he was praised for his courage and skill by his fellow warriors, and as they sang his praises his heart swelled with pride.

A single *Shemanese* had been taken prisoner. He was brought to the Shawnee village on the Scioto River. There he was condemned to death. Bound naked at the stake, he was burned alive, while Shawnee women and children danced and shouted and hurled insults at their victim.

Tecumseh watched the execution impassively. His features did not betray the almost overpowering disgust welling up inside of him. When the white man's charred body was finally motionless in death, his screams still echoed in the young warrior's head, and he could restrain himself no longer. Stepping forward, he raised his arms, indicating to the others present that he wished to speak, and all fell silent to hear what the young hero, the son of the great Pucksinwah, and brother of the legendary Blue Jacket, had to say.

"You may say that I am too young for my words to be given any weight," said Tecumseh, "but I tell you that I am not too young to feel deeply shamed because of what I have seen here. I am almost ashamed to call myself Shawnee. That is how strongly the feelings run within me.

"Why do you do this thing? What kind of courage does it take to burn a man at the stake? Are we so unsure of ourselves that we must hear our enemy scream in agony? I tell you, there is no honor in such an act. Only disgrace."

"He is our enemy!" shouted a warrior, infuriated by this dressing-down. "His kind have done as bad or worse to our own people."

"The *Shemanese* are barbarians," replied Tecumseh coldly. "We all know that. But must we lower ourselves to their level? Because they do such things, does that make them right for the Shawnee? And yes, he was our enemy. He deserved to die. But he should be given the opportunity to die like a man. If you were the prisoner of the Long Knives, would you not want the chance to die like a warrior? Or would you want to die like a dog? Yet I think today, having done this thing, we no longer have the right to call ourselves warriors, or even men.

"I am young, so I do not expect you to heed my

words. I will say only one thing more. Never again for the rest of my life will I participate in such an act as this. I will carry the shame of this day in my heart forever. I cannot believe that *Moneto* is smiling on us. He would expect better of his people. That is all I have to say."

Tecumseh braced himself for a storm of angry protest. Instead, there was a moment of stunned silence, broken only by the crackle of the flames licking at the blackened corpse.

Finally, Chiksika stepped up to place himself alongside his younger brother.

"Today, no one fought with greater courage than my brother, Tecumseh. For that reason I say we should all take his words to heart. He is much younger than I, yet I am in awe of him, for many times he has displayed great wisdom for one so young. I say this—that one day my brother Tecumseh will become a great chief of the Shawnee, greater than Black Fish, greater even than Cornstalk. Was he not born under the sign of the Panther Passing Across?"

A warrior stood. "Tecumseh has spoken true words. I for one vow never again to take part in such cruelty as we have committed this day."

Another warrior rose to his feet. "I, too, give my word never to do anything like this again."

Tecumseh watched in astonishment as one by one almost every Shawnee warrior present stood to make his own promise.

Already they follow his lead, thought Chiksika, bursting with pride. *Indeed, one day Tecumseh will be a great chief.*

II
(1787)

The Shawnees had long since given up mustering hundreds of warriors to march south into *Can-tuc-kee* and wage war. Since Point Pleasant, and throughout the war which the whites fought amongst themselves, they had tried that, and to no avail. Even with the assistance of the redcoats they had failed to achieve a meaningful victory.

So now they raided in small war parties, attacking isolated cabins while avoiding the strongly defended forts. They killed cattle and stole horses and sometimes they came home with scalps.

Time and again the Long Knives would pursue the war parties back across the Ohio River, but seldom did they manage to catch their elusive prey. In the summer of 1787, Colonel John Bowman led an expedition against the villages of the Shawnee Nation, but once he was deep in hostile country Bowman lost his nerve and beat a hasty retreat, much to the disgust of his Kentucky frontiersmen.

That year the new republic calling itself the United States of America established the Northwest Territory by passage of an ordinance that organized all the land north and west of the Ohio into a commonwealth. The Ordinance of 1787 was quite a unique document, for it absolutely forbade slavery in the new territory, thereby recognizing for the first time in history the right of every man to be free and enjoy an equal opportunity to prosper. The Ordinance also provided for complete religious freedom. It declared that the Northwest Territory would in time be divided into three, or possibly five, new states. Finally, and in a manner that resulted in great consternation among the Kentuckians, it addressed the Indian problem ...

> *The utmost good faith will always be observed towards the Indians; their lands and property shall never be taken from them, without their consent, and in their property, rights, and liberty they shall never be invaded or disturbed, unless in just and lawful wars authorized by Congress.*

No, the Long Knives of Kentucky did not like the taste of that one bit. Sounded like the government was forbidding them from striking back at the Shawnee devils who were making life a living hell for them and theirs. From one end of Kentucky to the other they talked it over—and everywhere came to the same decision: If the government in Washington thought they would stop protecting their homes and families then the government had misjudged them.

Meanwhile, in Salem, Massachusetts, the Ohio Company was chartered, purchasing vast tracts of land north of the Ohio from the government for the purpose of establishing settlements there.

It was just as Blue Jacket had predicted. He had tried to warn his people that the whites would never keep that part of the old agreements which guaranteed that they would never take Shawnee land for their own.

That same year, during the Hunger Moon, Chiksika and Tecumseh traveled south along the Great Mother of Waters for a winter sojourn with the Cherokees in a village in Tennessee. They were accompanied by ten other Kispokotha warriors. The Cherokees treated them as honored guests. And when it was decided in the Cherokee councils that the tribe would attack a white settlement that encroached upon tribal lands, the Shawnees agreed to fight alongside their southern brethren.

On the night prior to the attack, Chiksika informed his brother that he had had a vision.

"I will die tomorrow," said Chiksika calmly. "When the sun is high, a bullet will strike me here." He put a finger to his forehead. "The Cherokees will begin to lose their will to fight. It will be up to you, my brother, to rally them. If you can, you will lead them to a victory."

Tecumseh was in anguish, for he believed Chiksika's words. So it had been with Pucksinwah, and Pucksinwah's father before him. It seemed that the men of this family had a gift for seeing into the future. With some it was stronger than with others. Tecumseh knew of too many occasions when Chiksika had accurately predicted an event to doubt his brother now. Only a few months ago, Chiksika had informed him that he would break his leg in a fall from a horse. It had happened, during a buffalo hunt. A bull had charged Tecumseh's pony, knocking it down, and in the process Tecumseh had been thrown, breaking his hip bone.

The next morning the Cherokees, with their Shawnee allies, attacked the whites, who had been forewarned, and crouched behind hastily erected fortifications. The fight raged for hours. Three times the Indians attacked. Three times they were hurled back. Tecumseh and his brother fought valiantly, side by side, impressing the Cherokees. Then, when the sun was at its zenith, a bullet struck Chiksika in the forehead. It was a long shot, and the marksmanship of the Long Knives gave the Cherokees cause to falter. The death of their Shawnee friend was a bad omen. Tecumseh tried to rally them, but all the fight had gone out of the Cherokees. They withdrew. Tecumseh was the last to leave the field of battle. He carried the body of his dead brother, and his bronzed features betrayed no emotion. Chiksika had taught him well.

III
(1788–1790)

Often Tecumseh dreamed of his homecoming . . .

The Cherokees stood in awe of him. Following the death of Chiksika, Tecumseh became the leader of the small band of Shawnees. But in short order the Cherokees themselves began to look at him for leadership on the warpath. He demonstrated an uncanny knack for doing the right thing at the right time. Leading the Cherokees to victory after victory, he became a legend in the span of a year. His hosts looked upon him with respect bordering on awe. They offered to adopt him into the tribe, but he graciously declined.

He could not, however, decline the Cherokee maiden they offered him—not without insulting the entire village. She was pretty, and eager to please him, and she willingly saw to all his needs. The other young women envied her. But Tecumseh did not love her, and made it clear to her that one day he would be leaving.

He was homesick. Yet the Cherokees depended on him so much that he was compelled to delay his departure time and time again. Another winter passed, and it was not until the following spring that Tecumseh and the six Kispokotha warriors who were still alive departed the hills of Tennessee and headed north.

Black Hoof, the principal chief of the Shawnee Nation, personally welcomed Tecumseh home. Shawnee women provided him with fine new garments as gifts—shirt and leggins and a knee-length frock of soft doeskin, with fine bead- and quillwork. He was presented with a silver-mounted tomahawk, which he placed in his new elkhide belt.

His exploits in the land of the Cherokees had preceded him, and the Shawnees sang his praises at a great feast.

He learned of the great victory the Shawnees had won against federal troops under General Josiah Harmer. Four hundred soldiers and twice that many militiamen from Pennsylvania, Virginia, and Kentucky had marched into the Ohio country with orders from Secretary of War Henry Knox to deal with the pesky Indians once and for all.

A captured Indian informed Harmer that Shawnees under Blue Jacket were joining forces with Miamis led by Little Turtle at the confluence of the St. Joseph and St. Mary's rivers, at a place called French Store. Simon Girty had hurried north toward the lakes to gather more Indians for the purpose of resisting this invasion. Harmer advanced, but when a scouting party was ambushed and massacred, he lost his nerve and, to the disgust of many of his men, ordered a retreat.

To his dismay, Harmer found his path blocked by the Indians, over a thousand strong. Scouts informed the general that they had spotted Girty among the savages, wearing a long scarlet coat and riding a magnificent black stallion. This was faulty intelligence, but Harmer assumed that Girty had brought reinforcements from the north, and became firmly convinced that the hostiles outnumbered him two or three to one, when in truth the opposing forces were roughly equal.

Harmer was paralyzed by indecision. Some of the border captains serving as his subordinates insisted that an attack be made at once. The befuddled general made an incredible blunder. He split his army, sending six hundred men toward the Indians in what he would later call, in his dispatches, a reconnaissance in force. He promised to reinforce this detachment if a battle was joined.

The battle *was* joined, and a fierce battle it became. The six hundred fought valiantly against superior numbers, expecting Harmer to appear on the scene at any moment and turn the tide in their favor.

But a brilliant strategic move by Blue Jacket and Little Turtle froze the indecisive Harmer in place. They sent a small party of warriors to make a demonstration in front of Harmer's lines. The general was completely fooled into thinking that a major attack was underway against him. For three hours his "reconnaissance in force" held on—and Harmer did not move an inch. Losing a third of their number, the detachment finally broke off the engagement and retreated. The Indians pursued, and the retreat became a rout.

Harmer led his bloodied expedition out of the Ohio country, wrote the Secretary of War that they had won a great victory at French Store, and a fortnight later resigned his commission before it could be taken away from him. "A victory!" Knox reportedly exclaimed upon receipt of Harmer's communique. "If that was a victory I pray we may never know defeat."

As for the disgruntled Kentuckians who had marched with Harmer, they returned home, agreeing among themselves that if the good general ever set foot in Kentucky again, they would skin the cowardly fool alive. They also came to the conclusion that they could not count on the government in Washington, or the bluecoat soldiers, to help them win this fight. They were in it alone.

Spirits ran high in the Shawnee villages. Blue Jacket had won a great triumph in the north, while in the south Tecumseh had led the Cherokees on a brilliant campaign of hit-and-run tactics that had left the *Shemanese* bloodied and reeling. Perhaps now the whites would learn their lesson. Soon all the Long Knives would be gone from *Can-tuc-kee,* and things would be as they had been before.

Tecumseh sat in a place of honor at the council and solemnly listened for a long time without saying anything to all the optimistic talk and overconfident breast-beating. When it was finished he took Blue Jacket aside.

"The *Shemanese* will still be in *Can-tuc-kee* next year, *neethetha.* Another army will come, to take the place of the one which you defeated at French Store, and it will be stronger."

"What are you saying, Tecumseh? That there is no hope?"

"There is one way. When all the tribes—the Cherokees, the Creeks, the Miamis, the Mingos, the Wyandots, the Delawares, the Ottawas, the Iroquois, and the Shawnees—join together to wage war, only then will we have final victory."

Blue Jacket respected Tecumseh for his wisdom, and knew that he was endowed with a prophetic gift, like Chiksika and Pucksinwah before him. So he listened, and accepted what Tecumseh had to say.

"But who could bring all these tribes together?" he asked. "There is bad blood between the Creeks and the Cherokees, as between the Wyandots and the Delaware." He shook his head glumly. "No, I will not live to see that day."

"No, you will not," said Tecumseh, putting a hand on his adopted brother's shoulder. "But the day *will* come."

As Tecumseh walked away, Blue Jacket stared after him, wondering if Tecumseh meant that the day of salvation for the Shawnee Nation was far in the future—or if his brother was predicting his imminent death.

IV
(1792)

In his dreams lurked the Long Knife his people called *Metequa*—Flintlock.

It was from Blue Jacket that Tecumseh mastered English. Occasionally, books turned up as part of the booty taken in a raid, and it was with these that Blue Jacket taught his younger brother. Blue Jacket couldn't fathom why Tecumseh wanted to know how to read and speak English, and for quite some time all Tecumseh could tell him was that it seemed to be a good thing to know. Then, one day, a beaming Tecumseh brought a book to Blue Jacket and pointed out a passage: *Know thine enemy as thyself.*

"This is why I learn the language of the *Shemanese*," said Tecumseh.

Blue Jacket grunted, expressing skepticism. "I know

him by the color of his skin, and the blood of my people on his hands."

"From these books," insisted Tecumseh, "I will learn all I need to know about him, until I can think as he does. Only when we know his mind can we defeat him."

Some time later, Tecumseh led a horse-stealing expedition across the *Spay-lay-wi-theepi.* He was not so much interested in horses as he was in learning the lay of the land in *Can-tuc-kee,* and for that reason he traveled south at every opportunity. This time he returned with fifteen ponies—and a handbill boldly taken from the wall of a cabin occupied by an unsuspecting frontiersman and his family near the settlement called Boonesboro.

This notice, which he translated for the council, encouraged the chiefs to believe that their villages were safe for a time from the Long Knives. Written at the behest of the President of the United States, George Washington, it called on the Kentuckians to "forbear all hostility other than what may be rendered necessary in your own defense," since the government was attempting to give the "misled and deluded tribes of the belligerent Indians a last opportunity to save themselves by an honorable and substantial peace." To this end, the government was sending envoys to the hostile tribes in an effort to make arrangements for a treaty negotiation which, hopefully, would resolve the long-standing difficulties that existed between red man and white.

The Shawnees did not have high hopes for this new treaty. They had agreed to many treaties which, on their face, seemed eminently fair. Yet always the *Shemanese* broke their word. Still, they decided to treat the envoys from the Great White Father in Washington with respect. By engaging in, and if possible prolonging, the negotiations they could at least keep the Long Knives at bay.

They assumed the Long Knives would obey the Great White Father. But it didn't always work that way.

In ten years, Nathaniel Jones had become something of a legend among the Kentuckians. They spoke his name in the same breath with that of Boone and Kenton and Wetzel. Now he was on the trail of the Shawnee horse thieves, accompanied by eighteen other frontiersmen from the vicinity of Boonesboro. The trail was not difficult to follow. Spring rains had softened the earth. As they neared the Shawnee village they kept their eyes peeled for lookouts. But the Indians had dropped their guard. The first Shawnee they saw was a lone boy riding an old nag through the brush. He was looking for a stray horse. He found a bullet instead.

Nathaniel cursed the frontiersman who had fired the shot. "You haven't got the brains God gave a goose, Washburn. Do you want all our scalps hanging on a lodge pole?"

They approached the fallen boy. As he breathed his last, the young Shawnee, defiant even in death, said, "Tecumseh will avenge me." Then he was gone.

"What did he say, Flintlock?" asked one of the bordermen, knowing that Nathaniel had picked up some of the Shawnee lingo.

Nathaniel translated for them.

"Who's Tecumseh?" wondered Washburn.

Nathaniel shrugged. It was the first he had heard the name. But it would not be the last.

The Indians in the village heard the shot, but thought

little of it. A warrior out hunting. Only one shot, after all. Nothing to be concerned about. The handbill Tecumseh had read to them had lulled them into a false sense of security.

Nathaniel reconnoitered, and decided they should wait for nightfall. There would be no moon. He and half the men would swing around to the east and raise a commotion, in hopes of leading the Shawnees into a belief that they were being attacked by a large force from that direction. Meanwhile, the rest of the frontiersmen would slip in and gather up as much of the horse herd as possible. With any luck, they would be ten miles away before the Indians could collect their wits and figure out what had happened.

It might have worked—but Nathaniel had not counted on Tecumseh.

The young Shawnee listened to the shooting for a moment, and tried to organize the confused Indians. "They are not many!" he yelled. "Follow me!" He plunged into the darkness, straight at the blossoms of flame spouting from the long rifles of Nathaniel and his companions.

The first Long Knife Tecumseh confronted was Nathaniel himself. With a savage scream, the Shawnee put his rifle to Nathaniel's chest and pulled the trigger. Nathaniel was so startled that he did not have the chance to defend himself. But Tecumseh's rifle misfired. Both men were so disconcerted that they veered away from one another, going in opposite directions.

Other Shawnees followed Tecumseh in his fearless charge, and the frontiersmen scattered. Two of Nathaniel's men were slain, and two Shawnees. The bordermen met up some miles away from the village, at a prearranged place. They had managed to make off with only twenty ponies.

In the village a council was convened. The chief and the elders decided to evacuate the village at first light, taking their women and children north to safety, in case a large force of Long Knives was in the vicinity. Tecumseh argued against this decision, but to no avail. He realized for the first time that the older warriors had lost their will to fight. Once again they had been tricked by the *Shemanese*. They gave up too readily. He asked for and received permission to take two dozen warriors and try to catch the frontiersmen.

V

Tecumseh and his warriors left the village in the blue mists of dawn. The rest of the Shawnees were hastily preparing for flight northward. Tecumseh knew that was entirely unnecessary. He was convinced that the previous night's attack had been made by a small group of Long Knives. He couldn't explain how he knew—he just did.

The first thing they found as they began their search for the trail of the Kentuckians was the boy, the one Washburn had shot and killed. Tecumseh was furious. He did not think it right that war should be waged on women and children. That conviction set him apart from most of his brethren. The Indian believed that the women of his enemies had to die, for the simple reason that dead they could not produce more foes. There was some logic in it; nonetheless, Tecumseh abhorred the concept.

It was easy to find the trail of the Long Knives.

More precisely, the trails. The white men had scattered after the attack on the village. Tecumseh was confident that following one would lead them to all. Surely the Long Knives had established a rendezvous point in case one or more members of the party became separated.

As fate would have it, the trail the Shawnees followed belonged to the man named Washburn.

Washburn had had nothing but bad luck. In the confusion of last night he had fled west instead of southeast toward the prearranged rendezvous point. On top of that misfortune was piled yet another, when his horse stepped in a hole and broke its leg. Washburn did not dare shoot the horse to put it out of its misery, for fear the shot would bring a swarm of red savages down upon him. So he left the suffering horse and proceeded on foot, fearful that Flintlock and the others would give up on him and depart the rendezvous before he arrived.

When the Shawnees found the horse, Tecumseh grimly shook his head. He could understand why the Long Knife they were tracking would not want to shoot the animal, but there was no excuse for not using a blade—which Tecumseh proceeded to do. Cutting the horse's throat, he and his warriors pressed on.

Soon after, they spotted Washburn. One of the warriors let loose an exultant cry before Tecumseh could stop him, warning Washburn that death was hot on his heels. The frontiersman whirled. Unnerved, he fumbled with his long rifle. All the Shawnees but Tecumseh leapt from their horses and dived for cover. They worked on the assumption that every frontiersman was an uncanny marksman. But Tecumseh kicked his pony into a gallop, heading straight for Washburn.

Washburn got off a shot with Tecumseh less than thirty yards away. Watching from cover, the other warriors were astonished. Tecumseh did not fall! He had not been hit. It was a miracle. Indeed, *Moneto* was looking out for Tecumseh.

Inspired by Tecumseh's fearlessness, the Shawnees broke cover and rushed forward. Washburn tried to flee, but Tecumseh was on him quickly, leaping from his pony and bearing the frontiersman to the ground. A blow from Tecumseh's warclub knocked Washburn out.

The warclub was Tecumseh's weapon of choice. A stone, the size of a goose egg, was wrapped in rawhide, sewn about the stone when wet and dried to a hard finish, then secured to a hickory handle.

When Washburn came to he was lying flat on his back, hands and feet bound. He stared fearfully at the circle of fierce bronze faces above him.

"How many came with you to attack us?" asked Tecumseh.

Washburn was surprised to be alive. Tecumseh's good English also surprised him.

"Fifty," he said.

"You lie. Who leads you?"

"Flintlock Jones."

"Metequa!" exclaimed one of the warriors. "He is a great warrior."

"Is his hair yellow like the sun?" Tecumseh asked Washburn.

Washburn said it was so.

Tecumseh nodded. Then *Metequa* was the Long Knife he had had dead to rights last night—before his rifle misfired. Tecumseh had thought then that there was something special about the yellow-haired frontiersman. *Metequa*'s life was blessed. And, too, the clever and daring attack he had devised impressed Tecumseh.

"Where are you to meet your friends?" Tecumseh asked the prisoner.

"Go to hell."

"You are loyal. That is good. And it pleases me that your leader is the great *Shemanese* warrior, *Metequa*. He is a worthy foe. I know that he and I will meet again."

"That will be the day you die," said Washburn.

"Yes," said Tecumseh. "Three more times he and I will meet. Then we will both die."

Tecumseh turned to the other warriors, and ordered one to remain with Washburn while the rest followed him in pursuit of the Long Knives.

But the knowledge that *Metequa* was leading the Long Knives gave most of the warriors a bad case of cold feet. The fear in their eyes disgusted Tecumseh.

"Stay here, then, and tremble like little children afraid of the thunder and lightning. I will go alone."

This sufficiently shamed eight of the warriors, who vowed to follow Tecumseh to the death, if necessary. The others would not budge.

"I forbid you to kill this man," Tecumseh warned those who stayed behind.

He led the others a few miles into the woods when, suddenly, he stopped. Perplexed, the others watched him. Tecumseh seemed to be listening to something. But if so, it was something only he could hear.

"We go back," he said abruptly, and turned his pony around.

Arriving at the place where they had left the other

Shawnees and the prisoner, they came upon a grisly scene.

Washburn's head was impaled on a stout stick driven into the ground. His headless torso had been mutilated—the chest split open and the heart removed, the arms and legs hacked off.

Trembling with rage, Tecumseh stared for a long time at the corpse. Then he fixed such a cold gaze upon the warriors who had committed the deed that they shrank back from him in terror.

"Cowards!" he screamed. "You are not Shawnees. You are animals. You disgust me. You are so afraid of the Long Knives that you do this? I am ashamed to say that I know you. Come! We will go back. You will be safe with the rest of the village. Ride behind me, as I do not wish to see your faces. I refuse to take the warpath with such cowards."

VI
(1794)

He dreamed of war . . . and peace . . .

Harmer's defeat galvanized the United States government into action. General "Mad Anthony" Wayne was assigned the task of bringing peace and stability, once and for all, to the Northwest Territory.

When Wayne marched his troops across the mountains in the autumn of 1793 he realized that it was too late in the year to campaign. Eschewing old stockades left behind by his predecessor, Harmer, as totally inadequate if not downright indefensible, he built Fort Greenville, a long day's march due north of the Ohio River outpost called Cincinnati.

The fort built, Wayne proceeded to train his men to perfection. A veteran of the Revolutionary War, he was a hard taskmaster, as well as a brilliant strategist and administrator. Somewhat eccentric, it was true, but the men overlooked his peculiarities because it soon became apparent to them that Mad Anthony was smart and tough and would not lead them into disaster.

Wayne sent word to the Kentuckians: *Come and join me.* Aware of his reputation, the frontiersmen flocked to his banner. They were weary unto death of incompetent nincompoops like Harmer. Now, finally, here was a man who would rid them of the Indian pestilence once and for all. Rumor had it that Wayne was in possession of "unofficial" orders from the administration to march on Detroit and drive the British into Canada! The British had promised in the Treaty of 1783 to evacuate their strongholds in the Northwest, and so far they had failed to do so.

The general expressed a crying need for scouts—men who knew the Indian country and who weren't afraid of venturing deep into it. Among those who answered the call were Simon Kenton and Nathaniel Jones. Before long, Wayne could honestly claim to have the best company of scouts any American army had ever enjoyed.

While the swollen ranks of Wayne's army trained and trained some more, Kenton, Flintlock, and the scouts ranged deep into Shawnee territory. There were numerous skirmishes with the Indians. They tried to outdo one another in daring exploits. They didn't like being cooped up in the fort, and they were spoiling for a fight.

But Wayne refused to be rushed. He sent envoys under a flag of truce to all the Indian villages. These stalwart men bore his offer to the Shawnee: They could either establish a permanent peace or face destruction. None of the tribes chose peace, having experienced the duplicity and unfairness of the white man's peace many times before. A few of Wayne's envoys were never seen again.

Wayne hadn't expected it to be easy. Harmer's debacle had bolstered the confidence of the Indians, and they figured they could defeat his army, too. They turned once again to Little Turtle and Blue Jacket, the victors of French Store.

To every Indian's surprise, Little Turtle urged his people, the Miamis, to compromise with the *Shemanese*. But the majority of chiefs decided to fight. Peace meant giving up the whole of the Northwest Territory. Little Turtle declined to lead his warriors this time. So the honor fell to Blue Jacket.

The British in Detroit were alarmed by Mad Anthony Wayne's presence. As a consequence they built a stronghold, Fort Miami, on the banks of the Maumee River, blocking Wayne's approach to Detroit.

When spring came, Wayne's two thousand regulars had been augmented by three thousand mounted Kentucky volunteers. It was by far the largest army ever assembled west of the Appalachians. Still, Mad Anthony did not march. The frontiersmen became impatient. There were murmurs of discontent, growing louder with each passing week. Wayne ignored them. He just would not be rushed.

Finally, in the summer of '94, he marched, toward the Maumee. The Indians fled their villages before this host. Halfway to Detroit, Wayne paused to build yet another fort. His men groaned. The fort was erected in eight days, complete with ditches, fascines, pickets, and blockhouses. "Not all the devils in Hell could take this fort!" exclaimed the delighted Wayne. He called the place Fort Defiance.

Blue Jacket made ready to move against Wayne. The warriors under his command represented seven tribes—Shawnee, Delaware, Chippewa, Ottawa, Seneca, Miami, and Potawatomie.

"You see!" he boasted to Tecumseh. "Here is a great confederacy of tribes, just as you have described. And I am their leader. They will follow me to victory. Finally we will drive the *Shemanese* from our land forever."

Tecumseh merely shook his head.

Blue Jacket was not as confident as he appeared to be. He truly believed that Tecumseh had the gift of prophecy. And, if this was true, then it was also true that he, Blue Jacket, would not live to see the great confederation that would force the whites back across the mountains.

Trying to put aside his sense of foreboding, Blue Jacket took his warriors to Fort Miami. They encamped a few miles south of the British stronghold, near Presque Isle. Here, a devastating windstorm had torn the forest up by its roots, cutting a wide swath. Thousands of logs lay in a massive jumble. Blue Jacket judged this to be an impregnable defensive position. With luck, he would lure Wayne into attacking him here.

When his scouts returned with news of the Indians' disposition and the lay of the land, Wayne became a human dynamo. Eager for action, he rushed his well-trained army forward.

It would go down in the history books as the Battle of Fallen Timbers.

VII

Blue Jacket had chosen a very strong position in the fallen timbers, and at a glance Mad Anthony Wayne realized that it would be sheer madness to attack head on. He decided on a ruse. Sending several hundred mounted riflemen forward, he ordered them to feign confusion when the Indians opened fire, and then to fall back in disorder. The Indians could not resist giving chase, even though Blue Jacket did his best to restrain them. They were lured out into the open and cut to pieces by the balance of Wayne's army. The entire Indian force fled, leaving over a hundred dead on the rain-soaked field. Wayne pursued them to the very walls of Fort Miami.

The British refused to help their Indian allies during the battle, and closed their gate in Blue Jacket's face when he asked for assistance. The Indians nonetheless found what they thought was a safe haven beneath the stout walls and several cannon of the redcoats. Wayne had permission from the President himself to seize Fort Miami, but he could see that the fort was too strong to take by assault without incurring heavy losses.

Instead, he instructed his lieutenant, William Henry Harrison, to set fire to all the villages and crops of the Indians along a fifty-mile stretch of the Maumee River. Meanwhile, the British commander of Fort Miami sent a letter of protest to Wayne. How dare he besiege a post belonging to His Majesty? Wayne fired back a sharp reply. Since this was American soil, then that was an American fort the redcoats were occupying, and he insisted they surrender possession and march their scarlet-clad posteriors right back to Canada.

The British deemed it the better part of valor to vacate

Fort Miami under a flag of truce. Blue Jacket's Indian host was rapidly dwindling. They were slipping away every night by the dozens. The British commander advised Blue Jacket to disperse the rest of his warriors. Infuriated by what he considered British betrayal, Blue Jacket did just that. The British marched out of Fort Miami with flags snapping in the breeze and drums and fifes rendering a martial air. The Americans jeered at the redcoat columns. Wayne put the fort to the torch and returned to Fort Defiance to go into winter quarters.

Before long, emissaries from the Seven Nations came to him with offers of peace. The following summer, at Fort Greenville, the treaty was concluded.

Kentucky was one big celebration. This peace would last, they said. The Indians had been soundly defeated. They had agreed never again to attack the settlements in Kentucky, or to attempt to stop the settlers who were beginning to pour into the Ohio country.

Still, there were some Long Knives who did not put great faith in this peace. Among them were Simon Kenton and Nathaniel Jones.

"As long as Blue Jacket's alive there will be no lasting peace," predicted Kenton, and Nathaniel had to agree.

Blue Jacket's defeat at the Fallen Timbers cost him dearly in terms of influence. But Tecumseh's influence continued to grow, to the point that, on the day he announced his intention to move to a beautiful stretch of land along Deer Creek, and invited others to join him, several hundred warriors expressed a desire to accompany him with their families. The extent of the response surprised him. They weren't just Kispokotha, his own clan, but also Chalahgawtha, Maykujay, and Thawegila Shawnee.

Once the Deer Creek village was established

Tecumseh was chosen to be its chief. Second only to him was Lalawethika, his younger brother, who had been in Methotosa's tomb the day Pucksinwah died. Lalawethika was a medicine man. Like his brothers, he seemed to have the gift of prophecy. Yet early on it appeared to be strongest in him, so much so that in time the people would refer to him simply as The Prophet.

Tecumseh married a Peckuwa maiden called Monetohse. She was very attractive, and she bore him a son, but she attempted to dominate her husband while at the same time expressing precious little maternal interest in her child. Tecumseh could finally tolerate her no longer, and sent Monetohse back to her father's *wegiwa*, divorcing her, and giving his son to his sister, Tecumapese, to care for.

He refused to attend the signing of the peace treaty at Fort Greenville in the summer of '95. He would never, he said, be a party to the surrender of Shawnee rights to the land of their forefathers. But the treaty, while permitting the Indians to hunt in the Ohio country, pushed them back to a line that ran from the mouth of the Cuyahoga River southwest to the confluence of the Ohio and Kentucky rivers. That, in effect, gave twenty-five thousand square miles of Shawnee land to the *Shemanese*. For this cession, the Shawnees received goods valued at $1,666, and the promise of an annual stipend of $825.

Blue Jacket himself brought word to Tecumseh that by the terms of the Fort Greenville Treaty the land upon which the Deer Creek village stood now belonged to the white man. He had spoken against the treaty, said Blue Jacket but, he admitted ruefully, the people had stopped listening to him since the Battle of Fallen Timbers.

Tecumseh listened grimly to his brother. Then he spoke.

"The septs of the Shawnee nation are scattered, as are all the other tribes, like an armful of twigs dropped to the ground. But one day I will gather up all the twigs and bind them together, so that they will be as strong as an old oak. Then we will take our land back from the *Shemanese*."

Blue Jacket nodded. He believed that Tecumseh would do what he said. His only regret was that he would not live to see the day.

VIII
(1798)

It wasn't easy, but the Shawnee chief Black Hoof finally persuaded Tecumseh to move his village.

Tecumseh was loathe to go. The hunting was excellent at Deer Creek, and the crops they planted did well. And, too, there was the principle involved. But Black Hoof insisted that if he stayed it would violate the Greenville Treaty, and give the *Shemanese* an excuse to make war against the Shawnees. Then they would lose what little land was left to them. Tecumseh could not fail to notice that Black Hoof automatically assumed the Indians would lose if there was war. So it was with many of his people. Their spirit, their faith in themselves and the justness of the cause—even in *Moneto*—had been crushed.

In the end, Black Hoof prevailed. Tecumseh realized it was not time to defy the *Shemanese*. So he led his people to a new village at the headwaters of the Great Miami River.

Here he took a woman named Mamate. She adored him, but he did not love her, and when she died giving birth to his second child, Nay-tha-way-nah, he was sorry, but the grief was not overwhelming. Tecumapese gladly took on the responsibility of raising both of her brother's children.

Tecumseh would disappear from the village for days at a time. At first his people were concerned, but he never failed to return, though he also never spoke of his solitary sojourns in the forest. He did not tell them that often he went to the site of the once-great village of Chillicothe. Nothing remained of his boyhood home, but he could envision how it had once been—hundreds of lodges, thousands of smiling faces, the great horse herd, the cooking pots always full of meat. For hours he would sit on the banks of the river where he had dived to the bottom every morning, summer and winter, rain or shine, in preparation for his admittance into the warrior ranks.

Each time he returned from his visit to the site of Chillicothe he felt fresh resolve in his commitment to someday, somehow, restore the Shawnee Nation to its former splendor.

Three years passed.

Tecumseh accepted an invitation extended by the Delawares, who had themselves been transplanted to the Indiana Territory, to bring his people and live among them in their principal village on the White River. Hundreds more Shawnees, mostly young warriors, had by now joined Tecumseh. Like Tecumseh, they were disappointed in their old leaders, who had given up all hope of resisting the *Shemanese*. Worse still, many Indians were beginning to take on some of the ways of the white man. Wearing his clothes, adopting his religion, raising livestock for meat instead of hunting the wild game of the forests.

The Delawares, too, were dismayed by the defeatism of Black Hoof and other Shawnee chiefs. They turned to Tecumseh, son of Pucksinwah, brother of Blue Jacket, a great warrior in his own right, as their best hope for redemption. Almost all of them were ready to fight. Only a handful spoke out for keeping the peace. The most eloquent of these, in Tecumseh's opinion, was, ironically, one who could not speak at all. His name was Quashquame. He had lived much of the time among the Long Knives, and he impressed Tecumseh.

Tecumseh completely won over the hearts of the Delawares, to the point that they were ready to follow him anywhere. Then he began to travel among the other tribes. He spoke to the Wyandots and Ottawas, Miamis and Chippewas. He tried to make them realize that the Greenville Treaty would go the way of all the treaties of the past. Already the Ohio country was filling up with *Shemanese*. Soon the Long Knives would look with envious eyes upon this land that the treaty said would belong to the Indians forever.

"The white man will say, look there, so much good land wasted on red heathens. They do not deserve to have such good land. Soon they will want to take it from us. Every year they creep closer. There is a white man's settlement not an hour's ride from here. When the time comes, they will march against us, make war on us, burn our villages, kill our women and children, and all the time they are doing these things they will claim they only seek peace. Then there will be another treaty, and a new boundary line, farther to the west, and we will have to pack up the few possessions we have left to us and go away from here."

Tecumseh picked up a stick. "This is the Shawnee Nation. It is weak. So many of our warriors have given their lives to defend our country from the *Shemanese*. So many defeats have we suffered that our chiefs are weary and afraid of war. I cannot blame them. They have done all that is within their power to do. But their spirit is weak, and if the Shawnees tried to stand alone now, as they have so many times in the past . . ."

He snapped the stick in two and let the pieces fall to the ground.

Then he turned to Lalawethika, who gave him a bundle of sticks tied together with a strip of scarlet cloth.

Tecumseh held the bundle of sticks—as thick as a man's arm—for all those gathered to see.

"Behold, my brothers. A child can snap a single stick, but not even the strongest man can break *this*. All the tribes will one day join together, and they will fight until the Long Knives are driven back across the mountains."

"What does the scarlet cloth signify?" asked one of the warriors.

"It is Tecumseh, my brother," said Lalawethika, stepping forward. "He will lead all the tribes to victory."

"When?" asked another.

"When the time is right," replied the young shaman. "We must go and spread the word to many tribes. And we must wait for signs from *Moneto*. Without *Moneto*, we cannot win."

"What kind of signs shall we look for?"

"We will know them when they come. They will be as the sign *Moneto* sent at the moment of my brother's birth, when the Panther leaped across the night sky."

The Shawnees gave a great shout of approbation.

IX
(1800)

He dreamed of the years passing, and of the many nights spent in his *wegiwa* with Lalawethika, planning ... always planning ... and the many trips, to the various tribes, where he and his wily younger brother spoke with such eloquence that they stirred strong emotions in the hearts and souls of the warriors who listened, giving them new hope, restoring their battered pride.

They started with the remnants of the Iroquois Confederation—the Mohawks, the Oneidas, the Onandagas, the Cayugas, and the Senecas. Then too there were the erstwhile allies of the Shawnees—the Wyandots, the Potawatomies, Tuscaroras, Mingos, Hurons, Ottawas, and Chippewas. To the northwest were the Kickapoos, the Foxes, the Winnnebagos, and the Menominees. West of the Great Mother of Waters were the Iowas, the Omahas, the Osages, the Kansas, the Wichitas, the Pawnees, the Poncas, and the great Sioux Nation. To these Tecumseh said, "Come, help us fight for our land, or else one day soon the *Shemanese* will come to take your land away from you. Fight them now, or fight them later, alone."

He traveled to the south, as well, where his friends the Cherokees treated him like a king, and hung on his every word. Besides the Cherokees there were the Choctaws and Chickasaws, the Creeks and the Seminoles, the Catawbas and Santees and Alabamas. To the southeast were the Tawakonas, Natchez, Caddos, and Yazoos.

"Always in the past a few tribes have joined forces to fight the Long Knives," said Tecumseh. "But always they would fight but one fight, then, win or lose, the old quarrels between the separate tribes would return to divide them.

"If ten Indians fight ten *Shemanese,* the Indians always win.

"A few thousand warriors is not enough. I speak of tens of thousands. A few tribes joined together cannot prevail. I will bring fifty tribes together in a great Indian confederation.

"Until the time comes, we must keep the peace. We must not let the whites provoke us into a fight before we are ready. In the white man's Bible it speaks of turning the other cheek when your enemy strikes you. This we must do for the time being. Meanwhile we will grow stronger, and the *Shemanese* will become complacent. And by giving them no excuse for marching against us now, we buy precious time."

Time was Tecumseh's greatest ally. With tribes like the Delawares and the Cherokees, a single word from him and the tomahawk would strike the war post. But with other tribes, who knew him less well, he had to move slowly, winning their confidence and their respect.

Time was needed, as well, to bring about a change in the Indians. Tecumseh preached to them about setting aside their intertribal differences once and for all. There lay the key to victory. They had to stop thinking of themselves as Shawnees and Wyandots and Creeks and begin to think of themselves as brothers united in a common cause.

This was easier said than done. For generations before the coming of the white man the tribes had been warring among themselves. Tecumseh expended a lot of effort healing old wounds that festered between one tribe and another. He was a peacemaker, and his wisdom and compassion and impartiality became legendary. Tribe by tribe he began to cement his great confederation together. Step by step he drew closer to the day when, from north and south and west, all at once, the Indian would rise up in a mighty host numbering in the tens of thousands to wash the *Shemanese* from the land in a tidal wave of blood.

X
(1801)

Due in part to his involvement in Mad Anthony Wayne's successful campaign against the Indians, culminating in the victory at Fallen Timbers, William Henry Harrison found himself chosen to serve as territorial governor of the Northwest.

Harrison did his best to foster good relations with the tribes who resided in his bailiwick. He met with the most success among the Delawares who lived in the village of Wapakoneta. Their chief was called Beaver, with whom Harrison developed a strong friendship.

It was with dismay, then, that Harrison learned of Beaver's conviction, at the hands of a council of Delaware chiefs, for practicing sorcery. The charge had been leveled by a Delaware medicine man, but rumor had it that a Shawnee shaman named Lalawethika was really the one responsible, and Harrison couldn't help but suspect that Beaver's only crime was his friendship with the whites.

Many Indians believed that the problems which beset them—the loss of their lands, the scarcity of game, economic disaster, defeat and injustice, and the increasing prevalence of alcoholism among the people—were the workings of dark forces from within. The fear of witches and their evil power permeated their culture, and they were quick to believe a charge of sorcery.

But there was nothing Harrison could do to save Beaver, who met his end with great dignity. One of the last things Beaver did before going to his death was ask his friend Harrison to look after his ten-year-old son. Beaver and his entire family had converted to Christianity, and the old chief feared for his son's well-being if he remained with the tribe. Harrison was deeply moved, and promised to do everything in his power to care for the Indian boy, a promise that he faithfully kept for the rest of his days. Beaver's entire family, in fact, moved to Vincennes, Harrison's headquarters, where they prospered as the governor's wards.

Harrison was not the only one to suspect that Beaver was executed for reasons other than alleged sorcery. Quashquame boldly defended Beaver, but his efforts were for naught. Disgruntled, he did not fail to note that Lalawethika was present in Wapakoneta during Beaver's trial and subsequent execution. Quashquame did not trust this Shawnee shaman. He was sly, like the weasel. And he and his brother, the charismatic Tecumseh, were dangerous. It was obvious to Quashquame that they were luring the Delawares down the path to another war—a war that Quashquame was convinced would be disastrous for his tribe.

His suspicions regarding Lalawethika grew when he heard that upon the death of Penegashega, the head shaman of the Shawnee Nation, Tecumseh's brother asserted himself and took Penegashega's place as the undisputed prophet of the tribe. In this way Lalawethika became the conscience of his people, exerting in time almost as much influence as the principal chief, Black Hoof.

Aware of Quashquame's growing opposition,

Tecumseh attempted to win the mute warrior over. It could not be done. The spell that Tecumseh could cast upon so many of Quashquame's fellow Delawares had no effect on Quashquame himself. Lalawethika was of the opinion that he could discredit Quashquame by playing up the fact that he lived sometimes with the Long Knives. But Tecumseh advised his brother to leave Quashquame alone. He was a favorite son of the Delawares. As such, his opposition was troublesome, yet Tecumseh feared that an attempt to assassinate his character might backfire.

There were few like Quashquame who could resist Tecumseh's appeal for unity against the *Shemanese*. As the years passed, the Indians clamored for more precise information on these signs which, according to the young Shawnee and his shaman brother, would herald that the time had come to strike the whites.

The Prophet claimed he had visions, and he relayed what he saw to the others. When *Moneto* was ready for the great war that would drive the Long Knives back into the sea from whence they had come He would cause the earth to tremble. The ground would open up and swallow entire lakes. Whole forests would topple. Rivers and streams would all flow backward. By these unmistakable signs *Moneto* would let his people know that it was time for the warriors to pick up their tomahawks and join together under Tecumseh's leadership.

XI
(1805)

He dreamed of the years passing . . .

By 1805 Tecumseh had quite a few tribes aligned

with him, including the powerful Sioux Nation in the west, and the Cherokees in the south, as well as the remnants of the Iroquois Confederacy of the north. But it was among the Shawnees that he was having the most trouble. The old chiefs, Black Hoof and Little Turtle, were becoming more vocal in their opposition to him. While many of the brash young warriors heeded his words, the older men did not like it that he seemed to be challenging established authority. Tecumseh realized the seriousness of this problem. If his own people would not stand with him, the other tribes would begin to have second thoughts. Even his brother, The Prophet, was meeting with difficulty in holding onto his position as the chief shaman of the Shawnee Nation. Some dared to call him a charlatan.

Nonetheless, Lalawethika proved invaluable to Tecumseh in the long run.

From personal experience The Prophet knew that the Indian's most dangerous enemy was the white man's whiskey. Depressed by the state of affairs, more and more of his red brothers were drowning their misery in jugs of rotgut. The result was social chaos. The warriors quarreled among themselves. Husbands abused family members. Many fell victim to smallpox and other diseases, their body's natural resistance weakened by the liquor.

Lalawethika had himself been an alcoholic. He drank so heavily that on one occasion he collapsed, sinking into so deep a coma that his neighbors believed him dead. They swore that his heart ceased to beat. Then, to everyone's astonishment, Lalawethika regained consciousness. He announced that he had indeed died and visited heaven, where he was shown a glimpse of both Paradise and Hell. In Hell, Indians who had been alcoholics suffered more than most, for molten lead was poured down their throats. He renounced the use of frontier whiskey thenceforth.

Convinced that the Shawnee people had to embrace traditional moral values or perish, Lalawethika challenged the other medicine men with his preaching. Worst of all, in their eyes, he claimed to be the mortal spokesman of the Master of Life. They called him a religious fanatic. They said he was well named—Lalawethika meant "The Noisemaker." And he was dangerous. He condemned many old ceremonies. He said that these ceremonies no longer had power or meaning, and sought to replace them with new ones of his own devising. All shamans who opposed his doctrine were either fools or witches. And all those who took up the ways of the white man were most assuredly in league with the Great Serpent.

"The Master of Life made the *Englishmanake* and the French, but the Americans are the offspring of the Great Serpent. *Matchemenetoo,* the Bad Spirit dwells in their hearts. The sea is the home of the Great Serpent, is it not? Is he not the one who causes all strife and discord? Did not our forefathers warn that pale-skinned invaders would come from the sea? These Americans were spawned by the Great Spirit, and sent to destroy us.

"But do not lose hope. The Master of Life will restore the Shawnees. He will crush the Long Knives beneath his heel. We are His chosen people. But He gave us a set of laws to live by. If we obey these sacred laws we will prosper. But lately we have not obeyed them. So *Moneto* has turned His face away from us."

In *Pahcotai*—the autumn—there was a sickness in a village on the Auglaize River. Several people died.

Tecumseh and The Prophet arrived on the scene. They conferred with one another throughout the night, and the next morning Lalawethika announced that only three more people would perish. Those three were condemned by *Moneto* for practicing witchcraft. But his brother, Tecumseh, would intercede with the Master of Life on behalf of the rest of the village, and all others afflicted by the sickness would recover. *Moneto* was angry at the village for putting up with the evil ones in their midst, and had intended to wipe out every man, woman, and child to teach the other villages a lesson, but He would listen to Tecumseh's plea for mercy. Tecumseh was *Moneto*'s great favorite.

Some doubt was voiced regarding the accuracy of The Prophet's prediction. Lalawethika swore that if it did not happen as he had foretold then he would no longer be the chief shaman of the Shawnee Nation. But if it did happen as he predicted, then all the Shawnees must come to this village and listen to what he had to say.

Amazingly, only three more people died of the sickness. The rest recovered completely.

Word spread rapidly, and the Shawnees came to listen to The Prophet. Surely both he and his brother were looked upon with much favor by *Moneto*!

Lalawethika delivered the speech of his life, one that would be forever remembered, as long as a single Shawnee lived. Now, he said, no one should question his gifts. He was a true prophet, and everything he foretold would surely come to pass. He then proceeded to give the people new laws to live by. These laws came from *Moneto*, and in truth they were old and sacred laws that the people had drifted away from. If the people obeyed these laws, then *Moneto* would guarantee absolute victory over the *Shemanese*. So it was with Lalawethika, like Moses bringing the Ten Commandments to the tribes of Israel.

He told them that henceforth Indian women must not take up with white men, for that corrupted the purity of Indian blood. The Indian race was superior to all others, and so it must remain.

The people would no longer wear the wool and linen garments of the white man, a habit many had acquired. Nor were they to eat the meat of cattle or any other domesticated animal, as the white man did. *Moneto* had put *p'thu-thoi,* the bison, and *peshikta,* the deer, on this earth for his chosen people, so that they might fill their bellies with the meat of these wild animals, and clothe themselves with the skins. It was an affront to *Moneto* that the people were no longer content to partake of His bounty. And for those who said the bison and the deer were becoming scarce, if they had faith in the Master of Life he would restore the wild animals and provide for the Shawnees.

From now on, all Indians, regardless of tribal affiliation, would treat one another as brothers. The property of one Indian belonged to all Indians. The reason the *Shemanese* were so strong, said The Prophet, was because they considered themselves Americans no matter where they lived now or where they had come from originally. Whether their roots were English, Dutch, French, or Scotch-Irish mattered not. So it had to be with the Indians.

Most important, all Indians would have to devote themselves much more strenuously to the worship of *Moneto.* Was it not true that in the past, whether they won or lost a battle with the Long Knives, the end result was always the same—another bad treaty that took their land from them? *Moneto* allowed this to happen because He was displeased with his people. From now on they had to have complete faith in *Moneto* and what He had to say.

Of course, Lalawethika did not have to tell them that from now on *Moneto* would speak to them only through him.

The time was fast approaching when Tecumseh would lead the Indians to final victory over the Long Knives. For years now there had been peace. The white man was being lulled into a false sense of security. Soon they would strike.

"The Master of Life speaks through The Prophet," said many of the Shawnees, and even some of the Delawares. "He will lead us back to walking on the right path, so that we may please *Moneto*. Then *Moneto* will restore our lands to us, and the forests will teem with game once more."

Governor Harrison heard this talk. He blamed Lalawethika for the death of his friend Beaver. Some other prominent Indians who happened to be converted Christians had been burned at the stake like poor Beaver. Their blood was on Lalawethika's head. Harrison denounced The Prophet. "Tell him that if he is truly a prophet then he should cause the rivers to stop flowing, or make the dead rise from their graves, or the sun to stand still. If he does any one of these things you may rest assured that he was sent by God."

Lalawethika quickly accepted the governor's challenge. He recalled that in recent months several American astronomers had traveled through Illinois and Indiana, looking for observation sites from which to observe an imminent eclipse of the sun. The Prophet found out when this eclipse was supposed to occur, and then promised his people that he would darken the sun. Many

Indians came to his village on the appointed day, believers and skeptics both. Lalawethika remained in his lodge all morning and well into the afternoon, emerging only as the eclipse occurred. The crowd fell into a state of collective awe and dread. He reassured them that before the day was done he would restore the sun.

After that day, few remained unconvinced of The Prophet's power, and, if they were, they dared not say so.

Because of the eclipse, and what happened in the village on the Auglaize River, Tecumseh and his brother gained the support of a vast majority of the Shawnees. Old Black Hoof still spoke against them, but suddenly there didn't seem to be anyone listening.

XII
(1806)

Tecumseh knew that sooner or later the *Shemanese* would begin to suspect that something was amiss among the Indians—something that did not bode well for them. He was most concerned about Indians like the Delaware, Quashquame, who sometimes lived among the whites. The Prophet continued to suggest that they turn the Delawares against the mute warrior. They could say that *Moneto* had sent the Great Spirit to The Prophet while he slept, and the Great Spirit had given him the names of those who would betray the people. Not just Quashquame, but others like him, even some among their own Shawnee Nation, might be successfully dispensed with in this manner.

In the end, Tecumseh decided against this tactic. If "friendly" Indians began to turn up dead, would that not serve to inflame the suspicions of the whites? No, it was inevitable that the whites would hear more and more about him as time went by. And they would not like what they heard. The best course of action, he thought, would be to use his powers of persuasion on the *Shemanese* themselves. He remembered the lesson Chiksika had taught him. A Shawnee warrior never deceived his own kind, but there was no dishonor in lying to the white man.

Little did Tecumseh know that it would be none other than *Metequa*—Flintlock Jones—who raised the alarm.

Nathaniel was in Ohio, visiting a friend who had already moved from near Boonesboro to the new territory in a quest for elbow room. John McCarter had been a good neighbor, and his wife had been a friend to Amanda. While the women visited, McCarter and Nathaniel ventured forth to engage in a little hunting, as they had often done in Kentucky.

Less than ten miles from the McCarter cabin on the Mad River, right in the middle of his friend's long-winded singing of this new country's praises, Nathaniel made a sharp gesture to silence his companion. He seemed to be listening hard to something, but, try as he might, McCarter could hear nothing out of the ordinary issuing from the depths of the forest. Then Nathaniel motioned for him to follow, and proceeded with caution, on foot, deeper into the woods.

A short while later, McCarter found himself on a bluff overlooking a large meadow filled with an Indian encampment. In the middle of the camp stood a war post. Around it sat dozens of warriors in council. Every now and then one of them would rise and strike the war post with club or tomahawk. Black war belts were being passed around.

Nathaniel studied this scene for a time without saying a word. Finally, McCarter could stand it no longer.

"Looks like Shawnee," he whispered.

"Not just Shawnee. Delaware, Wyandot, and Mingo, too."

"Is it a war council?"

Nathaniel nodded.

"Christ," breathed McCarter, shocked that this host of hostile redskins was encamped so near his homestead.

"You had better go get your family and take them to the Springfield blockhouse. Amanda, too."

"What are you going to do?"

"Most of the other settlers in these parts are strung out along the Mad River, aren't they? I'll warn them, and meet you in Springfield."

True to his word, Nathaniel raised the alarm all along the Mad River, and brought the settlers into Springfield. Here they forted up, expecting the worst. A week passed without sign of a single Indian. The frontiersmen finally decided to send a small party out to the Indian encampment for the purpose of gauging their intentions. Nathaniel, whose reputation had preceded him into the Ohio country, was asked to accompany the group, and he could not decline, although he deemed the plan too risky by half.

As they neared the Indian village, a dozen warriors came out to meet them. The Indians were friendly enough, but they insisted that the Long Knives come no closer to the camp. Major Thomas Moore, by popular referendum Springfield's leader in this crisis, pointed out that the settlers were justifiably alarmed by news of a war council being held here. The Indians assured him that they had no intention of attacking their white friends. Returning to Springfield, Major Moore and the others concluded that the Indians were planning to make war on another tribe. But Nathaniel wasn't so sure.

The governor of Ohio agreed with the majority. He sent a letter to Major Moore, along with a belt of white wampum. He wanted the wampum presented to the chief of the village, and the letter read to that individual, as well.

Once again Nathaniel accompanied Moore to the Indian encampment. This time they were brought into the village and presented to the chief. Moore read the governor's letter aloud.

I cannot believe that our Red Brothers will be so lost to a sense of duty and their best interests as to desire to disturb the peace which exists between our two peoples. We wish only to strengthen the bond of friendship, to which purpose I offer you a fine white belt as a symbol of peaceful intent. But your white brothers are distressed, and as I wish to quiet their fears, I respectfully request that you inform Major Moore of any complaints that you may have against us, so that I may do all in my power to reconcile our differences. If you have no complaints, then I ask that you express your peaceful intentions, so that we may avoid any serious consequences. In hopes that the Great Spirit will incline your hearts to peace, I remain your true friend,

Edward Tiffin

The chief listened, nodded, and asked Moore and Nathaniel to wait while he composed a reply. An hour later he emerged from his *wegiwa* and presented a letter of his own to the white men.

Friend and Brother,
I have received your speech with great joy. We will never forget your goodness, and we give thanks to the Great Spirit for giving us such a friend. It has never been our intention to raise the warclub against the white man, and it never will be. It is true that a few of our warriors have gone on the warpath, but they are renegades. To our great surprise, we learn that the white settlers along the Mad River are preparing to come against us, all because of foolish lies told against us by bad people. Now our women and children live in fear. We beg you to inform your people of the truth about us, so that for the future we may no longer fear attack and live in peace with our white neighbors. We hope that you have a long and prosperous life, and that our peoples may live together in peace forever.

Tecumseh

On the way back to Springfield, Major Moore noted that Tecumseh had a remarkably firm grasp of the English language. He asked Nathaniel what he thought of the Shawnee chief.

"We've met before," said Nathaniel. "He would have killed me, but his rifle misfired."

"When was this?"

"About a dozen years ago. Some Shawnees had stolen a few of our horses and we came up here to fetch them back."

"Do you believe this letter?"

"Well, I don't tell foolish lies and I'm not a particularly bad man," said Nathaniel wryly. "They were holding a war council. I'd bet my eyeteeth on that."

"The governor will believe it," said Moore dryly. "He'll tell himself that those settlers along the Mad River were just suffering from a bad case of nerves. And most of my people will believe it, too, because they so desperately want to."

Nathaniel nodded. "That Tecumseh is one clever fellow."

Indeed, Tecumseh was immensely pleased with the way things had turned out. He had held the council in the vicinity of the settlers on the Mad River precisely to manufacture this crisis, using it as an opportunity to assuage *Shemanese* anxieties that had been exacerbated by recent raids against Ohio and Kentucky settlements by some young braves. As the days passed into weeks and no Indian attack materialized against the Springfield stockade, the whites would realize that they had misjudged the Indians, and they would not be so quick to jump to such conclusions in the future. Now Tecumseh was confident that war would not come before he was ready for it. In fact, some of the more gullible whites might even come to believe that he was a great peacemaker.

The chance to deceive the *Shemanese* pleased him. So many times the Long Knives had lied to his people. Now he had turned the tables on them.

Another year or two, maybe three on the outside— and then the Long Knives would discover that they had been deceived, even as they drowned in their own blood.

CHAPTER FIVE

Jonathan

February 6, 1811

Dearest Rebecca,

I have arrived safely in Washington. The trip was
pleasant enough. At least I could enjoy the company of
Mr. Clay. We met in Lexington, as prearranged, and
traveled by the road as far as Maysville, in his well-
appointed carriage. We then took a boat up the Ohio
River. During this leg of the journey I saw rather less
of Clay, as he devoted almost every moment to gambling
or gossiping in the saloon. The man never seems to sleep.
Being the engaging fellow that he is, he instantly
became the center of attention on the boat. Of course,
the foremost question on everyone's mind was whether
there would be war. Clay assured them that there would
be, if he or his traveling companion—meaning me—had
anything to do with it. I do not consider myself as
dedicated to the prospect of conflict with England as is
Clay, but I must confess that I found myself agreeing with
a whole heart when Clay told a congregation of fellow
passengers that the British lion had a mouthful of tail
feathers, and it was past time for the American eagle to
turn on its tormentor and pluck its eyes out. What a cheer
rang through the boat when Clay was done with his
inspirational oratory! I believe the man will be president

someday, and I certainly think the republic would profit from the experience.

Washington has not changed much at all since that day almost six years ago when I arrived here in response to a summons from President Jefferson. It is a city which one wit described—rightly so—as a place which many are willing to come to and all are anxious to leave. Let me attempt to describe it to you, though it defies description. Truly, one would have to see this place with his own eyes to believe it.

This federal city of ours, as envisioned by George Washington and planned by that quirky genius, L'Enfant, was of grand design. Yet where majestic boulevards were staked out there are fields of tree stumps instead. Where elegant townhouses were to stand there are barren hillsides, stripped of vegetation. Where noble monuments to tell of the glory of our young nation were to rise there remain foul-smelling marshes. Cows graze on the lawns of state buildings, and squadrons of hogs run hither and yon, rooting through the refuse. I have yet to enjoy a summer here, but I am told it is the next most pleasant thing to an eternity in Hell, with all manner of vermin to contend with, and heavy, humid air carrying every kind of sickness imaginable.

All roads lead to Rome, they say, but precious few will bring you here. It is even more difficult to find one's way in the city itself. There are no sidewalks, and no streetlamps, so if one ventures out after dark he may never be heard from again. In fact, several people have disappeared in the city's brief but sordid history, and the consensus is that if they did not fall victim to thugs and robbers, then their bones are resting at the bottom of one of our countless, mosquito-infested bogs.

It would avail you nothing to know if such-and-such

lived on a particular street, for there are no signs to direct you, and quite often a promising avenue will abruptly disintegrate into a brush-overgrown cowpath meandering into limbo. Only last year, I am told, a group of congressmen returning from a dinner party on the outskirts got completely lost and spent the rest of the night in their carriage, arriving finally at Capitol Hill as the new dawn broke.

Woe unto every inhabitant when it rains, for the streets, if such they can be called, are transformed into seemingly bottomless pits of black mire, and if a carriage is not suddenly overthrown, jeopardizing the limb if not the life of every passenger, then it will in all likelihood become mired up to the axletree, so that the passengers must sacrifice their shoes, stockings, and sometimes even trousers in wading through hip-deep muck endowed with a stench so foul that I cannot describe it.

As for the state buildings, they look quite magnificent from a distance—and so quite incongruous in this half-tamed wilderness they call a city—but closer inspection proves that they fall far short of deserving such an adjective.

The President's House is too large for a home, and too plain for a palace. Our first Chief Magistrates resided there while work was still being done on the interior, and I am told that Abigail Adams used the great audience hall, what they call the East Room now, to hang her clothes up for drying. The place was occupied for eight years before the staircase to the second floor was completed. Apparently the roof leaks in almost every room when it rains. The grounds are still covered with rubbish. One must be careful not to stumble into an open pit. There still stand the shanties and privies of the workmen, brick yards and kilns. The sight is a disgrace and an embarrassment to our country.

As for the Capitol, it dominates a splendid sight, atop the tallest hill in the federal district, and I suppose the view it affords would be magnificent indeed—were there anything to see except swamp and thicket and barren field. The Senate wing appears elegant indeed, a semicircular chamber with chairs of red Moroccan leather and two massive marble fireplaces. But this splendor masks poor construction. Part of the ceiling collapsed a few years ago, narrowly missing the Vice President as he presided over a session. The columns lining the gallery have a bad habit of splitting open.

As for the House chamber, where your husband will be spending a good deal of his time in the coming weeks, as he seeks to represent the needs and desires of the citizens of Madison County to the best of his ability, it is a glass dome which also leaks when it rains, so badly that the water flows like cataracts along the aisles. Furnaces were built below the floor, designed to heat the chamber, but instead the smoky fumes rendered so many representatives *hors de combat* that the furnaces are no longer used. As one of my colleagues, a veteran of several years' service, described it, he felt like an oyster baked in a Dutch oven when those furnaces were stoked. In both chambers the acoustics are horrible. A speaker in the well must shout himself hoarse to be heard in the gallery, while a whispered aside from the back row reverberates throughout the room.

I recall lamenting the lack of amenities at Frankfort, but in terms of entertainment that frontier village is an American Paris compared to this town. There is a theater, but one must be truly starved for diversion to endure the thick, eye-burning tobacco smoke, the rank stench of stale whiskey combined with the odor from an adjacent barn, and the disconcerting fact that at any moment a pack of local rowdies might lift up the warped floorboards under your feet for the purpose of gaining entry and making nuisances of themselves in the middle of a performance.

The consequence of this dirth of good entertainment is that one is constantly in the company of politicians, and the only subject discussed, morning, noon, and night, is politics. So one soon becomes sick unto death of political matters. My only escape is to walk in the woods, or along the river, and always my thoughts turn to you, dearest wife, and to our splendid young son. What a bright little man he is! I miss him terribly, and you, too. I wish you were here, but of course in your condition that just isn't possible. You must take plenty of rest to insure that the little blessing you carry inside you is born in perfect health. Don't worry! When the time is at hand I will be at your side. Meanwhile, let Trumbull handle the affairs of Elm Tree. He is an extremely capable man, and one you can trust completely.

Write soon.

Your homesick husband,

Jonathan

February 22, 1811

Dear Jonathan,

All's well at Elm Tree.

Your faith in Mr. Trumbull is not misplaced. He is an industrious, pleasant, and fair-minded man. The hands like him, and work well under his direction, and he has everything well in hand. The foundation of bricks for the new smokehouse has just been finished. The corn land is being plowed as I write. Duchess dropped a colt last night. The legs are almost black, the body is bay. The hogs got into my garden day before yesterday, disturbing all the seeds, and Mr. Trumbull is having a board fence put up to prevent a recurrence.

This morning the sky is overcast, and there was a heavy mist on the ground, but the sun is beginning to break through, and the day will be warm. We will have an early spring, it seems, and Mr. Trumbull assures me that it is safe to proceed with our planting, as there will not be a late frost this year. The man can tell whether it will be clear or cloudy tomorrow, windy or calm, and from which direction the wind will blow. I don't know how he does it, but he is seldom wrong. He is also full of new tricks, like soaking corn on the cob in salted water for feeding the horses. The horses then eat the corn, cob and all, and so require less corn in the long run. He also recommends placing a little hog's hair over the sets of Irish potatoes we have just planted to keep the varmints out. The cabbages and Dutch turnips have already sprouted, and the onions, too. In a fortnight I will plant some yams and peas and perhaps even muskmelons. I know what you are thinking—you are worried that I will over-exert myself, but I simply must get out of the house, and working with the soil is very soothing to me. Do not be concerned. I feel fine. After all, I am only two months with child.

A week ago an inquest was held in the death of an elderly Negro named Samuel, owned by Stephen Cooper. The poor man was placed in an open outhouse on a night which saw a very cold rain and strong gusting wind. He was without a stitch of clothing, shackled at the wrists, and chained to a bolt on the floor. There was another chain about his neck, which was attached to a ring in the wall, high enough so that the poor man could not sit down. Nor could he stand, chained as he was to the floor, so he had to squat on his heels all night. The next morning he was found, strangled to death. Murdered, I say, by that bloodthirsty demon in human form, Stephen Cooper.

When asked to explain why he had resorted to such extreme measures of punishment, Stephen explained that he had sent Samuel down to the creek in a small boat to fetch him some fresh fish. Samuel was late returning, because the creek was running high, and carried him far downstream. Worse still, for him, he returned without any fish. Stephen was convinced that Samuel had spent the entire day napping on the bank, and gave him a lashing. Apparently, Samuel howled so loudly in pain that it brought the other hands running, which infuriated Stephen even more, for some reason, and he ordered Samuel to be silent. Samuel replied that he could not be silent as long as he was being whipped, for which "insolence," as Stephen called it, he earned ten more stripes.

Later, Stephen's overseer, a man named Lewis, came to Stephen with news that he had overheard Samuel tell another field hand that he would not endure another whipping like the one he had just received, but would shoot Stephen down and turn his back on him. The field hand later said that Lewis misunderstood, that, in fact, Samuel said he was afraid that next time Stephen would just shoot him down, and if that happened then he, Samuel, would turn his back to him. Regardless of which version is true, the poor old man did not deserve the punishment which resulted in his death.

The inquest concluded with Stephen Cooper exonerated. He was within his rights to punish Samuel anyway he saw fit, they said, and it was not his fault that Samuel slipped from the position in which he had been placed, with the result that he strangled himself. I cannot help but wonder if Samuel was just too old and feeble to maintain an uncomfortable position throughout the long night, or if he committed suicide. I am shocked and angered by the verdict of the inquest jury, but console myself with the knowledge that Stephen will have to answer for this inhuman deed to the Lord Almighty on Judgment Day. I do not believe he will be exonerated then.

I miss you terribly, Jonathan, and long for the day when you can return to Elm Tree, but at the same time I am proud of you, and make but one request, that you remember your promise and endeavor to do all in your power to keep us from war with the British.

Your loving wife,

Rebecca

P.S. You are so right about Christopher! He is an extremely bright lad, and very energetic. Doubtless he can be anything he wants to be when he grows to manhood. I only hope he won't decide to be a soldier or a politician. Noble professions, yes, but they require such personal sacrifice, taking a man away from his home and family.

March 3, 1811

Dear Rebecca,

I was not surprised to hear of the cruel act perpetrated by Stephen Cooper upon that poor old slave. Nor, unfortunately, am I surprised by the verdict handed down by the inquest jury. Having been born in the Carolinas I suppose I should be accustomed to the sometimes barbarous treatment accorded the Negro. I saw the Barbary corsairs put people of all colors in chains to work in their galleys and in building coastal fortifications and the palaces of pashas. It disturbs me when members of my own race treat their Negro servants with the same inhumanity which was commonplace on the Barbary coast. I sometimes wonder if we shouldn't set them all free. I think most slaveholders would gladly do so, but for the fact that it is difficult to hire hands to work your fields when land is so plentiful, and there for the taking. Why would any man work another's soil when he could work his own?

It is a cold hard truth, Rebecca, but you will have difficulty finding a jury to convict a white man for the murder of a Negro. There are some in the northern states who say that slavery is a sin. Yet they do not want the Negro for a neighbor, and I venture to say if their land was such they could cultivate tobacco or rice or cotton, or any other crop which requires a large number of workers, they would not be so quick to judge. Personally, I believe it is wrong to keep a man in bondage, and have sometimes thought of giving the few slaves we have their freedom. Many, I think, would stay on at Elm Tree, and work for wages, which I would be happy to pay, but what of those who would prefer to move on, to have a piece of land of their own? Where could they go that they would not be shunned or beaten, cursed or burned out, or worse? At least with us they are treated decently, and, I would like to think, can live with at least a little dignity, though I imagine it is hard to have dignity when you have no rights before the law.

As for Cooper, he is a dangerous wretch, and it worries me that he lives so near Elm Tree. Please be cautious, and for God's sake never venture out alone! I have posted a letter to Trumbull with this one. In it I explained to him that Cooper was once your suitor, and harbors much resentment towards you for having married another. I think that is in fact the case. At any rate, I have instructed him never to let you leave the house unaccompanied. I suspect you will make trouble over this precaution, but I beg you to humor me in this, and try not to act in your usual headstrong way.

Three issues concern us in the present session: the recharter of the national bank, the Florida Question, and the continued embargo in the face of British—and French, I must add—violations of our sovereignty on the high seas. As to the first there is not much to say at present. We have postponed indefinitely the decision whether to recharter. As to the second there is a great deal of debate concerning our title to the country lying between the Mississippi River and the Rio Perdido, an area called West Florida for the sake of convenience.

When President Jefferson purchased the Territory of Louisiana from Bonaparte, the cession was to include every square mile which Spain had possessed, and which she had acquired from France according to the treaty which concluded the Seven Years War. At that time, the Floridas passed to Great Britain. Spain obtained them by dint of the 1783 treaty. All of that is agreed upon. The issue rests on one point. Did Spain reincorporate the Floridas into the Louisiana Territory after 1783? Mr. Clay, for one, believes she did. He recently delivered a very strong speech to that effect, addressing the problem as a lawyer might, building his case detail by detail going back to 1682 when LaSalle ventured down the Mississippi from Canada and claimed what we now know as the Louisiana Territory for his king. This included the Floridas, which were colonized by the French under D'Iberville in 1698 at the Isle Dauphine, which lies at the mouth of the bay at Mobile. In 1736 the French erected a fort on the Tombigbee. These facts, said Clay, prove that France held possession of the Floridas, or at the very least that portion now known as West Florida, since Spain, though she erected a fort at Pensacola, never ventured any further west. When Spain regained the Floridas from Great Britain in 1783, she made the governors-general of Mobile and Pensacola answerable to the governor of Louisiana at New Orleans. So, Clay argued, West Florida rightly belongs to the Louisiana Territory, and as a result belongs to us.

Unfortunately, the Spanish contend that West Florida did not pass into their possession with the purchase of Louisiana since France ceded only that territory west of the Mississippi to Spain in 1763, and there are quite a few of my colleagues who agree. They are, I should point out, Federalists for the most part.

Therein lies the problem. Our settlements on the Tombigbee and Alabama rivers require access to Mobile to prosper. Mobile is as good, if not better, a harbor than New Orleans. Furthermore, while Spain is stubbornly insisting that the Floridas remain hers, she exercises virtually no control over it, aside from a few undermanned forts. She has never made any effort to colonize the land, which is populated by Seminoles and mulattos who persist in raiding our southernmost towns, committing all manner of unspeakable atrocities, and then slipping back across the border beyond the reach of American retribution. And, if that were not bad enough, there is a rumor afoot among the diplomatic crowd that Spain may be forced to cede the Floridas to Great Britain! Can you imagine the consternation which that possibility had caused here? Since war looms between us and the British, such a cession would be a catastrophe.

President Madison has wisely accepted the argument made by his illustrious predecessor that we have, at the very least, a "natural right" to West Florida, and we have passed a bill which authorizes him to employ the army and the navy as he sees fit to occupy that territory in the event that Spain does in fact cede it to Great Britain. In the meantime we continue to negotiate with Spain for that which we believe must inevitably become part of this republic, if it has not already become so by treaty.

As to the persistence of the British in impressing our sailors into their service, and seizing our merchant ships, unless Great Britain rescinds her Orders in Council and respects our neutrality, I fear there must be war. Of course, Mr. Clay is all for it, as is Mr. Calhoun of South Carolina, and a number of other notables, but Clay is the ringleader, and yes I am included in the ranks of those called the War Hawks. I do not relish war, but if the honor of our country requires that one be waged, so be it. We are a youthful nation, and must earn the world's respect, or we shall perish from the face of the earth. But don't worry, dear wife. The British have their hands full with Bonaparte. I cannot believe they would be so foolhardy as to engage in a conflict on another front. We whipped them once, and can do so again.

Give my love to our son, and to our unborn child, whom I just know will be a girl. I only hope she has your beauty and not my looks! Consider her welfare before you go jumping fences on your favorite thoroughbred.

You have all my love and the truest devotion. I will be home soon.

Jonathan

March 18, 1811

Dear Jonathan,

I realize that you are concerned about Stephen Cooper and his intentions towards me, but your anxiety is uncalled for, really, as I am sure he would never harm me. But now you have put Trumbull to watching over me, and he is taking his new duty entirely too seriously. I cannot even stroll in my garden without turning to find him there, and he has even taken to carrying a pistol in his belt. This is too much. You must call him off, Jonathan. He will not listen to me, and even when I lose my temper he will not desist.

The horrible fate which befell that poor old slave, Samuel, has made me think long and hard about the holding of people in bondage, and I could tell by your letter that it has made you think, too. We have a dozen Negroes here, who do not enjoy their freedom. I seldom really think of them as slaves, but rather, in a way, as part of our family. But slaves they are before the law, and that makes us slaveholders in the eyes of God. How will we answer for that? By claiming that they are better off in bondage? That they could not survive free in this country? Our parents fought for their own freedom from the king's tyranny, and now we are the tyrants.

Mary Bucknell came by to visit, and I made similar remarks to her. She was quite shocked. She said I was talking like one of those addled Emancipationists. I replied that perhaps that was what I had become, and she was beside herself. "You be careful, Rebecca Groves, of the company you are in if you insist on saying such things!" she warned. But I shall not be careful. I have always said what I feel, and always will, the devil take the hindmost.

Dear Jonathan, I think we feel the same on this subject. You were exposed to the barbarity of slavery on the Barbary Coast, and I got a taste of it as captive of the Shawnees. Oh, they would have made a slave of me, and worse! I believe we should give our slaves their freedom. Most of them, I think, will want to stay on at Elm Tree, and your suggestion that we offer them wages is a wonderful idea. Let's do it! I know our neighbors may frown on us. They may complain that our actions have made their own Negroes more difficult to control. But I would say to them, do as we did, and you will have no more difficulties. And for those whose slaves all depart, then I would say, they would not all leave you had you treated them fairly, and if you are ruined because you can find no one to care for your horses or work your fields then I have no sympathy to waste on you.

Please consider it, Jonathan. It is a grave injustice we do, and we should make amends.

Our son is as headstrong as his parents. It is virtually impossible to keep him in the house. He is always with the horses. He will know everything there is to know about thoroughbreds when he grows up, but I fear that when the time comes to teach him how to read and write we will have the devil of a time.

As for the possibility of war, I tell you frankly, I dread the future. It is all they talk about here. War, war, war! You speak of the honor of our country. But what honor is there in war? It is one thing to fight for your freedom, as our parents did thirty years ago, but to fight over the seizure of a few ships, and the impressment of a few sailors? Why, there must be a better way to resolve our differences with the British. Remember that you promised me you would do all in your power to avoid such a calamity.

Tend to your health, and come home to us safe and sound.

Your Wife,

Rebecca

April 3, 1811

Dearest Rebecca,

This session will be over in a matter of days, and none too soon for my liking, as I have had my fill of Washington and this incessant chatter about politics. It is also the case that I feel uneasy being away while that scoundrel Stephen Cooper is loose. I am afraid you will just have to tolerate Trumbull acting as your shadow until I come home.

As for your idea about freeing our slaves, I fear I spoke rashly in my last letter, but will abide by your wishes if it will make you happy. You are quite right about the neighbors. Most of them will be very displeased. One consequence you should consider—I doubt very much that they will send me back here for another term. Not an emancipationist! No great loss, you might say, and I suppose this is a dubious distinction which I would do well to forsake.

But I cannot agree with you on the matter of our quarrel with Great Britain. The honor of our country is indeed of vital importance. It is more important than life itself! We fought the Barbary corsairs for our country's sake. We would not pay a cent in tribute to those pirates, just as we will not buckle under to the British. The seizure of a few ships, you say? The impressment of a few sailors? A few *thousand* Americans is closer to the truth. Imagine, our own countrymen, toiling under the lash on some British man-o-war, which by all accounts is the closest one can get to Hell on earth, perhaps never to see his homeland, much less his loved ones, again. Since by their Orders in Council the British forbid any neutral vessel from sailing into a port under the control of Bonaparte, and made any such vessel a good and lawful prize subject to seizure, we have lost several hundred ships.

My God, Rebecca, the British have the gall to lay off our own ports with their man-o-war, waiting to pounce on French ships. Remember the *Chesapeake*? One of our own frigates, fired on by a British warship as she left port, and several seamen killed. But for the fact that President Jefferson was committed to peace we would have gone to war then, four years ago, and rightly so, in my opinion. No, we must fight for our rights, for if we do not, we will be seen as a weak and vacillating people without pride, who are unwilling to defend their country. Then, very soon, we would have no country.

And what of the British in Detroit? For years they have been arming and instigating the northern Indians to strike terror into the hearts of Kentuckians, and would be doing so today had we not whipped the Indians soundly at Fallen Timbers. After all this time, Rebecca, you are still not completely safe from the Shawnees, even at Elm Tree.

Do not be deceived by the fact that the frontier has been quiet for a few years. Fallen Timbers was a decisive victory, and it dealt the Indians a severe blow, but perhaps not a fatal one. When your father returned from the country north of the Ohio a few years back, whence he had gone in search of his Delaware friend, he brought word of a scheme afoot among the tribes to join together in a great confederation for the purpose of driving us back across the Appalachians. Few would listen to your father, but Kentucky may rue the day. Mark my words, as long as the British remain in those outposts—which they promised about thirty years ago to abandon—we face the possibility of trouble with the Indians.

We have about run out of patience with the British. Mr. Clay has confided in me that when the next session convenes in November, the Congress will almost certainly authorize the President to raise a military force to the tune of 25,000 effectives. The British have 8,000 troops in Canada, by all accounts, and very strong fortifications at Quebec and other places, so that we will need a force of that size to invade Canada. And that we will most certainly do. Great Britain will pay for the damage she has done our merchant fleet, and our sovereignty, with her Canadian possessions. It has been said that the

Canadians, who are of French extraction for the most part, will rally to us. In addition, the Congress will appropriate sufficient funds to build several more frigates. The day of reckoning is fast approaching. So says Mr. Clay, and I believe that he is right, as usual.

I know that a few months ago my mind was not made up. But I just don't see any other way to solve this crisis. And if war comes, what should I do? That's what you are afraid of, Rebecca, and I can understand your fear, but how could I, an American, of sound mind and body, who once proudly held a commission in his country's navy, refuse to serve the republic in her hour of need? I would much prefer to be with you, my dear wife, safe at Elm Tree, than on some distant battlefield, or on a warship cleared for action, but I could not in all good conscience remain behind when others left hearth and home to fight for what is right.

Your Devoted Husband,

Jonathan

April 5, 1811

Dear Jonathan,

You may not able to read this, as my hand is trembling so.

This morning, a young Negro woman appeared at our doorstep. It was raining, and had rained all the night. She looked half-drowned, and completely exhausted. So exhausted, in fact, that she literally collapsed in my arms. She was with child, and well along. I had Trumbull carry her up to the spare room. Isaac fetched some brandy. I got her out of her wet clothes—and rags they were, Jonathan, tattered beyond repair and all decency—and into some dry clothes.

The brandy revived her. She told me that her name is

Cilla, and that she belonged to the Coopers of Hunter's Creek. And she said she knew what had happened to Gilly. She was very frightened, and when I asked her what she was afraid of, she said her master, Stephen Cooper. She had run away, and come to me, because she wished to unburden her heart of a terrible secret she had kept for two long years.

Remember that old Elisha said he caught a glimpse of a cloaked figure in a lightning flash the night Gilly disappeared? We all thought he was just seeing things, and dismissed it. But he wasn't seeing things, Jonathan. That was Stephen he saw. Stephen came and stole Gilly away.

The blood freezes like ice in my veins. Cilla says Stephen brought Gilly back to Hunter's Creek. That he did unspeakably bad things to her, and then killed her, and disposed of her body in Ruffian's Marsh, weighing her poor body down with stones.

I believe Cilla is telling the truth, but then I don't want to believe it. Yet it must be true. Why would she lie? Elisha said that the devil himself had come to steal Gilly away, and I suppose he was right all along.

Cilla says that Stephen was unaware that she saw what he did to Gilly, and she kept silent all this time for fear that he would kill her, too. Now she thinks he *does* plan to do away with her, but for another reason. The child she is carrying is his. She tried to conceal her condition from him as long as she could, and when it was no longer possible to do so she persuaded one of the field hands, a man named Jeff, to confess to being the father. Apparently, Stephen was suspicious from the start, and recently forced the truth out of Jeff. It was then that Cilla realized her life was forfeit if she remained at Hunter's Creek. She was convinced that Stephen would murder her, and the unborn child, perhaps in the same way in which he had disposed of poor Gilly. So she ran away, and came here.

Trumbull has dispatched Isaac to fetch the sheriff. But will they take Cilla's word against Stephen? Can a slave give evidence against her master? Oh, I wish you were here, Jonathan.

Rebecca

P.S. This evening Stephen Cooper rode up to the house. He said he was after a runaway slave. His overseer was with him, and two bloodhounds, who had tracked Cilla to our door. I told him he and his dogs were mistaken. He got angry, and insisted on entering our house and searching it. I thought he was going to strike me down, because I blocked the door and would not permit him to pass. Then Trumbull rushed up, and placed his pistol to Stephen's chest. I was never so glad to see anyone in my entire life. Trumbull told him to get off Groves land or be buried in it. I was afraid that Stephen would try to wrestle the pistol away from him. There was a mad gleam in his eyes. But then he turned to go, pausing only to tell Trumbull, with the most wicked of smiles, that he would rue the day.

Jonathan, I am certain that Stephen murdered our poor little Gilly. It was all because she spoke to him that day in town, when she and I were confronted by him. Now I fear he will try to murder Cilla, too. And even Trumbull.

Doctor Mattson came this afternoon to examine Cilla. I asked him to find a man in town who would ride to Boonesboro and deliver a letter I wrote today to my father. The doctor assured me that it would be done. In the letter, I asked my father to come immediately to Elm Tree, that I was in trouble and needed his help. But I need you, too, Jonathan. Please come home and hurry.

CHAPTER SIX

Nathaniel

I

Nathaniel Jones had visited his daughter at Elm Tree only once before. He admired the lay of land. Rolling hills of good grass for grazing horses, interspersed by fields for cultivation, and stands of fine timber. Good water, too, with two creeks converging on the property.

The main house was something to look at. Two stories high, with attic and basement, built in the federal style, not a large house, but with a gallery all the way across the front and four graceful pillars. Four big rooms upstairs, four down, and flanked by brick chimneys on either side. It was painted white, with dark green shutters, and looked pretty as a picture, in Nathaniel's opinion. There were other more elegant homes in the county, but to Nathaniel, who had lived thirty years in a log cabin—and was quite content to spend the rest of his days in one—his daughter's house was a palace and a wonder to behold.

He was proud of her. Every father wanted his child to fare better in life than he had done, and Rebecca had surely come a long way, that was certain. She'd married a good man in Jonathan Groves.

It was on account of Jonathan that Rebecca lived in such style. During his years fighting the Barbary corsairs, Jonathan had saved his pay, and managed in this way to put together a nice stake. All of that money had gone into Elm Tree. So too had several thousand dollars presented to Jonathan by some of Madison County's leading citizens, in a gesture of their appreciation for his endeavors in capturing the traitor, Burr. At first Jonathan had been loathe to accept the money, but he did so, reluctantly, only because he wanted Rebecca to have a home like Elm Tree.

Nathaniel had had no money to spare for his daughter's dowry, but he and Amanda had given Rebecca and Jonathan something worth a king's ransom— Gallivant, sired by Jumper. Most of the thoroughbreds Nathaniel could see grazing out on the hills beyond the house as he rode through the gate into Elm Tree were of Gallivant's bloodline, and Elm Tree horses were in high demand these days. Thanks to Gallivant, Rebecca and her husband prospered.

But on this warm spring day Nathaniel gave no thought to Elm Tree or thoroughbreds. Concern furrowed his weathered brow as he urged his lathered mount up to the gallery. Leaping from the saddle with long rifle in hand, he spared a quick glance for the buggy and the saddle horse in front of the house, then made for the front door.

The door opened just as he reached it, and Rebecca threw herself into his arms.

"Thank God you're safe," breathed Nathaniel.

She smiled, bravely, but the corners of her eyes harbored tears of relief.

"What has happened?" asked the frontiersman.

She shook her head. "Nothing. I'm just . . . just glad to see you."

She was frightened. Nathaniel could tell. But, of course, she would not admit as much to him.

"I came as fast as I could."

"I see." She looked past him, at his horse, and wagged a mock-scolding finger at him. "You ran the tallow off that three-year-old, Father."

"He was born to run. I guess you haven't heard yet from Jonathan."

"I received a letter from him day before yesterday. But he had not received mine when he wrote it. I'm sure he's on his way, though. It'll be several days, at least, before he can get here."

"All you told me in the letter was that you were in trouble, Becky. What kind of trouble?"

"It . . . it has to do with Stephen Cooper."

"Stephen Cooper! I didn't even know that he was still alive."

"Oh, yes. He's still alive. But he's not at all the Stephen we once knew. He . . . I'll tell you all about it, later."

Rebecca turned, having heard the two men descending the stairs to the hall.

"Who are they?" he asked.

"The sheriff, Mr. Ainsley. And Judge Dunston. They came to ask Cilla some questions."

Completely in the dark, Nathaniel realized that all he could do was wait, watch, and listen. Everything would come clear in time.

The two men were engaged in an earnest discussion as they descended the stairs. Seeing Rebecca and Nathaniel in the doorway, they abruptly curtailed their conversation and came forward.

Rebecca performed the introductions. Both the judge and the sheriff recognized her father's name, and shook Nathaniel's hand with enthusiasm.

"It isn't every day that one has the pleasure of

meeting a living legend," said Judge Dunston. He was a tall and portly gentleman, clad in a fine suit of black broadcloth. White side whiskers framed a round and ruddy face. He relied heavily on a gold-ferruled malacca walking stick.

"I'll be," said Ainsley, shaking his head and wearing a foolish grin. "Flintlock Jones, as I live and breathe."

"Judge, have you come to a decision regarding Stephen Cooper?" asked Rebecca.

"Why, yes, child. I have. I am going directly to Hunter's Creek with Sheriff Ainsley."

Rebecca's face brightened. "Thank you, Judge."

"I intend to have a long talk with Mr. Cooper," said Dunston, with a stern scowl.

"Talk?" Rebecca was stunned. "I thought . . ."

"You thought I would go straight over there and place him under arrest?" Dunston shook his head. "As much as I might be inclined personally to do so, I simply cannot. The only thing I have to hold against him is the word of a Negro woman."

Rebecca's cheeks seemed splotched with crimson. Nathaniel knew the signs. Dunston had just put a flame to his daughter's explosive temper.

"Oh, is that all?" she asked, her tone dripping with sarcasm. "Well, by God, I think that ought to be enough."

"Now Mrs. Groves . . ." said Ainsley, alarmed. Nathaniel could only assume that the sheriff knew Rebecca well enough to also know the signs.

"Don't you Mrs. Groves me . . ."

"That is quite enough," boomed Judge Dunston, in the voice he used to quiet an unruly courtroom. Never had it failed in the intended effect, for it might easily be mistaken for the voice of God speaking from on high, so filled was it with awesome majesty. It worked this time, too. "Listen to me, child. Don't you think I know all about Stephen Cooper? On occasion I have had the pleasure of dining with Doctor Mattson. He has confided in me his suspicions about Emily Cooper. A man who would abuse his wife, especially so delicate a creature as she, is lower than a snake's belly, in my opinion. And I was disgusted by what Cooper did to that poor old Negro . . . what was his name, Tom?"

"Samuel," said the sheriff.

"Yes, yes. Samuel. But Cooper was within his rights—"

"Within his rights!" gasped Rebecca. "To torture and murder an old man?"

Dunston grimaced and plowed ahead. "As to these allegations regarding your own servant, the one called Gilly, a jury would never convict a man of Cooper's stature in the community on the word of a slave girl. There is no evidence. There is no body. It would be his word against hers. Surely, my dear, you must see the facts of the matter. Put your emotions aside and look clearly at the situation."

The anger seemed to drain right out of Rebecca, leaving her slump-shouldered and resigned. "Then Cilla is doomed."

"Nonsense. There's no call for such talk. After I get finished with Cooper he won't dare lift a hand against her."

"Forgive me for saying so, Judge, but you won't be able to scare Stephen. You might as well not go to Hunter's Creek at all. It will only make matters worse."

"I insist on going. Now don't fret, Mrs. Groves. Let's be on our way, Sheriff. Good day to you folks."

"Mind if I go along?" asked Nathaniel.

The others looked at him in surprise.

"You, sir?" queried the judge. "For what purpose, may I ask?"

"I was acquainted with Stephen Cooper's father, and Stephen himself, when he was a lad. Maybe he'll listen to me."

Dunston glanced at Ainsley, brows raised in silent query. Nathaniel sensed that the sheriff was apprehensive of a confrontation with Cooper, and liked the idea of him tagging along, believing that there was safety in numbers.

Ainsley said, "Don't see how it could hurt none, Judge."

"Very well, then," said Dunston. "You may join us if you like, Mr. Jones."

"Be careful, Father," said Rebecca. "You just don't know what kind of man Stephen's become."

"I've known some pretty bad men in my time," replied Nathaniel, hoping to reassure his daughter. "Girty and Greathouse come to mind. Could Stephen be any worse?"

II

As magnificent as Nathaniel thought Elm Tree was, the mansion at Hunter's Creek made it look downright plain by comparison.

The lane leading up to the house from the road passed through an alley of green shade formed by double rows of stately oaks. Blackbirds, what seemed like hundreds of them, were in the trees, raising quite a racket. The house itself was a large colonial-style structure with six massive Doric columns across the front. There were L-shaped wings to either side, and a bevy of outbuildings behind. To the north and west of the house, stretching nearly three-quarters of a mile to a line of trees hazy in the distance, were row upon row of corn and tobacco in cultivation, where hands labored in the sultry heat of midday. To the south stood a pair of long stables that looked finer than most houses Nathaniel had seen. He counted twenty thoroughbreds on the rolling hills neatly segmented by white fences in a state of perfect repair.

"Mrs. Cooper's father is Dan Vickers," said Judge Dunston, as they neared the house. Nathaniel rode to one side of the judge's buggy, with Ainsley on the other. "That's where all this comes from. I thought you might be wondering, Mr. Jones."

"I was," admitted the frontiersman. "Stephen Cooper was born the son of a dirt-poor backwoods farmer."

"He married well. Vickers owns several plantations. He resides at one down near Nashville, I believe. I understand he gave Hunter's Creek to his daughter and her new husband upon their marriage. Not to say that Cooper hasn't done well running the place. It is no easy task, managing an estate this size."

"Lewis knows his business," remarked Ainsley. "He's one of the best overseers in Kentucky, what I've heard."

As they arrived at the foot of broad steps leading up to the veranda, a black youth in white and scarlet livery rushed out the front door to hold their horses. They dismounted, Ainsley giving Dunston some assistance in getting out of the buggy, and ascended the steps. A woman appeared in the doorway. She wore a pale yellow organdy dress. Very fine, straight yellow hair was done up in a French braid hanging long down her back. She was very pretty, with high cheekbones and rosebud lips in a heart-shaped face, and the saddest pair of eyes of bottle green that Nathaniel had ever seen. She looked as skittish as a young doe that hears the snapping of a telltale twig in the shinnery.

"Mrs. Cooper!" said Judge Dunston, doffing his hat and bending stiffly at the waist. "You are looking splendid, as always. How do you fare?"

"I am . . . well, Judge, thank you."

Nathaniel was sure he hadn't imagined the hesitation in her reply.

"Afternoon, ma'am," said the sheriff.

"Mr. Ainsley." She glanced curiously and with some trepidation at Nathaniel, this tall, dark, and rough-looking man with his travel-stained buckskin leggins and moccasins, linsey-woolsey shirt, and gray-flecked yellow hair curling long to the shoulders. Leaning on his Kentucky long rife, Nathaniel smiled pleasantly and nodded. She returned the smile, shyly, but the trepidation was gone. Nathaniel took an immediate liking to her.

"Oh, beg pardon," said Dunston. "I have been remiss. Mrs. Cooper, this is Nathaniel Jones, from Boonesboro. Mr. Jones, Mrs. Stephen Cooper. Mrs. Cooper, we have come to have a word with your husband."

"He is out riding." Anxiety pulled at the corners of her eyes and mouth. "What does this concern, may I ask? Is there anything the matter?"

"I think it would be better if we discussed it with Mr. Cooper."

"Damn right it would be better."

Nathaniel turned to see Stephen Cooper coming along the veranda toward them, taking long strides and flicking a riding whip against doeskin breeches tucked into high black boots. He wore a green clawhammer coat and a white muslin shirt open at the collar. He looked altogether different from the shy, gangly youth in homespun that Nathaniel remembered.

Reaching them, he glared, fuming, at Emily. "I've told you not to talk to anyone unless I was present."

"Stephen, I was only—"

"Go inside."

"Really, Mr. Cooper," said Dunston, shocked. "I don't believe there's any call to use that tone of voice with your wife."

"She's my wife, and I'll use whatever tone I wish. What—" Cooper had given Nathaniel a good look for the first time. "Don't I know you, sir?"

"It's been a few years, Stephen."

"Nathaniel Jones."

Nathaniel nodded.

Cooper's expression was unfathomable, but Nathaniel thought he saw a glimmer of fear in the back of the man's suddenly furtive eyes. *Why is he afraid?* wondered the frontiersman. *He hasn't done anything to me. Or to my daughter.* Then it dawned on him. Cooper's fear had everything to do with Rebecca. No, he hadn't done her harm. Not yet. But his intentions were evil. The act he was contemplating made him experience guilt before the fact in Nathaniel's presence.

Emily Cooper faded into the house and softly shut the door. Now Cooper placed himself in front of the door, as though prepared to keep them out by force if they tried to gain entry. *Here is a man who has a lot to hide,* decided Nathaniel.

"So what is it that you gentlemen wish to discuss with me?"

Dunston glanced at Ainsley. The judge did not much care for Cooper's arrogant tone. But Nathaniel watched the old gentlemen grind his teeth and bear it.

"The matter concerns a young Negro woman named Gilly. She was the property of Jonathan Groves of Elm Tree. Do you know the woman I mean?"

"I don't believe I've had the pleasure," snapped Cooper. Now his expression was as immutable as stone.

"She disappeared two years ago. There is evidence at hand to indicate that you kidnapped her, Mr. Cooper."

Dunston leveled a glower at Cooper which had, on occasion, melted the facade of some of the men who had stood as accused in his court. But Cooper was impervious.

"Me?" Cooper shook his head. "That's crazy. What evidence?"

"One of your own slaves, a girl named Cilla."

"A runaway slave, you mean. One which his daughter is harboring," said Cooper, pointing at Nathaniel with his riding whip. "Isn't there a law against giving aid to a runaway, Judge?"

"That is not the issue at present," barked Dunston. His dander was up.

"Oh, but it is. Cilla is lying. She's intent on making trouble for me. And, at the same time, she's protecting the real kidnapper, I'll warrant."

Dunston was thrown off balance by this new twist. "I ... I don't quite ..."

"Let me explain it to you," sneered Cooper, sensing that he had turned the tables. "Of course I heard about

Gilly's disappearance. My overseer, Lewis, mentioned it to me, as I recall. He, in turn, heard it in the quarters. He tells me everything the hands are talking about. Some said the devil came and took Gilly. But I suspect one of my own field hands of being the culprit."

"What?"

Cooper nodded grimly. "Yes. A boy named Jeff. He happens to be Cilla's lover, by the way. Has a hard time keeping his hands off the women."

"What makes you think he took Gilly?" asked the sheriff.

"The night Gilly disappeared from Elm Tree, Jeff wasn't where he was supposed to be. He showed up the next day. Told a ridiculous story. Said he heard something like a scream way back in the woods and went to investigate. Got lost in the storm. Ask Lewis. He'll vouch for the truth of what I'm telling you. I didn't believe Jeff then, and I don't today."

"Why didn't you send for me?" asked Ainsley.

"I had no proof against him. Unlike some people, I need solid evidence before I accuse someone of a crime."

Befuddled, Judge Dunston looked at Ainsley. The sheriff shrugged. Dunston breathed a sigh of resignation.

"Very well, then," he said. "We will trouble you no further, Mr. Cooper. Good day to you."

"Just a minute. What about Cilla? She's my property. Cost a lot of money. I want her back. I tracked her to Elm Tree, but Rebecca Groves refused to turn her over to me."

"She will be returned to you," muttered Dunston, and descended the steps to his buggy, followed by Sheriff Ainsley. Nathaniel lingered on the veranda.

"You've done well for yourself, Stephen."

Pinned by the frontiersman's piercing gaze, Cooper looked a little uncomfortable. "I've had some luck."

"Your father would be proud, were he still alive. He died a few years ago. I don't reckon you knew that. Leastways, he died not knowing where you were or even if you were still alive. His last words to me were asking about you."

"He worked me like a slave," rasped Cooper. "Had he treated me as a father should a son, I would have respected him as a father. If he died a lonely man, it was his own doing. He sent my mother to an early grave. I could never forgive him for that."

"Well, that's really none of my business."

"No, it isn't."

"But Rebecca is. The way I see it, you risked your life to save her five years ago, when the Shawnees came. I'm grateful to you for that."

"So was she," said Cooper, bitterly. "So grateful that she married another man."

Nathaniel simply nodded. "I'll be seeing you."

He went to his horse and climbed into the saddle. Dunston, in his buggy, with Ainsley alongside, had already started down the oak alley. Nathaniel rode after them. Looking back once, he glimpsed a pale, heart-shaped face in an upstairs window. Emily Cooper.

Catching up with the judge and the sheriff, Nathaniel said, "He's lying."

"I'm aware of that," said Dunston testily. "But my hands are tied. There is no evidence. Even if there were, Cooper has very neatly put suspicion on this boy Jeff."

"Yeah, and I'm sure Lewis will corroborate Cooper's story," added Ainsley.

"You're not serious about turning Cilla over to him, are you?"

"What choice do I have, Mr. Jones?" asked Dunston. "She's his property. Bought and paid for."

"It don't seem right," said Nathaniel. "He might kill her."

"It isn't right, perhaps, but it is the way of things."

"I don't relish having to tell Mrs. Groves," admitted Ainsley. "She won't cotton to it, not one bit." He glanced hopefully at Nathaniel. "Maybe you could tell her, Mr. Jones, you being her father and all, she might take it better coming from you."

"I'll tell her," said Nathaniel. "But she won't take it any better, I promise you."

III

"You must go away from here, Cilla," said Rebecca. "It's no longer safe for you to stay."

They sat at the long walnut table in the dining room of Elm Tree—Rebecca, Cilla, Nathaniel, and Trumbull. It was the evening following Nathaniel's visit to Hunter's Creek. He watched Cilla's face as Rebecca gave her the bad news. Her features, bathed in the buttery light of the candles in the brass candelabra at the table's centerpoint, were drawn taut with dread as she stared apprehensively out one of the windows into the dark shroud of night. The frontiersman thought he knew what she was afraid of. Was Stephen Cooper lurking somewhere out there in the darkness? In fact, he was wondering the same thing, convinced that Cooper was not only a threat to the pregnant slave woman, but to his own daughter as well.

"I gots nowhere to go," whispered Cilla.

It was all Rebecca could do to keep her composure. "You have no family?"

"I dunno, Mrs. Groves. I wouldn't know where to finds 'em if I did."

Rebecca looked at Nathaniel. At first she had rebelled against the idea of sending Cilla away. She was ready to put up a fight against what she perceived as a great injustice—fight Stephen, Sheriff Ainsley, even Judge Dunston and all the mighty power of the legal system, if need be. Nathaniel had finally brought her to her senses. She was going along with it now, but she still didn't like it, not one bit.

"One more reason to do away with the abominable institution of slavery," said Rebecca. "Sons are taken from fathers, daughters from mothers, brothers from sisters. It's not right, I tell you."

"I've learned it's best to fight one battle at a time, Becky," said the frontiersman.

She rose, a sharp and impatient motion, and went to the other end of the table to place a comforting hand on Cilla's shoulder. Her other hand appeared from beneath her apron with a small pouch, which she laid before the slave woman.

"I want you to take this, Cilla. It isn't much, but it ought to be enough to see you and your baby to a new start somewhere. But don't let anyone know you have that much money on you. They might think you stole it. Or they might try to steal it from you."

Softly weeping, Cilla clutched Rebecca's arm. "Nobody's ever been so kind to me, Mrs. Groves."

"Stop that crying, Cilla. Crying never helped anything." Rebecca looked across the table at Trumbull. "I want you to take her far away from here, Mr. Trumbull."

"Me? I don't think so, ma'am. Mr. Groves ordered me to stick close by you. I can't go anywhere."

Nathaniel smiled. He liked Trumbull. The craggy, big-shouldered bear of a man had an honest face, and he looked you straight in the eye. Besides, he was clearly loyal to Jonathan and devoted to Rebecca. A man, too, who looked like he could take care of himself in any kind of scrape.

"Mr. Groves will be here himself in a matter of days," replied Rebecca.

"I'll watch over her until then," promised Nathaniel.

"Well, I guess that'll be all right, then. But where do I take her?"

"Wherever she wants to go. Vicksburg, Natchez, somewhere a good long ways from here."

"New Orleans," said Cilla.

"New Orleans is it, then," Trumbull said. "You'd best write me out a bill of sale, Mrs. Groves, showing I bought Cilla fair and square."

"A bill of sale?" Rebecca frowned at the idea, but then saw the wisdom of it. "Yes. Yes, I will write one."

"You know that if the law catches you, you could be in a tight fix," remarked Nathaniel.

Trumbull chuckled. "I'll say. They'd probably hang me. But we'll make it through just fine, Cilla and me."

"I believe you will," said the frontiersman.

"Once we get to New Orleans and she's settled in somewhere safe and sound, then I'll set her free. Being her owner, I'll be within my rights to do that. And I know some folks down there, good folks. Maybe she'll be able to find some kind of work with one of them."

"You're a decent man, Mr. Trumbull," said Rebecca.

Trumbull looked down at his big hands. "I make my living workin' Negroes. I'm part and parcel of the system you despise, Mrs. Groves. I try not to bother myself with the right or wrong of it. But the Negroes I've known have been decent people, for the most part. And I do know that what Mr. Cooper done to this gal ain't right." He looked up at Rebecca, his expression melancholy. "I reckon I won't be coming back."

"Of course you'll come back. You have a job here for as long as you want it."

Trumbull shook his head emphatically. Nathaniel said, "He's right, Becky. Cooper will send the law here to fetch Cilla. You can't tell them what you've done."

"I *will* tell them," she said, defiant.

"No, ma'am," said Trumbull firmly. "You'll tell them I took Cilla without you knowing it. That'll put you in the clear." He forced a smile. "Of course, they'll be asking you which way I was headed when I took out. I'd be obliged was you to tell them I took off north."

"I'll tell them, Mr. Trumbull."

The overseer rose from the table. Nathaniel noticed the pistol in his belt. "Cilla," said Trumbull, "you'd best get a few hours sleep. We'll leave here a couple hours before sunup."

"Come along, Cilla," said Rebecca. "I'll take you to your room."

Trumbull lingered, waiting until the two women had left the dining room to say his piece.

"You're going to have to kill that Cooper fellow," he told Nathaniel.

"I hope not. He was a fine lad once. I knew his pa."

"That don't matter now. Whatever he was in his

younger days, he's pure devil now. And he means to do harm to Mrs. Groves."

"If he tries," said Nathaniel, "then I *will* kill him."

IV

The next several days were uneventful at Elm Tree, and Nathaniel used the time to good advantage, getting better acquainted with his grandson. Precious few had been the hours he'd spent with Christopher, and he was mightily impressed by the intelligence and energy of the rosy-cheeked, tow-headed lad. For one of such tender age Christopher knew a great deal about horses, and rode like one born to the saddle. Nathaniel fashioned for him a bow of Osage orange, and together they notched, tipped, and fletched a dozen arrows of mulberry wood, and they spent a lot of time at target practice.

"Is Christopher the son you never had?" asked Rebecca, kidding him.

"Becky," replied the frontiersman, "I have been twice blessed in my life. Once when I met your mother and the second time when you came into my life."

But for the circumstances that had brought her father to Elm Tree, these were some of the happiest days Rebecca could recall. Christopher was completely infatuated with Nathaniel. All three of them went riding every morning. And they laughed a lot. Yet she could not fail to notice that Nathaniel always had his long rifle within reach. And the rifle was a reminder of the cloud hanging over them.

Then Sheriff Ainsley appeared, as they knew he would, eventually, and the idyll was over. Cooper had lodged his complaint, and the sheriff, reluctantly, had come out to Elm Tree for the purpose of recovering Cooper's property. He was unabashedly pleased to learn that Cilla was gone. Asking no questions, he enjoyed a cup of coffee and a pastry, made a few casual remarks concerning the weather and the likelihood of war with the British, then prepared to take his leave.

"Aren't you going to ask me anything more about Cilla?" asked Rebecca, surprised.

"Did you want to tell me where I might look for her?" asked Ainsley, with a wink.

"I think she went north."

"North, eh? Good. Reckon I'll mosey on over to Hunter's Creek and tell Mr. Stephen Cooper she took off and headed north. Yes, sir, it's a fine day. Afternoon, folks."

"What do you think Stephen will do now?" Rebecca asked her father as they stood on the gallery and watched the sheriff ride off down the lane.

Nathaniel curled a brawny arm around her shoulders. "Don't worry about that."

"I'm not worried, really. Not while you're here. Not about Stephen. But I am worried about Jonathan, and what he'll do."

The next day Jonathan came home.

"I ought to kill him and be done with it," muttered Jonathan.

He sat slumped in a chair near the hearth in the parlor downstairs, swirling the brandy in his glass and staring pensively into the amber liquid. Rebecca had retired for the night, and Christopher had been asleep for hours.

Nathaniel sat in another chair, leaning forward,

hands clasped loosely between his knees, watching his son-in-law. He had not seen Jonathan for two years, and reflected on how much the man had changed from the youthful naval officer he had found lost in the wilderness. Jonathan Groves had aged considerably in that relatively short span of time, and Nathaniel supposed it was due to the weight of so much responsibility—a wife and family, Elm Tree, his duties as a representative of the people. Jonathan's face was long and deeply lined. His dark hair, brushed straight back from his face and grown long, nearly to the shoulders, had as much gray in it as Nathaniel's. *And he is not yet thirty years old,* mused the frontiersman. It made him glad he lived a simple life. Jonathan looked a lot thinner, too, clad in a dark blue clawhammer coat, with his white britches tucked into long black boots.

Nathaniel made no comment. Jonathan raised his head, as though it took much effort, and looked bleakly at him. "You're not going to tell me what you think I ought to do?"

"You didn't ask me."

Jonathan sighed. "I don't have to. And I know what Rebecca wants. That's why I would not make such a statement in her presence. But it's the way I feel."

"You're talking about a duel. An affair of honor, isn't that what you gentlemen call it?"

"Quite right." Jonathan rose to add another log to the pleasant fire crackling cheerfully in the hearth; the late April evening had turned cool. "The man has insulted my wife. He may have murdered one of my servants. He is a dangerous scoundrel. It *is* a matter of honor."

"Honor?"

"Yes, damn it. Honor."

"I've not found much honor in killing a man."

"I know what Henry Clay would do." Jonathan stirred the fire with an iron poker. "And I know what you would do."

"I'd do nothing."

"Rebecca lives in fear of him."

"Not as long as you're here."

"I'm to stay here and guard her the rest of my life? Never to let her out of my sight?"

"Would that be so bad?"

"I don't like waiting for my enemy to make the first move."

"I don't reckon you'd have to wait all that long, Jonathan."

"Why do you say that?"

"Cooper's got the devil in him. It's twisting his guts into painful knots, filling him up with hate. A man can't take much of that without doing something to try to ease it."

"Is it me that he hates?"

"Partly. He hates you for taking Rebecca away from him. That's how he sees it, anyway. And he hates Rebecca, too. I think he hates the whole world. Including himself. Maybe himself most of all. A man who hates so hard has to strike out. He can't help it. He won't wait long."

Jonathan glanced at the cutlass on the wall above the mantel. Of Tripolitan origin, he had taken it from a corsair while leading a boarding party that succeeded, after a fierce fight, in capturing a pirate galley. The corsair had almost cut him in half with that mighty curved blade. Instead, Jonathan had killed him, and used the cutlass throughout the rest of the fight, his own saber broken. From then on he had carried it—even into the wilderness when on the mission to arrest Aaron Burr. Jonathan never told anybody, but he believed that as long as he wore the cutlass no harm would come to him.

"I hope he doesn't wait too long to make his move," he said. "There will be war soon, Nathaniel. And I intend to serve my country when that happens. I can't stay here forever, waiting on Cooper."

Nathaniel shook his head. "War's not a good idea right now."

"Why? We can't just stand by and let the British ride roughshod over our rights. The honor of the republic demands action."

"Honor again."

"Precisely. The company of nations is like a pack of wolves. If one is perceived to be weak, the others will turn on it, and eventually destroy it. That is the law of nature, as well as the law of nations."

"We *are* weak," replied Nathaniel. "We could very well lose a war with the British."

"Nonsense. We beat them once."

"With French help, remember."

"In a way we'll have French help again. The British are engaged in a fight for survival against Bonaparte. They haven't soldiers to spare to send against us."

"They've got the Indians."

"The Indians? The Indians no longer pose a threat to us. We've whipped them. Fallen Timbers broke their will to fight."

"A Shawnee named Tecumseh has restored their will. You've been away too long, Jonathan, if you think the Indians are finished."

"Certainly there are isolated raids by hotheaded young braves. Like the ones who took Rebecca. But those raids are few and far between. You must admit it isn't anything like as bad as it was when you first came to Kentucky. And the chiefs are all for living in peace with us."

"I don't know. Tecumseh and his brother, The Prophet—"

Jonathan made a curt gesture of dismissal. "Nothing will come of that, Nathaniel."

The frontiersman grimaced. Too few wanted to hear his words of warning. He really couldn't blame them. The country had been aflame for twenty-five years, and Kentuckians were sick of the bloodshed—had become accustomed to peace. They heard what they wanted to hear.

"I thought you, at least, would heed my warning," said the frontiersman.

"The threat of another Indian war is useful in stirring up the people against the British. That's all."

Nathaniel stood, stretching like a big cat. "Reckon I'll turn in."

"Will you stay here at Elm Tree a while longer?"

"No. I need to get home to Amanda. Maybe another day or two, and then I must go." He started for the door, paused, and turned back. "I hope for your own sake, Jonathan, that you'll take a long look around at what you have here."

With that he was gone.

V

A storm rolled in the next day. Nathaniel decided he would leave on the morrow, if the rain had passed. He was suddenly anxious to get back to Amanda. She had wanted to accompany him to Elm Tree, but he had talked her out of it, not knowing what brand of trouble he was getting into by answering his daughter's urgent summons. And it occurred to him that there was irony in his advising Jonathan to think twice about leaving his family to fight a war. How often had he left Amanda to go off and fight the Shawnees? With Boone headed west to Missouri in search of more elbow room, his neighbors at Booneboro had increasingly turned to him in times of crisis. How could he refuse to help them when they asked? Perhaps Jonathan was compelled by a similar sense of obligation to his country. It wasn't that Nathaniel wasn't patriotic. But years in the Kentucky wilderness, fending for himself, without benefit of assistance from a government that at times seemed utterly indifferent to the fate of the pioneers in the Trans-Appalachian region, had made him—and all like him—rather independent-minded. In any case, he figured that if he was going to advise another to stay closer to home and family, he ought to try practicing what he preached.

All through the day the rain fell in silver sheets, and even as night fell the storm did not abate. The next morning, however, dawned clear. Nathaniel scarcely had time to notice. A hideous scream woke him. Snatching up the long rifle, he raced downstairs, barefoot and shirtless, colliding with Jonathan on the stairs. They bolted outside. The hoarse screams, accompanied now by the husky shouts of men, led them to the quarters of the slaves, a row of cabins some distance back of the main house.

A crowd of Negroes had gathered around one of the cabins. The horror etched on their faces made Nathaniel's blood run cold. They had every reason to be horrified. An old black man was hanging on the cabin door, pinned there by a cane knife, which had been plunged through his chest. The doorway was covered with blood. Nathaniel could tell by the color and consistency of the blood that the killing had occurred several hours ago.

"It's old Elisha," whispered Jonathan. It sounded as though he was strangling on something lodged firmly in his throat.

Nathaniel looked about him. The slaves were gripped in paroxysms of fear and grief and almost rapturous, supernatural dread.

Then he heard Rebecca's voice, calling out to her husband. He whirled, but Jonathan was faster, moving to stop her before she was halfway to the cabin.

"Jonathan, what's happened?"

"It's Elisha. He's dead."

"Oh my God!" sobbed Rebecca, and tried to get past him, but he held her fast.

"No, Rebecca! Go back to the house."

"What is it? What's the matter?"

"Rebecca, go back to the house!"

Never had he used that tone of voice with her. Rebecca was stunned. She stared at him a moment, then, without another word, turned and walked back to the house.

Jonathan rejoined Nathaniel. The frontiersman was

examining the corpse and the door, his face a bronze, stoic mask.

"The blade went clean through the door," he said. "It would take an exceptionally strong man to strike such a blow."

"The devil done it," wailed one of the Negro women.

Some of the others muttered their agreement. One of the women fell to her knees, moaning, clutching herself.

"Yes," rasped Jonathan. "The devil . . . and his name is Cooper."

Nathaniel peered at him. "Why would he do this? It makes no sense."

"Not to you. You're a straightforward man, Nathaniel, and expect others to be the same. But he's done this to torment my wife. To terrify my slaves." Jonathan made a sweeping gesture. "Look at them! Tomorrow half of them will be gone. The rest won't work. Cooper is intent on destroying us."

"Why not just kill you? Why kill an old man?"

"Because he's a brutal, sadistic monster. Killing me is too quick. He wants to do it slowly. He wants to make us suffer."

Nathaniel scanned the ground. He would have to pick up the trail, if that was possible, farther from the cabin, because here the sign had been obliterated by the slaves who had discovered the body.

"Help me get him down," said Jonathan.

While Nathaniel held the body, Jonathan grabbed the hickory handle of the cane knife and pulled with all his might. A woman cried out as the bloody blade came free. Nathaniel carried the corpse into the cabin and laid it gently on a narrow bed.

"I'm going to track the man who did this," he told Jonathan.

"It was Cooper, I tell you."

"Then the trail will lead me to Hunter's Creek."

"Then what will you do? Listen, Nathaniel. Cooper's mine. Give me your word you won't do anything to him."

Nathaniel hesitated. If indeed Cooper had committed this cold-blooded murder, he deserved to die. The frontiersman did not consider himself judge, jury, and executioner, but would justice be done in this case, if he left it to the courts? Would a jury hang Stephen Cooper in retribution for killing an old Negro man? Cooper was important. He had married into an important family. He had wealth, power, influence.

If he tracked Cooper down and killed him, justice would be served, but then he would be a murderer, wouldn't he? Would he hang? Still, that was better than leaving it to Jonathan. Jonathan had Rebecca and little Christopher and an unborn child who depended on him. Nathaniel couldn't take the chance that Cooper might kill Jonathan. For Rebecca's sake he had to be the one to confront Stephen.

Jonathan clutched his arm. "This is between Cooper and me. It has been from the very start. It's *my* fight, Nathaniel. If you kill him, they'll call it premeditated murder. But if I kill him on the field of honor, there would be nothing they could do. He has no honor, but there's no other way."

The frontiersman nodded grimly.

"Your word on it," insisted Jonathan.

"You have my word."

Jonathan released him.

* * *

He did not return until late in the afternoon, his buckskins and his horse splattered with mud. His first thought was for Rebecca.

"She's resting, finally," reported Jonathan, meeting him at the door to Elm Tree. "Elisha's death hit her hard. Where did the trail lead you?"

"Hunter's Creek."

"There, I told you. Did you see Cooper?"

Nathaniel shook his head. "But he's there. In the big house."

"You're sure?"

"Yes."

"You didn't kill him, did you?"

"I gave you my word," snapped Nathaniel, tired and confused.

Jonathan relaxed. "I will go tomorrow," he said with an almost deathly calm.

"If it's a duel, you'll need a second. Isn't that the way it's done?"

Jonathan simply nodded and turned to enter the house. Nathaniel followed him into the parlor, where Jonathan poured himself a brandy.

"You haven't told Rebecca what you plan to do, have you, Jonathan?"

"Not yet."

"She won't like it. Not one bit."

"Cooper must be stopped. I'll ... tell her in the morning."

VI

When morning arrived, Jonathan was still firm in his resolve. He came downstairs at dawn and found

Nathaniel sitting on the gallery, watching the cool white cottony mist cling to the fields and the trees, feeling its clammy dampness on his face, and listening to the querulous song of the birds. Jonathan had a pistol stuck under his belt, and he was carrying the Tripolitan cutlass.

"Where is everyone?" he asked. Apart from Elisha, the house staff consisted of young Nellie and a man named Isaac. But the house this morning was as quiet as a tomb.

"In their quarters. All but a couple of them. A man and a woman. They ran off during the night?"

"Ran off?"

"Scared, I reckon."

"As I feared. You didn't try to stop them?"

Nathaniel looked at him askance. "I'm not in the habit of keeping a person from going where he wants to go."

Jonathan swore under his breath. "That's no good, Nathaniel. Do you know what could happen to them? They don't have any papers. If they're picked up, they'll be counted as runaways, and runaways are often treated . . . roughly."

"It's something when folks have to have papers to take a walk."

"You're beginning to sound like Rebecca."

"Can't blame them for going. What happened to Elisha has got them all skittish."

"Well, it will be settled today."

"What if Stephen kills you, Jonathan?"

"My God, what would you have me do? I must defend my family."

Nathaniel nodded and picked up his long rifle.

"I'll saddle some horses," said Jonathan.

"Have you told Rebecca what you aim to do?"

"She's sleeping."

"Best wake her up, then. Tell her straight. She deserves that much. I'll fetch a couple of horses."

Nathaniel left the gallery and headed for the stables, permitting no debate by his abrupt departure. Jonathan tried to steel himself for what lay ahead—with Rebecca, not Cooper. Facing his wife would be by far the more difficult task.

When Jonathan emerged from the house a second time Nathaniel was waiting, astride one horse and holding the reins of another. Jonathan's face was drawn and pale. Nathaniel could tell by looking at him that the confrontation had been a stormy one. He didn't have to ask, and didn't.

Jonathan lashed the cutlass to his saddle with sharp, angry movements. Taking the reins from Nathaniel, he swung aboard the horse and without a word started down the lane at a canter. Nathaniel glanced at the door half expecting to see Rebecca. But his daughter was not to be seen.

He failed to notice her at an upstairs window, from which she watched her husband and father ride down the road. Tears coursed her cheeks. Sobbing quietly, she sank into a rocking chair near the window and cried some more, her hands covering her face, the tears seeping through her fingers. She leaned forward, rocking furiously. The chair creaked. The tears fell to the floor. After a time she leaned back, exhausted, and stared out the window without seeing anything. Staring at nothing, and feeling nothing. All she could think about was Jonathan—and Stephen. Before the day was out one of them would lie dead. In spite of what he had done to Elisha, she hated, for some reason, to think of

Stephen dead. There had to be another way. She remembered him as he had been before—before the Shawnees had almost killed him. Perhaps she had known him better than even his own father. And what if Jonathan was the one who fell? How could she go on without him?

A sudden, intense, unbearable agony wrenched a gasp from her lips. It felt as though someone was thrusting a stake into her midsection. She leaned forward, doubled over, fighting for breath. The pain would pass, she told herself. But it didn't. It got worse. So bad that when she wanted to call out for help she couldn't. Besides, the house was empty. No one would have heard her. She looked down at the floor and saw the blood. So much blood! Blood mingled with her tears. She had to get help. Tried to stand, but the pain was too much. Slipping to the floor, she tried to crawl, but she didn't get far. Halfway to the door she passed out. Her cotton wrapper was soaked with blood, and a trail of blood like a cord of scarlet, connected her crumpled form to the rocking chair, which still moved slightly over by the window.

They rode down the alley of oaks toward the house at Hunter's Creek, and as they drew near, a man Nathaniel did not recognize came from the stables to stand on the veranda at the top of the steps, a burly man, standing with legs braced well apart and his hands, curled into fists, on his hips. A scowl darkened his bearded features. Only then did Jonathan speak—nary a word had passed between him and Nathaniel since their departure from Elm Tree.

"That's Lewis. Cooper's overseer. Keep an eye on him."

"I will."

"Nathaniel . . ."

"Yes?"

"If I fall today . . ."

"I'll take care of things."

"No," said Jonathan brusquely. "Not what I meant. I don't want to die knowing Cooper is still alive. Still a threat to Rebecca."

Nathaniel kept his bleak gaze fixed on Lewis. He didn't like this. None of it. He had a bad feeling, creeping into the marrow of his bones. But he owed Jonathan an answer to that roundabout question.

"I said I'd take care of things, Jonathan."

It was all he could offer. Jonathan realized this, and did not press the issue.

Lewis stood there, like an unscaleable wall of flesh and bone and muscle, barring them from going any farther. Having been in his share of scrapes, Nathaniel could tell in a glance that this man was one to be reckoned with.

"What do you want?" asked the overseer, none too pleasantly.

"I've come for Stephen Cooper," said Jonathan.

Lewis didn't have to ask what for. The expression on Jonathan's face, the tone of his voice, the pistol in his belt, and the cutlass tied to his saddle spoke volumes about Jonathan's purpose for coming here.

"Stay where you are," said Lewis. "I'll get him."

He went inside. Nathaniel and Jonathan remained on their horses. The frontiersman took care to scan the windows in the front of the house. He didn't know what to expect from Cooper.

A moment later Cooper emerged from the house. He was coatless, and Nathaniel was confident he wasn't armed. But Lewis did not come out, and Nathaniel began to worry about the windows again.

"What do you want here?" asked Cooper, the query rank with disdain.

"I've come to kill you," rasped Jonathan.

Cooper raised an eyebrow. An aggravating smirk curled the corner of his mouth. He lifted his arms away from his sides.

"As you can see, I am unarmed."

"I have a pistol, and this." Jonathan grabbed the hilt of the cutlass riding beneath his leg. "I suggest you arm yourself in a like manner."

"Are you challenging me to a duel?"

"I am."

"Perhaps I will decline."

"Then you are a coward, as well as a murderer, and I will not hesitate to shoot you down like the animal that you are."

Strong emotion slithered behind Cooper's mask of arrogant disdain. He stared at Jonathan a moment, then glanced at Nathaniel.

"Why are you here? To finish the job if he can't?"

"He can finish it," said Nathaniel.

"What would my father think, to see you here after my blood?"

"If he knew what kind of man his son had become, he would kill you himself."

Cooper laughed, a harsh sound grating on Nathaniel's nerves. He had the feeling that Cooper was stalling, playing for time, and again he wondered what Lewis was up to.

"You *are* a coward," said Jonathan, trying to goad Cooper into action. "Only a coward would murder a defenseless man."

"I'm sure I don't know what you mean."

"Elisha, you bastard. You murdered him in cold blood."

"If you think so, get the sheriff. Have me arrested."

Jonathan shook his head. "I want the job to get done, so I'll do it myself."

Cooper made an impatient gesture. "If you want to die so badly, then I'll oblige you."

He turned on his heel and disappeared into the house.

Nathaniel dismounted. "Get down off that horse, Jonathan," he said quietly.

Jonathan obeyed. He was untying the cutlass from the saddle when Cooper reappeared, a pistol in each hand. There was a look of such dark towering rage, such twisted hate, on his face that he seemed utterly transformed.

"You took Rebecca away from me, you son of a bitch, and I'm going to kill you for that."

Nathaniel shouted a warning, but it was lost in the loud crack of one of Cooper's pistols as he brought it up, aimed at Jonathan, and fired from the top of the gallery steps. Jonathan was already moving, having anticipated Cooper, and threw himself to one side. The bullet struck Jonathan's saddle, pierced it, and dealt the horse beneath a serious but not fatal wound. The animal reared with a scream and bolted. The cutlass fell to the ground. Cooper was still coming forward. On the steps now, he raised the second pistol. Jonathan, on one knee, brandished his own pistol. They fired simultaneously.

Nathaniel saw movement in an upstairs window. Aware that it might be Emily Cooper, he hesitated. But it wasn't Emily. He heard the shattering of glass and caught a glimpse of Lewis's face behind the barrel of a shotgun. Nathaniel's Kentucky long rifle seemed to leap of its own volition to his shoulder, and in the next instant he fired. His aim was true. The overseer's face dissolved in a mask of scarlet, and the impact of the head shot hurled him backward out of sight.

Nathaniel turned to see what had become of Jonathan and Stephen Cooper.

Cooper was sprawled on his face at the bottom of the steps, motionless. Jonathan was getting slowly to his feet, clutching his left arm close to his body. A spreading stain of blood appeared on his sleeve. His face was drawn and ashen.

Moving to Cooper, Nathaniel wedged one moccasin-clad foot beneath him and rolled him over. Cooper's sightless eyes looked right through him. Jonathan had shot him through the heart.

"How bad are you hit?" Nathaniel asked Jonathan.

"I think . . . the bone is shattered. I don't . . ."

He slumped to his knees.

A sound from the door of the house drew Nathaniel's attention. It was Emily Cooper.

She spared her husband scarcely a glance. "Bring him inside," she told Nathaniel, referring to Jonathan. "I will send someone for the doctor."

"No time for a doctor. He's bleeding bad. I've got to see to his wound, quick."

She came down the steps to Jonathan's side. "I will help you," she said.

VII

Dusk was spreading a soft blue-gray blanket across the land, and it was pleasing to the eye and soul, but Nathaniel was not deceived. Today had reminded him that a man's world was a very fragile and sometimes unpleasant place indeed. Recent events, hitting him like a fence post smack across the eyes, had drawn his attention to this undeniable but oft-forgotten fact of life.

Sitting at a small table, gazing blindly out the window at the fields and rolling hills of Elm Tree, alive with the pyrotechnics of countless fireflies, he held a quill pen suspended an inch above a blank sheet of vellum. An hour ago, after Doctor Mattson left, he'd decided he would have to write Amanda, tell her all that had transpired, by way of explaining why he could not come home straightaway, and as a preface to the suggestion that she come to Elm Tree. An hour, and he had managed to write two words. *Dear Amanda.* That was all.

True, he wasn't much of a letter writer. How many letters *had* he written in his lifetime? None that he could remember. Oh, yes, there was that one to the lawyer in Virginia, about the sale of the tavern he had inherited from his father at that awful moment when one of Tarleton's Tory Rangers had killed Joshua Jones. But it wasn't so much his inexperience in the manufacture of epistles that stumped him; rather, it was the sheer, terrible enormity of the tragedy he would have to put into words. He had dipped the tip of the quill pen into the bottle of India ink, and now two drops of ink had dripped from the tip onto the paper, like indigo teardrops. He hadn't even noticed.

He wanted to tell her about Rebecca, of course, but that was the hardest part of the task, by far—how their daughter had miscarried, and so they were not destined to be proud grandparents, he and Amanda, a second time, at least not in the foreseeable future. The stress has just been too much for her—the anguish she had experienced watching her husband, and her father, riding off to kill a man, or be killed. All of that, added to the death of Elisha, and the news about Gilly's fate. The doctor had said Rebecca had lost a lot of blood, but would survive, as long as she remained in bed for a good long time and got plenty of rest.

And he could tell her how bravely Christopher was bearing up. How the little boy had informed Nathaniel that he need not worry, that he would make sure his mother and father got well. Yes, a brave boy for one so young. Not a tear, that Nathaniel could see.

He could tell her, too, about Jonathan's wound. The doctor confirmed that Cooper's bullet had smashed the bone. Nathaniel had removed the bullet at Hunter's Creek. Emily Cooper had helped him. One might have thought Jonathan was her own husband, so concerned was she for his welfare. And while they worked to remove the bullet and stop the prodigious bleeding, Stephen Cooper's corpse lay unattended on the gallery steps. Hours after the fact, Nathaniel still puzzled over the image seared into his memory—the image of Emily Cooper, fussing over Jonathan like a mother hen, or a loving wife, or a tender lover, and by the shine of her eyes, mysterious and serene and yet far away, one would be forgiven for assuming that the pale and unconscious man who lay bleeding all over her dining room table belonged to her.

It made no sense to Nathaniel. To be sure, he had seen many extraordinary sights in his life, but Emily Cooper took the cake. She ordered a servant to hitch up the wagon after Nathaniel insisted on taking Jonathan home to Elm Tree. She had argued against it at first, saying that the wound, just cauterized, would open up again, but Nathaniel had not wanted to return to Elm Tree and face Rebecca without her husband.

Emily had thanked him, too. *I have never been*

thanked in such a heartfelt manner for taking part in the killing of a man—especially by the man's wife! And as he drove the spring wagon down the lane away from Hunter's Creek, with the saddle horses tied on behind, he glanced back once at the mansion; Emily had been waiting for him to do so, and waved, and then turned and entered the house—and still the body of Stephen Cooper lay sprawled on the steps. *I would not be surprised if he lay there still . . .*

Doctor Mattson had told him in all likelihood Jonathan would keep his arm. "What did you use to cauterize?" "Gunpowder and a hot iron." The physician had nodded. "Crude but effective. I don't know that he will ever enjoy the use of that limb again—the bone is shattered beyond repair, but he won't have an empty sleeve." Mattson had looked with stricken sympathy at Nathaniel, shaking his head. "A sad day. A sad, sad day, sir," departing on that melancholy note.

Sitting by the window, with the twilight gradually deepening into night, Nathaniel lighted the lamp on the table. He wondered when the sheriff, Ainsley, would come. Surely he would. The frontiersman doubted that he and Jonathan would be in trouble with the law, but then you never knew, where the law was concerned. Ainsley and Judge Dunston would certainly be sympathetic, but the latter at least struck Nathaniel as a stickler when it came to the letter of the law, and it could not be denied that he and Jonathan had gone to Hunter's Creek with the intention—at least in Jonathan's case, the clear-cut intention—of killing Stephen Cooper.

Nathaniel wasn't sure even now what his own intentions had been. To make sure that Jonathan came to no harm, for certain, and he hadn't been completely successful in that regard. But deep down inside he had known that Cooper was going to have to die, had known as much ever since finding poor old Elisha pinned to the cabin door with a cane knife plunged through his brittle rib cage, and Nathaniel had been prepared to do the deed. Better he than Jonathan. Yes, eventually the law would come calling. Two men were dead. There would have to be an inquest. That was another reason he couldn't go home.

Nathaniel stared out into the night, a motionless figure in buckskin and linsey-woolsey, holding quill pen poised over ink-stained vellum, in a pool of butter yellow lamplight, and thinking about the new ghosts introduced this day into that limbo where spirits were thought to wander. Stephen Cooper, Lewis, and the unborn child. Add Elisha, and Gilly's spirit, too. Did they haunt that cypress swamp known as Ruffian's Marsh? Would Stephen Cooper's ghost have to confront the spirits of his own victims? Perhaps it was happening at this moment, in the shadows of the cool, wind-ruffled night beyond the window glass. If it was true that such happened, Nathaniel wondered if he would meet the ghosts of Stephen Cooper and Lewis—and all the others. How many Indians had he slain? And whose spirit would *he* haunt someday?

With a sigh, Nathaniel dipped the quill in the ink bottle and began to write, and the only sound was the sigh of the night wind against the window glass, and the scratch-scratch-scratching of quill on vellum.

Dear Amanda,
                 Terrible things happened today . . .

CHAPTER SEVEN

Tecumseh

I
(1811)

His name was Barron. He had been dispatched by Governor William Henry Harrison to Prophet's Town to deliver an important message to Tecumseh. He did not know what kind of reception he would find. The French trapper Harrison had sent to Prophet's Town last year to spy on the goings-on there had only recently returned to Vincennes with sobering news. Many tribes had sworn fealty to Tecumseh. All they were waiting for was some mysterious cataclysmic sign—a sign that Lalawethika, The Prophet, had promised would come, and which would tell the Indians that the moment had arrived when, with *Moneto*'s blessing, they would drive the Long Knives from their lands. Tecumseh could raise an army of ten thousand on a week's notice, three times as many in a fortnight.

The Frenchman had brought a single morsel of good news. One of the most feared of Shawnee warriors, Blue Jacket, had recently died of a fever.

Barron had been present when the trapper gave his report to the governor. And he had heard all the rumors that were beginning to sweep the frontier—rumors of a great Indian confederacy, unlike any that had come before. He had heard that a thousand warriors resided in Prophet's Town, and now that he saw all the *wegiwas,* stretching, or so it seemed, as far as the eye could see from one end of a smoke-hazed valley to the other, he knew this was no exaggeration. But Barron was endowed with steel nerve and extraordinary courage—which was why Governor Harrison had chosen him for the job.

Fifty Shawnee, Mingo, and Delaware warriors came out to meet him. They escorted him to the center of the village, where Lalawethika sat in a high-backed wing chair in front of his lodge, an Indian monarch on his horsehair throne. The Prophet scowled darkly at him. Rising from the chair, he swept a scarlet blanket robe aside and pointed an accusing finger at Barron.

"Harrison has sent another spy. Where you stand is where you will die, and where your bones will be buried."

Barron looked The Prophet square in the eye and did not flinch. "I have come to deliver a message to your brother," he said calmly, and his Shawnee was very good. "A message from the White Father."

"He is not *notha* to me," said Lalawethika. "He is Harrison. The slayer of Indian women and children. *Nineemeh, Shemanese!* Look, Long Knife! See the warriors all about you who only await my signal to fall upon you. Which one shall I let take your scalp?"

"I've come in peace. I thought the Shawnees still knew what honor meant. Perhaps I was mistaken."

"You were not mistaken."

Tecumseh spoke thus, as he passed through the circle of warriors to confront Barron. He looked sharply at Lalawethika. "This is no way to treat a guest." he said.

Still scowling, Lalawethika sank bank into his chair.

Tecumseh turned to Barron. "You are in no danger."

"I thought not. I said to myself, Tecumseh is *nenothtu oukimah,* a great warrior, and he would not suffer a man who had come to speak with him and smoke the *calumet* to be murdered."

Tecumseh's face might have been chiseled from stone for all the emotion it betrayed.

"Pe-e-wah," he said, with a curt gesture, and turned away. Barron followed him to the *wegiwa.* The Shawnee motioned for him to sit upon the buffalo robes near the center fire, and took his place opposite.

"Why have you come?" asked Tecumseh. "You are not here to spy on us like the Frenchman who came before?"

Barron saw no point in protesting the French trapper's innocence. Obviously the Indians knew the truth. Question was, why had they allowed the Frenchman to sojourn among them for a time, and then leave to carry his information to Vincennes? There could be only one answer. The rumors were true, the time of reckoning fast approaching, and Tecumseh did not care anymore about deceiving the whites because he believed there was nothing they could do to stop him now.

"I have brought a message written by the White Father in Vincennes to his friend, Tecumseh."

"Black Hoof is Harrison's friend," was Tecumseh's terse response as he held out a hand, a silent and vaguely imperious demand for the letter.

Barron took the letter from beneath his buckskin shirt, opened it, and began to read.

William Henry Harrison, Governor of the Territory of Indiana, to Tecumseh, chief of the Indians residing at Prophet's Town, otherwise known as Tippecanoe . . .

"I will read it."

Barron handed him the letter. Tecumseh read:

It has come to my attention that you have exerted yourself to lead the Indians astray, and that they are ready to raise their tomahawks against their father. Notwithstanding this, their father is not angry, and he is ready to embrace all of his children who will repent and ask forgiveness ...

Tecumseh glanced at Barron. The tone of the letter infuriated him. But his brother, Chiksika, had taught him well, and Barron could not discern anything by his expression. Tecumseh continued with the letter.

The chain of friendship which joins the Indian and the white man can be mended. All depends on you. Before you lie two roads. One leads to peace, security, and happiness. It is a straight and open road. The other road is narrow and crooked and leads to ruin. Do not deceive yourself. All the tribes joined together could not resist the force of the Seventeen Fires. Your warriors are brave, but so are ours. Our soldiers number more than you can count, and our hunters are like the leaves of the forest.

The redcoats will not protect you. Remember what happened at Fort Miami? And do not wait for them to go to war with us. If they did, you would soon see our flag above all the forts in Canada. You say we have violated the treaties we made with your people. It is not so. We have purchased the land. You say we bought it from those who had no right to sell it. But the chiefs who signed the treaties claimed to represent their respective tribes, and said it was their land, and they accepted the price we offered in good faith.

If you have complaints you should bring them to me. I have the authority to restore any property which you can prove was stolen. But should you wish to take your claims to the Great White Father in Washington, that can be arranged. Everything will be prepared for your journey, and you have my assurances of safe passage.

I earnestly believe that any differences which may now exist between the red man and the white can be resolved to the satisfaction of all concerned, and I heartily entreat you to work toward that end, rather than for war, and trust that since you have the best interests of your people at heart, you will heed my words.

William Henry Harrison
Governor, Territory of Indiana

Tecumseh carefully folded the vellum and handed the letter back to Barron.

"Harrison should know that everything I do is done for the sake of my people," he said gravely. "I do not intend to make war. Nor will I debate the matter of the chiefs who signed the treaties which gave away our land, or whether they had the right to do so. The land was not theirs to sell. The Great Spirit gave the land to his red children, and put the whites on the other side of the Big Water. But the whites were not content with what the Great Spirit had given them, and now they are taking our land. The land does not belong to the chiefs. It belongs to all the people. Would you let your White Father sell your land out from under your feet? No, you would not permit that to happen. In the same way, a chief may not sell or give away what belongs to all the people."

"You say you do not intend war," said Barron. "Do you speak for all the Indians? For years we have had peace between our peoples. Of late, though, some warriors had gone on the warpath again. War councils are being held in many villages. Do you deny that this is so?"

"I do not deny that councils have met, but they are not for war. That is how we govern, by the council. I have no say over what warriors in other villages do. They are angry because the Long Knives trespass on the lands promised to them by the treaties. Does Harrison send the Long Knives to trespass? Does he condone what they do? No. Nor do I condone what a few angry warriors have done. But I do understand their frustration."

"You say you do not want war. The same cannot be said for your brother, The Prophet. Will your people listen to him in their frustration, and turn a deaf ear to your wisdom, Tecumseh?"

Tecumseh smiled. "*Mattah*. No. They will do what I tell them. Even though they are angry, and have every right to be. Wouldn't you be angry, if you were driven from your home, where there was *alwameke*—good soil—and told to go live on some other land—land that is *melcheasiske*, poor and rocky, where the game is scarce? The plows of your farmers dig up the bones of our ancestors. Yes, you would be angry, too, if this had happened to you.

"But I am pleased with the words Harrison has sent to me. I think I should go speak to him, face-to-face, and tell him that he has been listening too much to bad men, who lie about me and my intentions. In one moon I will come to Vincennes, and smoke the *calumet* with Harrison."

Their talk concluded, Barron did not linger in Prophet's Town, and Tecumseh did not invite him to stay.

On his way back to Vincennes, Barron gave much thought to what Tecumseh had said. He was an astute man, who knew about Indians and their ways. When he gave his report to Governor Harrison he offered a well-studied opinion.

Tecumseh was lying. And he was stalling for time. He did intend to wage war against the Shemanese.

Harrison nodded. He thought so, too. And he figured Tecumseh was waiting for war to break out between the United States and Great Britain. Tecumseh was lying. Harrison didn't hold it against him. He had lied, as well, in the letter he had written to the Shawnee chief. The British *would* fight the Americans. They would have no choice. Any day now Harrison expected to hear that his country had declared war on the British.

And there would be hell to pay on the frontier when that happened.

II

One moon later, Tecumseh came to Vincennes. He was accompanied by four hundred warriors, traveling down the Wabash from Prophet's Town in eighty canoes. The appearance of such a large force of Indians alarmed the garrison at Fort Knox. They reported to Governor Harrison that the redmen were painted as though for war, and armed to the teeth.

Vincennes had grown to a fairly large settlement by

frontier standards, and in addition to the several hundred soldiers in the fort, there were hundreds more civilians in the town, including a goodly number of hunters and trappers, and a well-drilled militia, to boot.

"He would bring ten times that many warriors if he planned to attack us," Harrison assured the worried officers from Fort Knox. "No, this is naked intimidation, gentlemen."

William Henry Harrison was a border captain in the best sense of the word. His bravery and unflappable calm in times of crisis was a comfort to his subordinates. A tall and fierce-looking warrior in his own right, he was a stern man, but fair, honest, and straigtforward in his dealings with others. He was also well-versed in the military art, and acquainted with the Indian. Like most good soldiers, he placed a high value on peace. A decent man, he respected the Indians, which was more than could be said for many of the town's residents. While his self-assurance and cool head served to ameliorate the anxieties of the officers, it failed to soothe the collective fevered brow of the citizens of Vincennes. As Tecumseh and his fierce entourage encamped a mile from town, Harrison weathered a gale of protest from the civilians, and realized that he was seated squarely on a powder keg armed with a short fuse. One small misunderstanding, one careless word, might lead to an explosion.

The governor invited Tecumseh to his estate, Grouseland. They could hold their council in the cool shade of his spacious porch. Tecumseh accepted the invitation. On the appointed day, Harrison was attended by several officers and a platoon of soldiers from Fort Knox, as well as a number of the town's leading citizens—including three judges who sat upon the territorial supreme court. As there was some question of land rights, Harrison thought it would be well that the judges were present. When Tecumseh arrived, with at least a hundred of his warriors, he stopped well shy of the house. The Indians were painted as though for war, their faces and cheeks and backs bearing designs in red, white, yellow, and blue. Harrison sent his amanuensis, Barron, out to find out what was wrong. Barron had a lengthy conversation with Tecumseh, then returned to the porch of the governor's stately two-story home to convey the gist of it to Harrison.

"He says he doesn't care to hold a council beneath a white man's roof," Barron reported.

"Where then?"

Barron pointed to a grove of trees an arrow's flight from the house.

Harrison sighed. "There are no chairs for our distinguished guests beneath those trees."

"Tecumseh says he would prefer to sit upon the breast of his mother, the Earth."

"So be it." Harrison ordered chairs, benches, and a table carried out into the grove. The governor took his place in a comfortable armchair behind the table, the officers and judges on either hand, and the soldiers subtly arranged to provide a uniformed barricade between the spectators from Vincennes and the Tippecanoe Indians, who all sat upon the grass, with the exception of Tecumseh, who stood before the table and Harrison.

This was the first time Harrison had seen Tecumseh, and he was impressed by the Shawnee chief's appearance. Tecumseh was taller than most Indians, a strikingly handsome man with clean strong features and a magnetic presence. He was clad in a fine doeskin hunting tunic and leggins, fringed and beaded. The warclub dangling from his belt of elk leather was an impressive weapon, noted the soldier in Harrison, and it was the only weapon Tecumseh carried.

Following Harrison's introduction of the officers and judges to Tecumseh, the Shawnee leader launched into a long speech.

He had come here, he said, to try to reason with Harrison, as in retrospect he had concluded the governor could not fully understand his position based on the words exchanged with Barron in Prophet's Town a month ago. He did not want war, but on the other hand he did not see how war could be avoided, unless the *Shemanese* changed their ways. The white man persisted in taking the land away from the Indians. They were never satisfied with what they had. They broke their own commandment by coveting what belonged to others. Did they expect the Indian to simply sit idly by while the white man robbed him blind?

If there was trouble between the red man and the white, the blame rested squarely on the shoulders of the latter, because the white man was greedy; he was always pushing, pushing, pushing the Indian over the brink of exasperation into the chasm of violent retribution.

By what right, he asked, did Harrison interfere in the affairs of the Indian? He, Tecumseh, was trying to unite the tribes only for the purpose of making them perceive, as he did, that the land was the common property of all—hence, it could not be sold by any one chief or even any one tribe without the permission of all Indians. Yet Harrison was doing everything he could to divide the tribes. His motive was obvious. By telling each tribe that it owned a particular tract of land it would be easier to take their property. He could pit one tribe against another by playing on the old inter-tribal rivalries, and in Tecumseh's opinion he was doing precisely that.

As Tecumseh went on, his speech took on the trappings of a diatribe. He became increasingly overbearing in his attitude, while the mood of the warriors with him became ever more surly. The governor, a perceptive man, realized that Tecumseh had not come to settle differences but rather to put on a show. What did he hope to accomplish by this performance? *A better question,* mused Harrison, *is how do I turn the tables on him?*

"In your letter to me," continued Tecumseh, "you said you had the power to restore our lands to us if we could prove that those who had sold the land to you did not have the authority to do so. We intend to prove it. I will call a great council. All the tribes will be represented there. Then we will decide if the chiefs who sold our land to you for a handful of gold or a crock of whiskey or a thin blanket had the right to do so. If it is determined that they had no right, they will be put to death."

Harrison felt a sudden chill. Could Tecumseh really bring this off? If so, he had awesome influence among the various tribes.

"The warriors have given me the power to do this thing," said Tecumseh, as though he could read Harrison's mind. "I am the chief of them all, above all other chiefs. The Great Spirit speaks through me, and all Indians heed my words."

A mutter of wary discontent rose from the citizens of Vincennes as Tecumseh sat cross-legged on the grass in front of the warriors, indicating that he was done.

Harrison's eyes had never strayed from him during his entire harangue. Now, his gaze still fixed impassively upon Tecumseh, Harrison rose from his chair to have his say. As he spoke, Barron translated the words into Shawnee.

"The Indians are not one people," he said, having decided to be as blunt as Tecumseh had been. "If they were, they would not have different languages. The Great Spirit would have given them one tongue. And the land is not the common property of all. It has never been so. The Shawnees once lived in the south. But then the Creeks drove them off their land, and the Shawnees came north, to take the land of the Miamis. For centuries tribes have been taking land away from one another. Yet, to hear Tecumseh tell it, the white man is to blame for hundreds of years of Indian greed. The white man did not invent the sin of coveting what belongs to another, despite what Tecumseh would have us all believe."

Harrison made an impatient gesture, as though casting aside as worthless Tecumseh's argument. "My red brothers should consider this. Is Tecumseh uniting the tribes because he is concerned for the welfare of all Indians? Or is he doing it to acquire power? Tecumseh is an extremely prideful man. We have a saying: Pride goes before the fall. I am afraid that when Tecumseh falls, as he inevitably will, he will take all my Indian children with him."

Tecumseh leapt to his feet. "We are not your children!" he shouted, his face a mask of burning hate. He shook his fist in Harrison's face. "You are not our father, but our enemy. And you are a liar!"

The governor did not flinch. Beside him, one of the army officers from Fort Knox put a hand on the butt of his pistol, but Harrison made a sharp gesture that stopped him cold. As soon as Tecumseh sprang to his feet the other warriors did too, brandishing tomahawks and warclubs. Many of the citizens of Vincennes had come armed, and now filled their hands with their heretofore concealed weapons. The soldiers held their rifles at the ready. For an instant all was pandemonium, and bloodshed seemed imminent. In the midst of it all Harrison was an island of dauntless calm. Tecumseh saw a faint, self-satisfied smile touch the corner of the governor's mouth, and he knew then that Harrison had got the best of him. Rarely did Tecumseh lose his temper. Rarely did he forget the lessons Chiksika had taught him and betray strong emotion. Again and again his brother had told him that to do so would give your adversary a weapon to use against you. Harrison had provoked him for no other reason than to see how much provocation he could endure before coming unraveled.

Finally Harrison raised outstretched arms, and the whites fell silent. So did the warriors behind Tecumseh. It was obvious to them that Harrison had something more to say, and whether they knew it or not, they were impressed by the way he was standing up to Tecumseh, face-to-face, without flinching. There was not one among them who was not afraid of Tecumseh, but Harrison had no fear, and that was something.

"In effect, you have called me a liar," said Harrison coldly, glaring at Tecumseh. "Therefore, I see no point in continuing this council. You and your people will be allowed to go in safety, since you are here under my protection. But you must leave immediately."

With this summary dismissal, by which he demonstrated his power over the fate of Tecumseh and his Indians, Harrison turned on his heel and strode back up toward Grouseland, leaving Tecumseh fuming impotently.

III

Returning with his warriors to their camp, Tecumseh realized that Harrison had stolen the show at the council in the oak grove. With this realization came new-found respect for the governor. He was a worthy opponent indeed.

The next morning, Tecumseh sent a messenger to Harrison, applying respectfully for the opportunity to explain yesterday's outburst. The governor consented. The meeting occurred in the same location as before, in the pleasing shade of the big trees. This time Tecumseh came with only a handful of warriors. He apologized for losing his temper, and hoped Harrison would understand that it was due to his strong feelings about the injustice done to his people. He had not, however, changed his mind about the ownership of the land. All of the Ohio country belonged to the Indians. And he did have the right to speak for the Wyandots, the Ottawas, the Winnebagos, the Mingos, as well as the Shawnees. He would have the chiefs of all the other tribes come and confirm this to Harrison.

"That won't be necessary," replied Harrison. "You are not a man to lie, Tecumseh. I will present your claims to the President. You can rely on me to do so faithfully. But I tell you now, the President will never accept the idea that the land belongs to all the tribes together. He will say the lands belonged to the tribes which sold them to us. The title now resides in us. We made a fair purchase. We continue to pay annuities. That is something for the tribes who follow you to think about. If they go to war against us they will no longer receive those annuities."

"They will no longer accept them anyway," said Tecumseh.

"We hold title to the land," repeated Harrison sternly, like a tutor trying to drill a lesson into the skull of a backward student. "And if need be we will defend it with the sword."

The second council ended in this way.

The following morning, as the Indians prepared to break camp and return to Tippecanoe, Harrison appeared quite unexpectedly in their midst. Some of the warriors were of a mind to strike him down, as bad feeling was running rampant among them, but Tecumseh would not abide any harm coming to the governor. He admired courage, even in an adversary. So he went out to meet Harrison, and even shook his proffered hand.

"I have come," said Harrison solemnly, "to ascertain whether your intentions remain as before."

"They have not changed. They never will."

"You still intend to kill the chiefs who signed the treaties?"

"It is not what *I* want, but what *they* want." Tecumseh made a sweeping gesture, indicating the gathering, glowering warriors.

"But they listen to you. If you said to them, these chiefs will not be put to death after all . . ."

Tecumseh shook his head, and tried patiently to explain, for he could tell that Harrison's overriding concern at this point was to prevent bloodshed.

"The reason they follow me is because what I say to them meets with their approval. If it did not, they would cease to listen."

"I see," said Harrison, surprised by this revelation on Tecumseh's part. He wondered if it was sincere, or just sly obfuscation, Tecumseh's attempt to avoid responsibility. If sincere, it made of Tecumseh an unprincipled demagogue.

"My people feel betrayed," continued the Shawnee. "They are unhappy, and they are angry. I do not want to make war against the Seventeen Fires. All I want is the land of the Ohio Fire. Then our people could live in peace."

"Were it mine, I would give it to you. But there are many of my people upon that land, and they will not go away."

"Now you know how my people feel." Tecumseh smiled. "Their chiefs took their land and gave it away."

Harrison wasn't interested in semantics. "You could not possibly win this war, Tecumseh. Not even if the British helped you."

"I know the *Englishmanake* does not care about my people. His only wish is to use us against you."

"It would be a rash act to take the warpath against us. You can bring many thousands against us, but no matter how many waves beat angrily against the rocks along the shore of the sea, the rocks remain unmoved. Not even all your warriors could succeed against the Long Knives of the Kentucky Fire alone, much less against the whole of the Seventeen Fires. They would rise up, as many as the blades of grass in this valley. And they will fight to the death for their homes and families."

"As we will fight, if necessary, for our lands. It is too bad that the homes and families of your warriors are on our land. Will you send a letter to the Great White Chief, as you said you would do?"

"I will. But I don't think he will accede to your demands."

"I hope he will have the good sense to do so. But I have my doubts, too. He lives far away, by the Big Water, and perhaps he does not care if blood is spilled here. He will sit in his big house and we will have to fight it out, you and I."

They parted company with another handshake, and both men knew that when the day of reckoning arrived—and it was fast approaching—each of them would be faced by an adversary greater than either had ever known before.

IV

When Tecumseh arrived back in Prophet's Town he was immediately accosted by his brother, Lalawethika, who insisted on knowing when he would give the word and unleash the warriors who were aching to drive the Long Knives back across the mountains and even into the Big Water. When Tecumseh replied that it was not yet time something snapped inside Lalawethika, and he began to rant. Had they not been in the privacy of the Prophet's *wegiwa*—had Lalawethika behaved this way in public—Tecumseh would have been angered. Instead, he listened stoically, watching his brother with pity and disgust making a sour blend in his belly, and wondering if The Prophet was more of a liability than an asset.

It seemed to Tecumseh that of late his brother was becoming more and more unstable. Sometimes he caught what he perceived to be madness—just a glimmer—in Lalawethika's eyes. It was the power. Power was a black corruption in his soul. The Shawnees—and other tribes, as well—feared The Prophet. At his whim men died at the stake. He could blacken the sun. He could cure people of a killing sickness. But he treated everyone with the high-handed contempt of a petty tyrant, too.

Still, Tecumseh decided he still needed his brother—or rather, his brother's prestige—so he patiently tried to placate Lalawethika.

"In another year it will be time," he said. "I must go north to Canada and speak to the *Englishmanake*. Then I must go south and prepare the Creeks and the Choctaws and the Chickasaws, for when we do strike we must strike all at once, all the tribes, in the north and in the south."

"The Kickapoos and the Potawatomies are with us," said The Prophet. "As are the Iowas, the Sioux, and the Sacs and Foxes under their war chief, Black Hawk. The Wyandots are with us, and the Mingos, Ottawas, and most of the Delawares. We should strike now, brother, while all these are with us. They will be enough to kill all the whites in Ohio and Kentucky."

Tecumseh shook his head, remembering what Harrison had said about the long hunters being as numerous as the blades of grass.

"No, it will not be enough. We need our southern brothers. And we needs guns and powder from the *Englishmanake*. We must make it so that the white man never dares cross the mountains again."

"There are troublemakers we must deal with. Keokuk, among the Sacs and Foxes, speaks for peace, and when he speaks he is heard. The same is true of

Quashquame, the Delaware. Given time, they will convince their people to turn their faces away from us."

"As long as Black Hawk lives you need not concern yourself about Keokuk."

"But what of Quashquame? He is a great warrior. The other Delawares listen to what he has to say."

"Yes, he speaks eloquently for one who can make no sound," conceded Tecumseh. "I will think about it, and give you my decision before I leave to go north."

Tecumseh sent a messenger to Matthew Elliott, an old Britisher who had once been an Indian agent for the Crown, and now served as liason between Canada's Governor-General in Quebec and the northern tribes. He was one of the few white men that the Indians trusted without reservation. Elliott had married a Shawnee woman, and had lived much of his life among the Indians. Now he resided in a nice home called The Point, a mile down the Detroit River from Amherstburg. Nearby lived Simon Girty. The renegade was getting on in years now, and had recently retired to a farm near Amherstburg. They said he drank too much. He rode into town every day to while away the hours in a tavern there, telling tall tales about his lurid exploits, and every night they had to put him on his favorite mare and turn the horse loose, secure in the knowledge that the horse would take Girty home through the woods, even if the renegade was unconscious in the saddle, as was often the case.

While he waited for word from Elliott, Tecumseh pondered the problem of Quashquame. The majority of the Delawares had been won over to Tecumseh's way of thinking, and would not listen any longer to those who still advocated peace, but there was something about Quashquame that earned him the respect even of those who did not agree with him. It did not matter to the Delawares that Quashquame had once lived among the *Shemanese,* and even fought the Shawnees on occasion, side-by-side with *Metequa*—Flintlock—the legendary Long Knife from Boonesboro. What puzzled Tecumseh most was the fact that Quashquame had every reason to hate the whites. His sister—his last remaining kin—had not too long ago been murdered by the *Shemanese.* Yet Quashquame still urged his people to live in peace with the whites. Naturally, then, the Delawares believed that Quashquame had swallowed his hate and spoke for peace because he had the best interests of the people at heart. So they listened when he talked his silent talk.

Lalawethika was right about one thing. Quashquame *was* dangerous to their plans. The Prophet had long ago wanted to have Quashquame put to death. Always before, Tecumseh had prevented his brother from taking such action, afraid that it would backfire on them, and turn the Delawares against them.

Then, while Tecumseh waited in Prophet's Town for a reply from Elliott, something happened that seemed to put Quashquame right into their hands.

A party of Indians, Kickapoo and Shawnee, had raided an isolated homestead near the Kaskaskia River, killing the farmer, his wife, and two older children, and taking a five-year-old boy captive.

These random acts of violence infuriated Tecumseh, for though taken separately they seemed of little consequence, together they not only antagonized the whites but by so doing jeopardized his plans. Over the years Tecumseh had watched the *Shemanese* being lulled into a false sense of security, as the peace made by the treaty at Fort Greenville seemed to hold. Recently, however, such incidents as this one on the Kaskaskia alarmed the whites. Tecumseh knew that realistically he could not prevent such raids from occurring; still, they frustrated him.

This time, none other than Quashquame got involved. The Delaware, incensed by the murders, informed the *Shemanese* where to find the little boy taken captive. Bluecoat soldiers marched into the village and rescued the boy. In the process they arrested five warriors suspected of having been on the raid. They hauled the five Indians back to Vincennes, where Harrison hanged them.

The summary execution of the five warriors was causing quite a stir among the tribes. For one thing, the spirit of a hanged man could not escape the body because of the rope around his neck; hence, the spirits of five Indians put to death by Harrison were doomed to forever inhabit the rotting corpses.

Privately, Tecumseh did not blame Harrison. He was quite willing to sacrifice the lives of five hotheads if their deaths would placate the whites. That was a small price to pay, in Tecumseh's opinion, to maintain peace on the frontier until the time was right for war. Nor could he blame Quashquame for taking a hand in the affair. Tecumseh deplored the making of war on women and children, too.

Yet it did not take Lalawethika to tell Tecumseh that by this act, noble or not, Quashquame had endangered himself. Though he had not been physically present when the bluecoat soldiers arrested the five Indians, or when the Indians had been hanged, he was responsible, and his interference on the side of the *Shemanese* shocked and angered many Indians.

"This is no coincidence," insisted Lalawethika. "The

Great Spirit has given Quashquame to us. Here is the solution to our problem."

A messenger arrived from Matthew Elliott, inviting Tecumseh to The Point, where a representative of His Majesty's Canadian army would meet and parley with him. Tecumseh made preparations to leave Tippecanoe. From The Point he would proceed on his tour of the southern tribes. He told Lalawethika that he would be gone for several months, and gave his brother a stern warning.

"There must be no trouble here while I am away. You must do nothing to antagonize the Long Knives. Keep everything well in hand until I return. I will hold you personally responsible, *neethetha*. We are too close to realizing our dreams, and I will tolerate no one who jeopardizes my plans."

The Prophet did not like being spoken to in such a manner, but he held his temper in check, and managed to appear compliant, even while seething within.

"What is your decision regarding Quashquame?" asked The Prophet.

Tecumseh drew a deep breath. He felt it necessary to placate Lalawethika. Perhaps by doing so he could keep his brother leashed long enough to bring his plans to fruition.

"Tell our friends among the Delawares that Quashquame must be judged before the council and executed. Will that satisfy you?"

Lalawethika smiled like a fox.

Tecumseh leaned forward with a sly smile of his own. "I know you well, my brother. You do not hate Quashquame because he is opposed to what we are trying to do. You hate him because of the influence he has over our Delaware allies. You are jealous of his power."

Lalawethika did not bother denying it. "And while you are away, what will I tell those who ask me when we will strike against the whites?"

"Why, *Moneto* has not given us the signs *I* predicted, has he? When the earth trembles and opens up to swallow entire lakes, and forests fall, and the rivers run backward, then it will be time. Isn't that what *I* told you?"

Lalawethika stared blankly at him. This was Tecumseh's way of reminding him that almost all of the prophecy which he, The Prophet, had used to so impress the people had actually come from Tecumseh himself. It was their secret that though he was called The Prophet, Tecumseh's gift of prophecy was much greater than his.

Tecumseh left the lodge. The people had gathered to see him off. He rode with only a handful of warriors, who were astride their painted ponies, waiting for him. Tecumseh leaped with pantherlike agility aboard his own pony. Extending an arm, he made a sweeping gesture and cried, "*Moneto* be with you always!"

Many returned the blessing, a swelling chorus of voices punctuated by the yips of warriors, a sound that followed Tecumseh and his bodyguards as they rode north along a woodland trail.

Lalawethika did not emerge from the *wegiwa* to see his brother off. He sat alone, brooding, listening with envy in his heart at the adulation of the people for Tecumseh.

V

On his way to The Point, Tecumseh took a detour, calling on the villages of other northern tribes, inviting a select group of warriors from each to accompany him. All to whom he extended this invitation accepted, as they deemed it a great honor. By the time he reached his destination he was accompanied by over a hundred warriors, the cream of not only the Shawnee crop, but also of the Delaware, the Potowatomie, the Ottawa and the Winnebago. Tecumseh went to these lengths in order to demonstrate to the British his influence over *all* Indians.

Matthew Elliott greeted him effusively. On his own initiative the old Indian agent had made arrangements to provide Tecumseh's fierce honor guard with a profusion of valuable gifts—blankets, gunpowder, knives, and hatchets. He informed Tecumseh that a high-ranking officer in the British Army was at Fort Malden, only a few miles away, and that this officer, a great warrior in his own right, wished to present His Majesty's respects to the great Tecumseh.

While his warriors encamped on the grounds, Tecumseh accepted the hospitality of Elliott in his home, a French-style house with long galleries running the length of the structure, front and back.

That evening, several redcoat soldiers rode up to the house. Elliott and Tecumseh were on the gallery when they arrived. Elliott was drinking buttered rum, served by a young Negro manservant. They greeted the colonel who came up the steps with spurs chiming on his knee-high cavalry boots and his saber rattling against his leg. His uniform was resplendent, including a single-breasted surtout closed at the waist, with buff facings, a crimson waist sash, and silver epaulettes. He removed the shako from his head and held it under one arm as he snapped to attention and gave a smart salute.

Elliott introduced the officer as Colonel Peter Mc-Leod. Prior to the officer's arrival, the Indian agent had told Tecumseh what he knew of the man. McLeod had served in Bonastre Tarleton's Tory Legion during the colonial insurrection, and fought in several major engagements, not to mention dozens of lesser skirmishes. At present he was seconded to the staff of Sir George Prevost, Governor-General of Canada.

Tecumseh did not need to be told that McLeod was indeed a warrior. Though getting on in years—the Shawnee guessed that the man had seen at least fifty summers—McLeod was still in fighting trim. His black hair was thick with gray, and his mustache was flecked with it. The mustache and the distinctive scar on his face gave him a piratical appearance, and his eye was keen and angry as a hawk's.

"I have been instructed," said McLeod, "to extend the warmest felicitations from His Majesty the King to the supreme chief of all the Northern Tribes."

Tecumseh was flattered in spite of himself. Through Colonel McLeod the British monarch was extending his greetings to him as an equal. No mention here of a great white father and his red children!

Elliott hosted both Tecumseh and McLeod at his dinner table. A sumptuous feast had been prepared, and the agent was somewhat disappointed when his guests dined sparingly. They had things of greater import than their appetites to attend to.

Tecumseh related his experiences at the council with William Henry Harrison at Vincennes, and assured the

Britishers that as soon as he paid a final visit to the southern tribes he would be ready to strike.

"I recommend patience," said McLeod. "His Majesty is not prepared to war with the Americans at this time. Perhaps you would do well to wait until he is."

"Are you authorized to speak for your king?" asked Tecumseh.

"I am, through the auspices of Sir George Prevost. I am to assure you that when the time is right we *will* fight the Americans—and this time we will prevail."

"When will this happen?"

"At the moment our army is engaged in a great war against the French across the ocean."

Tecumseh smiled. "I think the *Tota* and the *Englishmanake* will be fighting each other until the end of the world."

"Our triumph is inevitable. Then we will unleash our full might against these insolent, upstart Americans. Once we have regained control of North America, we will guarantee the return of your ancestral lands to your people."

Tecumseh concealed his skepticism. He might have pointed out that even as British subjects the American colonies had dispossessed all the eastern tribes, pushing the remnants across the mountains. The Delawares were a case in point. Yet he held his tongue, betraying nothing of his true feelings.

"What if the Americans declare war on your king before he is ready to fight?" he asked McLeod.

"They would regret it."

Their dinner over, Elliott called for the table to be cleared, and requested cognac and cigars. McLeod watched the Indian agent's other house servant—a young half-breed woman, pretty in a dark and rather sullen way—with the eye of a connoisseur who drank deeply from many human vessels, then left them drained by the wayside.

"We do not need your help to take back what belongs to us," remarked Tecumseh. "So we do not need to wait for your king to decide to make war on the Americans."

McLeod was up from the table, over at the tall windows that were opened to the gallery and the night and the sounds from the Indian encampment, which was marked by the flicker of yellow tongues of flame, cookfires beneath the tall conifers.

"I know you thirst for revenge," said McLeod. "Yes, I know exactly how you feel."

"How can you know?"

"The same people who took your land from you also took mine. I was a loyal subject to the Crown even while my neighbors indulged their traitorous appetites. I had a fine home, good land, excellent horses, a loving wife. They weren't satisfied until my home lay in ruins, and the ravaged body of my murdered wife was buried beneath the ashes. I despise the United States. I cannot abide the greed and arrogance of its rabble citizenry. They sing their own praises, don't they? They claim their republic is the greatest in the world, and destined by God to be so. But it is in truth a country of thieves and traitors."

Tecumseh and Elliott did not respond. The Indian agent was stunned by the virulence running like a powerful undertow beneath the surface of McLeod's bitter discourse, so much so that he forgot momentarily about his cognac, poised halfway to his lips.

"You say you do not need us," said McLeod, turning from his bleak perusal of the night. "Well and good.

Nonetheless, we insist on helping our Indian friends. A pack train, laden with blankets, powder, food, and medicine will arrive in Tippecanoe within two months' time." He read Tecumseh's expression. "No strings attached."

"We are grateful to our English brothers," said Tecumseh. "I will send word to Lalawethika."

"How is your brother faring?" asked Elliott, and there was more to the inquiry than merely polite interest. Tecumseh sensed this immediately. Word of The Prophet's instability had reached this far, then. Even here his brother was a source of embarrassment.

"He is well," replied Tecumseh, but a glance at the Indian agent's white-bearded countenance warned him that this response was insufficient. Trusting Elliott, Tecumseh opened up. "But I am worried."

Elliott nodded sympathetically.

"I fear Harrison will do something to provoke him," admitted Tecumseh. "Harrison is suspicious, and clever." He paused, recalling how Harrison had gotten the best of him at the Grouseland council two moons ago. "I recently had a dream, that an army of American *shemaganas* marched on Tippecanoe, and Prophet's Town was destroyed."

Elliott glanced with cocked eyebrow at McLeod. He knew of Tecumseh's reputed powers of prophecy. Was this a manifestation of that gift?

"If Lalawethika is clever, he will not play Harrison's game," said Tecumseh, "but will turn the other cheek. If he does not, Harrison will have the excuse he seeks to move against us before I am ready. Then all my labors will be for nothing."

"If you cannot rely on a subordinate, be rid of him," said McLeod gruffly.

"The Prophet is his brother, Colonel," reminded Elliott, with mild reproof.

"Makes no difference. The stakes are too high."

Burdened by a premonition of disaster, Tecumseh looked thoughtfully at the fierce British warrior, and knew that he was right.

VI

Having spent several days at The Point, Tecumseh made ready to depart on a long journey to the south, expecting to be away for at least several months. Many of the warriors who had accompanied him to The Point were told to go home, for he wished to travel with a small and inconspicuous entourage—a dozen hand-picked Shawnee men.

He took with him several cedar wood slats, carefully wrapped in sheaths of leather and fur. Each slat was thirteen inches long and a half-inch at the top. Each slat was carved on one side with symbols.

Tecumseh had provided his brother, Lalawethika, with the basic design for these "sacred slabs" two years earlier, instructing The Prophet to make fifty cedar wood replicas. Lalawethika was to tell the people that he had been guided by the Great Spirit in the making of these slabs. The whites would be told that these "heavenly sticks" were religious artifacts designed to show the Indian the way to the next life. The symbols from bottom to top, read *family,* three horizontal bars, *earth,* a circle bisected by a horizontal bar, *water, lightning, trees, the four corners of earth* (a symbol which bore a striking resemblance to the cross of St. James), *corn, all animals and plant life, the sun, the blue sky,* and finally *heaven,* the topmost symbol on the slab. The true meaning of all these symbols had to be understood by the people before they could reach heaven—this, at least, was what the whites were led to believe.

In fact, the symbols had an entirely different meaning. *Family* was really *all Indians. Earth* was *both sides of the Great River*—the Mississippi. The single horizontal mark ostensibly symbolizing *water* in truth meant *a straight direction,* and the next symbol, the wavy line for *lightning* was to be read with the *speed of lightning. Trees* meant *weapons,* and the next several symbols—*corn, all animals and plant life*—really meant to *put aside the hunting of game and the harvesting of the corn.* The mark of the sun also symbolized unification, while the *blue sky* symbol actually meant *the Great Sign,* the trembling earth that had been foretold. The symbol for *heaven* was in truth that of *the Place of the White Man.*

Deciphered in its true meaning, then, the symbols on the sacred slabs read: *All Indians on both sides of the Great River are to come directly with lightning speed and with all their weapons, leaving the hunting of game and the harvesting of the corn, when the great sign reveals that it is time for all tribes to move against the place of the white man.*

Tecumseh intended to deliver several of these cedar slabs to the southern tribes, along with bundles of special sticks stained red with vermilion. Each stick was fifteen inches in length and a quarter-inch thick, with twenty-one sticks to a bundle. It would be The Prophet's responsibility to make sure the rest of the sacred slabs and red sticks were delivered during the Hunger

Moon to all the major tribes of the north and north-west.

Each red stick represented one month, or moon. Beginning with the Wind Moon, each chief entrusted with the red sticks was to discard one of them upon the rising of each full moon. When only one stick remained they were to begin watching the sky every night for Tecumseh's personal sign, the *Panther Passing Across*. When they observed this sign they were to cut the last stick into thirty pieces. Every night thereafter one of these pieces would be burned. When the final piece was burned the great sign would come. At that moment all the tribes were to take up arms and rendezvous—fifty thousand warriors, by Tecumseh's calculations, by far the largest army every to take the field in North America.

VII

Traveling south from The Point, Tecumseh and his Shawnee bodyguards crossed the *Spay-lay-wi-theepi* near its juncture with the Wabash, slipped through Kentucky and Tennessee without incident, and crossed the Tennessee River at Colbert's Ferry. His first stop was the Chickasaws.

As a whole, the Chickasaws were impressed by Tecumseh's charisma and eloquence. Even so, he could not cajole a commitment out of them. There were some, like the Colbert brothers, who prospered by their association with the whites, and were reluctant to take up arms against them. Chickasaws like George Colbert, who owned the ferry, and his brother, who operated a nearby inn on the Natchez Trace, lived and dressed and acted more like white men than Indians, and Tecumseh was contemptuous of them, yet careful not to let his true feelings show.

The Chickasaws provided him with an escort as he proceeded in a southwesterly direction to arrive at last at Red Pepper's Town, one of the principal villages of the Choctaw Indians. Red Pepper treated Tecumseh with cordiality, but directed him to a younger chief, a war mingo by the name of Mashulatubbe. He also plied Tecumseh's party with food and liquor. None of the Shawnees touched the whiskey, but the Chickasaws who were with them suffered no such inhibitions when it came to imbibing the white man's poison. Imbibe they did, becoming drunk and surly in short order, and picked a fight with their age-old enemies, the Choctaws. Tecumseh intervened, sent the Chickasaws packing, and used the incident as just one more example of the evil that would befall the Indian if he adopted the ways of the *Shemanese*.

Mashulatubbe was enthusiastic about a great Indian confederation, and arranged for a council of all the Choctaw mingos. Hundreds of warriors gathered. They were impressed by the fierce appearance of the Shawnees. All but Tecumseh were decked out for war. Their heads were shaved but for a band of hair stiffened with clay, running from forehead to the nape of the neck. Their faces were painted with red crescents beneath the eyes, and spots on their temples, and red circles on their chests. Tecumseh was clad in a plain buckskin tunic and leggins. His hair hung long and loose to his shoulders. A single white feather, tipped with scarlet, dangled from a scarlet flannel headband.

He warned the Choctaws that they had not yet been victimized by the whites as other tribes had been, but their time would come, and soon, because the land of the Choctaws was rich and pleasing to the eye, and the whites would covet it. Did the Choctaws intend to wait until that happened and then try to stand alone against the white interlopers? Their warriors were brave, but too few in number. The same fate that had befallen other tribes would be theirs as well.

No, if the Choctaws were wise, they would join the great Indian confederation that he was trying to forge. If they did not fight the whites now, they would either be destroyed or made slaves. Had they not seen how the whites made the black man and woman work in his fields? The Choctaws might be so enslaved, to toil on land that had once belonged to them, but which had been confiscated by the white man.

He saw a familiar pattern in the response of the Choctaws. Most of the younger men were inspired by his fiery rhetoric, his appeal to honor, courage, and glory. But the older chiefs were not so susceptible. The Choctaws had always been at peace with the white man, they replied. Tecumseh was just a troublemaker. Why should they fight for the Shawnees? If the Shawnees had lost their land, what concern was that of the Choctaws? If the Choctaws were foolish enough to fight the whites for the sake of the Shawnees, then most certainly the whites would take their land away from them.

One mingo, Pushmataha, went so far as to accuse Tecumseh of being a power-mad tyrant who had subjugated the Shawnees with his bogus magic and facile tongue. He would not rule the Choctaws as he did his own people, declared the truculent Pushmataha, preying on the superstitions of some while intimidating others. Was it not true that all those who dared speak out against Tecumseh were burned at the stake, or had their skulls crushed with the warclub? Tecumseh wanted to rule all the Indians. But if any Choctaws took up their weapons and went off to fight the Shawnee's war, they would be condemned as traitors. The other older chiefs concurred. Even the young firebrand, Mashulatubbe, was thoroughly cowed.

Dismayed, Tecumseh moved on, having failed now to win over the Chickasaws and Choctaws. Why, he wondered, now that he was so close to realizing his dream, after so many years of diligent labor toward that end, did it seem that everything was disintegrating before his eyes? His brother was acting in an erratic and untrustworthy fashion, alienating his own people. Harrison had got the best of him at the Grouseland council. The British were advising caution after thirty years of inciting them to war against the Americans. And now his words had fallen upon deaf ears among two of the most powerful of the southern tribes! What next?

To the villages of the Muscogees, the Alabamas, the Yazoos, and the Natchez Indians Tecumseh traveled, and to those of the Seminoles, the Apalachicolas, and the Creeks. Among the latter he made headway, despite the hostility and opposition of the tribe's established leaders, who did not cotton to the idea of this Shawnee coming in to usurp their power. He pulled out all the stops in his speeches. Never had his oratory been so inspired. Finally he felt as though he had won over the Creeks. He gave them one of the secret slabs and a bundle of red sticks and turned for Cherokee country.

Of all the southern tribes he expected the Cherokees to be most open to him and his ideas, yet to his surprise and chagrin he found that many stood adamantly against him. He was met by a party of warriors sent by the principal chief of the tribe, warning him that he was not to enter his village. The Cherokees were living and prospering at peace with the whites. Like the Chickasaws, they had begun to dress and act and even think like the whites. Many were farmers now. Some even owned slaves and raised money crops, just like the white man. They had taken the white man's religion. No, they did not want the Shawnee troublemaker in his midst, and if he entered the village of the principal chief he would be slain.

Tecumseh was enraged. Had the Cherokees forgotten that not too many years ago he and his brother Chiksika had fought side by side with their Cherokee friends against the whites? Chiksika had even given his life for their cause. Now it seemed his brother had made the ultimate sacrifice for nothing. Was the Cherokee so foolish as to think that just because they had taken up the white man's ways that the white man would leave them alone and let them keep their land? Yes, was the reply. The whites had promised as much. Tecumseh was bitter, derisive. The promises of the *Shemanese* were worthless. Indeed, the Cherokees had become fools. One day they would regret the faith they had put in these empty promises. One day the whites would come and force them off their land. The Cherokees would be herded west, like cattle, onto *melcheasiske,* poor land where their crops would wither and their livestock would perish for lack of good graze. He, Tecumseh, had come looking for true warriors with strong hearts to enlist in a just and noble cause. Clearly there were no such warriors among the Cherokees, not anymore.

Disgruntled, Tecumseh turned west, crossing the

Great Mother of All Rivers, and dwelling for a time among the Osage Indians. The Osage were good hosts, and liked his words, but too many of the tribes of the Northwest had been their enemies for too many generations for them to consider joining an Indian confederacy.

The early snows lay upon the ground when finally Tecumseh headed north, for home. His heart was heavy. His mission among the southern tribes had been a dismal failure. The Creeks would fight, and the Seminoles, and a few of the lesser tribes, but the Cherokees and the Chickasaws had adopted the ways of the white men and become corrupted, while the Choctaws were complacent, having thus far been overlooked by the avaricious whites. Only a few years ago the Cherokees had been the bitter enemies of the white men of the Tennessee Fire. What had happened to them was a demonstration of the insidious allure of the white man's way.

Still, he could count on twenty northern and northwestern tribes to stand with them. That would be enough, he told himself. He would have to make certain that nothing happened to jeopardize the confederation as it stood now.

On the road home, he was met by disastrous news The Prophet had been lured into battle by the wily William Henry Harrison, meeting with a crushing defeat in what would become known as the Battle of Tippecanoe.

CHAPTER EIGHT

Jonathan

October 23, 1811

Henry Clay, Esq.

Dear Henry,

You are probably already cognizant of the fact that I have resigned as a member of the United States House of Representatives. Due to your unflagging support in my rather short-lived political career, as well as your unconditional friendship, I feel as though I owe you an explanation. Rest assured this decision has nothing whatsoever to do with the affair of April last, when my duty as a husband and a gentleman required that I take the life of Stephen Cooper of Hunter's Creek. The coroner's jury completely exonerated me, as good and decent men were bound to do, and I have been privately congratulated by numerous people. While the particulars of the affair convinced the district attorney that Cooper and I had not engaged in a duel, and so precluded charges against me in that regard—which he, by the way, was not personally inclined to bring—I remain firm in the conviction that a duel of honor is precisely what occurred, albeit one attended by certain peculiarities, and apart from the fact that Cooper was by no means a gentleman, and a man who had not the vaguest concept of honor.

No, I resigned because I feel the time has arrived for me to fight in the defense of my country. As you may know, Governor Harrison of the Indiana Territory has issued an urgent call for volunteers to march against the Indians at Tippecanoe. There is no shortage of Kentuckians eager to respond. Harrison is well known among us as a hero of Fallen Timbers, Mad Anthony Wayne's most reliable lieutenant, and is highly respected in all quarters. In recent months, there have been several incidents of Indian atrocity, and it has come to the point where all of Kentucky, and Ohio to boot, is in a state of continual alarm. It seems that these rumors of a great Indian confederacy may have substance, after all. Only a few months ago I was telling my father-in-law, Nathaniel Jones, that there was nothing to worry about in that regard. Evidently I was wrong.

From the reports which I am privy to, the Indians congregated at the village of Tippecanoe, the troublemakers, have waylaid a shipment of salt which the United States government was transporting to other tribes located further west, as part of the annuities agreed upon by all signatories to one of the host of treaties we have executed with the various tribes. This has caused Governor Harrison no end of trouble, as the intended recipients of the salt shipment are up in arms over the failure of the government to deliver upon its promises. Also, five weeks ago, seven Indians—two Shawnees, two Kickapoos, a Miami, a Wyandot, and a Potowatomie, stole seven horses from settlers along the Wabash River. This was, it is said, hailed by the one they call The Prophet, who is by all accounts an egotistical madman of the first order, as a demonstration of the fact that Indians from different tribes can work together in a common cause, and when you think about it, that *is* rather alarming. From the beginning we have managed to use to good advantage the old hostilities existing between various tribes, playing one against another. Had the situation been different, had all the tribes been united in opposition against us, we may never have succeeded in establishing a foothold west of the Appalachians, or, for that matter, even survived in the early days of the colonies.

A party of settlers followed the horse thieves back to Tippecanoe and demanded the return of the stolen livestock. The Prophet surrendered the horses, but the next night fifty of his warriors surprised the settlers and absconded with the seven horses a second time, and took the fifteen the settlers had been riding for good measure. The settlers were warned that if they set foot in Tippecanoe again they would be killed, and apparently they took the warning to heart, for they walked directly to Vincennes and lodged a complaint with Governor Harrison.

In short order the governor had an army of almost a thousand men on the march. Upon hearing that The Prophet had several thousand warriors at Tippecanoe, Harrison halted to build a fort halfway to his destination and sent word into Kentucky that he needed volunteers. When this news reached Madison County a meeting was immediately convened, and the militia resolved to a man to take up arms and join Harrison. Due to my prior service in the navy, I have been what one might call an honorary member of the militia since establishing my residence in that county. I say honorary because my attendance has been sporadic, to say the least, with my other responsibilities taking precedence. Precisely for that reason, I offered to enlist as a private, and would have been perfectly happy to have done so, except that the others insisted that I not only remain an officer but accept promotion to captain of the company, as Mr. Josiah Noles, the esteemed gentleman who held that rank, was incapacitated by gout, and could not so much as raise himself from his bed, much less lead the cream of Madison County manhood into battle. I reluctantly accepted. In truth, Henry, I would have preferred to forgo the responsibility, but suppose it just as well, since, having the use of only one arm, I am better suited to wielding a sword than firing a musket.

This company of townsmen and farmers have for the most part applied themselves diligently to their training, and I would put them up against an equal number of regular soldiers any day. Motivated as they are by a desire to defend their homes and families against the threat posed by the hostile Indians of Tippecanoe, they will, I am confident, acquit themselves admirably.

Today we arrived at Fort Harrison, and I understand that in a few days we will march against Tippecanoe. I look forward to action, I must confess. I never realized how much I missed it. To be honest, I am happier now than I have been in some time. Things have not been the same at Elm Tree since the tragedy. Rebecca has remained aloof from me. She refuses to talk to me about what is bothering her, but I have a feeling she blames me for what happened. I am haunted by guilt. I sometimes wonder if the course I took was the proper one. As much as I miss my dear wife, it is in a way a relief to be far from Elm Tree, far from the unbearable silence. If only I could escape the guilt.

In strictest confidence, I must confide something else to you. On several occasions the widow of Stephen Cooper has sent me a letter, and twice even visited my house to inquire after my welfare. Upon my word, my friend, I believe the woman is grateful to me for killing her husband! She has confessed that while he lived she was in constant fear and torment. He was indifferent to her for the most part, but she told me that she came to prefer his ambivalence, for on the occasions when he *did* pay attention to her it was attention of the most cruel, even sadistic, nature. Although her attentions strike me as odd, I am always polite to her, even though the way she looks at me sometimes, with her velvet glances, makes me extremely uncomfortable. I feel compassion for her. She is a delicate, attractive, and immensely kind person. Perhaps you know her family. Her father is Daniel Vickers, a man of considerable means. I really did not know how to deal with the situation, which is yet another reason why I am much relieved to be embarked on this adventure.

It is growing late, and the candle is guttering out, so I will close, with best regards.

Your Obdt. Servant,

Jonathan

Washington
November 16, 1811

Dr Jonathan,

Hoping this letter catches up with you, I want to extend my deepest sympathy regarding your wife's condition. Although I have not had the pleasure of making her acquaintance, from everything you have told me about her I feel as though I know her quite well, and my heart is penetrated with grief by this sad misfortune. The strain which the events described in your letter have placed upon your marriage will be, I am confident, of short duration. In time your wife will realize that you are not to blame for the tragedy which has struck Elm Tree. There was no other recourse open to you, my good friend. Honor required the action which you took. A gentleman could not have done otherwise. Honor aside, this man Stephen Cooper clearly posed a most grievous threat to the security and happiness of your family, and you did your duty by dispatching the scoundrel to Hell.

I am indeed acquainted with Daniel Vickers, and if memory serves me, I met his lovely daughter Emily in Nashville a few years ago on the occasion of a horse race. The situation as you describe it to me, if your suspicions are correct, is quite extraordinary. A recent widow who would become infatuated with the man who has killed her husband exceeds my experience. If must be, as you say, that Stephen Cooper was perfectly malicious in his treatment of her, and she perceives you to be her savior. The only advice which I can give you is to steer well clear of the young woman. Do not allow your compassion for her plight to blind you, or lead you astray down a path which can only result in further misfortune. You have a wife and a son and your good name to protect. There is no limit to what a young man with your intelligence and daring and personality can accomplish in his career. But the merest hint of impropriety could render grave damage.

As for your decision to resign your position as the representative of the good people of Madison County, and go off to fight the Indians with Governor Harrison, I commend you. I only hope that you were not motivated by depression over the state of affairs at home, and of the heart, to place yourself in harm's way. If, instead, as I believe is the case, you are motivated by patriotism, then I wish you all the best. As for the Indians, I regret that they have fallen prey to charismatic demagogues and hate

mongers. I had hoped that the peace we had secured after
Fallen Timbers would endure, for the sake of white man
and red alike.

The war preparations are advancing with the support of
a majority. The spirit you witnessed in their favor while
you were here is not at all diminished. Our greatest
difficulty is revenue. War is an expensive undertaking. I
do not see how we can dispense with internal taxes.
Rumors are afloat that the Orders in Council will be
repealed, but I do not think we ought to pay that any
attention. It is entirely too late for that.

There is yet a difference of opinion whether the
additional military force proposed to be raised ought to
be 15,000 or 25,000 men. I fear 15,000 is too small a
number for war. Experience in military affairs has shown
that when a given number of men is authorized to be
raised you must, in counting upon the effective men it
would produce, deduct one-fourth for desertion, sickness
and other incidents to which raw troops are peculiarly
exposed. In measures relating to war it is wisest, if you
must err, to err on the side of the largest force. The
Secretary of War has stated that 12,600 men are necessary
for manning our coastal fortifications. We are told that
there are seven or eight thousand regular troops in
Canada, the whole of that force concentrated in Quebec,
and would you attempt that almost impregnable fortress
with less than double the force of the besieged?

As for volunteer militia, gentlemen who calculate upon
them as a substitute for regulars ought not to deceive
themselves. That is not meant as denigration of such fine
patriots as those in the company of militia which you
command, but while such men are admirably suited to
field operations, they are suspect when it comes to a
siege, or the garrisoning of forts. Then, too, there are

questions raised considering militia for foreign conquest. One of our goals in this war is to remove forever the threat of the British in Canada, a sword which has been hovering above our heads for many a year. The taking of Canada, therefore, must, it seems to me, be one of our principal military objectives. Some gentlemen say that the government has not the power to send militia beyond the boundary of the republic onto foreign soil, because the Constitution defines the purpose for which alone they shall be used, viz. "to suppress insurrections, execute the laws and repel invasions."

Gentlemen ask, will you carry the militia out of the U. States, for the purpose of conquest? That is not the purpose for which this volunteer force is wanted. They are wanted in a war of defense. While it may be argued, and I think justifiably so, that this war is waged in defense of our honor and sovereignty, the nature of things will require us to be on the aggressive, and drive the British out of Canada. There may be no other way of operating upon our enemy, but by taking possession of her provinces which adjoin us. The commander in the field who attempts to use militia for that purpose may find his troops refusing to set foot across the border. Your men, Jonathan, are proper militia, leaving their plows and shops and taking up arms in defense of their homes against the hostile Tippecanoe Indians. But would they march on Canada? I have my doubts on that score.

I have no wish to dwell upon the catalogue of injuries we have suffered at England's hands. You know them as well as I. A litany of woe indeed. Not content with seizing all our property which falls within her rapacious grasp, the personal rights of our countrymen—rights which forever ought to be sacred—are trampled upon and violated. The Orders in Council were pretended to have been reluctantly adopted as a measure of retaliation aimed at the French. Yet the French decrees, their alleged basis, are revoked, and now England resorts to the expedient of denying the fact of their revocation! England is said to be fighting for the world against Napoleon, and shall we, it is asked, attempt to weaken her exertions? If indeed the aim of the French Emperor be universal dominion, what a noble cause is presented to British valor. But how is her philanthropic purpose to be achieved? By scrupulous observance of the rights of others and by abstaining from self-aggrandizement, I should think. Then would she command the sympathies of the world. What are we required to do in her behalf? Bear the actual cuffs of her arrogance, that we may escape a chimerical French subjugation? We are invited to drink the potion of British poison that we may avoid the imagined imperial dose offered by Napoleon! We are called upon to submit to debasement, dishonor and disgrace—to bow our necks to royal insolence.

The real cause of British aggression against us is not to distress an enemy—France—but destroy a rival—us. A comparative view of our commerce with England and the continent will demonstrate the accuracy of this remark. Prior to the embargo, the balance of trade between this country and England was between eleven and fifteen millions of dollars in favor of England. We exported to her what she wanted most—provisions and raw materials—and received in return what she was most desirous to sell, nearly fifty millions of dollars of her manufactures. Our exports to France, Holland, Spain and Italy amounted to about 12 millions prior to the embargo. It is apparent that this trade with France, the balance of which was in favor of the U. States, was not of vital consequence to the French. Would England, then, solely to deprive her adversary of this commerce, relinquish her own valuable trade with us? No, sir, you must look for an explanation of her conduct in the jealousies of a rival. She sickens at our prosperity and beholds in our growth—our sails spread on every ocean—the foundations of a power which, at no very distant day, is to make her tremble for naval superiority.

I am fully persuaded now that war is the only alternative left to us by which the injustice of one of the powers may be remedied, and that the support and confidence of the people will remain undiminished. I, for one, am prepared to march on in the road of my duty, at all hazards, and urge all of my colleagues to do the same. Should we pusillanimously cling to our seats here, rather than boldly vindicate the rights of this glorious republic? While such heroic Americans as you, my dear Jonathan, and your gallant associates, exposed to all the perils of treacherous savage warfare, are sacrificing themselves for the sake of their country, shall we shrink from our duty?

Yrs Sincerely,

H. Clay

December 18, 1811

Henry Clay, Esq.

Dear Henry,

The battle has been fought, and a great victory won.

We left Fort Harrison on October 28th. The weather was good for so late in the year. We marched north towards Tippecanoe, which is located on the Wabash River approximately one hundred and seventy miles from Vincennes, as the crow flies. The governor wisely chose to move along the western bank, as the other side of the river is covered by a thick forest, where our scouts reported seeing small parties of Indians. It was ground conducive to ambush.

On November 5th we were within ten miles of Tippecanoe. Our scouts were instructed to invite the Indians they met to come in and submit in order to avoid needless bloodshed, but none availed themselves of the offer. The reports we received were that Tecumseh was absent from the village, and that instead of several thousand warriors, we faced less than a thousand. The inhabitants of the village were not only Shawnees, but of a dozen other tribes, and apparently many of the men were away visiting their home villages during Tecumseh's absence. I was told The Prophet had assured those who remained that he had received a vision from the Great Spirit, and this entity revealed to him that the bullets of the white man would pass harmlessly through their bodies in the battle to come. I feared they were in for a great shock.

The next day we camped a half mile from Tippecanoe. We learned from several prisoners taken during the battle that The Prophet had called a war council that night. He planned to send envoys to Harrison the following morning. They were to agree to submit without a fight. Then, while two returned to Tippecanoe, where The Prophet and his warriors would be waiting to launch the attack, the other two would remain in our camp, as close to Harrison as possible, and when the battle commenced, these two assassins would draw their tomahawks and fall upon the governor.

The night was overcast, with a miserably cold drizzle, which made our bivouac one of utter misery, and I was not the only one who found it impossible to get any sleep. As it turned out, that was just as well, because in the early morning hours the Indians began to creep through the woods towards our camp. The Prophet had changed his mind, and decided to attack under cover of night. They were spotted by one of our pickets. The shooting was sporadic at first, then became a crashing roar. Our pickets gave way. For one harrowing moment confusion reigned in our camp. Then we rallied, and for two long hours, we waged a battle in close combat, in darkness so complete one could scarcely see an arm's reach away, and punctuated by thousands of muzzle flashes, the endless beat of the Indian drums, and their blood-chilling war cries. We fought hand-to-hand, and it was nerve-wracking, to say the least, as you would not see one of the savages until he exploded out of the darkness and was upon you.

The Prophet stood above the fray, on a rocky rise from whence he could observe the entire field of battle. When his warriors realized that our bullets *did* have their usual effect upon flesh and bone, they began to falter, but The Prophet sent runners down to encourage them, and order them to rush straight into our barrels, for only by demonstrating their faith in the Great Spirit would they earn the right to his protection.

My company valiantly held its ground throughout the fight, and when the morning finally dawned the woods in front of our line were seen to be fairly littered with dead and wounded Indians. The drums fell silent, and the enemy withdrew. As they passed through their village they gathered up their families and a few belongings and continued on their way. We did not give chase, but rather strengthened our lines and buried our dead, sixty-two in number, with twice as many wounded. This number included four of my own company slain, and nine wounded. We were in the thick of the fight. Oddly enough, I did not receive so much as a scratch, although a bullet from an Indian musket passed through my sleeve. We found about fifty dead Indians, but believe their losses considerably greater, and that they had carried many of their dead and dying from the field. Once certain that their withdrawal was not trickery, we advanced into Tippecanoe and put the town to the torch, including about five thousand bushels of corn and beans, stored for the coming winter.

From prisoners we heard that the Tippecanoe Indians had scattered to rejoin their respective tribes. This information, which I am inclined to think is accurate, vouches for the success of our expedition. The Battle of Tippecanoe has crushed the Indian confederation. I suspect that Governor Harrison was looking for an excuse to justify a full-scale expedition for just that purpose, and used the theft of the salt shipment, and the incident involving the horses of the Wabash settlers, as that justification. Let me say that the governor was in the thick of the fighting, and seemed to be everywhere at once, encouraging his men with cool ardor under fire. A lesser man might have been unnerved by the attack in the hours before dawn, and called a retreat, or at worst led the rout, as that fellow Harmer did some years ago. Not William Henry Harrison. He has what I have heard referred to as "four o'clock in the morning courage."

The battle won, our job well done, we will return to Fort Harrison and, if all goes well, make our way back to Kentucky shortly thereafter. I must admit I dread going home much more than I did entering into battle. I dread it because I feel certain Rebecca will greet me with a cold and unforgiving shoulder, while Emily Cooper will welcome me back in the fashion of a wife and lover. What a twisted and sublimely ridiculous affair! Did I mention that a letter from her has caught up with me, in which she fretted about the danger I was in—yet, not a word from Rebecca. Ah, for more battles to fight. Perhaps soon.

I am posting this letter to Ashland, on the assumption that Congress is adjourned by now for the Christmas season, and that if you are not yet in Lexington you soon will be.

Yr. Obdt. Servant,

Jonathan

January 22, 1812

Dr Jonathan,

If it is a fight you want then I believe you will have it.

The measures of our government are taking on a decisive character, or rather their final cast. With England all hope of an honorable accommodation is at an end. Where is the motive for longer delay? The final step ought to be taken, and that step is WAR. By what course we have reached the present state is not now a question for freemen and patriots to discuss. It exists, and it is only by open and manly war that we can get through it with honor and advantage to the country. The wrongs we have suffered have been great; our cause is a just one by any standard, and if we are decided and firm, success is inevitable.

Let war therefore be forthwith proclaimed against England. Any further discussion, any new attempt at negotiation, would be as fruitless as it would be dishonorable. But it is said that we are not prepared for war, and ought therefore not to declare it. This is an idle objection which can have weight with the timid only. Our preparations are adequate to every essential object. From what quarter will danger assail us? From England, and by invasion? The idea is too absurd to merit a moment's consideration. Where are her troops? The war on the Spanish peninsula requires strong armies to support it. She maintains an army in Sicily, another in India, and a strong force in Ireland, and along her own coast, and in the West Indies. Where will she find the men to send against us? On the other hand, she has every reason to apprehend an invasion by us of her Canadian holdings. Now is the time to strike, while the iron is hot. Nor is there any serious danger from England's savage allies. You and your valiant comrades-in-arms have proven at Tippecanoe that our frontiers can be ably defended. No significant land force can be brought against us, because England has none to spare for such a service. Some of our towns along the coast may be exposed to danger from her ships-of-war, but we have taken steps to strengthen our navy. Aggressions upon our commerce have been committed by single vessels; a force of 20 or 30 frigates would be capable not only of defending our important coastal towns but inflicting great injury upon English commerce. Such a force, aided by privateers, to whom we should issue letters of marque, would be formidable.

There are some gentlemen who fear that a stronger navy will produce collisions with foreign nations and plunge us into other wars. I say that if they want to avoid foreign collisions they had better abandon the ocean, surrender all our commerce, give up all our prosperity. It is the thing protected, not the instrument of protection, which involves you in war. The only obstacle to increasing our navy is the state of our finances, and the only solution is a resort to taxes. By what I have lately seen of the temperament of our citizens, they would gladly reach deeper into their pockets for this cause, as they know it is not only just but also necessary.

And what of you, Jonathan? Would you not consider the command of one of our frigates? You are amply suited for the task, with your considerable experience. All you need do is say the word, and such a command will be yours. I will see to it.

On my return home I found the public sentiment in Ohio and Pennsylvania entirely in favor of the war. In Kentucky the measure has been received with enthusiasm. Indeed, I have almost been alarmed at the ardor which has been displayed, knowing how prone human nature is to extremes. As one means of preserving the present tone of public opinion here I am extremely desirous that the Govt. should employ the volunteers. The recruiting service has been conducted with a success which surpasses my expectations. Such is the structure of our society however that I doubt whether many can be engaged for a term longer than six months. In this nation of farmers, there is leisure for every kind of enterprise until the commencement of Spring, but then it becomes another story entirely.

Allow me to comment that as for Governor Harrison, no military man in the U. States combines more general confidence in the Western Country than he does, and rightly so. I hope the President will see fit to bestow upon him a well-deserved brigadier's appointment. The people here in Lexington are all enthusiasm when his name is pronounced. A number of resolutions have been proposed and carried; one affirms our ability to bring the Indian war to a speedy conclusion under the guidance of the governor. I understand now that he has prevailed upon the volunteers who conducted themselves with such distinguished valor at Tippecanoe to remain with him, as he seems to be convinced that the Indian problem was not resolved by that recent stunning victory, for the fact that the Shawnee named Tecumseh is still at large. Apparently he is certain that unless and until that man is under our thumb the Indians will fall upon our frontier with all their fury.

I have received disturbing reports from other sources that your courage during the battle bordered on the suicidal. I apologize for speaking bluntly to you on this subject. I hope you will not allow domestic strife to lead you to a reckless flirtation with Death. Do not make the Reaper too many offers—he may take you up on it! Your personal life, of course, is no affair of mine, but I pray that you will take to heart the advice of a man who holds you in high regard, and who has had his share of personal misfortunes. Do not fall prey to melancholy. All things work out in time. Women are mysterious creatures, and no man can fathom that mystery, try as he might. The best he can do is proceed through life, following the course he has set for himself, and he must not make the mistake of allowing the actions of a woman to distract him, for there is little logic to follow in them. You have many productive years ahead of you, many achievable goals, many adventures, many pleasures yet to sample. Do not throw your life away, Jonathan. You would not live to regret it!

Come to Ashland, if you are afforded an opportunity to do so, and keep me informed of the campaign against Tecumseh's Indians as it unfolds.

Yrs Sincerely.

H. Clay

_____

CHAPTER NINE

Nathaniel

I

She saw the rider coming up the long, snow-clad slope, breaking out of the strip of trees that stood like an evergreen barricade between the Boonesboro road and the hill upon which the remote cabin had stood for thirty years now, and despite the fact that Nathaniel had made it clear that he had every intention of "sticking close" from now on, she had a premonition about this rider and his purpose for coming, and she was uneasy.

Watching from a window, wringing the apron she wore between her hands, Amanda tried to convince herself that she had no reason for anxiety. Nathaniel had come home over six months ago, home from Elm Tree where terrible things had happened, and he had seemed a changed man, in what way she could not have actually described, had she been asked to do so, but changed nonetheless, in a very subtle way, and perhaps the best evidence of this was his determination to stay here with her despite several opportunities to go. First there had been that time, in early summer, when the irate men of Boonesboro came asking him to join in the pursuit of several Indians who had made off with a dozen horses and killed a few cattle, apparently just for sport, or maybe out of spite. Always before, the

Boonesboro men had turned to Nathaniel on such occasions and he had succumbed to a sense of obligation to them, yet this time he refused, and the men were flabbergasted—but none more so than Amanda herself. Nathaniel had been smiling yet firm in declining; he gave two of the men some powder and shot because he thought they were a little short on these necessities, and he provided the group on the whole with some sound advice on the best route to take, a route that would give them the best chance of catching the horse thieves, since he had a suspicion regarding where they would go. Then he had sent the men on their way with his best wishes.

Then, a couple of months ago, the governor of the Indian Territory had spread word that he was mounting an expedition against the Tippecanoe Indians, and asked for all able-bodied Kentuckians who wanted to rid the country once and for all of the threat that the Indians posed against their farms and families. Again the Boonesboro men looked to Flintlock Jones, expecting him to respond to the call, as he had always done before, and wanting him to be their leader on this adventure, a role he had modestly accepted and filled to everyone's satisfaction on previous occasions. But again he disappointed them. "I am getting too old for war," he told them, by way of explanation, figuring he owed them at least that much, because he was letting them down, since they felt invincible when Flintlock Jones was leading them, and it was a sobering blow to feel something less than invincible when going up against hostile Indians.

Nathaniel made no promises. He let his actions speak for himself. Clearly he was committed, and Amanda thought, *he is hoping to make up for lost time, all that time we could have spent together but didn't because he was away, and making amends, too, for the promise he made thirty years ago, when we were youngsters who had come overmountain, looking for a future and knowing, or thinking, that the future would be together.* She wanted to believe that he would not go away again, and comprehended the silent commitment made by his actions these past six months, yet still lived with apprehension, as she had always lived, apprehensive that their time together was short and that he would be going away, because by now she had concluded that God had charted their life in this fashion, moments together and eternities apart, and had resigned herself to a possibly divine plan. She was even apprehensive after he had gone away, because there was always that chance that he wouldn't come home this time. *Maybe,* she thought, *I've made such a habit of being apprehensive that I don't know any other way to live.*

Now here came a lone rider, and there was an urgency about him, and she was afraid. He had come, in a sense, to lure her husband away from her, and the question was, would Nathaniel keep his silent commitment? She'd never asked him what had happened to change him. Was it the fate that had befallen their daughter and her husband? Jonathan and Rebecca were estranged. It had something to do with Stephen Cooper and the miscarriage and honor, she supposed, but she couldn't be certain, because Rebecca refused to talk about it to anyone, and she and Nathaniel had agreed that it would be best if they stayed out of it, it was none of their affair. They would help if Rebecca, or Jonathan, asked for their help, but they would not interfere unbidden. Amanda had a feeling, just by remarks her husband had made, that Nathaniel thought the source of the problem was Jonathan's frequent and sustained absences from Elm Tree. That maybe the situation there would not have spun so out of control had he been home more often, and it occurred to Amanda that perhaps this was what Rebecca was thinking, too, and blaming Jonathan for. Maybe Nathaniel had learned a lesson from it all.

The rider was near the house, and he raised an arm and shouted "Halloo," sounding cheerful, which Amanda immediately hated him for, and she saw Nathaniel appear in front of the cabin, an axe racked on his shoulder. He had been out chopping firewood. Amanda could identify the rider now, that Ames boy, apprenticed to Lindsay, the blacksmith at Boonesboro. Amanda thought, *I ought to make the boy a cup of hot tea, because it's very cold outside, and he must be frozen clean through.* But she couldn't bring herself to leave the window. Her feet seemed rooted to the cabin's worn-smooth puncheon floor, worn especially smooth at the window where for so many days in all these years she had paused there as she went about her chores to gaze hopefully down the long slope in the direction of the Boonesboro road, hoping to see her absent husband break out of the trees on the last leg of his journey home. Horse and rider both were breathing hard, their exhalations thick white vapor-like smoke in the frozen air, and there were little icicles on the horse's chin, and on the bit chains, too.

Nathaniel walked out, high-stepping in the snow that came up almost to his knees, and then he stood alongside the winded horse, and the Ames boy was leaning slightly sideways in the saddle to speak to him, his reddened face taut with excitement. Nathaniel listened for a moment, nodding twice, and then gestured toward the cabin, but the Ames boy shook his head emphatically, throwing a thumb over his shoulder in the general direction of Boonesboro. Frustratingly, Amanda could not make out anything he'd said. The Ames boy turned his horse and started down the long slope where the bluegrass lay buried beneath a blanket of snow. Nathaniel turned for the cabin. He didn't notice Amanda at the window. He walked to the door with his head down, and looking at him Amanda knew something was terribly wrong.

He came through the door and when he looked up Amanda could see her future in his eyes.

"You're leaving," she said softly, a statement of fact, because she knew it was so, he didn't have to say it.

"Remember Beaver, the older Delaware chief? His squaw lives near Vincennes now. Governor Harrison's been looking out for her and her children ever since they put Beaver to death. She's heard that Quashquame is to be executed. Just like her husband was."

Amanda gasped. Her hand flew to her throat, as though to catch the sound there, but too late. "Quashquame? Executed? Why?"

"She thinks The Prophet's behind it. Quashquame's been speaking out against him and his brother Tecumseh. And now it looks like Quashquame helped the settlers up there catch some Indians who murdered a family somewhere along the Kaskaskia. The Indians were executed by Governor Harrison's order. Now Quashquame is on trial for his life before a Delaware council, on account of his helping the whites."

Seeing the anguish etched deeply into his weathered features, and knowing the source of that anguish was as much her as Quashquame, Amanda decided she had to make this easy for Nathaniel, even though that made it much more difficult for her.

"Then you must go," she said quietly. "I will pack you some venison and corn dodgers. You won't have time to stop for hunting."

"Amanda . . ."

She was already turning away, going to the fireplace, not wanting him to see the tears welling up in her eyes. "You should take several horses. You can make better time by riding one until it's bottomed out and then switching over to another. You can leave the horses with folks along the way and pick them up on the way back." She thought, *if you come back,* but she didn't say it.

Nathaniel moved up behind her, put his strong arms around her. In his embrace was the only time she felt fully content and completely safe. He held her that way for a while, and then gently turned her around, and she was looking down, her eyes almost closed, still trying to hide the tears, and fighting them back, too, and failing on both counts. He cupped her chin in one hand and lifted her head, and kissed her lips, tasting the salt of her tears. The kiss was a lingering one, and the passion built up around them like a hot electric cocoon, and she threw her arms around his neck, drawing him down to the buffalo rug in front of the fireplace, down on top of her. They made love, and all the magic of the very first time was there, but with none of the clumsiness. Their bodies fused in a long slow deep graceful dance, and the heat they generated in their cocoon of passion kept building hotter and hotter, until the cocoon could no longer contain it, and exploded with such violent ecstasy that she screamed as though dying. Spent, they lay entangled, he with his face nestled in the soft warm curve of her neck, and she crying silent and apprehensive tears.

II

For Nathaniel it was a case of déjà vu.

He reached the Delaware village where Quashquame lived, and where he had come two years earlier, and captured the renegade Simon Girty, there by the rollicking—and now ice-rimmed—river, only to have Girty escape his clutches and chase him all the way to the Ohio River. Rumor had it that Girty was living up near the lakes these days, a drunkard, a warrior no longer. That was too bad, mused Nathaniel, as he slipped through the thick woods near the place he had fought and vanquished Girty, because it meant the renegade would probably never face the justice, Kentucky-style, which he so richly deserved.

Nathaniel found a good spot from which to view the Delaware village, on a long hill to the west of the meadow where the lodges were scattered. The sun was just coming up, touching the wooded heights around him with its golden light, but the valley below was still filled with dusky blue shadows, and a pall of gray wood smoke from dozens of lodge fires. Even so, Nathaniel could see the post driven into the ground near the council lodge at the center of the village. The post rose up out of a mound of deadwood. The frontiersman was relieved to see this. Clearly the Indians were preparing to burn someone at the stake, and he figured that someone had to be Quashquame. So maybe he had made it here in time, having come close to ruining two good horses to do it.

Watching the waking village begin to stir, Nathaniel turned his thoughts to the problem at hand. Getting here before Quashquame's execution was all well and fine, but it wouldn't do his Delaware friend any good if he couldn't figure out a way to rescue him. One idea he had was to wait until nightfall, then to slip into the village, hopefully undetected, and reaching Quashquame while the rest of the Indians slept. But within the hour Nathaniel witnessed things which convinced him that by nightfall Quashquame would be beyond saving.

The Delawares began to gather around the post. The members of the village council entered the council lodge, to emerge a short time later to spread their blankets on the ground and sit in a semi-circle in front of the lodge, facing the post. Then Quashquame was brought from his lodge, hands bound behind his back, head held high—brought to stand before the council. The villagers gave a great shout when they saw him. By the tone of that hue and cry Nathaniel could tell that his friend's people had turned against him. He could not, at this distance, hear what words passed between Quashquame and the council members. He didn't really need to. Quashquame was being given the death sentence again—again, because he had no doubt been condemned the day before, and given the span of the night to make his peace.

Desperation growing inside him, Nathaniel cast about for a plan. He was running out of time. When his gaze fell upon the Delawares' horse herd in the valley north of the village it came to him. The horses were pawing at the foot-deep snow, trying to get to the grass buried beneath. Two hundred ponies at least. Nathaniel saw a single herd guard, a lone rider with a red wool blanket over his head to shelter him from the morning's bitter cold.

The frontiersman didn't waste time trying to calculate the odds of his plan working, or seeking a better alternative. Instead, he left his vantage point and raced back to his horse, secured down near the river at the base of the hill. He ran for all he was worth through the trees, a tall, lean blur clad in a fur-lined deerskin coat. There was not a moment to lose.

Reaching the horse, he rode north, keeping the long hill between himself and the village. Circling the northern end of the hill, he paused at the edge of the trees, and found the horse herd directly ahead. He spotted the guard in his red blanket. Pony and rider were facing south. If he was awake, the guard could look over the herd and see the distant village, where now someone was beating a drum, a methodical *thump-thump, thump-thump,* like the rhythm of a heart, but beating much slower than the heart pounding in Nathaniel's chest.

Removing the fringed deerskin sheath from his Kentucky long rifle, Nathaniel kicked the horse into motion, holding it to a short-rein walk. The herd guard was a shade over a hundred yards away. As easy shot, but Nathaniel did not want to forsake the element of surprise. Except for the pulse of the drum in the village, and the occasional whicker of one of the ponies in the herd, and the crunch of snow beneath the shod hooves of his horse, and the distant screech of a hawk, a cold and heavy silence lay upon the valley.

Fifty yards now. The herd guard had not moved. Could he be sleeping? Nathaniel dared not hope. But he had to be weary, after long hours of vigil in the darkness, patrolling the perimeter of the herd, on a job left usually to boys who were not quite men, boys who had to prove themselves worthy. A herd guard was to raise an alarm if strangers came to thieve, or a wolf pack prowled in search of colt meat to take the edge off winter hunger, or a catamount came slinking down off the wooded heights on a similar mission. Now that the sun had risen, rolling back the shades of night, a false friend providing a dangerous sense of security with its illumination, the guard would be most susceptible to the weariness that had tormented him for hours, with the bitter cold its willing accomplice, making every joint ache, and the eyelids heavy like iron, dulling the brain.

Nathaniel was more concerned about the horses in the herd than he was the guard. Some of the ponies had turned their heads to look in his direction, but there was nothing to unduly alarm them in his slow and measured approach, just as apparently there was nothing in their actions that served to alert the motionless guard. Only when the guard's own pony turned its head to look and then whicker querulously did the guard move; removing the blanket from his head, he draped it around shoulders hunched against the cold, and when he saw Nathaniel the dull, sleepy, dark eyes flared open with surprise, and the mouth gaped to form a shout, but at the guard's first sign of life Nathaniel had kicked his horse into a lunging gallop and loosened his grips on the reins. Even as he shouted—more of a strangled croak than a full-throated shout—the Indian swung his horse around, a reflex action, because no one likes to have his back turned to death when it comes slipping up. But he should have tried to run for it. Precious seconds escaped before he realized his mistake. Seeing the frontiersman bearing down on him, he pulled harshly on the braided reins, jerking the pony's head around toward the village.

It was too late. Nathaniel was on him, swinging the long rifle. As he struck, Nathaniel was aware of two things: The herd guard, as he had suspected, was a youngster—had probably fourteen maybe fifteen summers but certainly no more—and he wasn't armed with a rifle, but rather a knife and a bow, the former in a sheath on his elkskin belt, the latter, along with a quiver of arrows, strung on his back beneath the red blanket. The Indian seemed to have altogether forgotten about his weapons. Consumed by an overpowering urge to flee this sudden apparition, so much more frightening than a pack of gaunt wolves, the guard gave no thought to putting up a fight, associating such an attempt with suicide, and rightly so. But because he was young, and wasn't making a move to brandish either of his weapons, Nathaniel did not strike as hard as he might, letting up just enough in that instant before the brass-mounted point of the long rifle's stock made contact with the guard's skull, striking now to disable rather than to kill. The blow fell true. The Indian youngster somersaulted backward off the haunches of his pony, to land facedown in the snow, sprawled and still, but not lifeless, of that Nathaniel was sure. His pony galloped away, into the herd, which was already beginning to stir nervously.

Nathaniel rode right into them, shouting at the top of his lungs, and like one creature the ponies turned and ran away from him, running south, straight for the village. He gave chase, still yelling like a banshee. A few of the ponies veered off into the gray and green line of trees to the west, but most preceded him into the village, a tidal wave of thundering hooves and vapor-spewing nostrils and flashing manes, a wave of brown and red and dun and spotted white, breaking around the lodges, pouring inexorably through the open spaces in a cloud of snow churned up by those thundering hooves, and nothing was going to stop this wave until it had spent itself, no obstacle was sufficient to divert it.

The Indians sensed this. A few were foolhardy enough to stand in the path of the stampeding herd, shouting and waving their arms, only to be trampled. Most scattered, running for their lives. A few of the lodges came crashing down. A woman screamed. Nathaniel thought, *God, I hope no women or children are harmed.* The herd reached the center of the village where the council lodge stood, and where they had lashed the naked Quashquame to the post already, and set fire to the mound of deadwood. Tongues of hungry flame were just now beginning to lick at the tangle of branches. In a matter of minutes, perhaps seconds, the fire would take hold and consume the wood and the man tied to the stake. As the herd broke around the post Nathaniel rode straight at it, though his horse balked, as all creatures will in the face of fire, whether they have ever seen or felt it before. Straight into the mound he rode, scattering the smoldering branches. The blade of the knife he drew gleamed for an instant in the cold hard silver light cast by the heatless winter sun, and then Nathaniel was slashing at the bindings that held Quashquame to the post.

Freed, the Delaware grabbed Nathaniel's arm and vaulted lithely astride the horse behind the frontiersman. As the horse leaped away from the post and the burning pile of wood, a warrior appeared suddenly out of the smoke, screaming at the top of his lungs and racing straight for them, a tomahawk raised as though he intended to hurl it. He never got the chance. Nathaniel's rifle spoke. The impact of the bullet stopped the Indian, stopped him as though he had run full speed into an invisible wall and bounced backward off of it.

They rode on, catching up with the tail end of the stampeding herd, and now, behind and on both sides of them the guns began to talk their deadly talk, a ragged volley of rifle fire crackling like the flames in the deadwood, only louder. Several ponies came galloping around a lodge, stragglers from the main body of the herd, and Quashquame saw his chance. Nathaniel felt his Delaware friend make ready to jump, and veered the horse closer to the running ponies, right alongside a fleet-footed young paint, and Quashquame made his leap, grabbing handfuls of mane to use in lieu of bridle and reins, bending low to present a smaller target as the bullets whined angrily in their search for him.

South of the village the stampeding herd scattered before them, and in losing cohesion the herd also lost its velocity, so that now only a few were still running, while others trotted in long and aimless circles, and others arched their backs and kicked their hind legs out like the wild mustangs they were not so far removed from being, while still others stopped altogether and looked about them in a baffled and wary manner, like sleepwalkers who sleep in one room and wake in another and don't understand how it all happened.

Through them rode Nathaniel and Quashquame, scattering them like leaves, their horses running stretched out, kicking up plumes of powdery snow. Some of the warriors ran a short distance out from the village in a spirited but futile pursuit, hurling curses and hot lead after the frontiersman and his Delaware friend. The bullets seemed to have as little effect as the epithets. As grim resolve replaced blind rage, the warriors gathered up their scattered ponies.

Nathaniel and Quashquame rode more than two miles before slowing their horses to let them cool down. By this time they had put the valley behind them and were deep in the wooded hills. They listened for pursuit, heard none, but were not fooled. The warriors of the village would come. Then, again, Nathaniel had that feeling of déjà vu. Two years ago the Indians had pursued him to the banks of the Ohio. It would go the same way today. Of that he was certain.

He gave Quashquame his long coat and they rode on. Nathaniel said nothing, and the mute Delaware made no sign. There was a time and a place for talking, and this wasn't it. Though they could not see the warriors, they knew they were coming. This was the time for running.

For hours they rode through the hills, and it was slow going, but there was no other way to go, and they had to take care to avoid the deep snow drifts gathered in the low places, where a horse could flounder, and after a while the idea crept into Nathaniel's head that there wasn't anybody else in this white winterland except the two of them, but he knew that idea for what it was—the perilously false allure of the serenity of this snow-clad forest, pristine and sparkling in the sunlight, where it did not seem that anything bad could happen, or anything evil or lethal could exist. He had been lulled into that false sense of security two years ago—and then Girty and his Indians had exploded out of this very same serene forest and damn near killed him.

Then, sometime in the early afternoon, Nathaniel

leaned forward until his forehead was touching the bowed neck of his horse, and a moment later slipped slowly sideways out of the saddle to sprawl unconscious in the snow.

Quashquame leapt from his pony to kneel at the frontiersman's side. Seeing the unhealthy pallor of his friend, and his buckskin leggins soggy with blood, the Delaware for the first time realized that Nathaniel had been shot. All this time Nathaniel had concealed the fact that he had taken a bullet in his left thigh. Always the frontiersman had ridden to the left of him so that Quashquame could not see the blood. The Delaware rose and walked along their backtrail a hundred feet. Yes, there was the trail of blood, drops of scarlet vivid against the white snow. He returned to his fallen friend. Hooking Nathaniel under the arms, he dragged him beneath the heavy sweeping boughs of a spruce. Then he went back to retrieve the frontierman's horse and the long rifle lying in the snow. The paint was nowhere to be seen, having vanished into the forest, heeding the wild call its ancestors had lived by as soon as it was rid of its unwelcome rider. Back at Nathaniel's side, he used his friend's knife to cut open the leggins so that he could examine the wound. The bullet had not passed through, lodging deep.

Nathaniel regained consciousness.

"You better get going," he said.

Quashquame signed *We go*.

Nathaniel shook his head. "I've come as far as I can." He raised his head and looked at his leg. "Deep?"

Quashquame nodded.

Nathaniel sighed. "Get moving. They're not far behind us."

You stay I stay.

"Now listen," snapped Nathaniel. "I reckon I can hold them off until nightfall. Ride all night and you'll be safe. They'll never catch up. Might not even try. Go on, Quashquame. You don't, and I've died for nothing."

Quashquame shook his head, striving to mask his emotions. But this once the mask slipped.

"We can't leave Amanda alone," said the frontiersman. "I promised I never would. I can't get back to her now. But you can. You've got to promise me you'll look out for her, my friend. There is no one else I'd trust—or her either. Please."

Quashquame knew this was no ploy to get him to go. Nathaniel was sincere. The request came from the heart—and it was one he could not refuse.

I go, he signed. And added, *My friend.*

He rode away on Nathaniel's horse, looking back only once, and Nathaniel was waiting for him to do that. The frontiersman raised a hand in farewell.

Quashquame had gone no more than a mile when he heard the distant crack of a rifle, then a flurry of shots, followed by at least a dozen more, spaced well apart, and finally three in quick succession, about a half hour after the first report, and now so faint he could scarcely hear them at all. Then the silence of the forest closed in on him, and he rode blindly on.

III

Much to Nathaniel's surprise they did not close in for the kill, even though they knew his shot pouch was empty. Instead, they spent more than two hours circling him, inching ever closer, keeping to the cover, so that he did not see hide nor hair of them until they were almost upon him. He didn't need to see them to know where they were. The more time they took the better he liked it. The day was waning. As the sun sank, purple shadows reached across the snow for him. Their timidity gave Quashquame a better lead. And it gave him the chance to enjoy the cold, clear air so sweet it tasted like wine, and to gaze upon the wooded heights, and marvel for the last time at how blue the sky could be. He scooped up a handful of snow and squeezed it in his fist, listening to the crunching sound it made, and he realized that he had always wondered why snow, when compressed, made such a distinctive sound. He used the snow to slake a raging thirst.

In short, he gave all his senses free rein, sampling the world in all its wonder, at least all the wonder he could see, taste, feel, and hear from this spot in the blood-stained snow beneath the spruce, figuring it would be his last chance to do so. He tried not to think about his life, as men who are about to die will do, if given the time, because his life was wrapped tightly around the image of a willowy flaxen-haired woman. Amanda *was* his life, had been since his earliest childhood remembrances almost, and he couldn't bear to think of her now.

Finally they worked up the nerve to break cover and come for him, two of them, anyway, from different sides, with bloodcurdling screams and tomahawks raised. Halfway to him they stopped dead in their tracks. He simply lay there, propped up against the trunk of the tree, the long rifle across his lap, looking at one and then the other, with a remarkable calm. One of the warriors called out, and six more appeared, surrounding the spruce beneath which he lay. They discussed the situation, and since he knew enough of the lingo to comprehend the gist of what they were saying he knew that at least one among them had recognized him as *Metequa*—Flintlock—the great Long Knife. More Delawares appeared to join the eight sent forward to stalk him until, by his count, thirty-six warriors stood, or sat their horses, in a circle around the tree.

"What are you waiting for?" he asked. "An invitation? I have killed six of your brothers today. Don't you want to avenge them?"

One of the warriors moved cautiously closer, to sit on his heels beneath snow-weighted branches of the tree.

"I am Pimoacan," he said. "You are Flintlock. You were once friend of the Delaware."

"Once. But then the Delaware decided to listen to the Shawnee named Tecumseh, who tells them to turn against the whites. Tecumseh's friend becomes my enemy. So you might as well kill me, Pimoacan, and be done with it."

Pimoacan glanced at Nathaniel's blood-soaked leggins. "We have decided not to kill you, Flintlock."

"Why not?"

"We are afraid of The Prophet."

"I don't understand."

"Quashquame has escaped. We will never catch him now. The Prophet wanted him dead. He will be angry with us when he discovers that Quashquame still lives. Maybe he will not be quite so angry if we give you to him. You are *Metequa,* a great prize."

Nathaniel was relieved to know that he was not going to die, at least not today, but the prospect of being handed over to the Shawnees, his mortal enemies, was a very unpleasant one. He wasn't sure if it wouldn't be better to perish here than by the hand of The Prophet, or his brother, Tecumseh.

"I may not live long enough for you to bring me to Tippecanoe," he said, with a curt gesture indicating his wound.

"Flintlock will live," replied Pimoacan confidently.

They made a travois, a blanket spread across a frame fashioned from limber saplings, the contraption lashed to the pony of one of the warriors he had killed that day. In this way they transported him to the village. It was a painful ordeal for Nathaniel. The slightest motion of the travois sent bolts of pain lancing through his body. Halfway there he passed out.

He awoke to find himself on a comfortable pallet of buffalo robes inside a smoky, warm deerskin lodge. Pimoacan was looming over him with a knife, and Nathaniel's first thought was that the Delaware had changed his mind about giving him to The Prophet as a consolation prize.

"The bullet must be removed," said Pimoacan, "or the poison will spread within you and you will die." He turned his head and barked a command. Four men entered the lodge. Two took hold of Nathaniel's legs, two his arms. A young woman was squatting by the fire, heating a very long thin-bladed knife. Nathaniel broke into a cold sweat so profuse that it ran down his forehead through the deep furrows of the bridge of his nose and into his eyes. The woman brought the knife to Pimoacan, who handed her his own blade, which she took back to the lodge fire to heat in the flames. Pimoacan placed a strip of rawhide between Nathaniel's teeth, and without further ado began to probe the bullet hole in the frontiersman's thigh. Nathaniel clamped down hard on the rawhide and tried his best to stifle the guttural scream that came rattling out of his throat as the blade pierced his already torn and tortured flesh.

Suddenly the ground seemed to fall away beneath him and he was plummeting down through a black hole, leaving the scream and the pain somewhere up above. The snarling scream faded, even though he could still feel it in his raw throat, and the pain lessened, even though he could feel the blade in his flesh, and then there was a quick flash of white light and he was gone.

An eternity—or was it a minute?—later he heard, very faintly, someone shouting at him. He could not distinguish the words and he could not see anything except an inky blackness, as though he were down in the guts of a cold, clammy cavern a thousand feet beneath the surface of the earth, except that there did not seem to be any gravity, and he was floating—upward? downward?—and the shouting was somehow drawing him toward it. Slowly it drew nearer, or he got closer, and he realized it was not one person shouting, but many, and it sounded like a chant of sorts, but still he could not quite make it out, not until he was much closer, and he could detect a diffuse light, and he opened his eyes to see the dusty shaft of sunlight through the smokehole at the top of the deerskin lodge, and the face of the young Delaware woman who had been heating the knives in the fire. Now he could understand what the people, outside the lodge, were shouting.

Tecumseh! Tecumseh!

"He is here," she said, with a kind of reverence.

Nathaniel was too tired to care, and went to sleep.

IV

"I am Tecumseh. Do you remember me?"

The Shawnee sat cross-legged on the other side of

the lodge fire from Nathaniel, who was stretched out on the buffalo robes.

"I remember," said the frontiersman. "You would have killed me, but your rifle misfired."

"I knew then that we would meet again, three times. This is the second time. The first was when you came to my village with Major Moore, who was chief of the *Shemanese* at Springfield."

"Three times?"

Tecumseh nodded.

Nathaniel had to smile at that. "That's good news, I reckon. If you're right, I'll survive this meeting."

"You will."

"You speak good English."

"My brother, Blue Jacket, taught me. I have read many of your books."

"Blue Jacket. Wasn't he born white?"

"The Great Spirit sometimes likes to play jokes on people. Blue Jacket was born to be an Indian, but he had white skin. Tell me, *Metequa*, why were you willing to die to save the life of Quashquame?"

"He is my friend."

"*Ne-cana*? But he is an Indian."

"You don't have any white friends?"

Tecumseh shook his head. "None that I would die for."

"It's a mistake to hate all red men if you're white, or all white men if you're red. There's both good men and bad of both colors."

"You may be a good man," mused Tecumseh. "But you have killed many of my Shawnee brothers."

"None as I recall that weren't trying to kill me."

Tecumseh nodded. "That is always so, isn't it?"

"I reckon. Wonder sometimes how different things

might have been if the first time a white man and red man met they'd shaken hands instead of trying to kill each other."

"No different. Because your people want to own all the earth."

"There's some truth in what you say," conceded Nathaniel. "My people always figure it's greener on the other side of the fence. I'm a fair example, myself. I stood to inherit a tavern and a piece of land over Virginia way, but I'd always wanted to see what was on the other side of the mountains. I don't know why, exactly. My feet fairly itched to walk that Wilderness Road."

"My people nurture the land," said Tecumseh. "so that the land which our forefathers lived on could nourish their children, and their children's children. Your people ruin the land. They graze their livestock and plant their crops with no thought for tomorrow, and when the land has been rendered useless they are not concerned—they merely move to another piece of land, and stay until it, too, is ruined, then move on again. I have given this much thought, and I think I know why this is. For some reason the white man looks upon our land and says to himself, 'No one lives here. This land is mine for the taking.' Does he not have eyes to see my people? If someone moved onto your land, *Metequa,* what would you do? Would you not tell them to go away, that this land belongs to you? How would you feel if they looked right through you, as though you were an invisible spirit, and did not hear your words, and began to live on your land, and destroy it? Would you tell yourself, 'I will just move to another piece of land and let them have this one?' What if the blood of your forefathers had irrigated that land? What if their bones lay beneath the land and made it sacred? Would just walk away and leave the blood and bones of your forebearers to the keeping of strangers who have no respect for them? You see, there is the problem. The white man does not understand how the land can be made sacred by the blood and bones of their ancestors, because they never stay in one place long enough. No, they are restless, always moving, always wanting what they do not have. Where the blood and bones of our forefathers are, there also reside their spirits. The spirits of my father and his father before him and his father before him and so on wander now in the Ohio Fire, searching for their people. But their people are nowhere to be found. The living can move from one place to another, but the spirit remains. And the spirits of my forefathers are searching, and they are confused, because where once there were the *wegiwas* of the Shawnee stand now the cabins of the *Shemanese*. Where once the buffalo and the elk roamed freely, now there are the white man's cattle. Where once the trees stood tall, holding up the sky, now there is but a wasteland. We want only our land back. Then the spirits of our forefathers will smile again. They will be content, and at peace. And when those of us who live now die, then our spirits will be greeted by the spirits of our fathers, and walk with them upon the land that is unchanged, instead of wandering in a strange land. We belong to the land, the land does not belong to us."

Tecumseh fell silent, to stare pensively into the burning embers that danced in the rising smoke between them, thinking about Pucksinwah and Chiksika and their spirits. Nathaniel did not interrupt his thoughts, though he was of a mind to tell Tecumseh that God had given the land to man to use as he saw fit, that the earth without man had not satisfied the Almighty, that trees grew to replace those cut down for the building of the cabins, that the field left behind as barren by the farmer inevitably restored itself in time, that *his* ancestors had come from a place referred to as the Old Country where they had been forced to work for the great land-owners, so that when they arrived in the New World, being born to work the soil, who loved the soil and what grew out of the soil, they decided they would work their own land for the change, and it was this ownership that made them free, and beholden to no man. Possessing a piece of land was their dream. They wanted to make their mark, and have something they could pass down to their children. They were a nation of farmers for the most part, and by their labor the land yielded up its bounty, and that was God's plan, after all.

But he said nothing, and after a while Tecumseh blinked and raised his eyes, emerging from his brooding trance.

"Tomorrow I must go on to Tippecanoe. I have been gone too long. I will tell the Delawares to take you north when you are healed enough to travel, and give you over to the British."

"What would the British want with me?"

"You are their enemy. Your people have declared war on the *Englishmanake.*"

"They have?"

"You did not know?"

"I did not."

"It was as inevitable as night following day. You white men have your own tribes, with their old rivalries. War was bound to come."

"It's what you've been waiting for."

Tecumseh smiled. "It is what I have lived for." He

got to his feet. "I leave you now. Goodbye, *Metequa*. We will meet again—once more."

And then we both shall die.

V

A fortnight after Tecumseh's visit, the Delawares judged Nathaniel fit to travel. A dozen warriors were chosen by lot to have the honor of delivering him to the British as Tecumseh's gift. They tied him to a horse, his hands bound behind him. Then, amidst much ado and fanfare, they left the village and headed north. Their destination was The Point, Matthew Elliott's home near Amherstburg.

Nathaniel was treated as well as a prisoner could expect to be. The Delawares shared their venison and pemmican with him, and no one laid a hand on him. He made no trouble, though he kept his eyes open for a chance to make a break for it. The chance never came. The warriors stayed alert, respecting his prowess, and fearing the consequences of failing Tecumseh.

He talked to them, having long ago mastered the Delaware tongue, and they spoke freely, giving him much information about Tecumseh and his plans for a great Indian confederacy, about the secret slabs and the red sticks and the great signs that would come soon. He did not argue with them, or endeavor to change their minds, or chide them for becoming the willing victims in what he perceived to be a blatant grab for power on the part of Tecumseh and his brother. He knew he would learn a lot more by just asking questions and listening respectfully and appearing to be impressed by what he heard.

The nights were cold, but the weather held, and the modest heat of the winter sun warmed the days, and they made good progress. When they were but a day's ride from The Point one of the Delawares rode on ahead to inform Elliott of their imminent arrival. The warrior returned that evening with Colonel Peter McLeod.

"By God, it is you," exclaimed McLeod when he saw Nathaniel. "Flintlock Jones."

"You have me at a disadvantage," replied the frontiersman. "I remember your face. You were with the traitor Burr. I guess that makes you a traitor, too. But I never caught your name."

McLeod threw back his head and laughed harshly. "You've got plenty of gall, calling *me* a traitor. I am Peter McLeod. And you, sir, you and all your kind, are the traitors."

Nathaniel looked him over, from the shako on his head to the boots on his feet. "You're an American by the sound of it. Yet you wear the King's scarlet."

"You were a British subject once and you will be again."

"It will be a cold day in Hell."

"It will happen sooner than you think."

They made camp in the woods, and McLeod told the Delawares that he intended to stay with them until they reached Fort Malden.

"I did not, of course, know who you were that day on the Natchez Trace," McLeod told Nathaniel as they sat hunched close to the campfire. "But you and that friend of yours, Lieutenant Jonathan Groves, became celebrities after Burr's capture, and from that moment on I have taken a keen interest in your career. His, as well. Hoping that the day would come when we could finish what was started on the Trace."

"We could have finished it then, but you ran away, as I recall."

The firelight glittered in McLeod's dark, cold eyes. "You should practice keeping a civil tongue in your head, Jones, bearing in mind that you will be my guest indefinitely. I could make your life bloody miserable."

"I reckon you will anyway."

"It's your friend, Groves, whom I am particularly keen on meeting again. You see, he killed a young woman of whom I was rather fond."

"He told me about that. A woman and two men tried to waylay him on the road out of Washington. She tried to shoot him."

"Yes. She was doing it for me."

"So you were behind the ambush. Then her blood's on your hands."

"As will be the lieutenant's, I assure you," snapped McLeod. In the living light of the dancing fire his face looked deeply lined and pocked, as though the acid of his hate was eating through his flesh.

Nathaniel shrugged, feigning indifference. "So what are your plans for me?" he asked.

"Were it my decision, you would die," replied McLeod with naked malice. "By my hand."

"A fair fight, of course."

"Naturally. Unfortunately, Sir George Prevost will want to keep you alive. You may be more useful to us as a prisoner of war. For the time being you will enjoy the hospitality, such as it is, of the guardhouse at Fort Malden. You may even reside there for the duration of the war. I will have to derive what pleasure I can from watching you rot behind bars. Or perhaps the prison hulk off Halifax would be more to your liking."

The following morning they arrived at The Point,

dallying there long enough for Matthew Elliott to have a look at their famous captive, then proceeding on, past Amherstburg, to Fort Malden, where Nathaniel, with shackles on his wrists, was cast into the guardhouse, a row of stone cells. The only ventilation was a small square cut into the door of heavy timbers reinforced with strap iron. The square was cross hatched with stout iron bars. The cell was dark and damp and bitterly cold. Nathaniel was given a thin blanket and a bucket for his bodily wastes. They fed him once a day, a sour gruel with, sometimes, a piece of rancid meat. They brought him a bucket of water every day. Otherwise they left him alone with his bleak thoughts. For three days he took it, sitting huddled and shivering in the blanket, but he was a man accustomed to roaming free, fond of the wide open spaces, and he could not long abide this confinement. On the third day he rose, stared at the cell door for quite some time, and then launched himself against it. Time and time again he threw his body against that unyielding door.

Drawn by the noise, the redcoat soldiers came. They were alarmed at first, and then annoyed, and finally amused. They laughed at him, because he would not stop slamming his body against the door, even though he had to know, as they did, that the door would withstand the bludgeoning, that in fact the door would outlast the man. Finally, exhausted, Nathaniel slumped to the ground and passed out or went to sleep—the soldiers weren't sure which. The show over, they drifted away. But an hour later Nathaniel was at it again, and three more times during the night, and in the morning Colonel McLeod came to see for himself.

A soldier surmised that the prisoner had lost his mind. McLeod wasn't so sure. He stepped closer to the door, up to the bars in the small square cut into the thick timbers. Nathaniel's body *thumped*! against the door, *thumped*! again. *Thump. Thump. Thump.* As if the guardhouse possessed a slow measured heartbeat of its own. The door rattled a little on its hinges. To his amazement, McLeod saw that a couple of the hinge bolts driven deep into the stone had been moved, albeit only a millimeter or two. He peered through the bars. The heart had stopped beating. Nathaniel stood in the center of the cell, breathing hard, swaying slightly. His buckskin tunic was torn and bloodied. He stared at McLeod with a blaze of defiance in his bloodshot eyes. Standing there, bleeding, torn, starving, bearded, filthy, exhausted, ragged, he was the most formidable foe McLeod had ever faced. McLeod knew that Nathaniel could never break the door down, and he knew that Nathaniel realized this too. That was precisely what made this exercise in futility so frightening, because it was a demonstration of indomitable will. Here stood a man who refused to surrender to his fate.

McLeod backed away from the door.

"He'll stop soon enough," said one of the soldiers. He said it as he would a prayer, because he and his colleagues were no longer laughing—they had sensed what McLeod had seen with his own eyes in that dank cell, something fearsome, something primeval, something their minds could not quite comprehend but their nerve-endings could. "He's got to . . . doesn't he, Colonel?"

He wanted reassurance, wanted it badly, but McLeod could not oblige him.

"He won't stop until he's dead."

McLeod turned on his heel and walked away, and the soldiers congregated near the guardhouse all jumped nervously as Nathaniel's body *thumped*! against the cell door again . . . and again . . . and again.

CHAPTER TEN

Tecumseh

I

When Tecumseh arrived at Wildcat Creek his face was as grim as anyone could remember having ever seen it. Recently he had passed through what remained of Prophet's Town. The blackened ruins of the village represented the ruination of his plans, or so he feared.

Following the Battle of Tippecanoe, many of the Indians who had been dwelling in Prophet's Town returned to their own tribal villages. The rest established the camp at Wildcat Creek—some two hundred warriors and their families. When word spread that Tecumseh was coming, the entire village turned out to meet him. They cheered and called out happy greetings when Tecumseh emerged from the forest on the trail from the southwest, but fell silent when, as he drew closer, they saw the expression on his face. Reaching the center of the village, he and his small bodyguard dismounted.

"Where is my brother?"

He was taken to a lodge where Lalawethika had been bound to a post driven into the ground at the center of the *wegiwa*. Fury flashed in Tecumseh's eyes like cold steel in bright sunlight when he looked upon his brother. As he stepped toward the post he drew the warclub from his elkskin belt. Lalawethika's eyes widened with terror. He struggled ineffectually against the bindings. Tecumseh grabbed him by the hair. Wrenching The Prophet's head back, he raised the warclub as though to strike. It was then that Lalawethika began to babble incoherently and lost control of his bodily functions. But Tecumseh came to his senses just in time. He lowered the warclub, trembling with unspent rage.

"You are not worth killing," he sneered.

Even in the grasp of a black and blinding fury Tecumseh managed to see past the moment, through the fog of strong emotion, to the consequences of the action he wanted to take so badly he could taste it, like copper in his mouth. For years he had preached to all his red brothers that they had to stop killing one another and focus their wrath upon the *Shemanese*. Now, if he slew his own brother—no matter that he might be fully justified in doing so—he would be guilty of failing to practice what he had preached, which was fatal for a leader. How could he expect others to do his bidding, to set aside their jealousies and their desire for vengeance and even their most petty quarrels, if he could not live by his own rules?

"Cut him loose," he told the warriors who stood just inside the entrance of the lodge.

As the knives slashed the rawhide bindings, Lalawethika sank to his knees. Tecumseh sat on his heels in front of him and spoke softly but with great intensity of feeling.

"In one day you have managed to destroy what has taken me ten years to create. Brother, you are a fool. You have allowed your thirst for power to destroy the hopes of all our people. You care only for yourself. You have no concern for others. From this day on you are no longer The Prophet. You are no longer even a

Shawnee. You have no honor, so you cannot be one of us. I banish you from our midst. I will not kill you, *neethetha,* and I forbid any other Shawnee from doing so. But I also forbid any Indian from giving you food or clothing or a place to lay your head when you are weary. You will wander the land, friendless and homeless. Henceforth, all people will treat you with the scorn you deserve. They will curse your name. They will spit on you when they see you. They will treat you with more contempt than they would a diseased dog. They will despise you as they despise no other living thing. You will wish you were dead, Lalawethika, and when death does come for you no one will be there to mourn your passing. I have spoken. Now go! I wish never to see your face again."

"Tecumseh," whispered Lalawethika, "I am your brother . . ."

"You are my brother no longer. I do not know you."

Lalawethika got to his feet and moved sluggishly, like a man who is weary from a long day's work without respite, shuffling out of the *wegiwa.* All of the inhabitants of the village had congregated outside the lodge. Tecumseh had passed sentence on Lalawethika in a voice intentionally loud enough for all assembled to hear. Now Lalawethika looked at the loathing in their hardened faces, and bowed his head. The silent crowd parted to let him pass. He knew they would have fallen upon him and torn him to pieces but for Tecumseh. As he walked they cursed him under their breath, and spat upon him, because suddenly their fear of him was gone, and that had been his only hold over them. For such a prideful man this was a gauntlet far worse than had they struck him with sticks and cast stones at him.

Inside the lodge Tecumseh, too, bowed his head, still sitting on his heels before the post. One of the warriors, a Wyandot named Stiahta, came forward and placed a hand on his shoulder.

"Tecumseh, I speak for all here when I tell you that we are ashamed. Our hearts are filled with regret because we have failed you."

"No," he replied. "Lalawethika failed me. He was The Prophet. What else could you do but follow him? How could you have known that *Moneto* had already forsaken him? The Great Spirit knew the evil in my brother's heart. Knew that he cared nothing for his people, only for himself. No, you are not to blame. Lalawethika is, and I am, because I knew *Moneto* had abandoned my brother, and yet I did not want to believe it, and I left Tippecanoe without doing what I should have done to protect the people. So *Moneto* is punishing me because I put my own interests and my brother's before the interests of my people."

He stood and turned to face the warriors, forcing a smile, and shaking his head when he saw their stricken expressions.

"But I do not believe that *Moneto* will forsake his people," he added. "Perhaps there is yet a way we can achieve victory."

"We will follow you to the death," vowed Stiahta.

"It is not death I seek, but life. A life for all our people like that which our fathers and their fathers lived."

"As you can see, many have departed."

"But some will return, now that you are back," said another of the warriors.

"Yes, some will return," agreed Tecumseh. "But because of what happened at Tippecanoe many others will lose faith. Only those whose faith was strongest will follow me now. I tell you, my brothers, that as I passed through the ruins of Tippecanoe I was reminded of the destruction of Chillicothe, where as a boy I had lived. Often I would visit the place where Chillicothe once stood, and each time my desire for vengeance waxed stronger. When I saw Tippecanoe burned to the ground I stood yet again among the ashes of my home and heard the spirits of all the fallen warriors of the Shawnee nation call out to me. I could even smell their blood, a bitter fragrance rising up from the soil which they had died defending, and I knew then that I could not fail them. I *will* not."

"Tell us, Tecumseh," said Stiahta, greatly moved. "Are the prophecies of Lalawethika still to be believed? Will the earth still tremble? Will the forest still fall, and the rivers reverse their direction?"

Tecumseh nodded, and this time it was he who placed a comforting hand on Stiahta's shoulder.

"These things will come to pass. *Moneto* has shown me." He refrained from telling them that it was he, not Lalawethika, and had been all along, who had seen these visions. That subterfuge was better left unrevealed. "My brother possessed a real gift. His sin was using that gift to further his own ends, with no thought to the welfare of his people."

The others were visibly encouraged by these assurances.

"Then truly many will return to us when those signs occur," said one.

"But *when* will they occur?" wondered Stiahta. "We have waited a very long time."

"The whites believe that the Son of God will someday descend from heaven to create a paradise on earth," said Tecumseh, "where there will no longer be any death or disease or famine or evil. I have read this, in a book they call the Bible. You will not easily find a *Shemanese* cabin which does not contain this book. They have faith that this Son of God, the one they call The Christ, will return. Christians have clung to this faith for almost two thousand years. Surely our people can hold onto *their* faith for just a few years. But do not cast your eyes down, my brothers. I am not scolding you. I am only saying that what a white man can do, surely we can do. And I tell you, the day is fast approaching. Not many more suns will rise and fall before *Moneto* gives us the signs we have long awaited."

"We will be as strong as before."

"No. Many of our brothers to the south have been corrupted by the *Shemanese*. They profit from their association with the whites. Some even try to live and dress like the white man. They will not follow us. And there are some among the western tribes, on the other side of the Mother of All Rivers, who do not believe me when I tell them that if the white man is not stopped now they will one day find themselves being robbed of *their* land. They say, 'We have no quarrel with the white man, so why should we fight your fight?' They also say, 'If and when the time comes that the white man does try to steal our land we will kill him.' They cannot comprehend how many white men there are, and so they think that one tribe can defeat the Seventeen Fires. They will not follow us. And now, because of my brother's stupidity and greed, even some of the northern tribes will turn their backs on us. Even the signs of which I speak will not suffice to restore their faith."

"So what are we to do?" asked Stiahta.

"I have been told that war has broken out between

the *Shemanese* and the *Englishmanake*. The only choice left open to us is to join forces with the British. The British will supply us with guns and powder, food and medicine."

"Black Fish learned that the Shawnee cannot depend on the *Englishmanake,*" said one of the warriors.

Tecumseh knew that he was referring to that summer, thirty years ago, when Black Fish, principal chief of the Shawnee nation, had relied on his British allies to aid him in an invasion of Kentucky. But the British, repulsed by the brutality of the Indians, had abruptly curtailed the campaign, leaving much hard feeling in their wake. Then, too, the British had failed to support Blue Jacket at the Battle of Fallen Timbers, cowering behind the walls of their fort while the Indians fought Mad Anthony Wayne's *shemagana*.

"They will not fail us this time," he said. "Tomorrow, all the men who remain with us must ride to their home villages and tell the people what they have seen here today. Tell them it is true that The Prophet has betrayed their faith in him, but that I, Tecumseh, never will. Tell them, too, that I am going to return to Tippecanoe. I am going home. A new village will rise from the ashes of the old. Those who believe in me must take up their weapons and join me there."

Tippecanoe, he thought, would stand as a symbol of the survival, the durability, the unquenchable spirit of the dream for the future of his race that had inspired him for fifteen years, a dream that had shaped his life, and would give meaning to his death.

II

It was the biggest earthquake anyone could remember, and it came on the day following the thirtieth night after the sign of the Panther Passing Across. Chiefs from the Tombigbee River in the south to the Wabash and Sandusky to the north had just burned the last—the thirtieth—piece of the final red stick in the fire.

The epicenter of the earthquake was near the river town of New Madrid. The ground opened up in gigantic, jagged chasms. New lakes appeared in vast sinkholes, while whole lakes were drained in a matter of minutes, leaving thousands of stunned fish flapping helplessly in the stinking mud exposed for the first time to the sunlight. The rivers, even the mighty Mississippi, flowed backward, and tidal waves of muddy, debris-cluttered water leaped over the riverbanks and swept across the land. Trees snapped like brittle sticks by the thousands. Whole forests toppled over. Houses collapsed all at once. Bridges, shaken into rubble of stone and timber, fell into the madly swirling rivers. Entire bluffs disintegrated, and massive landslides buried everything in their paths. Shock waves reached westward, and on the prairie whole herds of buffalo were knocked off their feet. Tremors were felt as far away as the coast of the Gulf of Mexico and in the city of Charleston, South Carolina, and were reported a thousand miles from the epicenter.

The noise was terrifying: the tortured grinding of the earth and the thunder of the landslides and the hissing of the rivers in turmoil and the cracking of the trees as they split open and fell like a ceaseless volley of musket fire, only louder, and the bellowing of livestock and wild creatures rolling helplessly on the trembling bosom of the earth, and the screeching of millions of birds who darted wildly in the sky, darkening the sun, afraid to alight anywhere.

In the villages of the Creeks and the Choctaws and the Cherokees in the south, and of the Delawares and Wyandots and Potowatomies and Sauks in the north, the terrified Indians stumbled from their collapsing lodges and cowered together in the choking dust that filled the air, and there was only one word on the lips of thousands.

Tecumseh!

And when the dust cleared at Fort Malden near Amherstburg, the guardhouse was nothing but a pile of rubble, and Colonel McLeod paced and fumed while soldiers searched for the body of the prisoner Nathaniel Jones. There was no body to be found. McLeod hurled indiscriminate invective and ordered a search party out, accompanied by reliable Huron scouts. When the officer in charge of the search party assured McLeod that they would track down the frontiersman the colonel scoffed.

"Somehow I doubt it. But go ahead and do your best."

The Hurons were superb trackers, but they soon lost the trail. So many trees had fallen in the forest that Nathaniel could literally travel for miles without moccasin touching the ground.

As soon as the quake spent itself Simon Girty left his badly damaged cabin and rode his favorite mule into Amherstburg. The town was a scene of shocking devastation, but the old renegade paid little attention to anything besides the tavern, which had lost two walls and its roof. In the aftermath of the earthquake a heavy silence lay upon the land, in stark contrast to the hellish din that had accompanied it. Down in the town the people wandered aimlessly, staring blankly at the destruction, and if they spoke at all it was in hushed tones, as though they feared that by speaking loudly they might trigger an aftershock. The birds, which had recently filled the sky, all seemed to have disappeared. Dogs huddled, panting hard and watching wild-eyed, but did not bark or howl. The whole world was holding its breath.

Girty found no one in the vicinity of the tavern, and stumbled upon no bodies in the debris, and he was glad for that, but gladder still when he discovered an undamaged crock of corn liquor, which he confiscated. If he didn't take it, someone else would. Sorely in need of nerve medicine, he sat on the stoop of the tavern. The front wall had collapsed, leaving only the door frame, and the door was hanging drunkenly on one leather hinge behind him. He took several long swigs from the crock and felt better about things, but then he thought about his cabin and how much hard work would be required to render it habitable again, and he helped himself to a few more swigs, after which the condition of his home struck him as a matter of great inconsequence. The liquor helped him put his priorities in the proper order. At least he was alive, and at least some of the tavern stock had survived the earthquake. And his favorite mare was alive, too, though his other horses and his dog had run off into what used to be a forest but was now a great jumbled pile of fallen trees. He drank some more in a toast to his favorite mare.

Eventually, thoroughly drunk, he decided to take his leave. Since the tavern keeper was not going to make an appearance and prevent him from absconding with the crock he felt free to take the corn liquor with him. If he left it on the stoop, somebody would come along and drink it, undoubtedly someone who did not appreciate good corn liquor the way he did. So he managed, with some difficulty, to climb into the saddle, took another swig for the road, and kicked the mare into motion, not bothering to use the reins because the mare knew its way home and because Girty needed one hand to hold the crock and another to clutch the saddlehorn in order to steady himself, since he did not want to fall off the horse and possibly shatter the crock.

The road that led to his cabin passed through a stretch of used-to-be forest, and here there were a number of fallen trees lying in the mare's path. It stopped before the first obstacle and waited for some direction from its rider, but Girty was too befuddled even to realize that they weren't still moving. So the mare, sensing that it was up to her, snickered softly and went around the tree. On several occasions it jumped a smaller obstacle, and when it jumped Girty managed to stay glued to the saddle, an old instinct, an accomplished horseman's reflex. In Girty's opinion each successful jump was cause for self-congratulations, bestowed in the form of another pull off the crock. After a half-dozen jumps and subsequent rewards, the renegade was lost in an inebriated fog, to the extent that all he could do was stay in the saddle and hold onto the crock. He was not aware of doing either, nor of anything else.

Which made him easy prey for Nathaniel Jones.

III

It was not mere coincidence that brought the frontiersman, in his flight from Fort Malden, to this point in the devastated forest. Knowing that his chances of eluding pursuers would be enhanced were he mounted rather than afoot, he had made his way toward Amherstburg, hoping that in the confusion wrought by the earthquake he might be able to steal a horse. He muttered thanks to God Almighty when he saw the lone rider. Not recognizing Girty at first, he assumed by the slumped posture of the rider that the man was either hurt, asleep, or drunk—and as he moved in closer and saw the crock he knew it to be the latter case. Nathaniel did not want to hurt the man if he could help it, but he made up his mind to have that horse.

He had to get home—had to let Amanda know he wasn't dead, after all.

Seeing that the horse—clearly the rider had very little to do with it—was keeping more or less to the road, Nathaniel galloped through the woods, hurtling over fallen trees with the agility of a gazelle, or running along their trunks as sure-footed as a cat. As he ran he held the eighteen-inch iron chain that connected the heavy shackles on his wrists, to prevent it from jangling. Having his wrists bound in this way made running and jumping more difficult, but he managed. He had to.

Girty's mare heard him—though he moved as quietly as he could he had to sacrifice a degree of stealth for the sake of speed—and her head jerked up, and her ears swiveled this way and that as she whickered as though disgusted by this new and as yet unseen complication in what was already a most exasperating day. Girty, on the other hand, was blissfully drunk and heard nothing. Nathaniel was able to secret himself among the fragrant green boughs of a fallen pine lying athwart the road well in advance of horse and rider. Here he waited, crouched, scarcely breathing, among limbs that had only hours before swayed to the susurrant whisper of the wind eighty feet above the earth, now lying broken and tangled upon the ground.

By the time the mare had reached the fallen tree among whose limbs the frontiersman lay in wait she had lost track of him entirely—unable to see him, or hear him, or pick up his scent, she forgot all about him. Nestled in his green and bristly cocoon, Nathaniel noted that the reins lay knotted together upon the mare's neck. The rider was clutching the saddlehorn with one hand and the crock with the other. So when he exploded from his place of concealment he went for the reins first, rather than the rider. Caught by surprise, the mare snorted and reared. Nathaniel had prayed it would rear before bolting, and his prayer was answered. When the mare came down on all fours he grabbed the reins. To his surprise, the rider was still in the saddle, as though only an act of God could pry him loose, because gravity and the antics of a spooked horse apparently could not do the trick.

The mare's violent reaction to Nathaniel's sudden appearance did manage to penetrate Girty's liquor lethargy. For an instant his bloodshot eyes met Nathaniel's. The frontiersman recognized him then.

"Girty!"

Reins in his grasp, Nathaniel grabbed hold of the saddlehorn and vaulted onto the mare's back, his body colliding with Girty's and knocking the renegade out of the saddle. The befuddled Girty sprawled on the ground, stunned by the fall. Nathaniel climbed the reins and got the mare under control. Then he dismounted and secured the leathers to a stout limb before turning to the renegade. Girty was on his hands and knees now, staring with sheer horror at the shattered crock, its precious contents staining the dust of the road. Nathaniel grabbed him with both hands by the back of the collar and hauled him to his feet. Girty still didn't recognize Nathaniel. He wasn't too clear about what had just happened. But he blamed his assailant for breaking the crock, and with a sob of sodden rage he took a wild swing at Nathaniel. Nathaniel blocked the swing and hit Girty with both hands clasped together, striking the side of the head. Girty crumpled. Nathaniel pulled him upright again and pinned him against the trunk of the fallen tree, holding him there, and having to do it because it seemed as though Girty's knees no longer had any bone in them.

"God has truly blessed me today," said the frontiersman, jamming a forearm against Girty's throat and bending him backward over the log.

"Who the hell are you?" wheezed the renegade.

"Surely you remember me."

Girty stared blankly, searching his memory, but great big chunks of his memory were gone now, lost forever, and he hadn't even been aware of that loss until this moment, and the realization both shocked and frightened him. Nathaniel could read it in his eyes even before he responded. The renegade who had chased him for an entire night and day, from Quashquame's village to the banks of the Ohio, accompanied by a passel of warriors out to skin him alive, did not know him from Adam now.

"What's your name?" asked Girty.

"Nathaniel Jones."

"The one they call Flintlock. I've heard of you. We've never crossed paths ... have we?"

"We have." Nathaniel gave him the details, pared down to the bone. Girty listened, brows knit, then sadly shook his head.

"I just don't recall."

Nathaniel eased the pressure on Girty's throat, realizing that the renegade was not at all the man he had once been, the terror of the woodlands, the bogey man that pioneer women warned their children about. Now he was just an empty rotting shell, a shadow of his former self, and maybe not even that, a man who in a few short years had become old and soft and forgetful. He was no threat now. It scared Nathaniel some, seeing Girty like this, how a man could come unraveled so quickly, and how he could still be walking and talking and breathing and yet be already dead, for all practical purposes. He derived no pleasure from seeing a once-hated foe in such a state of decrepitude.

"I'm going to take your horse," said Nathaniel.

"Don't, I beg you," gasped Girty. "She's the only friend I got."

"God, Girty, what's become of you?"

The renegade shrugged. "I just woke up sick and tired one day. Not bone tired. Soul tired, I guess you'd say. Like during the night while I slept somebody snuck in and took all the will to live right out of me." Girty noticed for the first time the shackles on Nathaniel's wrists. "You broke out of the guardhouse at Fort Malden, didn't you?"

"I didn't break out. There was no guardhouse left after the earthquake."

"God, I need a drink . . ."

"I almost feel sorry for you, Girty."

The renegade did not have enough pride left to bristle at the notion that he needed sympathy.

"If you were half the man you once were, I'd kill you," continued Nathaniel. "You'd be obliged to pay the debt you owe all those of your own race who lay cold in their graves on your account."

"I *am* paying the debt," muttered Girty. "Don't you think I know that? I wish you *would* kill me. Go ahead and do it. I don't care. Nobody else will either. Got no one to mourn over my grave, Jones. Indians used to like me well enough when I was strong and fast and would kill for them. But they got no use for me now. I'm paying for my sins, and I ain't even got to Hell yet."

"You will. But not by my hand."

"You might beat me there," said Girty, with a crooked half smile exposing yellowed teeth. "You'll have to go up against Tecumseh now, and all the Injuns, northern and southern alike, 'cause you know all this"—he gestured at the fallen forest—"the earthquake and everything, is the sign they been waiting on. We done wrong by them, Jones, our kind has. It's the day of reckoning. They'll sweep across Kentucky like a red wave of death."

"You're wrong on two counts, Girty. There was always more than enough land for all of us. More than the red man would ever use. You can count them by the thousands. We number in the millions. Yet there was never any room for us as far as they were concerned. And when we put down our roots they took to the warpath. The Indian says he doesn't own the land, yet he doesn't want anyone else to partake of its

288

bounty. Too bad, I say. If they don't own it, then it's up for grabs. We're a nation of free men, Girty, free to hack out a living for ourselves and our families in this wilderness, and we're free because of the land. I reckon we're more free than the Indian, in that respect. When you own a piece of land you don't have to work for anybody else. Just yourself. The sweat of your brow belongs to you, and falls for your sake. No one else's. No one's got a claim on you, and you can live on your own terms, as long as the way you live don't trespass on somebody else's freedom."

"We have trespassed on the Indian."

"This land we're standing on, how many tribes have laid claim to it? A tribe would live here until a stronger one came along and drove the first one out, and then that tribe would linger until an even stronger bunch came along. We're the strongest tribe yet, Girty, and it's no use pretending that this is any different from all those other times. More Indians have been killed by their own kind than by our people. We're here to stay, and Tecumseh and all his signs and all his warriors won't make a bit of difference. When the smoke clears we'll be the ones left standing. And you know why? Because we're free. Had the Indian felt the pride and responsibility of ownership of the land and put down roots, things might've turned out another way entirely. But he hasn't, he doesn't, and he won't. He's a wanderer. Tell him he needs to stay put in one spot and he'll spit in your eye and be gone before you can blink. Thing is, if you don't have roots down deep in the land, you just get blown away by the first strong wind that comes along."

"That's your opinion," said Girty.

"Yes, by God, that's my opinion."

"I'm glad I won't be there for this fight. Because it is hopeless, like you say, and I would hate to see them fall. But against such men as you what chance does Tecumseh have?"

"None at all." Nathaniel turned to the mare.

"Jones," said Girty, as the frontiersman climbed into the saddle. "They're not savages, no more than we are. They are an honorable people."

"What's honor got to do with it?"

"You can make out like it's of no consequence to you because you have it and to spare."

"It's those who don't have it, or wonder if they do, who make a big noise about honor. Good-bye, Girty. God knows, I hope we never meet again."

As Nathaniel rode away on the mare, the renegade slumped to the ground among the fallen timbers, and in a little while tears streaked his dusty cheeks as he wept over the wasted liquor.

IV

True to his word, Tecumseh re-created the village of Tippecanoe. He meant the village's rebirth to be a symbol of hope and faith for all those who followed him, and for those who had once followed him but did no longer because of The Prophet's defeat. Many Indians converged on Tippecanoe after the Great Sign. By April, a thousand Indians lived in the village, and every day more were coming in—not just Shawnees but also Potowatomies and Delawares and Wyandots and Miamis and Sacs and Foxes and Winnebagos and even a few Iroquois. The winter had been a difficult one, because Harrison's soldiers had destroyed all the stores of corn and grain. They would not have made it but for the generosity of the British, who sent two pack trains of food and ammunition to Tippecanoe. Matthew Elliott served as a trusted go-between.

Back at Vincennes, William Henry Harrison offered amnesty to Tecumseh and his followers if they promised never again to take the warpath against the white man. In return, Harrison reiterated his offer to see to it that Tecumseh received an audience with James Madison, the President of the Eighteen Fires—eighteen now, as Louisiana had recently entered the Union as the eighteenth state. Not wishing to provide Harrison with an excuse to launch a second attack against Tippecanoe, Tecumseh's response was cordial, side-stepping the matter of amnesty—which of course he had no desire for, being disinclined to make the promise Harrison wanted from him, a promise he would have to break anyway—but expressing an interest in seeing the President. Tecumseh was stalling for time. Yes, he would like to speak with the Great White Father in Washington, but he could not possibly go before the end of the summer. Until then his presence was required in Tippecanoe.

Praised for his great victory, Harrison was given command of all troops stationed in Illinois and Indiana Territories, and was authorized to call upon the Kentucky militia if he deemed it necessary, which was perfectly acceptable to the Kentuckians, who thought they had finally found a man in Harrison they could proudly follow. Harrison kept some of the Kentucky border captains and their companies of Long Knives with him at Vincennes, for he was wary of Tecumseh and the Shawnee's true intentions, rotating long furloughs so that the Kentuckians could go home and till their fields and do their spring planting and give their wives and children a kiss or two.

War had been formally declared by the United States on Great Britain. In the towns the church bells tolled and in the cities cannon boomed and the citizens celebrated in the streets. The entire population seemed to heave a vast sigh of relief. Since 1807, with the firing of HMS *Leopard* on the USS *Chesapeake* and Jefferson's embargo, the tension had been building and the pressure had become unbearable. Now the deed was done, the die was cast, and the devil was left to take the hindmost. Thirsting for glory, young men rushed to enlist in the army, while at the "War Mess"—the Washington club of War Hawks that customarily convened to plot their bellicose strategies in a boardinghouse dining room—Henry Clay leapt upon the table and danced an Indian war dance, whooping at the top of his lungs. No one had worked more diligently than he to bring the conflict about. He had not the slightest doubt that his country would prevail, and he fully expected her to reap a bountiful harvest, in particular the whole great uncharted vastness of Canada, rich in untapped resources. Great Britain would finally be ousted from the continent.

Meanwhile, William Hull, governor of the Michigan Territory, was awarded the rank of brigadier general and the command of a newborn entity called the Northwestern Department of the Army. Hull was authorized to raise an army of twelve hundred men and march north to Detroit, capturing Fort Malden near Amherstburg on the way, the first stage in an invasion of Canada.

Unfortunately, Hull proved to be Harmer reincarnated. He knew next to nothing about military affairs, and demonstrated as much from the start. Nonetheless, volunteers flocked to his banner. There were parades and speeches and dress reviews galore. Hull himself was a rather pompous man, better suited for politics than the field of battle. He named his own son, an unreliable drunkard, as his aide-de-camp. The troops had a good laugh at young Abraham Hull's expense upon the occasion of their very first river crossing, when Abraham, intent on demonstrating to the others how an officer handled such a situation, spurred his horse off a cutbank into the stream. Abraham had been drinking since before breakfast, and could not stay in the saddle. The commanding general was quite humiliated when his aide-de-camp son had to be fished out of the waters and saved from drowning.

It would be only the first of many mishaps.

Hull refused to believe that the Indians posed any threat, even though almost fifty people had been murdered on the frontier since the Battle of Tippecanoe. He wanted to believe that they weren't a factor because Indians terrified him. Failing to utilize his scouts to full advantage, he was blissfully ignorant of the fact that Tecumseh had departed Tippecanoe with three hundred warriors, making for Amherstburg, where the Shawnee leader intended to help the British army defeat Hull's army.

Tecumseh sent belts of black wampum to other villages, urging all those who still believed in his vision of the future to join him. Some answered the call, drifting north in groups of ten, twenty, fifty. Others did not like the idea of an alliance with the British, and refused to participate. They remembered how the British had failed to help Blue Jacket at Fallen Timbers. The redcoats had huddled safely behind the walls of their fort and let their Indian allies fight it out alone. Tecumseh wasn't happy with the situation, either, but he had no alternative. It was a case of being in league with one devil to defeat another.

Hull crept northward, giving the British ample time to prepare a hot reception. By the first week of July, while the Americans toiled through the steaming heat of the verdant Maumee Valley, Tecumseh could count nearly a thousand warriors in his encampment not far from The Point, Matthew Elliott's home. Three hundred Sioux and Sacs had just arrived from the west. Colonel McLeod asked Tecumseh to dispatch scouts to spy on the slowly advancing enemy column. The scouts supplied McLeod with excellent and encouraging intelligence. There seemed to be a shocking lack of discipline among Hull's volunteers. The army was really just an armed mob, two thousand strong.

Against this number McLeod could rely on three hundred well-trained redcoats in the garrison of Fort Malden—elements of two crack regiments—as well as over a hundred French-Canadian Rangers and, of course, Tecumseh's Indians. He thought it was enough to do the job. Hull finally reached Detroit. On the Canadian side of the Detroit River, McLeod and Tecumseh prepared an ambush, laying the groundwork for what would become only the first of many disasters for the Americans in a war that started out as a lark but would quickly deteriorate into a grim and desperate struggle for the survival of the young republic.

V

Belatedly aware of the presence of Tecumseh's Indians, Hull lost what little in the way of nerves that he possessed. The devil's children as he called them, were terrifying, and few were fooled by his feeble attempt to demonstrate a proper disdain for them. It was natural, then, for him to magnify his scout's reports of the Indian presence tenfold, imagining the woodlands filled with a redskin horde waiting to descend like locusts on his army were he so foolhardy as to venture out of the fortifications at Detroit, much less proceed on an invasion of Canada.

His amateur soldiers were quickly becoming disenchanted with this adventure. The march north through the sweltering woods had taken a lot out of them, and there was precious little glory to be found in digging trenches. The more experienced border captains in the army prevailed upon Hull to proceed with training the raw recruits, and Hull, whose politician's instincts could detect discontent among the masses, readily agreed. But it was very difficult now to get the men to knuckle under to the discipline required to whip them into fighting shape. Desertions were soon on the rise. The inhabitants of Detroit inundated Hull's headquarters with complaints about the unruly mob of patriots. Hull finally concluded that he had to act, though he had no stomach for it. In the stifling heat of mid-July, a large portion of his army crossed the river below Hog Island in a flotilla of small boats and occupied the deserted Canadian village of Sandwich. The crossing caught Tecumseh—and, therefore, McLeod—completely by surprise. In spite of himself Hull had done well. Then, without realizing it, he made another right move.

On the evening of July seventeenth Tecumseh responded to a summons from Colonel McLeod to meet him at The Point. McLeod was drinking heavily, putting Matthew Elliott's well-stocked liquor cabinet to good use, and giving the young half-breed woman, the old Indian agent's house servant, dark and speculative glances each time she appeared soundlessly to refill his empty glass, and Tecumseh could sense that the colonel desired her, like a vulture perched in a tree desires the carrion on the ground below, and was just waiting for the right moment to spread his wings and launch himself.

"Hull has issued a proclamation," said McLeod. Though he had been drinking heavily he had a tremendous capacity for hard liquor, and the amber poison—that was the way Tecumseh perceived it—seemed to have no effect whatsoever. His eye was clear, his voice strong. "Matthew has a copy."

"Just tell me," said Tecumseh.

"He has offered amnesty to all the French-Canadians," said Elliott. "Urged the residents of the town of Sandwich to return to their homes in safety. But he has also made it clear that any white man caught fighting alongside your Indians will be executed."

"A clever ploy," sneered McLeod. "I didn't know the old fool had it in him, frankly. Someone must have put him up to it."

"Half of the French-Canadian Rangers have deserted," announced Elliott, his voice flat and emotionless, like that of a man who has removed himself from the issue, the referee of a bare-knuckle donnybrook who has no stake in the outcome. "Many of the civilians *have* returned to Sandwich. Some, even, have crossed the river to Detroit."

Tecumseh nodded grimly. "That explains the Chippewas leaving."

"Leaving?" McLeod, moodily gazing into his glass now that the half-breed girl was gone and he did not have her to undress with his eyes, looked up sharply.

"Two hundred of them."

"Perhaps Hull is smarter than we gave him credit for," acknowledged Elliott.

"No, he is a coward," said Tecumseh. "He wants to fight this war with words."

"So far it's working," replied the Indian agent. "He put the fear of God into the Chippewas and the French-Canadians."

"My people are tired of waiting for him to attack," said Tecumseh. "But his people are also tired of waiting. Soon they will make a mistake. Impatient men always do. Then I will strike. We need a victory to encourage our people."

Two days later Tecumseh's prediction came true. One of Hull's captains convinced the reluctant general to let him reconnoiter with one hundred and fifty volunteers down the River Road toward Amherstburg. They marched as far as the bridge across the Canard River. Tecumseh had hidden his eighty warriors in the woods, where they were joined by a like number of French-Canadian Rangers, intending to strike the Americans as they debouched from the bridge. Yet the Americans refused to cross the Canard. Frustrated, Tecumseh turned to Stiahta.

"I will go out and try to draw them across."

"You will not go alone," said Stiahta. "I am going with you."

"I will go too," said Main Poche, a war chief of the Potowatomies and one of Tecumseh's staunchest supporters.

Going on foot to present smaller targets to the enemy, the three Indians trotted out of the woods and across the bridge. The startled Americans began shooting at them from their ragged lines two hundred yards away. Their bullets whined around Tecumseh and his two companions, kicking up spurts of dust in the road. With some surprise, Stiahta realized that Tecumseh was laughing. They ran fifty yards out from the bridge before Tecumseh called a halt. Then all three raised their rifles and fired at the Americans, before turning to run back toward the bridge. They were nearly to the river when a bullet struck Main Poche in the neck. The Potowatomie was older and heavier than his companions, and so had lagged behind. Tecumseh, turning at the bridge, saw his friend sprawled in the road. Without a moment's hesitation he tossed his rifle to Stiahta. "Get across!" he shouted, and raced back to Main Poche. The Americans were coming now, running with whoops and hollers, baying like hounds on the spoor of a fox. Tecumseh reached Main Poche unscathed and, lifting the wounded Indian onto his shoulders, ran back to the bridge.

The Indians and rangers in the woods were inspired by Tecumseh's heroic act. They burst from cover, moving to the south bank of the Canard and firing into the ranks of the advancing Americans. The air around him angry with bullets, Tecumseh crossed the bridge unhurt. The Americans drew up in shoddy formation on the north bank, and for the next several minutes a fierce firefight raged. The Indians and the rangers lay on their bellies in the tall sunbrown grass while the half-trained Americans milled about in the acrid powder smoke hanging heavy on the sullen summer air. It was the Americans who got the worst of the exchange.

Tecumseh carried Main Poche into the woods and laid him gently on the ground. He was relieved to see that the wound, amazingly, was not a mortal one, having passed through the neck, missing both the spine and the carotid artery. He rushed back to the river and stood there, impervious to the bullets of the Americans, and disdainful of them, too. His cool courage under fire and his apparent invincibility impressed the Indians, and they held their ground until the Americans, bloodied and discouraged, withdrew.

The history books would record the fight at the Canard River bridge as a minor skirmish, if they recorded anything about it at all. But Tecumseh hailed it as a decisive victory, and it proved to be useful propaganda, bolstering the flagging confidence of the Indians under his command. There were no more desertions.

The River Road was the only practical route for Hull to take in an advance on Fort Malden and Amherstburg, and though his captains insisted that the bridge over the Canard could be taken and the way made clear, Hull refused to budge. He knew he was facing Tecumseh, and the very thought rendered him indecisive. In time he returned to Detroit, where he felt a lot safer. He took most of his muttering army with him, leaving but a token force on Canadian soil.

Meeting again with McLeod at The Point, Tecumseh learned that British reinforcements commanded by Major General Isaac Brock were on the march from Niagara.

"This is good news," said Tecumseh. "My people will cross the Detroit River and cut off the Americans' supply line. Hull will not leave Detroit. We will surround him, and he will surrender his army."

Neither Elliott nor McLeod questioned this bit of prophesy.

Tecumseh had been right too often in the past.

VI

In mid-August General Brock arrived with four hundred soldiers and sixty Iroquois warriors loaded onto ten bateaux. He was greeted with good news compliments of Tecumseh. The Shawnee leader had successfully turned back two attempts by the Americans—at Maguaga and Brownstown—to resupply William Hull and his army which, for all practical purposes, were trapped in Detroit.

Of course Hull could have broken out to the south or the west if he had wanted to. The British and their Indian allies were not strong enough to prevent that from happening. Hull's scouts told him this was so, and the border captains under his command pestered him to act, but Hull refused to believe the reports of the former and considered the latter woefully lacking in knowledge and judgment.

The truth of the matter was that Hull was terrified of Indian ambush. By now Tecumseh knew this, and a swarm of Indians seemed to infest the woods around Detroit, so that in a few weeks' time Hull was firing off frantic dispatches insisting on reinforcements and justifying this request with the claim that he was confronted by ten thousand hostile Indians, when in fact

Tecumseh had considerably less than one-fifth that number.

For Tecumseh, Brock's energy and aggressiveness were gratifying to see. The redcoat general immediately tightened the noose around Detroit, and British batteries began to pound Hull's defenses. A few days later Tecumseh was called to a meeting with the new British commander at The Point. Tecumseh was glad Brock had assumed command from McLeod. The colonel was too interested in Elliott's liquor and Elliott's half-breed house servant. Hate and bitterness were eating away at McLeod's insides, and his devotion to the basest passions were clouding his judgment. He was not interested in winning, only in destroying. He was a killer, thought Tecumseh, but not really a soldier. Brock, on the other hand, was all business.

"I believe we can take Detroit, and General Hull's entire army," said Brock. "We must strike quickly and decisively. If we can put enough pressure on Hull, his own fear will finally break him."

Tecumseh wholeheartedly agreed.

"Tomorrow morning," continued Brock, "my troops will begin an assault on the American fortifications to the south. Tecumseh, you will cross the river unseen during the night and enter the town from the north. They will not be expecting an attack from that quarter, and resistance will be light. When Hull learns that Indians are in the streets of Detroit he will buckle."

"It is a good plan."

"But you must give me your word that your people will not put the inhabitants of Detroit to the knife. There must be no massacre. I do not make war on civilians, and I will not tolerate it."

"Neither will I," replied Tecumseh. "I never have. You have my word."

"That's good enough for me," said Brock. He removed the scarlet sash from his waist and presented it to the Shawnee leader. "Accept this, please, as a token of my regard for you, my trusted ally."

Tecumseh was deeply moved, and accepted the sash. "I will wear it proudly into battle tomorrow, and all the battles to come."

"With you on our side, Tecumseh, I believe we will win this war."

"We fight to get our land back. That is all."

"And you shall have it back."

That night, Tecumseh and seven hundred warriors, wearing only moccasins and breechclouts and painted for war, slipped across the river. When dawn broke and the British bombardment commenced in the south, Tecumseh gave the signal, and the Indians rushed into Detroit, overwhelming the pickets Hull had placed to the north of the town, catching the Americans completely unawares.

Panic spread like wildfire through the town as the Indians roamed the streets, facing only light resistance. A few townsmen tried to fight, but were quickly overcome. The rest cowered behind locked doors. The Indians broke into a number of houses, stealing food and knickknacks that caught their fancy. To the astonishment and relief of the townspeople no one was struck down, apart from the handful who had tried to put up a fight. There was no massacre. Tecumseh had warned his warriors that they were permitted to kill only in self-defense, and that if one white person was slain or molested, the Indian who had done the deed and thereby disobeyed his express order would suffer greatly—before he died.

General Hull had been drinking all night. When he heard that the Indians were in Detroit he began to shake uncontrollably. Spittle dropped from his chin. A British cannonball crashed into his headquarters. That was the last straw for William Hull. The flag came down the headquarter's flagpole and a white bedsheet was run up—much to the disgust and chagrin of Hull's soldiers.

Brock had little respect for Hull, but he tried to act as though he did when he accepted the man's sword. Tecumseh was present at the formal surrender, resplendent in a blue breechclout and red leggins, his face and chest painted with vermilion circles and crescents, a look of fierce exultation on his face. This was a stunning defeat for the *Shemanese*. This time the British and the Indians had worked together and achieved a tremendous victory. This time had been different from all those times before. The doubting Thomases would see that he had succeeded where Cornstalk and Black Fish and Blue Jacket had failed.

He could see a clear image in his mind's eye— Chillicothe, the once great Shawnee capital on the banks of the Scioto River, standing in all its former splendor once more.

CHAPTER ELEVEN

Jonathan

Henry Clay, Esq.

Sept. 16, 1812

Dear Henry,

I am writing from Fort Harrison to keep you up to date on the situation here. Since the disgraceful surrender of Detroit by that coward William Hull, the entire frontier has erupted into bloody warfare. Much encouraged, the Indians have taken to the warpath, and the incidents of depravity and butchery which they have perpetrated on innocent people are too numerous to mention. Suffice it to say that dozens of cabins have been put to the torch, and I would estimate that a hundred men, women, and children murdered. Reports have come in from Michigan, Illinois, Indiana, Ohio, and even Tennessee and the Mississippi Territory. The Sauks, Sioux, Wyandots, Delawares, Potowatomies, and Ottawas in the north as well as the Upper and Lower Creeks and some of the Cherokees to the south have risen up against us. Of course, as you know by now, the Shawnee Tecumseh is the one most responsible. He played a key role in our defeat at Detroit. I am told his brother, The Prophet, has been completely discredited, but that members of the numerous tribes, north and south, look upon Tecumseh as something of a god. He is our most dangerous foe by far.

As for Hull, the circumstances attending the surrender, the most mortifying and humiliating event in the history of our republic, being well known at this juncture, assure us that there was no justification for it. I believe he was seized by panic, and his army of stalwart men were victims of the man's want of energy and prompt decision. He allowed his line of communication to be cut off with the states of Ohio and Kentucky and without making any active movement to reopen them, he remained tranquil instead, evincing a want of confidence, and giving the enemy time to consolidate its forces. No intelligence justifies the belief that he gave battle in a single instance. His surrender was very much premature. His men were paroled, and we have heard from some of them that the surrender caught them completely by surprise. They insist that a vigorous counterattack would have cleared the streets of Tecumseh's Indians. But no such effort was made. Hull's defenders say he was concerned for the safety of the civilians, and that he assumed the Indians were falling upon the defenseless inhabitants of the town, and he feared that to prolong the contest would result in the annihilation of the entire population. In truth—and this must be credited to Tecumseh—the Indians did not touch a single hair on the head of one citizen of Detroit, apart from those who vainly attempted to repel the Indian onslaught. Hull could have drawn his troops from their fortifications in the south and swept the Indians before him. The British were pounding away with their cannon, but by all accounts there was no immediate threat of an attack by redcoat infantry, who were delayed in their crossing of the river. Unfortunately, this is pointless conjecture. The fact remains that Hull surrendered, and should be court-martialed. That degree of incompetence is criminal, if not traitorous.

The enemy followed his success at Detroit with another at Chicago. The garrison at Fort Dearborn had been ordered to evacuate that post and march to Fort Wayne. Virtually the entire civilian population of Chicago joined this evacuation. On the shores of Lake Michigan a large body of Indians, hidden in the sand dunes, fell upon them in ambush as they passed. Nearly a hundred of our people were struck down, including many women and children.

As you might imagine, these events have prompted hundreds, if not thousands, of warriors to flock to Tecumseh, even some of those who have gone to great pains to profess their friendship to us. But do not despair. I suspect Tecumseh must be surprised by the reaction of our race to these recent disasters. Fort Harrison has been inundated with volunteers. They come from Kentucky, Ohio, Virginia, Maryland, and Pennsylvania. I am told that several thousand men have congregated at Urbana. Baltimore has promised to raise an entire regiment for the defense of the frontier. Virginia has sent fifteen hundred of her native sons to our aid. Your colleague, Colonel Richard M. Johnson, has raised a Kentucky regiment of five hundred mounted rifles. Governor Shelby has entrusted the command of the thousands of Kentuckians who have responded to this crisis to William Henry Harrison. I believe we are in good hands. His victory at Tippecanoe last year is a source of national pride, and all of us who have had the privilege of serving with him do now without hesitation place our lives in his keeping. We are going to have to beat these damned Indians again, Henry. It was our great misfortune that Tecumseh was absent from the Battle at Tippecanoe. He will, I am sure, be with his warriors when next we fight. There is not a man among us who has not vowed to kill him if the opportunity arises. We had peace on the frontier until he began to stir up trouble. All of us know that our homes and our families will remain at risk as long as that man draws breath. The fate of this country, at least that portion that lies west of the Alleghenies, will be, I think, determined by our next battle. Rest assured, we will triumph or perish in the attempt.

Your friend,

Jonathan Groves

October 9, 1812

My Dear Jonathan,

I would like to include for your perusal a portion of the letter I recently received from your General Harrison:

"The rumoured disasters upon our northwestern frontier are now ascertained to be correct. The numerous northwestern tribes of Indians in arms against us is the distressing picture which presents itself to view in this part of the country. To remedy all these misfortunes I have an army competent in numbers and in spirit equal to any that Greece or Rome have boasted of but destitute of Artillery, of many necessary equipments, & absolutely ignorant of every military evolution. But I beg you to believe my dear Sir that this retrospect of my Situation far from producing despondency produces the contrary effect. And I feel confident of being able to surmount them all. The grounds for this confidence are reliance on my own zeal and perseverance & a perfect conviction that no such raw materials for forming an invincible army ever existed as the volunteers which have marched from Kentucky on the present occasion."

* * *

I have the utmost confidence in you, Jonathan, in your army, and in the man who commands it. A park of heavy artillery has been sent in to Pittsburgh, to be forwarded thence towards Cleveland, for the use of the army. I assure you that we here in Congress will pay the utmost attention to the needs and wishes of you and your valiant comrades-in-arms. Everything depends on you. Yet I am not concerned. If the fate of this fair republic rests on Kentucky shoulders then we may all sleep soundly in our beds.

A salutary effect has been produced on the public mind by the events which have occurred. Misfortune has diminished the influence of foreign attachments and party animosities, and contributed to draw the people closer together. The disaster at Detroit has awakened new energies and roused the whole people. The Indians have shocked us with some of the most horrid murders. Within twenty miles of Louisville, I am told, on the headwaters of Silver Creek, twenty-two people were massacred a fortnight ago. Our policy must be changed towards these savages. They have commenced an unprovoked war. They must be made to feel the utmost vigor of the Government. The President, I have no doubt, has been deceived as to their dispositions. They are not of the pacific and admirable character which certain Gentlemen would represent them. The fact is our frontiers have enjoyed one of the longest intervals of Indian peace that has occurred since the first settlement of Virginia. The inevitable progression of our people westward, the death of the old warriors, the springing up of a new race of young ones, the natural propensity of savage man to war—all these factors are sufficient to account for Indian hostilities, without recurring to that most fruitful source of them, British instigation.

It is in vain to conceal the fact—at least I will not

attempt to disguise with you—that Mr. Madison is wholly unfit for the storms of War. Nature has cast him in too benevolent a mold. Admirably adapted to the tranquil scenes of peace, he is not suited for the rough and rude blasts which the conflict of nations generate. On the part of this Legislature, never was there a body assembled more disposed to adopt any and every measure calculated to give effect and vigor to the operations of the war than are the esteemed members of the Twelfth Congress. If he is wise, the President will leave the details of the war's prosecution to us who are eager to pursue it. Would that I could be there with you and the other courageous sons of Kentucky to take up arms against the scourge of Tecumseh's Indians. But, as Speaker of the House, I can perhaps best serve my country here. Rest assured, though, that I am with you in spirit.

We have had news of several victories at sea. Brilliant as they are, however, they do not fill the void created by our misfortunes on land. Nonetheless, the justness of our cause, the adequacy of our means to bring it to a successful issue, the spirit and patriotism of the country will bring us through. There is still some political opposition. They become the friends of peace and of commerce now that it is no longer possible to abstain from war—a war which is identified with our independence and sovereignty. They tell of the calamities of war, the squandering of resources, the waste of the public treasure, the spilling of innocent blood. They tell us that honor is an illusion! They were for war when the administration was for peace. They are for peace now that the administration is for war. You find them, sir, tacking with every gale. Do not listen to them. Pay them no heed. The champions of war—the proud, the spirited, the sole repository of the nation's honor, the men of vigor and energy—*they* will prevail. I must remain here and fight these "gentlemen" of the opposition, as much as I long for the field of battle. If we stand united we are too powerful for the mightiest nation in Europe, or even all of Europe combined. If we are divided we shall become easy prey. This war was announced, on our part, to meet the war which Great Britain was waging on her part, a war waged by her arrogating to herself the pretension of regulating our foreign trade under the delusive name of retaliatory Orders in Council and by the practice of impressing American seamen & by instigating the Indians to commit hostilities against us.

It is true, the disgrace of Detroit remains to be wiped off. It was the parent of all the subsequent misfortunes we have experienced. An honorable peace now is only attainable by a successful war. We must prosecute this war with the utmost vigor, strike wherever we can reach the enemy, at sea or on land, and negotiate the terms of a peace at Quebec or Halifax. We are told that England is a proud and lofty nation. Proud as she is, we once triumphed over her, and if we do not listen to the councils of timidity and despair we shall again prevail. In such a cause, with the aid of Providence, we must come out crowned with success; but if we fail, let us fail like men and expire together in one common struggle, fighting for our rights.

Am respectfully,

H. Clay
Washington, D.C.

———————————

October 26, 1812

Nathaniel Jones, Esq.

Dear Nathaniel,

I am writing you from an encampment in the vicinity of Grouseland, Governor Harrison's estate on the outskirts of Vincennes. We moved here at the end of August from Fort Harrison, as there were alarming rumors afloat to the effect that the Indians intended to attack the town, which at the time was undefended. Then, too, Vincennes is a central location well-suited for a military concentration. I think there are at least five thousand men here now, almost all of them volunteers, with hundreds more coming in every day. Needless to say it is utter Pandemonium. We must endeavor to whip them into some semblance of order as quickly as possible. The Governor has employed me, along with others, to accomplish as much in the way of training as time will allow. I do not have much experience with infantry, I confess. Were we aboard a man-o-war I could teach them how to beat to quarters, but infantry tactics are something else entirely. Still, I am doing my best.

No sooner had we left Fort Harrison than the Indians attacked, there and at Fort Wayne. Captain Zachary Taylor had a garrison of only fifty men at Fort Harrison. Some Kickapoo and Miami warriors appeared with their women and children and pleaded for admittance into the fort, claiming that they were peaceful Indians and in dire need of food. Captain Taylor did not fall for this transparent ruse. The Indians then dropped all pretenses and launched an attack, which was heroically repulsed. They moved on to easier prey, & massacred twenty men, women, and children who had settled along Pigeon Roost Creek.

The Indians then laid siege to Fort Wayne, commanded

by Captain Oscar Rhea and garrisoned with but seventy men—this against six hundred savages. The defenders managed to get word to us here at Vincennes, and Harrison immediately dispatched a relief force and sent a message back to Rhea, instructing him to hold on at all costs. Nonetheless, Rhea was prepared to surrender, and would have done so, but for an officer of singular and steadfast courage, one Lieutenant Joseph Curtis, who threatened to kill Rhea where he stood if he so much as made the suggestion again. Curtis later relieved Rhea of command, on the grounds that Rhea was in a constant state of inebriation. The brave garrison held out against overwhelming odds long enough for the relief force to arrive and drive off the Indians.

We have only just now received word that General Dearborn crossed the Niagara River into Canada and defeated the British at a place called Queenston. The British general, Brock, was killed in the action. I am told that Brock and Tecumseh had become fast friends, and so I imagine that Brock's death will be a heavy blow to the man some Indians are calling the King of the Woods. It was a great blow to the British, as well, of course, since Brock was one of the few officers in His Majesty's army who knew how to wage war on the frontier.

As a consequence of our victory at Queenston, and the failure of their attacks on Forts Harrison and Wayne, many of the Indians have become discouraged. There is one crucial difference between us, I believe. If things do not go in his favor, the Indian will lose faith in his cause. In our case, misfortune engenders renewed determination to succeed. At any rate, our scouts and spies report that hundreds of warriors have abandoned Tecumseh, who has gone into winter quarters near Amherstburg with a force substantially diminished.

The reason I am writing, Nathaniel, is because the governor has asked me to prevail upon you to come to Vincennes in time for the campaign he intends to launch next spring. The objectives of this campaign are twofold: to recapture Detroit and crush Tecumseh once and for all. While it is true that at least six thousand of our fellow Kentuckians have volunteered, none of them are endowed with your skills as a scout, or your knowledge of the Indians. Harrison wants you to captain his company of scouts. You are the best-qualified man for the job. The only two men who are your equal in the requisite ability are Boone and Kenton, and neither of them is available. He asked me if he thought a letter by his own hand, exhorting you to volunteer, would suffice to sway you, but I told him I would be glad to write you myself. I know you are a patriot, and will give this request the serious consideration it deserves, without permitting personal matters to color your judgment. I do not know what you think of me at this point, or what your daughter has told you concerning the problems which have come between the two of us. I admit I have not heard from Rebecca since I left Elm Tree so many months ago, although I have written countless letters to her. It is clear to me now that my presence at home is not desired, and I will respect her obvious if unspoken preferences in that regard. I am still at a loss to explain why she is acting this way, or what I could have done differently and retained not only her respect, and my son's, but my own, as well. I do love her, Nathaniel, and will until the day I die, no matter what happens, but I do not hold out much hope for a reconciliation.

Please respond. Respectfully Yrs,

Jonathan

November 30, 1812

Captain Jonathan Groves
Dear Jonathan,

I am not much for writing letters, but you must know
I cannot leave Amanda and go off to fight Indians. She
has not yet got over the shock of thinking I was dead.
A piece of her died when Quashquame told her the
Delawares had killed me, and I cannot bring it back to
life. If I left her again, I am afraid the rest of her
would die too. I am sorry but you will have to
handle Tecumseh without my help. I have no doubt
you and Genl Harrison can do it. I only hope you will
watch out for yourself. A man named Hoke Tuller
showed up at my door a month or so ago. He said he was
on leave from your company and was going home to see
his family back in Madison County, only he came a good
piece out of his way to tell me that he was worried about
you. He said all the men in the company held you in high
regard, and none more than he, and that while he was not
in the habit of sticking his nose into another's business he
felt obliged to break that rule this once. He said that in
his opinion you were bound and determined to get
yourself killed, that after the battle at Tippecanoe you
looked right disappointed for being still alive. Lately, said
he, you have taken to strong drink, that while he was not
one to judge others by the quantity of spirits they
consumed, seeing as how he could consume as much as
the best, or worst, of them, he said you were drinking like
a man who has made up his mind that if he cannot get
himself killed in battle or any other way he will drink
himself into an early grave. Hoke Tuller also asked me
not to tell you about his visit unless I had to, and I would
not be doing it now except that I feel as though I know
you well enough to say that you are a man who will

understand that his intentions are good. He is your friend, and came to me with this out of concern for your welfare, and I trust you will not hold it against him.

If you love Rebecca as you say—and I for one believe that you do—you will not let whatever differences separate the two of you now keep you apart forever. You must not forget your son, Christopher. He needs you as much as he does his mother. If what I suspect is true, and you see no purpose in living for yourself, then picture your young son in your mind's eye and I believe you will find that purpose you are lacking. I know you are a man of great courage, Jonathan, I knew that from the moment I first saw you, when you were fighting a she-bear with that cutlass of yours. Nor do I doubt that you are a decent man, a man of integrity, and for that reason, no matter what happens with you and my daughter, I will always think highly of you.

Sincerely,

Nathaniel Jones

December 5, 1812

Capt. Jonathan Groves
Vincennes
Dearest Jonathan,

I am departing Hunter's Creek today, bound for Vincennes, and thought you should be made aware. There has been a heavy snowfall, and the roads are difficult, but not impassable, and it would not matter to me if they were, because I can no longer bear to be so far away from you. I have hired a man who swears he can get me safely to my destination, and I believe he will, because he desperately wants the gold I have promised him if he is successful.

Perhaps you don't want me to come to Vincennes. If this is so, you have only yourself to blame. Had you answered my letters I might not feel compelled, as I do now, to make the journey. But I simply must be sure you are safe, and if you will not communicate with me by letter you will have to do so face to face. I cannot help myself. Oh, if Father knew he would be so outraged at my conduct! I know it is wrong. I realize that you are a married man. Yet I do not believe your wife loves you as I do. No one could. Perhaps you will refuse to speak to me, or acknowledge me in any way once I have arrived, but it won't make any difference, and won't change the way I feel, and I know you are a gentleman and would not treat a lady in such a cavalier manner. I am coming to you, and nothing will prevent me, and I will be content just to set eyes on you again if that is all I can have.

Emily

———————————

CHAPTER TWELVE

The Reckoning

I

Nathaniel did not range far from the cabin anymore when he went hunting. Sometimes he went alone. Sometimes Quashquame went with him. Either way it mattered not—he still stayed close to home, and it wasn't so much Amanda's safety that concerned him, as this was winter and no hostile Indians had been sighted anywhere in the vicinity of Boonesboro for months now, but rather her sanity. He did not know all the details of what had transpired that day when Quashquame had appeared wearing his coat and bearing bad tidings of the kind Amanda had been dreading for thirty years. The Delaware hadn't enlightened him and neither had Amanda, and he had never asked, didn't need to. All he had to do was look into Amanda's eyes for the answer. It lurked there still, behind the eyes, the terror, the grief, the dying she had endured in those weeks when she had known that he would never be coming back to her. It had blunted her smile and deepened the very fine lines at the corners of her mouth and darkened the shadows under her eyes as though some deadly illness had struck her down, an illness that she had barely survived and from which she would never fully recover. So that was the reason, when he had to go hunt something to put in the pot he never ventured far. She was walking on thin ice now, and he had to be careful that it did not crack on his account.

On this bitterly cold February day he returned with two rabbits—game was hard to find these days because in the thirty years they had lived here in these hills the land had filled up with settlers. When he saw the two strange horses standing in the snow in front of the cabin he was at first alarmed, then annoyed, because he surmised that they belonged to men who had come to ask for his help in some part or another of this damned war. It wouldn't be the first time. Things were not going well for the United States. He had tried to warn them, but had they listened? The young republic had been like a brash boy feeling his oats, all a swagger and cocky with overconfidence as he got into the ring with John Bull, and so far John Bull had been whipping the tar out of him.

But it wasn't at all what he thought. Stepping into the cabin with his jaw grim-set, ready to tell them that hell would freeze over before he left his wife and went off to fight in this foolish war, he was shocked to see his daughter. The four of them sat at the table—Rebecca and Amanda, Quashquame and a young black man whose name Nathaniel thought was Isaac. Rebecca rose from the table, stood there, looking unsure of herself, or rather unsure of the reception she would receive from her father.

"Becky . . ."

He rushed forward with a grin, embraced her, long rifle still in one hand, rabbits in the other, and he scarcely noticed Quashquame taking the game and the gun from him.

"It's good to see you," said Nathaniel, half laughing

with the joy of it. "How are you? How's Christopher? Where is he? What a wonderful surprise."

"Christopher is fine. I'm sorry I didn't bring him. But I didn't know what kind of weather we would run into. So I thought it wiser to leave him home."

"And you? You look fine, Becky."

"I'm ... well."

He knew right then that she was lying, and knew, too, what was ailing her, the same old thing, even though two years had passed. Suddenly he was discomfited, wondering what to say, and looking at Amanda, a silent plea for rescue.

"I told her we had a letter from Jonathan a few months ago," said Amanda. "That he is safe."

"I'm glad of that, truly," said Rebecca, trying to come across ambivalent, but doing a poor job. "I ... just came for a visit. I miss this place. I miss the two of you. Do you remember Isaac, Father?"

" 'Course I do."

"I set them all free. I sleep better now, having done it, though I must confess some of my neighbors refuse to have anything to do with me anymore. My friend, Mary Bucknell ... well, I guess you wouldn't say she was my friend any longer. She doesn't come to Elm Tree like she used to. I saw her in town once, but she was in a big hurry to get somewhere, and didn't have time to talk, and I suppose that if I chance to meet her again she'll still be in too big of a hurry to pass the time. You know how it is. I guess I'm not really surprised. I'm glad I did it. Of course, most of them stayed on, like Isaac."

"Elm Tree's mah home," said Isaac.

"He's free, but old habits are hard to break," said Rebecca. "He didn't want to come into this house, and didn't want to sit at this table with us. Said it wasn't proper. I keep telling him he has the right to sit anywhere he wants. But he's stubborn—almost as stubborn as I am."

"That's hard to believe." Nathaniel smiled. "You're always welcome in our house, Isaac."

"Thankee, suh."

"And Quashquame," said Rebecca, turning to smile at the silent Delaware. "It's so wonderful to see him again, too. He's always been like a brother to me. And I suppose something like a son to you, Father."

"I reckon something like that," replied Nathaniel, the furrows deepening between his eyebrows. Rebecca had changed. She was high-strung, nervous, too garrulous, just rattling on and on, as though she was afraid to stop for fear the talk would turn to a subject she desperately wanted to avoid.

But she had run out of things to say now, and lapsed into an uncomfortable silence. Amanda came to her rescue. "Looks like rabbit stew tonight," she said, taking the game from Quashquame. "Come along, Becky, you can help me."

That night after dinner, when Quashquame and Isaac had gone out to the stables, where Quashquame slept when the weather was inclement, and where he and the black man would sleep tonight, Rebecca joined her mother and father to sit near the fire, and Nathaniel settled back in his chair with his ankles crossed and fingers laced together, waiting to hear what Rebecca had come all this long way in the heart of winter to tell him, because by now he was certain that she had come on a mission.

"A man named Hoke Tuller came to Elm Tree a few

weeks ago," she said. "He talked a lot about Jonathan."

"That feller gets around," remarked Nathaniel.

"He said he'd been up here to see you. I suppose he must have told you the same things about Jonathan that he told me. How Jonathan's turned to drink. And . . . and how he's been trying to get himself killed."

"That's just Hoke's opinion."

"I believe him. I do. Don't ask me how, but I just know it's true. I just know."

"Do you want him back, dear?" asked Amanda gently.

Rebecca's troubled gaze was lost in the fire. "I still love him. But I . . . I've lost him. I'm not sure I know how it came to be this way. It didn't really start with Stephen Cooper. Not really. No, it started, I think, when Jonathan went to Frankfort, to complete Elisha Ferguson's unexpired term in the assembly. Then he went on to Washington. But at first he'd sworn that he didn't like the work, and wouldn't serve again if the people reelected him, and yet he always did go back. He spent less and less time at home. And when he promised me he would do all within his power to avoid this idiotic war he didn't mean it. He was one of Henry Clay's War Hawks. He worships the ground Clay walks on. Wants to be just like him. Clay fought that duel with Humphrey Marshall with Jonathan as his second, so Jonathan had to fight a duel, too."

"That's not why he fought Cooper, Becky," said Nathaniel.

"Isn't it? It was all about honor, wasn't it? Not my honor. His. Those years in the public eye changed him. He began to care what people thought of him. When I told him I wanted to free our slaves he was cool toward the idea, worried what our neighbors would think. He said he didn't care, but he did. And he tried to kill Stephen, and do it face-to-face, when he could have let Sheriff Ainsley handle it. But no. That would be like letting another man fight his battles for him, and that just wouldn't do. He knew I didn't want him to go. But he refused to listen. He was listening instead to voices in his head, imagining what others would say about him if he didn't abide by that damned code of honor!"

"Rebecca," said Amanda sternly. "No cussing under this roof."

"I'm sorry."

"So what do you want, Becky?" asked Nathaniel.

Rebecca's eyes flashed. "I want that woman to stay away from my husband."

"What woman?" asked Amanda.

"I reckon she means Emily Cooper," said Nathaniel.

"Yes," said Rebecca. "Emily Cooper. She's left Hunter's Creek, you know. Gone to Vincennes to be near him!"

"Oh my," breathed Amanda.

"It's not his doing," said Rebecca. "I'm certain of that. But she is after him. It doesn't make any sense, does it? After all, he made her a widow."

"He saved her, the way she sees it," said Nathaniel.

Rebecca buried her face in her hands. "I was wrong to blame Jonathan for my losing the baby. He was wrong to care more about his honor than about his family. We were both wrong. I . . . I want to put it all behind us. I don't know if that's possible, but that's what I want. And I don't want him to die. Even if we never . . . I can't bear to think of him dead. But I'm afraid to go." She looked up tearfully at her father. "I'm afraid he hates me now . . ."

Nathaniel looked at Amanda, who had come around behind Rebecca's chair and leaned over to put her arms around her daughter. And Amanda looked him straight in the eye and said, "You must go to Vincennes."

"Amanda . . ."

"You must go. Leave in the morning. Bring him back alive."

Nathaniel nodded. He wasn't surprised. He had known all along that he would leave again.

II

The peninsula of Ontario between Lake Huron and Lake Erie is bisected by the Thames River, which from its mouth at Lake St. Clair rambles one hundred and fifty miles to the northeast. It was on the banks of this river that Tecumseh's Indians were encamped on the evening of October 4th, 1813. The British army commanded by General Henry Proctor was camped nearby. Recently they had abandoned Amherstburg and Fort Malden and were now in full retreat.

In the center of the Indian encampment Tecumseh sat at a fire with his most trusted lieutenants. There was the faithful Stiahta of the Wyandots, and Black Partridge, the Potowatomie, and Black Hawk of the Sauks and the Winnebago war chief Carrymaunee. The Ottawa chief, Naiwash, was present, and the Chippewas were represented by Ooshawanoo. There, too, was his most trusted Shawnee adviser, Sauganash, as well as his old friend Wasegoboah.

Invisible in the black void of a starless night sky

winged flocks of geese, heading south. Winter was coming, a winter that promised to be as bleak as their hopes for the future. All were silent, solemn, waiting for Tecumseh to speak. They knew in their hearts that their cause was lost. But for a long time Tecumseh did not speak, staring morosely into the fire, not feeling its warmth. There was a chill in the air, but that was not what made Tecumseh cold. He thought about everything that had transpired during the year, a year which had opened with such promise, and yet here they were, ten months later, hounded by the *Shemanese* at every turn, their dreams turned into ashes, and on the eve of a battle Tecumseh knew in his heart they could not win.

A year ago Tecumseh had kept his word by rebuilding Tippecanoe, intending the new village as a symbol of the resurrected hopes and dreams he shared with thousands of Indians seeking the return of their homelands. But when the new redcoat general, Proctor—who had replaced Isaac Brock—refused to give them enough supplies to last out the winter, most of Tecumseh's followers were forced to disperse to their tribal villages, leaving Tippecanoe weakly defended and, therefore, easy prey for a force of Kentucky Long Knives dispatched by Harrison from Vincennes. A second time Tippecanoe was burned to the ground, while Tecumseh was forced to flee to the north and the protection of the British. Another disaster followed quickly on the heels on this one. Six hundred militia led by Colonel John Campbell undertook a campaign against the villages of the Miamis, some of Tecumseh's staunchest supporters, and when Campbell was done the Miami tribe, for all practical purposes, ceased to exist.

Nonetheless, the new year had opened with a victory over another of Harrison's contingents, at the River Raisin. Five hundred British troops and eight hundred Indians led by Stiahta launched a surprise attack against the American fortifications at Frenchtown. The outnumbered *Shemanese* put up a valiant if futile resistance, and surrendered after receiving Proctor's assurances that they would be provided protection from the Indians. Proctor took six hundred prisoners with him as he set out for Fort Malden, leaving two hundred wounded Americans in Frenchtown in the charge of a single British officer. As soon as Proctor was gone the Indians struck. Stiahta later told Tecumseh that he had been powerless to stop them. An irresistible blood lust seemed to have his warriors in its grasp. Half the Americans were burned alive in the houses that had been converted into hospitals. The rest were butchered with knives and tomahawks. Though the massacre flew in the face of everything Tecumseh had preached about making war, he let it go, so elated was he by news of the great victory.

In May, Tecumseh and Proctor laid siege to Fort Meigs on the Maumee River. Harrison himself was in the fort. The valley echoed with the thunder of a British battery of mighty 24-pounders, but the American fortifications withstood the pummeling, and with fifteen hundred stalwart Long Knives under his command, Harrison refused to even consider surrender. Tecumseh was eager for a fight with Harrison, and even went so far as to send a message through the American lines offering to face Harrison one-on-one. Instead, Harrison sent several hundred men on a daring raid against the British artillery emplacements located on both sides of the Maumee. On the north side, the

Americans managed to seize the whole battery. They spiked the guns, rendering them useless. Tecumseh led his warriors against them, hoping to cut them off from the flotilla of small boats that had ferried them across the river from Fort Meigs. In the battle that ensued, a great many Long Knives were slain, and hundreds more captured. The American commander, Colonel William Dudley, surrendered to General Proctor, demanding that the British protect his men now that they had put down their weapons. Proctor responded by contemptuously turning his back on Dudley. A Chippewa warrior standing nearby rushed forward and split Dudley's head open with a tomahawk, then hacked the American's chest open and took out his heart, which he and several of his friends proceeded to eat.

The Indians fell upon the rest of the prisoners with a vengeance, shooting, stabbing, tomahawking, and then mutilating the bodies. Only one British officer tried to intervene. He too was struck down. Tecumseh arrived on the scene and tried to stop the carnage. He went so far as to slay a Chippewa who refused to listen to his order to desist. With his bloody warclub raised, Tecumseh told the Indians they would have to take his life if they wanted to kill the remainder of the prisoners. Only then did the Indians take heed. Only then did the slaughter stop.

Enraged, Tecumseh confronted Proctor, asking the British officer why he had not tried to stop the massacre. A bitter argument followed, marking the beginning of an estrangement between the two leaders that would prove fatal to their cause.

A few days later British headquarters received word that a large force of Kentuckians was marching to the rescue of Fort Meigs, and Proctor ordered a withdrawal

to Amherstburg. Tecumseh had no choice but to abandon the siege. He was deeply troubled, not only by
their failure to capture Harrison, but also by the massacre. Now, too late, he realized that by tacitly condon-
ing the butchery at Frenchtown he was in large
measure responsible for what had happened on the
banks of the Maumee. He and his followers had done
wrong, and displeased *Moneto*. There would be consequences, and they would be dire.

This summer, encamped near Amherstburg, Tecumseh's ranks were swollen with new recruits who had
heard of the great victories at Detroit and Frenchtown.
Six hundred Ottawas and Chippewas came, and a considerable number of Sioux. Even some Chickasaws and
Choctaws had arrived from the south, so that by mid-
summer Tecumseh could count no less than three thousand warriors.

But there was bad news, as well. Harrison had finally convinced the United States government to use
friendly Indians as allies. Hundreds of Delawares, Wyandots, and even Shawnees had agreed to take up arms
and fight on the side of the Americans. The idea of Indian fighting Indian was a blow to the morale of the
warriors who followed Tecumseh. So too was the long
summer of inactivity. Proctor flatly refused to even
consider taking the offensive. He seemed to be perfectly content sitting tight in Canada, while every day
Harrison waxed stronger at Fort Meigs. It was late in
August before Proctor stirred and struck halfheartedly
at Fort Stephenson, a small stockade on the banks of
the Sandusky manned by only two hundred Americans
commanded by a twenty-one-year-old major in the
U.S. Army, George Croghan. Against this puny force
Proctor arrayed four thousand redcoats and Indians. He

was confident of quick victory. After a spirited bombardment of the fort, Proctor sent Matthew Elliott, the old Indian agent, under a flag of truce to demand the surrender of the Americans.

"You may tell General Proctor that we are resolved to hold this fort or bury ourselves in its ruin," said Croghan.

"That's fool's talk," said Elliott. "If we have to take the fort by storm, there will be no restraining our Indian allies."

"There never is."

"For God's sake, surrender and avoid a terrible slaughter."

"When—and if—this fort is taken, there will be none left to massacre," was Croghan's icy reply, and his final word on the subject.

Frustrated, Proctor ordered a full-scale assault on the following day. Croghan correctly surmised that the main attack would come against the northwest angle of the fort. A wide ditch lay in front of the angle, and Croghan moved his single cannon to the blockhouse from whence it could command the ditch. When the British 41st Regiment attacked, Croghan waited until the redcoats were tight up to the stockade, filling the ditch. Then his little six-pounder, loaded with grapeshot, spoke. A hundred redcoats were mowed down in a matter of minutes. When they withdrew in complete disorder the ditch was left filled with scarlet-clad corpses. Shaken, Proctor ordered a withdrawal. Tecumseh was beside himself with rage. Proctor was a weak and cowardly man, and Tecumseh told him as much to his face, widening the gulf between them. Major Croghan reported the loss of one man.

As the British retired, many of Tecumseh's followers

melted away, vowing never again to fight with the red-coats. It was a stunning defeat, snatched from the jaws of certain victory, and a complete reversal of fortune for Tecumseh. His Indian army dwindled to less than two thousand men. And when Harrison finally marched out of Fort Meigs, advancing on Amherstburg, the last leg of the long-awaited invasion of Canada, Proctor abandoned Fort Malden and withdrew to the Thames River, and Tecumseh realized that all was lost.

Now, sitting moodily at the campfire, gazing blindly into the crackling flames, he realized that really he had known all was lost even before that, and tried to pinpoint exactly when, acknowledging to himself that for weeks now, if not months, he had been in a state of denial. He retraced his steps along the dark road to disaster and came to the Battle of Tippecanoe, the betrayal of their dream by his brother, Lalawethika. That had been the turning point, he thought. Even last year, a year of great victories, all had been lost, and he had been deluding himself. *Perhaps,* he thought bitterly, *I have been fooling myself all along.* But what of his visions? *Moneto* could not have misled him. No, that could not be. The opportunity had been there. But he had missed it, or lost it, or it had been taken away from him, and if the latter were the case, then it must mean that somehow he had betrayed *Moneto*'s trust, just as The Prophet had betrayed his. So perhaps Lalawethika wasn't to blame after all. Maybe it had been his fault all along.

Tecumseh lifted his eyes and scanned the circle of grim faces, his friends, his confidants, his trusted lieutenants, and their eyes reflected his own despair. They were looking to him, as they had now for years, for words of comfort and encouragement. They wanted to be reassured. They had trusted him to lead them to final victory, and all their dreams were entwined around him, only now they were strangling the life out of him.

"My brothers," he said, "tomorrow we will go into battle. In this battle I will be killed."

They were all talking at once then, saying that it could not be so, but knowing it must be since Tecumseh had the gift of prophecy. Tecumseh listened for a moment, a faint, wistful smile on his lips, and raised his hand for silence.

"The Americans outnumber us," he said. "The British are unreliable. I love all my people too well to see them sacrificed needlessly. But all of you have said we must stand and fight."

"It is our only hope," said Stiahta. "With every mile we retreat the more discouraged our people become. Every day some of them slip quietly away. If we do not fight, all is lost."

"Are we lost anyway?" asked Ooshawanoo, the Chippewa. "Is that what you are telling us, Tecumseh?"

Tecumseh sighed. Beside him, on the red sash Brock had given him, were his personal weapons—the sword Brock had presented to him on the day the general had left Amherstburg, having turned his command over to Proctor, the tomahawk his brother Chiksika had carried into his last battle (one of Tecumseh's most cherished possessions,) two Mortimer pistols he had received from Blue Jacket, a flintlock rifle that had belonged to the great white warrior, *Metequa,* and which the Delawares who had captured that legendary Long Knife had given to him as a gift. These he now distributed among his friends, along with other personal items, so that each received something of his. He gave all his weapons away, keeping only his warclub. The others accepted these gifts with gratitude and profound sorrow. For a time no one spoke. Tecumseh sat motionless, eyes closed, head tilted back and a little to one side, as though he were listening to something no one else could hear. They watched him, wondering if he had fallen into a trance. Finally he opened his eyes, rose, and went to Wasegoboah, to whom he had given the flintlock rifle. He drew the ramrod from its place beneath the barrel and held it out to Wasegoboah.

"My friend, hear me well. Tomorrow, stay by my side in the battle. I will fall, and when I do, if you can reach me, and strike my body four times with this, I will rise up and, resurrected, lead our people to victory."

The others had no doubt that what Tecumseh said was true, and they were cheered. Clearly *Moneto* had just spoken to Tecumseh. And they were certain that if their warriors saw Tecumseh fall and then rise from the dead, the effect would be dazzling and decisive, and victory would be theirs after all.

III

After reporting to General Harrison, Nathaniel prowled the camp to find Jonathan and his Madison County militia. He found him with Hoke Tuller and a couple of others, around a campfire, one of a thousand campfires in the bivouac. There were eight thousand men here, and yet it was astonishingly quiet. The men were subdued by the knowledge that the enemy had stopped its retreat and turned at bay and tomorrow there would be a big fight, and many would perish. The men were thinking about their loved ones as they cleaned their rifles and sharpened their knives and hatchets, the sound of steel on whetstones similar to the sound of thousands of crickets, or they wrote letters, those that could write, and if they talked at all it was in a subdued way, as though they were attending a funeral. There were no rousing speeches tonight, no bold talk, no cheers or bands playing martial airs, no dress parades. That was all finished. It was down to business now.

Jonathan had been drinking. Nathaniel could tell as soon as he hunkered down to warm his hands above the flames. Jonathan looked up at him and then his hooded eyes slid back to the fire. He was wrapped in a cocoon of private thoughts and he could do no more than acknowledge Nathaniel's presence. But Hoke Tuller was full of questions.

Nathaniel shared everything he knew. He and several other scouts had just returned from a reconnaissance of the enemy lines. Proctor's right wing straddled a carriage road and was anchored to the banks of the Thames. The river here was deep and wide and unfordable. His left wing was hinged to a swampy thicket. Here Proctor had placed his six hundred British regulars. His single cannon commanded the road. On the north side of the swampy thicket was a strip of dry woodland, and to the north of that more swamp. In these woods hid Tecumseh and probably a thousand Indians.

"A good place to make a stand," Harrison had said. "We cannot turn either flank. So we will have to go straight at him, gentlemen. Our losses may be high. But we have the numbers. There can be no excuse for failure in these circumstances."

Those present in the general's tent agreed whole-heartedly. There was Isaac Shelby, who had come to fight with the four thousand Kentuckians who had recently elected him their governor. And there was Richard Mentor Johnson, big and bluff and bold, who had organized a regiment of mounted riflemen, most of whom were from Kentucky, too. Also present was Beaver, the son and namesake of the Delaware chief who had been Harrison's good friend. Beaver was one of about two hundred Indians who had come to fight with the Americans, and no one wanted this fight more than Beaver, who had sworn to avenge his father's death. Harrison gave his orders for tomorrow morning's attack in a crisp, confident manner.

"What about you and the other scouts?" Hoke asked Nathaniel.

"We've been given leave to fight wherever we want."

"You gonna fight with us, Flintlock?"

"Reckon so."

"Good!" Hoke slapped his knee. "Ain't that good news, Cap'n? Ol' Flintlock Jones'll be fightin' with us."

"Huh," said Jonathan.

Nathaniel looked at Hoke and made a short sideways motion with his head and Hoke understood, and gathered up the other two Madison County men who were hunched over the fire. "C'mon boys. Let's go spread the good news 'bout Flintlock here. Dog-dammit, c'mon!"

When they had gone Jonathan reached under his blue cloak and brandished a silver flask, offered it to Nathaniel, who declined. The frontiersman watched Jonathan take a long drink.

"The Cooper woman gave you that, didn't she?"

Jonathan eyed him suspiciously. "How did you know?"

"You had it when you came back to camp from one of your visits to Vincennes. Didn't have it before."

"You're supposed to be spying on the British, not me."

"Wasn't spying. I just notice things."

Jonathan stood up. "I've got something I want to give you. Wait."

When he came back he had the Tripolitan cutlass, and he held the weapon out to Nathaniel.

"I want you to have this. I've got no use for it."

"That's your good luck, isn't it?"

"I won't need luck tomorrow. Nothing's going to happen to me. Besides, I've got three pistols, and only one good arm. Take it."

"Obliged, but I'll stick with this." Nathaniel patted the flintlock rifle. "You keep it. You'll be wanting it to hang over the fireplace when you get home to Elm Tree."

"Home." Jonathan sat back down, cross-legged, the cutlass in his lap, and resumed staring morosely into the fire. It was all he said.

"With any luck, tomorrow will see an end to this campaign. Then we can all go home."

Jonathan didn't respond. He didn't hear the Indian, either—didn't hear anything except the crackling of the fire and off somewhere in the night someone making a fiddle wail a melancholy melody and the sibilant whisper of a hundred blades on a hundred whetstones. But he looked up and saw Quashquame standing at the rim of the firelight.

"You're here to look out for him," said Jonathan, "and he's here looking out for me." He found the scenario amusing, and smiled wryly.

"You love Becky," said Nathaniel. "If you didn't, you wouldn't be this way."

"Yes, it's affected me. You can't help but be affected when your wife refuses to talk to you, even look at you." Jonathan drank again from the flask.

"She wants you to come home."

"Does she? Might be too late."

"On account of Emily Cooper?"

"Vickers. Emily Vickers. She doesn't use his name anymore. No, it has nothing to do with her. Not really. Leave her out of this, Nathaniel. She's a good person. A real lady."

"Does a lady try to steal a married man away from his wife?"

Jonathan leaped clumsily to his feet, fists clenched. The cutlass clattered against his boot tips.

"That's not how it is. Not at all. This wouldn't have happened if Rebecca hadn't—"

"That's enough," said Nathaniel. "I thought you put a lot of stock in honor, Jonathan. Where's the honor in what you're doing?"

Jonathan's laughter rang hollow. "Honor? Look what it's got me. I tried to do what I thought was right. This is my reward?"

"The preachers say our reward is in Heaven."

"Or Hell," amended Jonathan.

Nathaniel rose and walked away, vanishing into the darkness, the Delaware at his side.

IV

Many of the great battles in history have proved to be the anticlimax rather than the climax of a campaign. Weeks or months or even years in the making, a battle may last a day, a few hours, or even only a few minutes. The Battle of the Thames, at which so much was decided, lasted hardly more than an hour.

Tecumseh was summoned to General Proctor's headquarters in the gray twilight prior to dawn, and Proctor did his best to reconcile their differences, yet succeeded in making matters worse by asking for Tecumseh's assurance that the Indians would stand fast. By a great effort of will Tecumseh remained civil. How ironic, he thought, that Proctor would ask that question. In all the long history of the association between the British and the Indians it had always been the redcoats who retreated or refused to fight. Tecumseh returned to the place in the woods where Stiahta, Wasegoboah, and Black Hawk sat on a log, smoking their pipes. Their warriors were spread out in the strip of forest between the two swampy thickets. Tecumseh looked about him with grim satisfaction. No one would know that a thousand Indians lurked in these woods just by looking.

"What did Proctor want?" asked Stiahta.

"To know if we will run away or stand and fight."

Stiahta demonstrated his contempt for Proctor by spitting on the ground. "The British will run before we do. We have nowhere to run. They can go home across the Big Water whenever they want."

"They *will* run," predicted Tecumseh. "I see it in Proctor's face. He does not have the stomach for this fight. The *Englishmanake* soldiers are as brave as their commander. If he stands, they will stand to the last man. If he runs, they will run. The *Shemanese* will strike the redcoats first. They will want to silence the cannon. Then they will turn on us."

"But we will stand and fight, no matter what," said Stiahta.

"Yes. As long as I am alive. If I fall and do not rise, you must try to save yourselves."

Tecumseh shed his buckskin tunic. Wearing only leggins, breechclout, and moccasins of buffalo hide, with a red headband knotted at the back to keep the long hair out of his face, there was nothing to distinguish him from the lowliest warrior.

Suddenly there was the sound of a single gunshot. Oddly, it seemed to come from all directions at once. They heard distinctly the angry whine of a bullet. Then Tecumseh made a sound and staggered, grabbing his left side, high up, close to the heart.

"Tecumseh!" cried Wasegoboah, jumping up. "Have you been hit?"

Tecumseh took his hand away. There was no wound, and the pain left him as quickly as it had come. He looked at his friends. Their eyes were wide with superstitious awe. No words were needed. They were all thinking the same thing. There had been no rifle shot, no bullet. It had been a sign, an omen. And a bad one, at that.

A rolling crash of rifle fire from the south, over near the river, punctuated by the throaty roar of the lone cannon, signaled the beginning of the battle. The sun was just now peeking over the hills to the east. The Americans were attacking the British line, just as Tecumseh had said they would.

Harrison had hit upon a rather novel idea for getting as many of his troops into action as he could. Each of Colonel Johnson's mounted riflemen would take another man on the back of his horse. Riding double, four thousand strong, the Americans charged straight into the British lines. Johnson was quick to see that there was no room between the river and the swamp for more than one of his battalions to advance at a time. He saw, too, that one battalion would be enough to deal with the redcoats. So he led his second battalion to the north, skirting the swampy thicket and launching an assault on the Indian position in the woods. Tecumseh had told his warriors to hold their fire until the *Shemanese* were almost upon them. This they did, and when they fired it was a devastating fusillade, nearly a thousand rifles speaking at once, and the woods were filled with muzzle-flash, like a thousand giant fireflies flaring in the blue-shadow of night which yet clung stubbornly to the bosom of the earth beneath the trees. The noise was deafening. The hail of lead cut down men and horses by the dozen, obliterating the entire first line of the Kentucky mounted rifle battalion.

Bullets struck the man behind whom Nathaniel rode, and several more struck the horse beneath him, killing both man and horse. Nathaniel jumped clear as they fell, rolled and came up in a crouch, rifle in hand. Then he saw Jonathan, who was also riding double with one of Johnson's men, about to gallop by him. Nathaniel leaped forward, launching himself at Jonathan, and bore him to the ground. Johnson's rifleman looked back and shouted something lost in the din of battle, but rode on into the woods. Jonathan lay in the tall grass, stunned by the fall. Nathaniel paused only long enough to make certain that Jonathan had not been seriously injured by the fall, before hitting him, a good solid measured blow to the point of the chin, knocking him out cold.

Plunging into the trees, Nathaniel found himself in the midst of desperate hand-to-hand fighting. Many of Johnson's men had dismounted to fight on foot. Others hurled themselves from their saddles to bear Indians to the ground, or else were plucked from their saddles by Indians leaping out of nowhere. A Shawnee brave charged him with a piercing war cry, tomahawk raised. Nathaniel whirled and fired, the rifle held at hip level. The Indian fell dead at his feet. His back to a tree, Nathaniel quickly reloaded. A bullet struck the tree. Wood shrapnel gashed his cheek. He moved at a running crouch, looking for Quashquame, shot another Indian who had dehorsed one of Johnson's men and, straddling him, was about to deliver the *coup de grâce* with his warclub. Before he could reload another warrior came at him, and Nathaniel used the empty rifle as a club, shattering the stock on the Indian's skull. Not twenty feet in front of him, a mounted rifleman and his horse fell in a barrage of bullets. Nathaniel cast aside the ruined rifle, hurtled the corpse of the Indian whose head he had just bashed in, and darted through the dying horse's flailing hooves to snatch up the dead Kentuckian's rifle. Another shrill war cry scraped along his nerve endings as he turned to see one more Indian bearing down on him.

It was Tecumseh, brandishing his warclub.

Nathaniel triggered the rifle.

Misfire!

Quashquame suddenly appeared, flying at Tecumseh, carrying him to the ground. Tecumseh pitched him head over heels, leapt to his feet and pounced on the Delaware. Nathaniel felt a hoarse and incoherent cry well up from his throat as he watched the warclub rise and fall. Then one of Colonel Johnson's young officers ran up to aim a pistol at Tecumseh's back. Before he could fire Stiahta killed him with a rifleshot. The Wyandot and Wasegoboah had been staying close to

Tecumseh throughout the fight, doing their best to protect him. As the officer fell, the pistol was flung from his dying hand and dropped to the ground almost at Nathaniel's feet. Nathaniel scooped it up. Stiahta was coming straight for him. Nathaniel fired at point-blank range. Stiahta's face disintegrated in a spray of hot scarlet blood and white fragments.

Tecumseh saw his friend die. Rising from the body of Quashquame, he stood there for just an instant, stunned by the loss. Then two bullets struck him simultaneously, piercing his left side and exploding his heart, slamming him to the ground.

Wasegoboah saw him fall. Drawing the ramrod from the flintlock rifle Tecumseh had given him the night before, he tried to reach the side of his fallen leader. *Strike my body four times with this, and I will rise up* . . .

Nathaniel drew the tomahawk from his belt and hurled it. Wasegoboah fell, the hatchet buried between his shoulder blades. He tried to stretch out and touch Tecumseh's body with the ramrod, but he could not quite reach him, a matter of inches, and the life drained swiftly out of him.

"Tecumseh is dead!"

Nathaniel heard the cry from somewhere nearby, spoken in Shawnee, and it was taken up throughout the woods, in the tongue of the Wyandot, and the Delaware, and a number of others. The effect was startling. The firing slackened. The Indians drifted away like ghosts unseen and unheard. The Battle of the Thames was over.

As he knelt beside the body of Quashquame, Nathaniel was dimly aware of several Kentuckians wandering through the woods nearby. They gathered around the bodies of Wasegoboah and Stiahta. The latter had dressed in full regalia for the battle. There were silver armbands and a necklace of bear claws. His buckskins were adorned with exquisite beadwork, as befitted a Wyandot war chief.

"Is it him?" asked one of the Kentuckians. "Is this Tecumseh?"

"No, this is him," said another, standing over the body of Wasegoboah.

"No it ain't," said a third. "This is the devil right here." He pointed at Stiahta.

"Hey, Flintlock," called a fourth. "You know Tecumseh. Is *this* him?"

Nathaniel glanced at the body of Tecumseh, laying facedown across Quashquame's legs. Then he rose and pointed at Stiahta.

"That's Tecumseh," he said.

"So it *is* him!" chortled one of the Kentuckians. "He's a good Injun now, ain't he?"

"The necklace is mine."

"I claim them moccasins."

"Gimme them bracelets!"

Several more men appeared. They gathered like vultures. Sick at heart, Nathaniel watched as they stripped Stiahta's corpse and then, with bloody long knives flashing in the yellow sunlight slanting through the trees and muted by the drifting powder smoke, they took the scalp, and strips of flesh for razor strops and coin purses, butchering Stiahta as they would a deer.

Nathaniel turned away from this grisly spectacle. He rolled Tecumseh's body off Quashquame's legs and left it lying facedown. Then he lifted Quashquame up in his arms. He felt empty. Quashquame had been his one true friend. Next to Amanda and Rebecca and Christopher, the Delaware had been the most important person in his life. Like a son, in a way. Now he was dead and something inside Nathaniel had died with him.

He carried him out of the woods, and there met Jonathan, staggering, still dazed.

"Why?" cried Jonathan, in a bitter shaking rage. "Why did you . . . ?"

"Go home," said Nathaniel, and walked on.

V

When the news reached Boonesboro, riders went out to carry the word. A great victory had been won! The frontier was finally safe! Tecumseh was dead! The Indian confederacy was crushed! The British were on the run!

And Amanda waited. There were many things to do around the place to keep her busy, but she couldn't bring herself to do them now. Days passed, agonizingly slow in their passage, and as bad as the days were, the nights were infinitely worse, because she knew somehow that someone had died, she could feel it in her bones and in her heart.

The victors began to return, coming home alone, or in pairs, or in bunches, the conquering heroes. The campaign was over, the battle won, and winter was setting in. Time to go home. Sometimes she would go down through the ribbon of trees to the road and there she met some of them, and she would ask the question tearing at her heart, but no, no one knew for sure. Most of the time, though, she sat by the window, gazing down the long slope where the bluegrass lay beneath the first snow, which had come a week ago. As the days passed the fear became conviction, and with every hour her heart bled more.

I cannot live alone, without him. And she thought about the crazy old woman she and Nathaniel had met over thirty years ago, when they were crossing the mountains, through the Cumberland Gap, the woman whose long-dead husband, buried out under the trees, called to her in the night when the wind was high. *I cannot live alone.*

She wasn't really aware of when she started doing it, but she began to carry a knife with her as she wandered aimlessly about the cabin. She would stand sometimes for hours staring blankly at the bed with the pretty quilt she had made long ago, now old and faded, and she did not sleep for the duration of her long vigil, having made up her mind without knowing that she had done so that she would lie down on that bed one last time when the news, that dreadful news, came, as she knew by now that it would, and then she would sleep forever, and she would look at the knife.

Then she saw them, one man coming through the trees, up the long snow-clad slope, carrying another man in his arms, and her heart seemed to stop, seemed to turn into lead heavy in her chest. She stepped out of the cabin, still willowy after all these years in her plain dress, and she did not feel the cold, did not feel anything, holding the knife behind her back, staring, and not even able to cry, relieved in a way that she would never have to endure the waiting again.

"Hello, Amanda," he said, and she saw the tears on his cheeks, tears he had held in check for five hundred miles and could not restrain any longer, and she ran to him, leaving the knife to lie in the unblemished snow at the front of the door.

Glossary of Shawnee Words

calumet—pipe of peace
Can-tuc-kee—sacred hunting ground (Kentucky)
cut-ta-ho-tha—condemned
dai-na-tha—daughter
Englishmanake—Englishman
mattah—no
Matchemenetoo—Bad Spirit
msi-kah-mi-qui—council house
melcheasiske—poor land
metequa—long rifle
Moneto—God
ne-cana—friend
neequithah—son
neethetha—(my) brother
nenothtu—warrior
nenothtu oukimah—great warrior
nineemeh—look, see
notha—(my) father
Pahcotai—Autumn
pe-e-wah—come, follow
peshikta—deer
p'thu-thoi—bison
Seventeen Fires—United States
shemagana—soldiers
Shemanese—Long Knives, Americans
Spay-lay-wi-theepi—Ohio River
Tota—Frenchman
wahsiu—husband
wegiwa—lodge

You are invited
to preview
the third volume of
the Flintlock Series
by acclaimed author
Jason Manning . . .

Gone to Texas

available from Signet
in 1995.

The dinner hour commencing at one o'clock in the afternoon every single day of the year, was the only time between dawn and dusk that a West Point cadet had to spend on his own pursuits. While most of his fellow cadets returned to their quarters, or gathered in small groups on the commons to indulge in idle conversation, Christopher Groves liked to walk. The serene beauty of the site of the United States Military Academy never failed to soothe his sometimes troubled soul.

Leaving the mess hall, Christopher walked briskly along a path which led him past the Post Office and Laboratory, then under the guns of the Siege Battery and to the river where the Long Dock jutted like a fat, upsidedown *L* into the river. The trail narrowed as it wound in serpentine fashion across steep wooded slopes to the point, above which loomed the old fort, now falling into a disgraceful state of disrepair. It was nearly summer. The cool shade of the trees was a pleasure.

Gazing out at the wide blue-green expanse of the Hudson, nestled between forested heights, Christopher noticed several white-sailed skiffs on the water. He thought of his father. It never failed—he always did when he saw a sailing ship, be it skiff or schooner. Jonathan Groves had first made a name for himself as a valiant young naval officer in the war against the Barbary pirates almost thirty years ago.

346

A frown creased Christopher's brow. Having just turned twenty-three, he was of medium height and slender build. Broad across the shoulders and slender at the hips, he cut a fine figure in his uniform—regulation gray tunic and white trousers and, of course, every cadet's pride and joy, the bell-crowned black leather cap with the polished leather visor and the yellow scales and eagle which could be fastened under the chin. By anyone's standards he was a handsome young man. His chin was square and strong, with more than a hint of stubbornness. His mouth a testament to determination, could flash in an easy white grin. His nose was aquiline, his brow high. And his eyes, a startling sea-green in color, were keen and intelligent. In spite of his deceptively slender build, he was endowed with an agile strength. Physically he was resilient—a cadet had to be to endure the constant drill which was a feature of the Academy. His constitution was cast-iron, which was lucky, as the worst thing about West Point was the food. A cadet's diet was atrociously poor. Yet Christopher thrived. Food was of no importance to him except as fuel for the body. His face was facile, a sponge which soaked up the heavy doses of French and mathematics which inundated the cadets in the Point's sand-floored "academies."

Now in his second year, Christopher was a popular member of the Corps of Cadets. Though reserved, sometimes to the point of reticence, he was amiable and reliable and eminently fair-minded. Apart from that, he was at the top of his class in horsemanship—which was little wonder considering his upbringing at Elm Tree, where some of Kentucky's most prized thoroughbreds were raised—and near the top in swordsmanship and academics.

And yet he often wondered if he was not here under false pretenses. These self-doubts plagued him whenever his thoughts turned to his father.

To say that Christopher hated his father would be too

strong a statement, yet Christopher had never been able to forgive what had been done to his beloved and long-suffering mother. Since the age of five Christopher—and his mother, Rebecca—had seen precious little of Jonathan Groves. But it was on the strength of the hero's name that Christopher had been accepted into the Military Academy. Ironically, nearly everyone here had a higher opinion of his father than did he.

Nearly everyone. Christopher knew of one exception. Adam Vickers hated the very name of Jonathan Groves, and by virtue of blood kinship, Christopher as well. Considering the circumstances, Christopher could scarcely blame him. But Vickers's hate put Christopher in an uncomfortable position of having to defend the indefensible—his father's honor.

Christopher walked on with long brisk strides, hands clasped behind his back. There was no time to dally. At precisely two o'clock there was formation, and no one wanted to be awarded the demerits which being even one minute late for that daily ritual would bring.

Breaking out of the trees, he turned south along the path below the ramparts at the rim of the plateau. Straight ahead was the Battery Knox, named after the republic's first secretary of war, and beyond that the Stables and Riding Hall, near the road which led down to the South Dock. The sun beat warmly on his face, and a breeze swept up from the river carrying the fragrance of spring flowers which bloomed in profusion on the slope near the water's edge. Due west of the Riding Hall stood the Cadet Barracks, and having timed his daily walk down to the minute, Christopher was confident he would arrive just in time to join his company for formation. He was never late.

Few were his demerits after two years. Only three cadets had a better record in that respect. Demerits were devilishly easy to acquire. There were a great many "thou shall nots" at the Military Academy. Cadets were not permitted to drink, smoke, or play cards—nonetheless, Christopher had never seen so much tobacco use in his life, and gambling was widespread. The countryside was infested with civilians who made a good living in a brisk black market which supplied the cadets with forbidden merchandise.

Demerits were also received for loitering, being late for class, bathing in the river, answering for another at roll call, or standing at guard duty in another's stead. Pranks and fist fights were also forbidden, which is not the same thing as saying that they did not occur on a regular basis—they were inevitable when two hundred proud, high-spirited young men were thrown together into an extremely competitive and stressful environment. Those unfortunate enough to be caught in a flagrant dereliction of these commandments were often punished, but seldom court-martialed and dismissed.

The worst crime a cadet could commit—one which inevitably resulted in dismissal—was to engage in the *duello*. If a cadet so much as heard of a rendezvous with pistols or blades to settle an affair of honor, he was duty-bound to report it.

"Christopher! Christopher Groves!"

Two cadets stood on the ramparts above him, silhouetted against the bright blue afternoon sky. They had to call several times before he heard them, so lost in brooding thoughts was he.

"Stay there! Wait for us!"

Christopher waved acknowledgment. He recognized them both—Gil Bryant and John O'Connor. Like Christopher, they were second-classmen, and his roommates. Of the ninety-one cadets who had entered West Point with Christopher the summer before last, nineteen had dropped out before the end of the first year, and a dozen more had failed to make the grade this year. Such a high mortality rate created a strong camaraderie between the surviving classmen, and Christopher considered both Gil and O'Connor friends. Especially O'Connor. The redheaded son of an Irishman was often brash, and sometimes bold to the point of sheer recklessness. His temper was notorious. But he was an engaging, outgoing, and fiercely loyal friend. His academic marks left much to be desired, but Christopher knew that O'Connor was capable of much better. He was just the kind who exerted the minimum effort necessary to squeak by.

A hundred feet north of where the two cadets stood was a footpath which connected the ramparts with the broader path upon which Christopher was walking. The cadets negotiated this treacherous descent at breakneck speed. Christopher rocked slightly back and forth on his heels, falling prey to impatience; his keenly accurate mental clock ticked away precious seconds. He did not fancy a demerit just because Gil and O'Connor wanted to pass the time of day with him.

But it was much more than that, as Christopher soon discovered.

"The Superintendent wants to see you," gasped O'Connor, breathing hard from what had been a long run from the mess hall.

"What? Now?"

"Right away. He sent us to fetch you."

"But what about formation?"

O'Connor flashed that rakehell grin of his. "There's no way out of it, bucko. When Old Silly wants you, your goose is cooked."

Christopher grimaced at the butterflies in his stomach.

"What have you done?" asked Bryant, who looked more than a little worried for his friend.

"That's what I'm wondering."

"Oh, come on," said O'Connor, with a sly wink. "You can tell us." He didn't look the least bit worried. Christopher didn't take that personally. O'Connor never worried about anything. He took everything life threw at him with devil-may-care aplomb.

"I'd tell you if I knew," said Christopher, wracking his brain for the answer.

"Oh, yes, pure as the driven snow," jibed O'Connor. "I tell you what I think, Gil. It has something to do with Miss Inskilling."

"What about her?" asked Bryant, seeing that O'Connor intended to have some fun at Christopher's expense—good-natured fun—and playing his role as the Irishman's foil to the hilt.

"Well, you must be aware that Miss Greta's father and Superintendent Thayer are very good friends. You are also undoubtedly cognizant of the fact that our friend here has been seeing a great deal of the lovely lady. Maybe you've seen a bit more of her than her father thinks proper, eh, Christopher, you sly devil?"

Christopher would have taken offense at the remark and all it implied, had it come from anyone else. But he knew O'Connor meant no disrespect.

"You're just jealous, O'Connor."

"Aha! You see, Gil? He admits it."

"I don't admit anything."

"Well, you didn't deny it."

"I wouldn't dignify such an absurd statement with a denial. You're green with envy, that's all, because a young lady of Greta Inskilling's caliber wouldn't give you the time of day."

"You think not? Why, I take that as a challenge, Cadet Groves. I have made a point of not exerting my considerable charms upon the lady in question, out of respect for your tender sensibilities. But if you challenge me, as you most certainly have—and Gil here is a witness—then perhaps I ought to teach you a lesson in humility. I daresay that in a fortnight I could make Miss Inskilling forget you even exist."

"That will be the day."

O'Connor laughed heartily. His joviality was contagious, and Christopher, despite the sobering prospect of being called before Superintendent Thayer, laughed along with him.

"Come on, Johnny," said Bryant. "We'll be late for formation."

"Right." Putting on a somber face, O'Connor offered his hand to Christopher. "It's been a pleasure knowing you, Cadet Groves. I shall always treasure our friendship. Rest assured I will perform an annual pilgrimage to your final resting place."

Christopher scoffed and slapped away the proffered hand. "I'll dance a jig on your grave."

It was a long-standing, if somewhat morbid, joke between the two of them.

"Let's go, Gil," said O'Connor, and took off running down the path in the direction of the Riding Hall.

Christopher watched them go. What could Thayer want with him? Whatever it was, no doubt it meant trouble. There was but one way to find out. Christopher ascended the steep footpath to the ramparts. At the top he squared his shoulders and marched resolutely across the parade ground, making for the Superintendent's house.